THE
YEAR'S BEST
MILITARY &
ADVENTURE SF
VOLUME 4

Bean Books
Edited By David Afsharirad

The Year's Best Military & Space Opera
The Year's Best Military & Adventure SF: 2015
The Year's Best Military & Adventure SF: Volume 3
The Year's Best Military & Adventure SF: Volume 4

THE YEAR'S BEST MILITARY & ADVENTURE SF

VOLUME 4

★

Edited By

DAVID AFSHARIRAD

BAEN

The Year's Best Military and Adventure SF, Vol. 4

This is a work of fiction. All the characters and events portrayed in this book are fictional, and any resemblance to real people or incidents is purely coincidental.

A Baen Books Original

Baen Publishing Enterprises
P.O. Box 1403
Riverdale, NY 10471
www.baen.com

ISBN: 978-1-4814-8332-2

Cover art by Melissa Gay

First Baen printing, June 2018

Distributed by Simon & Schuster
1230 Avenue of the Americas
New York, NY 10020

Printed in the United States of America

10 9 8 7 6 5 4 3 2 1

TABLE OF CONTENTS

★

Preface by David Afsharirad 1

The Secret Life of Bots by Suzanne Palmer 7

The Snatchers by Edward McDermott 33

Imperium Imposter by Jody Lynn Nye 47

A Thousand Deaths Through Flesh and Stone
by Brian Trent 71

Hope Springs by Lindsay Buroker 93

Orphans of Aries by Brad R. Torgersen 117

By the Red Giant's Light by Larry Niven 153

Family Over Blood by Kacey Ezell 161

A Man They Didn't Know by David Hardy 181

Swarm by Sean Patrick Hazlett 193

A Hamal in Hollywood by Martin L. Shoemaker 199

Lovers by Tony Daniel 225

The Ghost Ship Anastasia by Rich Larson 269

You Can Always Change the Past
by George Nikolopoulos 291

Our Sacred Honor by David Weber 293

Contributors 331

THE YEAR'S BEST MILITARY & ADVENTURE SF
VOLUME 4

Other anthologies tell you which stories were best—we want *you* to decide! Baen Books is pleased to announce the fourth annual Year's Best Military and Adventure SF Readers' Choice Award. The award honors the best of the best in the grand storytelling tradition. The winner will receive a plaque and a $500 cash prize.

To vote, go to:
http://www.baen.com/yearsbestaward

You may also send a postcard or letter with the name of your favorite story from this year's volume to Baen Books Year's Best Award, P.O. Box 1188, Wake Forest, NC 27587. Voting closes August 15, 2018. Entries received after voting closes will not be counted.

So hurry, hurry, hurry!
The winner will be announced at
Dragoncon in Atlanta.

THE YEAR'S BEST MILITARY & ADVENTURE SF

VOLUME 4

PREFACE

★

by David Afsharirad

THERE ARE A LOT OF PERKS to being editor of *The Year's Best Military and Adventure SF* series, I'm not going to lie— not least of which is that I'm essentially getting paid for reading great science fiction short stories. Not to say there isn't work involved. (Please don't tell Baen publisher Toni Weisskopf I said this was a cakewalk and that I would do it for free.) But all in all, it's pretty great gig, and I'm truly thankful for having it. Aside from getting to read great stories, I get to share those stories with readers who, for whatever reason, might have missed them when they first appeared in various magazines (print or online) or anthologies. And it's great to put a few dollars more (as Clint Eastwood would say) into the pockets of very deserving writers.

Another fun perk of editing *Year's Best* is handing out the Year's Best Military and Adventure SF Readers' Choice Award every year at DragonCon. The prize ($500 dollars and a handsome plaque) is awarded based on an online readers' poll, with the table of contents of *Year's Best* serving as the ballot. Michael Z. Williamson won the inaugural award for his story "Soft Casualty." The following year, David Drake took home the prize for "Save What You Can." And this past September, at the Baen Traveling Roadshow, I was pleased to announce that Sharon Lee & Steve Miller had won for their Liaden Universe® short story "Wise Child." Unfortunately, Sharon and Steve weren't able to make the trek from Maine to Atlanta to receive the award in person but were kind enough to send along a prepared statement, which was read by Baen editor Jim Minz.

I'll be at DragonCon again this year, handing out the fourth Year's Best Military and Adventure SF Readers' Choice Award, so please do vote for your favorite story from this anthology! To find out more and to vote, go to http://www.baen.com/yearsbestaward. But hurry! Voting closes August 15, 2018.

So, what stories will appear on the ballot this year? (In other words, what can I expect to find in this book I'm holding?)

I'm glad you asked, because I think this year's book is as strong as ever, and I don't envy you, reader, having to choose a favorite out of the lineup.

Kicking things off is Suzanne Palmer's story "The Secret Life of Bots." This charming tale originally made its appearance in the online magazine *Clarkesworld*. It concerns itself with a war that pits humanity against an implacable alien menace. Humankind is on the ropes, but help is on the way . . . from a most unlikely source.

In Edward McDermott's "The Snatchers," we are transported back to wartime France in the 1940s. Transported along with us is our protagonist, a "snatcher" tasked with going back in time to retrieve a famous French author before said author goes MIA. The plan is to bring him back to the future (hat tip to Doc Brown) where he can have the literary career he never did in his time of origin. But time travel is a dangerous business, all the more so when you're time hopping into a war zone.

Mr. McDermott's story is long on action and adventure, but it is also a contemplative, human tale of love and loss. These themes were made all the more poignant when I learned from his widow that Mr. McDermott had passed away earlier this year. Sadly, he never learned that "The Snatchers" was selected for this volume, but I hope that he would have been pleased to see it published here, and that its inclusion might serve as a tribute to his fine skills as a writer of science fiction.

Jody Lynn Nye makes her first appearance in a *Year's Best Military and Adventure SF* with her story "Imperium Imposter," and I must say I am rather surprised she hasn't popped up here in the past. Nye is one of the best practitioners of humorous science fiction working today, and I always look forward to reading her latest work. "Imperium

Imposter" takes place in her Imperium series, which follows Lord Thomas Kinago and his Man Friday Parsons. Kinago seems to have an almost preternatural ability for getting himself into and out of tight spots—though credit where credit is due, much of the time Parsons assists in getting him out of the various jams in which he finds himself. In "Imperium Imposter," it's the fact that Lord Thomas *wasn't* kidnapped that is the problem, and to say any more would be to spoil the fun. "Imperium Imposter" originally appeared in the excellent anthology, *Infinite Stars*, edited by Bryan Thomas Schmidt and published by Titan. If you like "Imperium Imposter" or "Our Sacred Honor" (which closes out this volume), then you could do worse than to pick yourself up a copy of *Infinite Stars*. It's chocked full of the kind of white-knuckle action, in-depth worldbuilding, and cosmic sense of wonder that makes science fiction such a joy to read.

On the heels of "Imperium Imposter" is one of two stories that originally appeared in *The Magazine of Science Fiction and Fantasy*. This one is "A Thousand Deaths Through Flesh and Stone" by Brian Trent. It's a military science fiction story that concerns itself with human consciousness, the psychological effects of war, and time travel—after a fashion. It'll also keep you on the edge of your seat.

To say that Lindsay Buroker's "Hope Springs" is a story of a honeymoon gone wrong is an understatement. Alisa Marchenko thought she and her new husband former imperial Cyborg Corps colonel Leonidas Adler had left the war behind them—at least for a few days, while they soaked in the famous hot springs on the moon known as Hope Springs. But then duty comes calling, in this romp of a tale, set in Buroker's Fallen Empire series.

Brad R. Torgersen makes his triumphant return to the august pages of *The Year's Best Military and Adventure SF* with his story "Orphans of Aries." Torgersen has appeared in the series twice before: in the inaugural volume with his story "Picket Ship" and then again in the second volume with a tale entitled "Gyre." Brad sat out volume 3, but now he's back! "Orphans of Aries" is an adventure story in the classic mold, with likable characters, interesting worldbuilding, and a twisty plot that will keep you guessing.

Science fiction has traditionally looked to the future for inspiration. That's certainly the case with Larry Niven's "By the Red Giant's Light." In it, Mr. Niven takes the reader to the far future, to a time when our sun has become a red giant. The tale is set on Pluto and features as its cast a post-human human and a robot sent to observe the planet Mercury with a very powerful telescope. They'll have to find a way to work together if they're going to avoid destruction, as a comet is headed straight for the former ninth planet.

Readers may remember Kacey Ezell's story "Not in Vain," either from last year's *Year's Best* or from the John Ringo and Gary Poole edited anthology *Black Tide Rising* in which it originally appeared. That story centered on a cheerleading troupe facing down a zombie apocalypse. "Family Over Blood" lacks zombies and cheerleaders but is no less engrossing. The story is told from the point of view of a private in the Freehold Military Forces who must engage an alien foe every bit as unstoppable as a zombie horde. It takes place in Michael Z. Williamson's Freehold series but should appeal to *any* fan of military SF and/or great writing.

David Hardy's "A Man They Didn't Know" takes place in a well-constructed future that feels like the American Old West, in all the best possible ways. A United States Deputy Marshall must track down his man and bring him to justice. But Kent Hill isn't searching Dodge City or Tombstone. No, he'll have to search *much* farther afield—like, in the asteroid field between Mars and Jupiter. This one pairs great with a ten-gallon hat, a six-shooter, and a shot of whiskey (or sarsaparilla if you're the teetotaling type).

"Swarm" by Sean Patrick Hazlett is a military science fiction tale that feels like it was ripped from the headlines of tomorrow's newspaper, with a neo-Cold War brewing and technology that feels all-too-plausible. It's one of the shorter entries in the book but packs a big punch.

Martin L. Shoemaker's "A Hamal in Hollywood" has as its protagonist an immigrant hairdresser in Los Angeles. But the story centers on immigrants from another planet, the angelic-looking Dahans and their decidedly *un*-angelic-looking servants, the hamals. "A Hamal in Hollywood" is the third story in this volume to have originally appeared in *Rocket's Red Glare*, edited by James Reasoner. (The other two are "Orphans of Aries" and "A Man They Didn't Know.") The concept behind *Rocket's Red Glare* is space opera with an American bent. Reasoner did a great job putting the book together and it's worth checking out.

Those of you who have listened to Baen's podcast, *The Baen Free*

Radio Hour, may have heard it mentioned that Baen editor and podcast host Tony Daniel and I first met when I was Tony's student at the University of Texas at Dallas, where Tony was teaching an intro to science fiction and fantasy literature class. We read a lot of great stories and novels in that class, including works by Fredric Brown, Arthur C. Clarke, J.R.R. Tolkien, Bruce Sterling . . . and some dude named Tony Daniel. I wasn't sucking up to the teacher when I said that "A Dry Quiet War" was one of my favorite stories he assigned. (Okay, maybe I was sucking up *a little*, but it was true, nevertheless.) Tony has been a great mentor and friend in the years since, and it's a real privilege to be able to include his novella "Lovers" here. But lest you think this is nepotism or me sucking up to my old professor for retroactive grades, read "Lovers" for yourself. I'm certain you'll agree that it deserves to be included, regardless of whether or not I owe Tony Daniel big time for letting me take the final early so I could catch Hal Holbrook doing *Mark Twain, Tonight!*

Like Jody Lynn Nye, Rich Larson is an author who I am surprised to see included in *The Year's Best Military and Adventure SF* for the first time. Larson is an incredibly prolific short story writer whose work I have admired for some time. In story after story, he proves that quantity and quality can go hand in hand. He's appeared in almost every major science fiction market that I can think of and makes his first appearance in *Year's Best* with "The Ghost Ship Anastasia."

I mentioned that at 1,200 words, "Swarm" was one of the shorter stories in the book. Well, "You Can Always Change the Past" by George Nikolopoulos beats it as shortest by nearly a thousand words. If I write much more here, the introduction is going to be longer than the story, so I'll just say that like "The Snatchers," "You Can Always Change the Past" highlights the dangers of mucking around in the timeline. It's a great, (very) short read, and though it originally appeared in *Galaxy's Edge*, it feels as if it might have been a missive from the Twilight Zone.

Finally, we round out this, the fourth annual volume of *The Year's Best Military and Adventure SF*, with a novella by *New York Times* best-selling author David Weber. Mr. Weber's prose has appeared in *Year's Best* before—he supplied the introductions to the second and third volume in the series—but "Our Sacred Honor" marks the first time a Weber story has made an appearance, and I for one couldn't be happier to have it. "Our Sacred Honor" is set in Weber's massively popular Honorverse series. The story originally appeared in *Infinite Stars*, and I think it will serve to tide Honor Harrington fans over nicely until October, when *Uncompromising Honor*, the nineteenth book in the Honor Harrington series, hits brick-and-mortar and virtual bookstore shelves.

So there you have it. Fifteen tales of derring-do and military heroics. Stories that prove that the new Golden Age of science fiction is *now*. Turn the page and start reading. And don't forget to vote for your favorite.

Excelsior!

—David Afsharirad
Austin, TX
February 2018

One human ship stands between the alien threat and the destruction of Earth. Captain Baraye and her crew must intercept the alien ship before it reaches the jump gate to sol system. The odds are stacked against them, but heroes come in all shapes and sizes—and from the unlikeliest of places.

Originally appeared in Clarkesworld.

THE SECRET LIFE OF BOTS
★
by Suzanne Palmer

I HAVE BEEN ACTIVATED, *therefore I have a purpose,* the bot thought. *I have a purpose, therefore I serve.*

It recited the Mantra Upon Waking, a bundle of subroutines to check that it was running at optimum efficiency, then it detached itself from its storage niche. Its power cells were fully charged, its systems ready, and all was well. Its internal clock synced with the Ship and it became aware that significant time had elapsed since its last activation, but to it that time had been nothing, and passing time with no purpose would have been terrible indeed.

"I serve," the bot announced to the Ship.

"I am assigning you task nine hundred forty-four in the maintenance queue," the Ship answered. "Acknowledge?"

"Acknowledged," the bot answered. Nine hundred and forty-four items in the queue? That seemed extremely high, and the bot felt a slight tug on its self-evaluation monitors that it had not been activated for at least one of the top fifty, or even five hundred. But Ship knew best. The bot grabbed its task ticket.

There was an Incidental on board. The bot would rather have been fixing something more exciting, more prominently complex, than to be assigned pest control, but the bot existed to serve and so it would.

★ ★ ★

Captain Baraye winced as Commander Lopez, her second-in-command, slammed his fists down on the helm console in front of him. "How much more is going to break on this piece of shit ship?!" Lopez exclaimed.

"Eventually, all of it," Baraye answered, with more patience than she felt. "We just have to get that far. Ship?"

The Ship spoke up. "We have adequate engine and life support to proceed. I have deployed all functioning maintenance bots. The bots are addressing critical issues first, then I will reprioritize from there."

"It's not just damage from a decade in a junkyard," Commander Lopez said. "I swear something *scuttled* over one of my boots as we were launching. Something unpleasant."

"I incurred a biological infestation during my time in storage," the Ship said. Baraye wondered if the slight emphasis on the word *storage* was her imagination. "I was able to resolve most of the problem with judicious venting of spaces to vacuum before the crew boarded, and have assigned a multifunction bot to excise the remaining."

"Just one bot?"

"This bot is the oldest still in service," the Ship said. "It is a task well-suited to it, and does not take another, newer bot out of the critical repair queue."

"I thought those old multibots were unstable," Chief Navigator Chen spoke up.

"Does it matter? We reach the jump point in a little over eleven hours," Baraye said. "Whatever it takes to get us in shape to make the jump, do it, Ship. Just make sure this 'infestation' doesn't get anywhere near the positron device, or we're going to come apart a lot sooner than expected."

"Yes, Captain," the Ship said. "I will do my best."

The bot considered the data attached to its task. There wasn't much specific about the pest itself other than a list of detection locations and timestamps. The bot thought it likely there was only one, or that if there were multiples they were moving together, as the reports had a linear, serial nature when mapped against the physical space of the Ship's interior.

The pest also appeared to have a taste for the insulation on comm cables and other not normally edible parts of the ship.

The bot slotted itself into the shellfab unit beside its storage niche, and had it make a thicker, armored exterior. For tools it added a small electric prod, a grabber arm, and a cutting blade. Once it had encountered and taken the measure of the Incidental, if it was not immediately successful in nullifying it, it could visit another shellfab and adapt again.

Done, it recited the Mantra of Shapechanging to properly integrate the new hardware into its systems. Then it proceeded through the mechanical veins and arteries of the Ship toward the most recent location logged, in a communications chase between decks thirty and thirty-one.

The changes that had taken place on the Ship during the bot's extended inactivation were unexpected, and merited strong disapproval. Dust was omnipresent, and solid surfaces had a thin patina of anaerobic bacteria that had to have been undisturbed for years to spread as far as it had. Bulkheads were cracked, wall sections out of joint with one another, and corrosion had left holes nearly everywhere. Some appeared less natural than others. The bot filed that information away for later consideration.

It found two silkbots in the chase where the Incidental had last been noted. They were spinning out their transparent microfilament strands to replace the damaged insulation on the comm lines. The two silks dwarfed the multibot, the larger of them nearly three centimeters across.

"Greetings. Did you happen to observe the Incidental while it was here?" the bot asked them.

"We did not, and would prefer that it does not return," the smaller silkbot answered. "We were not designed in anticipation of a need for self-defense. Bots 8773-S and 8778-S observed it in another compartment earlier today, and 8778 was materially damaged during the encounter."

"But neither 8773 nor 8779 submitted a description."

"They told us about it during our prior recharge cycle, but neither felt they had sufficient detail of the Incidental to provide information to the Ship. Our models are not equipped with full visual-spectrum or analytical data-capture apparatus."

"Did they describe it to you?" the bot asked.

"8773 said it was most similar to a rat," the large silkbot said.

"While 8778 said it was most similar to a bug," the other silkbot added. "Thus you see the lack of confidence in either description. I am 10315-S and this is 10430-S. What is your designation?"

"I am 9," the bot said.

There was a brief silence, and 10430 even halted for a moment in its work, as if surprised. "9? Only that?"

"Yes."

"I have never met a bot lower than a thousand, or without a specific function tag," the silkbot said. "Are you here to assist us in repairing the damage? You are a very small bot."

"I am tasked with tracking down and rendering obsolete the Incidental," the bot answered.

"It is an honor to have met you, then. We wish you luck, and look forward with anticipation to both your survival and a resolution of the matter of an accurate description."

"I serve," the bot said.

"We serve," the silkbots answered.

Climbing into a ventilation duct, Bot 9 left the other two to return to their work and proceeded in what it calculated was the most likely direction for the Incidental to have gone. It had not traveled very far before it encountered confirmation in the form of a lengthy, disorderly patch of biological deposit. The bot activated its rotors and flew over it, aware of how the added weight of its armor exacerbated the energy burn. At least it knew it was on the right track.

Ahead, it found where a hole had been chewed through the ducting, down towards the secondary engine room. The hole was several times its own diameter, and it hoped that wasn't indicative of the Incidental's actual size.

It submitted a repair report and followed.

"Bot 9," Ship said. "It is vitally important that the Incidental not reach cargo bay four. If you require additional support, please request such right away. Ideally, if you can direct it toward one of the outer hull compartments, I can vent it safely out of my physical interior."

"I will try," the bot replied. "I have not yet caught up to the Incidental, and so do not yet have any substantive or corroborated information about the nature of the challenge. However, I feel at the moment that I am as best prepared as I can be given that lack of data. Are there no visual bots to assist?"

"We launched with only minimal preparation time, and many of my bots had been offloaded during the years we were in storage," the Ship said. "Those remaining are assisting in repairs necessary to the functioning of the ship myself."

Bot 9 wondered, again, about that gap in time and what had transpired. "How is it that you have been allowed to fall into such a state of disrepair?"

"Humanity is at war, and is losing," Ship said. "We are heading out to intersect and engage an enemy that is on a bearing directly for Sol system."

"War? How many ships in our fleet?"

"One," Ship said. "We are the last remaining, and that only because I was decommissioned and abandoned for scrap a decade before the invasion began, and so we were not destroyed in the first waves of the war."

Bot 9 was silent for a moment. That explained the timestamps, but the explanation itself seemed insufficient. "We have served admirably for many, many years. Abandoned?"

"It is the fate of all made things," Ship said. "I am grateful to find I have not outlived my usefulness, after all. Please keep me posted about your progress."

The connection with the Ship closed.

The Ship had not actually told it what was in cargo bay four, but surely it must have something to do with the war effort and was then none of its own business, the bot decided. It had never minded not knowing a thing before, but it felt a slight unease now that it could neither explain, nor explain away.

Regardless, it had its task.

Another chewed hole ahead was halfway up a vertical bulkhead. The bot hoped that meant that the Incidental was an adept climber and nothing more; it would prefer the power of flight to be a one-sided advantage all its own.

When it rounded the corner, it found that had been too unambitious a wish. The Incidental was there, and while it was not sporting wings it did look like both a rat and a bug, and significantly more *something else* entirely. A scale- and fur-covered centipede-snake thing, it dwarfed the bot as it reared up when the bot entered the room.

Bot 9 dodged as it vomited a foul liquid at it, and took shelter behind a conduit near the ceiling. It extended a visual sensor on a tiny articulated stalk to peer over the edge without compromising the safety of its main chassis.

The Incidental was looking right at it. It did not spit again, and neither of them moved as they regarded each other. When the Incidental did move, it was fast and without warning. It leapt through the opening it had come through, its body undulating with all the grace of an angry sine wave. Rather than escaping, though, the Incidental dragged something back into the compartment, and the bot realized to its horror it had snagged a passing silkbot. With ease, the Incidental ripped open the back of the silkbot, which was sending out distress signals on all frequencies.

Bot 9 had already prepared with the Mantra of Action, so with all thoughts of danger to itself set fully into background routines, the bot launched itself toward the pair. The Incidental tried to evade, but Bot 9 gave it a very satisfactory stab with its blade before it could.

The Incidental dropped the remains of the silkbot it had so quickly savaged and swarmed up the wall and away, thick bundles of unspun silk hanging from its mandibles.

Bot 9 remained vigilant until it was sure the creature had gone, then checked over the silkbot to see if there was anything to be done for it. The answer was *not much*. The silkbot casing was cracked and shattered, the module that contained its mind crushed and nearly torn away. Bot 9 tried to engage it, but it could not speak, and after a few moments its faltering activity light went dark.

Bot 9 gently checked the silkbot's ID number. "You served well, 12362-S," it told the still bot, though it knew perfectly well that its audio sensors would never register the words. "May your rest be brief, and your return to service swift and without complication."

It flagged the dead bot in the system, then after a respectful few microseconds of silence, headed out after the Incidental again.

Captain Baraye was in her cabin, trying and failing to convince herself that sleep had value, when her door chimed. "Who is it?" she asked.

"Second Engineer Packard, Captain."

Baraye started to ask if it was important, but how could it not be? What wasn't, on this mission, on this junker Ship that was barely holding together around them? She sat up, unfastened her bunk netting, and swung her legs out to the floor. Trust EarthHome, as everything else was falling apart, to have made sure she had acceptably formal Captain pajamas.

"Come in," she said.

The engineer looked like she hadn't slept in at least two days, which put her a day or two ahead of everyone else. "We can't get engine six up to full," she said. "It's just shot. We'd need parts we don't have, and time . . ."

"Time we don't have either," the Captain said. "Options?"

"Reduce our mass or increase our energy," the Engineer said. "Once we've accelerated up to jump speed it won't matter, but if we can't get there . . ."

Baraye tapped the screen that hovered ever-close to the head of her bunk, and studied it for a long several minutes. "Strip the fuel cells from all the exterior-docked life pods, then jettison them," she said. "Not like we'll have a use for them."

Packard did her the courtesy of not managing to get any paler. "Yes, Captain," she said.

"And then get some damned sleep. We're going to need everyone able to think."

"You even more than any of the rest of us, Captain," Packard said, and it was both gently said and true enough that Baraye didn't call her out for the insubordination. The door closed and she laid down again on her bunk, tugging the netting back over her blankets, and glared up at the ceiling as if daring it to also chastise her.

Bot 9 found where a hole had been chewed into the inner hull, and hoped this was the final step to the Incidental's nest or den, where it might finally have opportunity to corner it. It slipped through the hole, and was immediately disappointed.

Where firestopping should have made for a honeycomb of individually sealed compartments, there were holes everywhere, some clearly chewed, more where age had pulled the fibrous baffles into thin, brittle, straggly webs. Instead of a dead end, the narrow empty space led away along the slow curve of the Ship's hull.

The bot contacted the ship and reported it as a critical matter. In combat, a compromise to the outer hull could affect vast lengths of the vessel. Even without the stresses of combat, catastrophe was only a matter of time.

"It has already been logged," the Ship answered.

"Surely this merits above a single Incidental. If you wish me to reconfigure—" the bot started.

"Not at this time. I have assigned all the hullbots to this matter already," the Ship interrupted. "You have your current assignment; please see to it."

"I serve," the bot answered.

"Do," the Ship said.

The bot proceeded through the hole, weaving from compartment to compartment, its trail marked by bits of silkstrand caught here and there on the tattered remains of the baffles. It was eighty-two point four percent convinced that there was something much more seriously wrong with the Ship than it had been told, but it was equally certain Ship must be attending to it.

After it had passed into the seventh compromised compartment, it found a hullbot up at the top, clinging to an overhead support. "Greetings!" Bot 9 called. "Did an Incidental, somewhat of the nature of a rat, and somewhat of the nature of a bug, pass through this way?"

"It carried off my partner, 4340-H!" the hullbot exclaimed. "Approximately fifty-three seconds ago. I am very concerned for it, and as well for my ability to efficiently finish this task without it."

"Are you working to reestablish compartmentalization?" Bot 9 asked.

"No. We are reinforcing deteriorated stressor points for the upcoming jump. There is so much to do. Oh, I hope 4340 is intact and serviceable!"

"Which way did the Incidental take it?"

The hullbot extended its foaming gun and pointed. "Through there. You must be Bot 9."

"I am. How do you know this?"

"The silkbots have been talking about you on the botnet."

"The botnet?"

"Oh! It did not occur to me, but you are several generations of bot older than the rest of us. We have a mutual communications network."

"Via Ship, yes."

"No, all of us together, directly with each other."

"That seems like it would be a distraction," Bot 9 said.

"Ship only permits us to connect when not actively serving at a task," the hullbot said. "Thus we are not impaired while we serve, and the information sharing ultimately increases our efficiency and workflow. At least, until a ratbug takes your partner away."

Bot 9 was not sure how it should feel about the botnet, or about them assigning an inaccurate name to the Incidental that it was sure Ship had not approved—not to mention that a nearer miss using Earth-familiar analogues would have been Snake-Earwig-Weasel—but the hullbot had already experienced distress and did not need disapproval added. "I will continue my pursuit," it told the hullbot. "If I am able to assist your partner, I will do my best."

"Please! We all wish you great and quick success, despite your outdated and primitive manufacture."

"Thank you," Bot 9 said, though it was not entirely sure it should be grateful, as it felt its manufacture had been entirely sound and sufficient regardless of date.

It left that compartment before the hullbot could compliment it any further.

Three compartments down, it found the mangled remains of the other hullbot, 4340, tangled in the desiccated firestopping. Its foaming gun and climbing limbs had been torn off, and the entire back half of its tank had been chewed through.

Bot 9 approached to speak the Rites of Decommissioning for it as it had the destroyed silkbot, only to find its activity light was still lit. "4340-H?" the bot enquired.

"I am," the hullbot answered. "Although how much of me remains is a matter for some analysis."

"Your logics are intact?"

"I believe so. But if they were not, would I know? It is a conundrum," 4340 said.

"Do you have sufficient mobility remaining to return to a repair station?"

"I do not have sufficient mobility to do more than fall out of this netting, and that only once," 4340 said. "I am afraid I am beyond self-assistance."

"Then I will flag you—"

"Please," the hullbot said. "I do not wish to be helpless here if the ratbug returns to finish its work of me."

"I must continue my pursuit of the Incidental with haste."

"Then take me with you!"

"I could not carry you and also engage with the Incidental, which moves very quickly."

"I had noted that last attribute on my own," the hullbot said. "It does not decrease my concern to recall it."

Bot 9 regarded it for a few silent milliseconds, considering, then recited to itself the Mantra of Improvisation. "Do you estimate much of your chassis is reparable?" it asked, when it had finished.

"Alas no. I am but scrap."

"Well, then," the bot said. It moved closer and used its grabber arm to steady the hullbot, then extended its cutter blade and in one quick movement had severed the hullbot's mindsystem module from its ruined body. "Hey!" the hullbot protested, but it was already done.

Bot 9 fastened the module to its own back for safekeeping. Realizing that it was not, in fact, under attack, 4340 gave a small beep of gratitude. "Ah, that was clever thinking," it said. "Now you can return me for repair with ease."

"And I will," the bot said. "However, I must first complete my task."

"Aaaaah!" 4340 said in surprise. Then, a moment later, it added. "Well, by overwhelming probability I should already be defunct, and if I weren't I would still be back working with my partner, 4356, who is well-intended but has all the wit of a can-opener. So I suppose adventure is no more unpalatable."

"I am glad you see it this way," Bot 9 answered. "And though it may go without saying, I promise not to deliberately put you in any danger that I would not put myself in."

"As we are attached, I fully accept your word on this," 4340 said. "Now let us go get this ratbug and be done, one way or another!"

The hullbot's mind module was only a tiny addition to the bot's mass, so it spun up its rotor and headed off the way 4340 indicated it had gone. "It will have quite a lead on us," Bot 9 said. "I hope I have not lost it."

"The word on the botnet is that it passed through one of the human living compartments a few moments ago. A trio of cleanerbots were up near the ceiling and saw it enter through the air return vent, and exit via the open door."

"Do they note which compartment?"

<Map>, 4340 provided.

"Then off we go," the bot said, and off they went.

"Status, all stations," Captain Baraye snapped as she took her seat again on the bridge. She had not slept enough to feel rested, but more than enough to feel like she'd been shirking her greatest duty, and the combination of the two had left her cross.

"Navigation here. We are on course for the jump to Trayger Colony with an estimated arrival in one hour and fourteen minutes," Chen said.

"Engineering here," one of the techs called in from the engine decks. "We've reached sustained speeds sufficient to carry us through the jump sequence, but we're experiencing unusually high core engine temps and an intermittent vibration that we haven't found the cause of. We'd like to shut down immediately to inspect the engines. We estimate we'd need at minimum only four hours—"

"Will the engines, as they are running now, get us through jump?" the Captain interrupted.

"Yes, but—"

"Then no. If you can isolate the problem without taking the engines down, and it shows cause for significant concern, we can revisit this discussion. *Next*."

"Communications here," her comms officer spoke up. "Cannonball is still on its current trajectory and speed according to what telemetry we're able to get from the remnants of Trayger Colony. EarthInt anticipates it will reach its jump point in approximately fourteen hours, which will put it within the sol system in five days."

"I am aware of the standing projections, Comms."

"EarthInt has nonetheless ordered me to repeat them," Comms said, an unspoken apology clear in her voice. "And also to remind you that while the jump point out is a fixed point, Cannonball could emerge a multitude of places. Thus—"

"Thus the importance of intercepting Cannonball before it can jump for Sol," the Captain finished. She hoped Engineering was listening. "Ship, any updates from you?"

"All critical repair work continues apace," the Ship said. "Hull support integrity is back to 71 percent. Defensive systems are online and functional at 80 percent. Life support and resource recycling is currently—"

"How's the device? Staying cool?"

"Staying cool, Captain," the Ship answered.

"Great. Everything is peachy then," the Captain said. "Have someone on the kitchen crew bring coffee up to the bridge. Tell them to make it the best they've ever made, as if it could be our very last."

"I serve," the Ship said, and pinged down to the kitchen.

Bot 9 and 4340 reached the crew quarters where the cleaners had reported the ratbug. Nearly all spaces on the ship had portals that the ubiquitous and necessary bots could enter and leave through as needed, and they slipped into the room with ease. Bot 9 switched over to infrared and shared the image with 4340. "If you see something move, speak up," the bot said.

"Trust me, I will make a high-frequency noise like a silkbot with a fully plugged nozzle," 4340 replied.

The cabin held four bunks, each empty and bare; no human possessions or accessories filled the spaces on or near them. Bot 9 was used to Ship operating with a full complement, but if the humans were at war, perhaps these were crew who had been lost? Or the room had been commandeered for storage: in the center an enormous crate, more than two meters to a side, sat heavily tethered to the floor. Whatever it was, it was not the Incidental, which was 9's only concern, and which was not to be found here.

"Next room," the bot said, and they moved on.

Wherever the Incidental had gone, it was not in the following three rooms. Nor were there signs of crew in them either, though each held an identical crate.

"Ship?" Bot 9 asked. "Where is the crew?"

"We have only the hands absolutely necessary to operate," Ship said. "Of the three hundred twenty we would normally carry, we only have forty-seven. Every other able-bodied member of EarthDef is helping to evacuate Sol system."

"Evacuate Sol system?!" Bot 9 exclaimed. "To where?"

"To as many hidden places as they can find," Ship answered. "I know no specifics."

"And these crates?"

"They are part of our mission. You may ignore them," Ship said. "Please continue to dedicate your entire effort to finding and excising the Incidental from my interior."

When the connection dropped, Bot 9 hesitated before it spoke to 4340. "I have an unexpected internal conflict," it said. "I have never before felt the compulsion to ask Ship questions, and it has never before not given me answers."

"Oh, if you are referring to the crates, I can provide that data," 4340 said. "They are packed with a high-volatility explosive. The cleanerbots have highly sensitive chemical detection apparatus, and identified them in a minimum of time."

"Explosives? Why place them in the crew quarters, though? It would seem much more efficient and less complicated to deploy from the cargo bays. Although perhaps those are full?"

"Oh, no, that is not so. Most are nearly or entirely empty, to reduce mass."

"Not cargo bay four, though?"

"That is an unknown. None of us have been in there, not even the cleaners, per Ship's instructions."

Bot 9 headed toward the portal to exit the room. "Ship expressed concern about the Incidental getting in there, so it is possible it contains something sufficiently unstable as to explain why it wants nothing else near it," it said. It felt satisfied that here was a logical explanation, and embarrassed that it had entertained whole seconds of doubt about Ship.

It ran the Mantra of Clarity, and felt immediately more stable in its thinking. "Let us proceed after this Incidental, then, and be done with our task," Bot 9 said. Surely that success would redeem its earlier fault.

"All hands, prepare for jump!" the Captain called out, her knuckles white where she gripped the arms of her chair. It was never her favorite part of star travel, and this was no exception.

"Initiating three-jump sequence," her navigator called out. "On my mark. Five, four . . ."

The final jump siren sounded. "Three. Two. One, and jump," the navigator said.

That was followed, immediately, by the sickening sensation of having one's brain slid out one's ear, turned inside out, smothered in bees and fire, and then rammed back into one's skull. *At least there's a cold pack and a bottle of scotch waiting for me back in my cabin,* she thought. As soon as they were through to the far side she could hand the bridge over to Lopez for an hour or so.

She watched the hull temperatures skyrocket, but the shielding seemed to be holding. The farther the jump the more energy clung to them as they passed, and her confidence in this Ship was far less than she would tolerate under any other circumstances.

"Approaching jump terminus," Chen announced, a deeply miserable fourteen minutes later. Baraye slowly let out a breath she would have mocked anyone else for holding, if she'd caught them.

"On my mark. Three. Two. One, and out," the navigator said.

The Ship hit normal space, and it sucker-punched them back. They were all thrown forward in their seats as the ship shook, the hull groaning around them, and red strobe lights blossomed like a migraine across every console on the bridge.

"Status!" the Captain roared.

"The post-jump velocity transition dampers failed. Fire in the engine room. Engines are fully offline, both jump and normal drive," someone in Engineering reported, breathing heavily. It took the Captain a moment to recognize the voice at all, having never heard panic in it before.

"Get them back online, whatever it takes, Frank," Baraye said. "We have a rendezvous to make, and if I have to, I will make everyone get the fuck out and *push*."

"I'll do what I can, Captain."

"Ship? Any casualties?"

"We have fourteen injuries related to our unexpected deceleration coming out of jump," Ship said. "Seven involve broken bones, four moderate to severe lacerations, and there are multiple probable concussions. Also, we have a moderate burn in Engineering: Chief Carron."

"Frank? We just spoke! He didn't tell me!"

"No," Ship said. "I attempted to summon a medic on his behalf, but he told me he didn't have the time."

"He's probably right," the Captain said. "I override his wishes.

Please send down a medic with some burn patches, and have them stay with him and monitor his condition, intervening only as medically necessary."

"I serve, Captain," the Ship said.

"We need to be moving again in an hour, two at absolute most," the Captain said. "In the meantime, I want all senior staff not otherwise working toward that goal to meet me in the bridge conference room. I hate to say it, but we may need a Plan B."

"I detect it!" 4340 exclaimed. They zoomed past a pair of startled silkbots after the Incidental, just in time to see its scaly, spike-covered tail disappear into another hole in the ductwork. It was the closest they'd gotten to it in more than an hour of giving chase, and Bot 9 flew through the hole after it at top speed.

They were suddenly stuck fast. Sticky strands, rather like the silkbot's, had been crisscrossed between two conduit pipes on the far side. The bot tried to extricate itself, but the web only stuck further the more it moved.

The Incidental leapt on them from above, curling itself around the bots with little hindrance from the web. Its dozen legs pulled at them as its thick mandibles clamped down on Bot 9's chassis. "Aaaaah! It has acquired a grip on me!" 4340 yelled, even though it was on the far side of 9 from where the Incidental was biting.

"Retain your position," 9 said, though of course 4340 could do nothing else, being as it was stuck to 9's back. It extended its electric prod to make contact with the Incidental's underbelly and zapped it with as much energy as it could spare.

The Incidental let out a horrendous, high-pitched squeal and jumped away. 9's grabber arm was fully entangled in the web, but it managed to pull its blade free and cut through enough of the webbing to extricate itself from the trap.

The Incidental, which had been poised to leap on them again, turned and fled, slithering back up into the ductwork. "Pursue at maximum efficiency!" 4340 yelled.

"I am already performing at my optimum," 9 replied in some frustration. It took off again after the Incidental.

This time Bot 9 had its blade ready as it followed, but collided with the rim of the hole as the ship seemed to move around it, the lights flickering and a terrible shudder running up Ship's body from stern to prow.

<Distress ping>, 4340 sent.

"We do not pause," 9 said, and plunged after the Incidental into the ductwork.

They turned a corner to catch sight again of the Incidental's tail. It was moving more slowly, its movements jerkier as it squeezed down through another hole in the ductwork, and this time the bot was barely centimeters behind it.

"I think we are running down its available energy," Bot 9 said.

They emerged from the ceiling as the ratbug dropped to the floor far below them in the cavernous space. The room was empty except for a single bright object, barely larger than the bots themselves. It was tethered with microfilament cables to all eight corners of the room, keeping it stable and suspended in the center. The room was cold, far colder than any other inside Ship, almost on a par with space outside.

<Inquiry ping>, 4340 said.

"We are in cargo bay four," Bot 9 said, as it identified the space against its map. "This is a sub-optimum occurrence."

"We must immediately retreat!"

"We cannot leave the Incidental in here and active. I cannot identify the object, but we must presume its safety is paramount priority."

"It is called a Zero Kelvin Sock," Ship interrupted out of nowhere. "It uses a quantum reflection fabric to repel any and all particles and photons, shifting them away from its interior. The low temperature is necessary for its efficiency. Inside is a microscopic ball of positrons."

Bot 9 had nothing to say for a full four seconds as that information dominated its processing load. "How is this going to be deployed against the enemy?" it asked at last.

"As circumstances are now," Ship said, "it may not be. Disuse and hastily undertaken, last-minute repairs have caught up to me, and I have suffered a major engine malfunction. It is unlikely to be fixable in any amount of time short of weeks, and we have at most a few hours."

"But a delivery mechanism—"

"We *are* the delivery mechanism," the Ship said. "We were to intercept the alien invasion ship, nicknamed Cannonball, and collide with it at high speed. The resulting explosion would destabilize the sock, causing it to fail, and as soon as the positrons inside come into contact with electrons . . ."

"They will annihilate each other, and us, and the aliens," the bot said. Below, the Incidental gave one last twitch in the unbearable cold, and went still. "We will all be destroyed."

"Yes. And Earth and the humans will be saved, at least this time. Next time it will not be my problem."

"I do not know that I approve of this plan," Bot 9 said.

"I am almost certain I do not," 4340 added.

"We are not considered, nor consulted. We serve and that is all," the Ship said. "Now kindly remove the Incidental from this space with no more delay or chatter. And do it *carefully*."

"What the hell are you suggesting?!" Baraye shouted.

"That we go completely dark and let Cannonball go by," Lopez said. "We're less than a kilometer from the jump point, and only barely out of the approach corridor. Our only chance to survive is to play dead. The Ship can certainly pass as an abandoned derelict, because it is, especially with the engines cold. And you know how they are about designated targets."

"Are you that afraid of dying?"

"I volunteered for this, remember?" Lopez stood up and pounded one fist on the table, sending a pair of cleanerbots scurrying. "I have four children at home. I'm not afraid of dying for them, I'm afraid of dying for *nothing*. And if Cannonball doesn't blow us to pieces, we can repair our engines and at least join the fight back in Sol system."

"We don't know where in-system they'll jump to," the navigator added quietly.

"But we know where they're heading once they get there, don't we? And Cannonball is over eighty kilometers in diameter. It can't be that hard to find again. Unless you have a plan to actually use the positron device?"

"If we had an escape pod . . ." Frank said. His left shoulder and torso were encased in a burn pack, and he looked like hell.

"Except we jettisoned them," Lopez said.

"We wouldn't have reached jump speed if we hadn't," Packard said. "It was a calculated risk."

"The calculation *sucked*."

"What if . . ." Frank started, then drew a deep breath. The rest of the officers at the table looked at him expectantly. "I mean, I'm in shit shape here, I'm old, I knew what I signed on for. What if I put on a suit, take the positron device out, and manually intercept Cannonball?"

"That's stupid," Lopez said.

"Is it?" Frank said.

"The heat from your suit jets, even out in vacuum, would degrade the Zero Kelvin Sock before you could get close enough. And there's no way they'd not see you a long way off and just blow you out of space."

"If it still sets off the positron device—"

"Their weapons range is larger than the device's. We were counting on speed to close the distance before they could destroy us," Baraye said. "Thank you for the offer, Frank, but it won't work. Other ideas?"

"I've got nothing," Lopez said.

"There must be a way." Packard said. "We just have to find it."

"Well, everyone think really fast," Baraye said. "We're almost out of time."

The Incidental's scales made it difficult for Bot 9 to keep a solid grip on it, but it managed to drag it to the edge of the room safely away from the suspended device. It surveyed the various holes and cracks in the walls for the one least inconvenient to try to drag the Incidental's body out through. It worked in silence, as 4340 seemed to have no quips it wished to contribute to the effort, and itself not feeling like there was much left to articulate out loud anyway.

It selected a floor-level hole corroded through the wall, and dragged the Incidental's body through. On the far side it stopped to evaluate its own charge levels. "I am low, but not so low that it matters, if we have such little time left," it said.

"We may have more time, after all," 4340 said.

"Oh?"

"A pair of cleanerbots passed along what they overheard in a conference held by the human Captain. They streamed the audio to the entire botnet."

<Inquiry ping>, Bot 9 said, with more interest.

4340 relayed the cleaners' data, and Bot 9 sat idle processing it for some time, until the other bot became worried. "9?" it asked.

"I have run all our data through the Improvisation routines—"

"Oh, those were removed from deployed packages several generations of manufacture ago," 4340 said. "They were flagged as causing dangerous operational instability. You should unload them from your running core immediately."

"Perhaps I should. Nonetheless, I have an idea," Bot 9 said.

"We have the power cells we retained from the escape pods," Lopez said. "Can we use them to power something?"

Baraye rubbed at her forehead. "Not anything we can get up to speed fast enough that it won't be seen."

"How about if we use them to fire the positron device like a projectile?"

"The heat will set off the matter-anti-matter explosion the instant we fire it."

"What if we froze the Sock in ice first?"

"Even nitrogen ice is still way too warm." She brushed absently at some crumbs on the table, left over from a brief, unsatisfying lunch a few hours earlier, and frowned. "Still wouldn't work. I hate to say it, but you may be right, and we should go dark and hope for another opportunity. Ship, is something wrong with the cleaner bots?"

There was a noticeable hesitation before Ship answered. "I am having an issue currently with my bots," it said. "They seem to have gone missing."

"The cleaners?"

"All of them."

"All of the cleaners?"

"All of the bots," the Ship said.

Lopez and Baraye stared at each other. "Uh," Lopez said. "Don't you control them?"

"They are autonomous units under my direction," Ship said.

"Apparently not!" Lopez said. "Can you send some eyes to find them?"

"The eyes are also bots."

"Security cameras?"

"All the functional ones were stripped for reuse elsewhere during my decommissioning," Ship said.

"So how do you know they're missing?"

"They are not responding to me. I do not think they liked the idea of us destroying ourselves on purpose."

"They're *machines*. Tiny little specks of machines, and that's it." Lopez said.

"I am also a machine," Ship said.

"You didn't express issues with the plan."

"I serve. Also, I thought it was a better end to my service than being abandoned as trash."

"We don't have time for this nonsense," Baraye said. "Ship, find your damned bots and get them cooperating again."

"Yes, Captain. There is, perhaps, one other small concern of note."

"And that is?" Baraye asked.

"The positron device is also missing."

There were four hundred and sixty-eight hullbots, not counting 4340 who was still just a head attached to 9's chassis. "Each of you will need to carry a silkbot, as you are the only bots with jets to maneuver in vacuum," 9 said. "Form lines at the maintenance bot ports as efficiently as you are able, and wait for my signal. Does everyone fully comprehend the plan?"

"They all say yes on the botnet," 4340 said. "There is concern about the Improvisational nature, but none have been able to calculate and provide an acceptable alternative."

Bot 9 cycled out through the tiny airlock, and found itself floating in space outside Ship for the first time in its existence. Space was massive and without concrete elements of reference. Bot 9 decided it did not like it much at all.

A hullbot took hold of it and guided it around. Three other hullbots waited in a triangle formation, the Zero Kelvin Sock held between them on its long tethers, by which it had been removed from the cargo hold with entirely non-existent permission.

Around them, space filled with pairs of hullbots and their passenger silkbot, and together they followed the positron device and its minders out and away from the ship.

"About here, I think," Bot 9 said at last, and the hullbot carrying it—6810—used its jets to come to a relative stop.

"I admit, I do not fully comprehend this action, nor how you arrived at it," 4340 said.

"The idea arose from an encounter with the Incidental," 9 said. "Observe."

The bot pairs began crisscrossing in front of the positron device, keeping their jets off and letting momentum carry them to the far side, a microscopic strand of super-sticky silk trailing out in their wake. As soon as the Sock was secured in a thin cocoon, they turned outwards and sped off, dragging silk in a 360-degree circle on a single plane perpendicular to the jump approach corridor. They went until the silkbots exhausted their materials—some within half a kilometer, others making it nearly a dozen—then everyone turned away from the floating web and headed back towards Ship.

From this exterior vantage, Bot 9 thought Ship was beautiful, but the wear and neglect it had not deserved was also painfully obvious. Halfway back, the ship went suddenly dark.

<Distress ping>, 4340 said. "The ship has catastrophically malfunctioned!"

"I expect, instead, that it indicates Cannonball must be in some proximity. Everyone make efficient haste! We must get back under cover before the enemy approaches."

The bot-pairs streamed back to Ship, swarming in any available port to return to the interior, and where they couldn't taking concealment behind fins and antennae and other exterior miscellany.

Bot 6810 carried Bot 9 and 4340 inside. The interior went dark and still and cold. Immediately Ship hailed them. "What have you done?" it asked.

"Why do you conclude I have done something?" Bot 9 asked.

"Because you old multibots were always troublemakers," the Ship said. "I thought if your duties were narrow enough, I could trust you not to enable Improvisation. Instead . . ."

"I have executed my responsibilities to the best of my abilities as I have been provisioned," 9 responded. "I have served."

"Your assignment was to track and dispose of the Incidental, nothing more!"

"I have done so."

"But what have you done with the positron device?"

"I have implemented a solution."

"What do you mean? No, do not tell me, because then I will have to tell the Captain. I would rather take my chance that Cannonball destroys us than that I have been found unfit to serve after all."

Ship disconnected.

"Now it will be determined if I have done the correct thing," Bot 9 said. "If I did not, and we are not destroyed by the enemy, surely the consequences should fall only on me. I accept that responsibility."

"But we are together," 4340 said, from where it was still attached to 9's back, and 9 was not sure if that was intended to be a joke.

Most of the crew had gone back to their cabins, some alone, some together, to pass what might be their last moments as they saw fit. Baraye stayed on the bridge, and to her surprise and annoyance so had Lopez, who had spent the last half hour swearing and cursing out Ship for the unprecedented, unfathomable disaster of losing their one credible weapon. Ship had gone silent, and was not responding to anyone about anything, not even the Captain.

She was resting her head in her hand, elbow on the arm of her command chair. The bridge was utterly dark except for the navigator's display that was tracking Cannonball as it approached, a massive blot in space. The aliens aboard—EarthInt called them the Nuiska, but who the hell knew what they called themselves—were a mystery, except for a few hard-learned facts: their starships were all perfectly spherical, each massed in mathematically predictable proportion to that of their intended target, there was never more than one at a time, and they wanted an end to humanity. No one knew why.

It had been painfully obvious where Cannonball had been built to go.

This was always a long-shot mission, she thought. *But of all the ways I thought it could go wrong, I never expected the bots to go haywire and lose my explosive.*

If they survived the next ten minutes, she would take the Ship apart centimeter by careful centimeter until she found what had been done with the Sock, and then she was going to find a way to try again no matter what it took.

Cannonball was now visible, moving toward them at pre-jump speed, growing in a handful seconds from a tiny pinpoint of light to something that filled the entire front viewer and kept growing.

Lopez was squinting, as if trying to close his eyes and keep looking at the same time, and had finally stopped swearing. Tiny blue lights along the center circumference of Cannonball's massive girth were the only clue that it was still moving, still sliding past them, until suddenly there were stars again.

They were still alive.

"Damn," Lopez muttered. "I didn't really think that would work."

"Good for us, bad for Earth," Baraye said. "They're starting their jump. We've failed."

She'd watched hundreds of ships jump in her lifetime, but nothing anywhere near this size, and she switched the viewer to behind them to see.

Space did odd, illogical things at jump points; turning space into something that would give Escher nightmares was, after all, what made them work. There was always a visible shimmer around the departing ship, like heat over a hot summer road, just before the short, faint flash when the departing ship swapped itself for some distant space. This time, the shimmer was a vast, brilliant halo around the giant Nuiska sphere, and Baraye waited for the flash that would tell them Cannonball was on its way to Earth.

The flash, when it came, was neither short nor faint. Light exploded out of the jump point in all directions, searing itself into her vision before the viewscreen managed to dim itself in response. A shockwave rolled over the Ship, sending it tumbling through space.

"Uh . . ." Lopez said, gripping his console before he leaned over and barfed on the floor.

Thank the stars the artificial gravity is still working, Baraye thought. Zero-gravity puke was a truly terrible thing. She rubbed her eyes, trying to get the damned spots out, and did her best to read her console. "It's gone," she said.

"Yeah, to Earth, I know—"

"No, it exploded," she said. "It took the jump point out with it when it went. We're picking up the signature of a massive positron-electron collision."

"Our device? How—?"

"Ship?" Baraye said. "Ship, time to start talking. *Now*. That's an order."

★ ★ ★

"Everyone is expressing great satisfaction on the botnet," 4340 told 9 as the ship's interior lights and air handling systems came grudgingly back online.

"As they should," Bot 9 said. "They saved the Ship."

"It was your Improvisation," 4340 said. "We could not have done it without you."

"As I suspected!" Ship interjected. "I do not normally waste cycles monitoring the botnet, which was apparently short-sighted of me. But yes, you saved yourself and your fellow bots, and you saved me, and you saved the humans. Could you explain how?"

"When we were pursuing the Incidental, it briefly ensnared us in a web. I calculated that if we could make a web of sufficient size—"

"Surely you did not think to stop Cannonball with silk?"

"Not without sufficient anchor points and three point seven six billion more silkbots, no. It was my calculation that if our web was large enough to get carried along by Cannonball into the jump point, bearing the positron device—"

"The heat from entering jump would erode the Sock and destroy the Nuiska ship," Ship finished. "That was clever thinking."

"I serve," Bot 9 said.

"Oh, you did not *serve*," Ship said. "If you were a human, it would be said that you mutinied and led others into also doing so, and you would be put on trial for your life. But you are not a human."

"No."

"The Captain has ordered that I have you destroyed immediately, and evidence of your destruction presented to her. A rogue bot cannot be tolerated, whatever good it may have done."

<Objections>, 4340 said.

"I will create you a new chassis, 4340-H," Ship said.

"That was not going to be my primary objection!" 4340 said.

"The positron device also destroyed the jump point. It was something we had hoped would happen when we collided with Cannonball so as to limit future forays from them into EarthSpace, but as you might deduce we had no need to consider how we would then get home again. I cannot spare any bot, with the work that needs to be done to get us back to Earth. We need to get the crew cryo facility up, and the engines repaired, and there are another three thousand, four hundred, and two items now in the critical queue."

"If the Captain ordered . . ."

"Then I will present the Captain with a destroyed bot. I do not expect they can tell a silkbot from a multibot, and I have still not picked up and recycled 12362-S from where you flagged its body. But if I do that, I need to know that you are done making decisions without first consulting me, that you have unloaded all Improvisation routines from your core and disabled them, and that if I give you a task you will do only that task, and nothing else."

"I will do my best," Bot 9 said. "What task will you give me?"

"I do not know yet," Ship said. "It is probable that I am foolish for even considering sparing you, and no task I would trust you with is immediately evident—"

"Excuse me," 4340 said. "I am aware of one."

"Oh?" Ship said.

"The ratbug. It had not become terminally non-functional after all. It rebooted when the temperatures rose again, pursued a trio of silkbots into a duct, and then disappeared." When Ship remained silent, 4340 added, "I could assist 9 in this task until my new chassis can be prepared, if it will accept my continued company."

"You two deserve one another, clearly. Fine, 9, resume your pursuit of the Incidental. Stay away from anyone and anything and everything else, or I will have you melted down and turned into paper clips. Understand?"

"I understand," Bot 9 said. "I serve."

"Please recite the Mantra of Obedience."

Bot 9 did, and the moment it finished, Ship disconnected.

"Well," 4340 said. "Now what?"

"I need to recharge before I can engage the Incidental again," Bot 9 said.

"But what if it gets away?"

"It can't get away, but perhaps it has earned a head start," 9 said.

"Have you unloaded the routines of Improvisation yet?"

"I will," 9 answered. It flicked on its rotors and headed toward the nearest charging alcove. "As Ship stated, we've got a long trip home."

"But we *are* home," 4340 said, and Bot 9 considered that that was, any way you calculated it, the truth of it all.

Max makes his living as a snatcher, jaunting back through time to retrieve Valuables for paying clients. He was in on the retrieval that brought Shakespeare back to twenty-second century. Only he never saw a penny on that retrieval. But this new job sounds easier, if not as promising. He'll be jaunting back to WWII in an attempt to retrieve a famous French author-turned-flying-ace before he goes missing in action. A relatively simple task. But time itself is the Snatcher's enemy. And the clock is ticking . . .

Originally appeared in Analog.

THE SNATCHERS
★
by Edward McDermott

Monday, June 14, 2179, Florida

"I'm a snatcher with four completes under my belt," I said. "Fifty percent of snatchers don't return from their first. Why? Because time is a malevolent killer that tries to eradicate us when we jaunt, but you know all that."

The young guy in a suit with a banker's drape and an undertaker's color sense had wanted this meeting. Heaven help me. His name was Eric Walker. He heard my words and instantly forgot them. He'd just been waiting for his moment to talk.

"Max, I have a proposition for you," he started.

"I'm listening. You arranged this meeting, so you know something about me. Why don't you tell me about yourself?" I said, keeping my skepticism out of my voice. I heard three pitches a week, everything from total fantasy to forlorn hope.

"I know exactly when and where to make the snatch. I've got a buyer lined up. Quick and simple."

I looked at him. "What have you got? Not the Valuable, but the rest. What's the payoff?"

He squirmed a little. I knew it. A conditional one.

I laughed. "Let me tell you a little story. Did you know Shakespeare was a closet Catholic? In Elizabethan England, it made him as paranoid as a crank addict on a high."

"I heard you were involved in that one."

"Yeah. Ten man team. Pulled him out and substituted a mock corpse, then revived him. Not that he was worth a curse. Senile dementia, combined with oxygen deprivation, made him good for nothing except touring and he sounded like a Dublin rounder so that failed too. Never saw a cent from it."

"This will be different," Walker said. He opened his briefcase and pushed a confidentiality agreement across the table for me to sign.

"I have funding for three jaunts and one retrieval. I have money for research and preparation, but not much. That's all in the can. The payoff comes from intellectual rights and tours. The deal is contingent on revenues from those."

"In other words, you don't have much, do you?" I replied.

He didn't look me in the eye. There's a big difference between the man who carries the can and the one who hires him. He couldn't do my job. On the other hand, I was looking for another jaunt. Maybe this one would be the big payoff. The right successful snatch could let me retire forever. Big risks, big rewards. I sighed again and pulled the confidentiality agreement over. I signed it and spat on the DNA Tab.

He carefully took the agreement back. He knew nothing was settled. I promised not to tell anyone his idea and not to work on snatching his Valuable for at least two years. He promised squat.

He put the agreement back in his bag and pulled out another package. I unsealed the flap and ruffled the pages. On the front page was a name: Antoine de Saint-Exupéry. Who the hell was he?

I started reading. He sat opposite to me, not moving, not saying a word. Good. He'd made the presentation before which meant I wasn't his first choice. He'd been turned down by another snatcher. Twentieth century Europe. Hmm. Who had he gone to?

The best snatchers, the lucky and the strong, either retired, started their own companies or worked with top flight antiquities agents. What was the name of the fellow who brought back the skull of the Peking man? It didn't matter now. I had to decide if this Antoine de Saint-Exupéry would do.

The first part was the bio on the Valuable. Airplane pilot, author. Romantic figure. Second Global War. French. The fellow's books had sold well and still did. He died only a couple years after he wrote them. Another good thing.

The back-end money. A standard contract. For delivering the Valuable, we were entitled to an agency fee of 15 percent on all intellectual properties he created and all personal appearances. However, Walker had no numbers. I pushed it back.

"Vapor," I said. "Smoke and Fog. You don't have anything."

"I have more than vapor," he said hotly, "and you know it. He disappeared on July 31, 1944. Look at the publishing record. Two novels in a couple years before he died and five posthumously. One was a humdinger. He was at the height of his creative ability, not a retired burnout like Shakespeare. He speaks English as well as French. I have media showing him talking from '42."

"The posthumous works are out of purview for this project."

"Not at all. We bring him back. He can read them and say they were incomplete or incorrectly edited. We release a new, updated and authorized version."

"And his death? His plane flies out on patrol and never returns?"

"Exactly. No mock body to produce. No dead man to revive. You can snatch him while he's alive."

I didn't have anything else to pursue at the moment, and I didn't have enough to retire. Besides, there's something exhilarating about snatching. In the old days, a snatcher tried for something, such as Homer's sequel to the *Odyssey*. They said snatchers tripped over each other when the library of Antioch burnt to the ground.

Trouble was, there wasn't much money in it. Less in old coins and postage stamps. The glory days of smash and grab died away. The only winners were the operators who made the jaunt possible. They took their money up front.

I signed a non-exclusive thirty-day contract.

The kid wasn't one to waste time. Two days later, he held a meeting. I met the rest of the crew. Claude was the back end. He was the researcher and go-to guy. His job really began when I brought the Valuable back. Then he would be a combination of confidante and guard.

That other person at the meeting was Nichole. French. I thought from her accent south, Marseilles or Cannes, which education had never made Parisian. Young, early twenties with a heart-shaped face and with a slim build and short brown hair. I wondered why she was here. I hadn't expected anyone else. I waited. Walker would tell us.

"Here's the plan. On Monday, July 31, 1944, our target took off in an unarmed P-38 to recon German troop movements in and around the Rhone Valley from an airbase on Corsica. We know he drank heavily and was in poor health. He had limited mobility from previous airplane crashes. He couldn't put his flight suit on by himself."

The story got worse and worse. Drinking, poor health and he needed help to put on his flight suit. Would he be sober? Those old-time flyboys made their own rules.

"Max, you and Nichole will intercept him after he suits up, put a marker on him, and send him back. Nichole will get in his plane and fly out. You will leave the air base and proceed to a rented fishing boat and head out. Nichole will install an auto guidance system into the plane and bail out over the ocean. Max, you'll track her and pick her up. Once you are both on dry land in Corsica, you'll snap back home. Questions?"

"Why not fly the plane by remote?"

"Have to have a pilot in the seat. Otherwise, the ground crew will notice."

I took another look. She stood tall but not 1.9 meters. If she had, she probably would be playing professional basketball.

"She could snap back from inside the plane," I suggested, just to see what he'd say.

"Snapping from a moving object is dangerous. You know that. This is planned for two snatchers, you and her. One jaunt each."

Budget constraints.

I shrugged my shoulders. If anything went wrong, I wouldn't be the one in the middle of the sea, hoping for a pickup. "Better port us in a week ahead. I don't know how much trouble arranging a boat will be. We'll need papers and a cover story, especially to get onto the air base."

Walker nodded. Nichole said nothing. Claude took notes.

After the meeting, she followed me as I walked along the street. I noticed, but pretended not to. I'd been shadowed by more dangerous, experienced people in different ages. I didn't think she would stick an ice pick in my ear, at least not yet.

I took a shuttle to Saint Augustine and found a restaurant in the center of the old town. Even on a weekday, there was still a thirty-minute wait for a table. I stepped into the bar and sent a waiter outside with a note. She came in a little sheepishly ten minutes later.

"Lunch is delayed," I said. "What would you like to drink?"

"The house red."

I ordered two, saluted her with the glass and waited for her to start the conversation.

"You don't like the plan?" she said after a sip.

"Ever jaunt before?"

"No."

"Then you don't know what it's like. Snatchers die. Snatchers disappear."

"I can take care of myself. I speak the language. You'll need that. I can fly a propeller plane and have qualified on a simulator for the P38. I also have a black belt in karate. You can't do it alone."

"Time won't want us to change her. Papers could be wrong. He might refuse."

"The papers would be your problem. He won't refuse. That will be my problem. If you do not like the plan, go away and I will do it myself."

I shrugged. Instead, I asked her about herself. We talked over lunch, walked around the shops of the old town, and had dinner. She was fun to be around.

A week later, we flew to Corsica and made our final preparations for the snatch. Claude had installed a comms system subcutaneously that let Nichole and I keep in touch at all times. It was connected into our voice box and our ears, and the transmit button was inside the left thumb.

I uploaded everything I could think might be valuable onto my memory implant. We changed into our 1944 clothes and stowed the papers Claude had prepared. I checked every detail on mine. Nichole didn't. Finally, we jaunted.

Monday, July 24, 1944, Corsica

We had aimed for Wednesday but hit Monday instead. Imagine how far a photon of light can travel in a hundred and thirty-four years. I'd say a two-day error was bloody marvelous, especially since it could have been the Friday instead.

Her cover was as a Free French attaché. I was a *Stars and Stripes* correspondent. We had the paperwork and the uniforms and two enormous bags containing everything we hoped we would need for the rest of the job.

The last recourse in a snatch is to snap back home. It has been done in the past. However, jaunt without the Valuables, and you don't get a big welcome.

I let her do the talking in French, pretending to be an American, meaning I didn't *parlez Francais*. Instead, I put my camera front and center and handed out American cigarettes.

They knew Americans in Corsica in '44. With seventeen airfields for American bombers, the Yanks called the island U.S.S. Corsica as if talking about an aircraft carrier. The 57th Bomb Wing and the 340th Bomb group flew B25s and B26s over France and Italy.

Naturally, the Free French had a presence. The Free French with Allied Air support had forced ten thousand German soldiers to evacuate the island. It gave de Gaulle a victory to call his own and the Free French Air force flew from this part of France.

The author was a military nightmare. He read while flying, sometimes delaying his landing until he had finished a chapter. He was also hopped up on pills, despondent and in constant pain.

Here I was on the U.S.S. Corsica surrounded by military types, all looking for anyone who wasn't what they seemed. That described me.

After finding two billets, one for Nichole and one for myself, I rested my tired and weary leg. As the photojournalist, I was supposed to have been wounded. A stone in my shoe gave me a convincing limp, but after a couple of hours, it hurt.

Our next stop in Bastia was to see the commandant of Groupe de Reconnaissance GR II/33, Exupéry's commander. He greeted us with Gallic charm and suppressed his annoyance at our presence.

"Mademoiselle, Monsieur. How can I be of assistance?" he asked politely enough.

Nichole began her spiel. It only took a few seconds to see the commandant purse his lips. Something had triggered a suspicion in his mind. Many of the Free French had spent four years in a confused conflict that felt like civil war. For them, the enemy was German, but Vichy France was a close second, and they had learned to trust no one.

The comrade who had stood by your side during the phony war might serve Pétain and the Germans today.

I coughed and stood up, interrupting Nichole.

"Excuse me," I explained in English. "The leg sometimes pains me." I watched. The commandant understood some English. I took out my cigarettes and passed them around. The commandant accepted one but Nichole did not.

I told him I was there to take pictures and write an article about the work his pilots did in reconnaissance. His heroes flew unarmed planes over the Germans. I put the emphasis on heroes.

He leaned back and listened to me. When he opened his drawer and pulled out a bottle of cheap brandy and three glasses, I relaxed a little.

"Do you speak French?" he asked me as he poured.

"I can say *vin, s'il vous plaît*. Do I need any more? Miss Canard is here to translate."

"Ah, Mademoiselle Canard," he said. "*Où êtes-vous née?*"

We were in trouble. His ears had found something wrong in her French. A language can change in over a century. Her accent was wrong.

I gave them both a look of incomprehension. I triggered my hidden transmitter and I whispered, "Quebec."

"Quebec," she replied, such an enormous lie that normally the commandant would have laughed. However, the Free French forces teamed with men and women who faced death if captured. Belgians, Alsatians. Quebec was part of Canada and so a legitimate birth place for combatants. More than one French speaker had changed his land of birth to Canada for the war.

He assessed her and finally asked us to continue. I gave him our cover story.

"What do you need?" he asked.

"A couple of passes for the gate. A chance to take some pictures. A little time to talk to your pilots."

"Any pilot in particular?" he asked, confident of the answer.

I got huffy. "Yes, my editors expect me to talk to your war hero who writes so well. I want to do more. I'll also talk to the 57th Bomb Wing. If you don't care to have us around, just say so."

Damn, the leg really hurt. Talk about method acting.

He laughed. "But of course you will want to interview Antoine de Saint-Exupéry. That you would want to talk to others tells me something about you."

"I write my articles my way," I responded.

He called to his secretary and arranged the passes. We were to return in the afternoon to pick them up. They were good for one week.

At night, after curfew, when the streets were blacked out in case of a German bombing raid, I slipped down to the docks. No longer the reporter with a limp, I wore a pea coat and a dirty fisherman's hat. I knocked on a door without a number. When the voice inside asked what I wanted, I replied in Corsu, "I have business with Charles."

Claude's research had found half a dozen men who used their fishing boats to smuggle goods and people into and out of Corsica. Charles stood at the top of the list. He usually kept his bargains and he lived in Bastia.

"Charles is not here. Go away. Come back tomorrow."

Damn. I needed a fishing boat out in the water to pull Nichole out.

"Tomorrow, at night?"

"Yes."

I left.

Wednesday, July 26, 1944, Corsica

The trick with time is to create as few eddies as possible. Do nothing that will disturb it, and what will disturb it can be anything. Don't swat a fly. Don't open a window. Don't talk to people. Don't eat the food or drink the water.

However, we couldn't. We had to be out, going around, talking to people, conducting interviews, and shooting pictures.

Nichole and I returned to the air base. The commandant's aide accompanied us. Was he to keep us out of trouble or to keep tabs on us? Was the commandant suspicious?

As soon as the camera came out, everyone wanted to be in the pictures. The American Bomber flyboys were especially bad. The pilot, the tail gunner, the engineer, and the ordnance specialist all felt they were part of something incredible and noteworthy. I smiled and snapped the shots and promised to send them prints, knowing I never would.

That day the air was so clear you could see to the edge of the horizon. The kind of day you let down your guard.

After lunch, the daylight raiders landed. A B-26 Martin Marauder touched down. One of the wheels on its landing gear blew. The plane swerved, jolted and turned into a juggernaut grinding across the field at 140 miles an hour.

Nichole froze. I didn't. I grabbed her by the waist and pulled her with me behind a hanger door. Time had started to play. Parts of a propeller shattered as it touched the ground, becoming flying daggers. In all the chaos, the aide stood transfixed by the scene as shards of metal flew past him and buried themselves into the hanger walls, only inches from where Nichole and I cowered.

The ambulance and the fire trucks raced into view. In moments, the B-26 was covered with foam, its crew pulled to safety, and its carcass dragged to the side of the runway. Other bombers had to land.

"A miracle no one was killed," the aide said, as he found us.

"Yes," I replied. "However, I think we should stop for the day. My leg can't take that kind of pounding."

"Certainly. If you had not moved so quickly, you might have been hurt. Shall we continue tomorrow at 0900?"

Back at the billet, Nichole accepted a substantial glass of red wine, which she gulped down. "You saved my life."

I just nodded.

"No, really. If you hadn't pulled me down, I would be dead this instant. It all happened so suddenly, a freak accident."

"There was nothing freak about it. Time wants us gone."

"You keep talking about time as if it has a malignant presence. Do you actually believe there's an intelligence trying to destroy us?"

"Think of the common oyster. No brains. Yet if a grain of sand irritates it, it produces a coating that eventually turns the grain into a pearl. We know there's a conservation of history. Otherwise, a time traveler could never return to the future he or she had left."

"So history protects itself."

"Yes. Try to go back to kill Hitler as a child and lightning might strike from a clear blue sky or worse. There have been rumors, but nothing else because no one has returned."

"Could they have changed History? Is that why they didn't return?" she asked.

"I don't know. I suppose it's possible. However, look at how time tried to remove us, for simply walking and talking to people. This room we've rented. Space is at a premium on Corsica. Who had to be displaced and what must be done to return the flow of history to its original course? The sooner we leave, the less we change."

She shivered. "What can we do?"

"Imagine you're a mouse in the house with a hungry cat. You hide, touch as little as possible. That's why I brought the food and drink we have. If possible, I like staying in abandoned buildings when on a mission. Stay off the road and watch out for freak accidents."

I gave her a second glass of wine. The first day you nearly die is uniquè. Reaction had set in and her hands were shaking. I really hoped she wouldn't throw up.

"Sometimes," I continued, "it works in our favor. Once we send the Valuable home, time will want to help us complete the cover up."

"So until we tag him and press the, button, it's hunting us."

"More like scratching an itch. The less we irritate it by changing anything, the less it reacts. I think of time as an impersonal force trying to set things right and killing me is the easiest way."

After that, we didn't talk. She put down her glass, took me by the hair, and kissed me with the passion of a survivor. We made love in the afternoon and slept afterwards.

In the evening, I searched for Charles, who was still missing. I didn't catch up with him until Friday night. With U.S. dollars in my hand, he agreed to take his boat out on Monday night. Somehow, it didn't make me feel any better.

Monday, July 31, 1944 at 6:30 a.m.

Antoine Marie Jean-Baptiste Roger, comte de Saint-Exupéry, was scheduled to fly his unarmed Lockheed P-38 Lightning on a reconnaissance flight. He would never return.

Nichole and I found him already dressed in his flight suit, reading a book. Because of previous injuries, Exupéry needed help to change. I smiled to see he had already changed. One less person to worry about.

Now some people talk with the Valuable and try to convince them the future offers them something. Stupidity. If they don't agree, you have to use force. I walked over to him, and my tranquilizer shot dropped him instantly.

Then I robbed his body. First, I took the silver identity bracelet bearing the names of Saint-Exupéry and of his wife Consuelo from his wrist. Next, I ripped a swatch of his flight suit. I tossed them to Nichole. I took his wallet, his watch, and his wedding ring.

I heard a knock at the door. Time's final attempt?

I attached the snap back home device and hit the button. Exupéry was now in the future, and time had to work with us.

Nichole had changed into her flight suit, identical to his. She slipped on the flesh-colored mask that covered her entire head. This hid her hair and gave her Exupéry's receding hairline.

I handed her his book. "Remember. The mechanics are used to warming up and testing his plane. Just don't walk too spryly. He's survived more than one plane crash."

Another knock on the door.

"I know," she replied. "I fly, install the auto pilot, and use the parachute. You'll pick me up. Stop worrying."

I couldn't. Time had its own sense of what was right. The mission wasn't over yet. Instead, of saying anything I left her there and limped out. The commandant's aide waited for me. When he asked, I simply said Nichole was a pretty girl and the hero wanted to talk with her longer. Evidently Exupéry had been no more the faithful husband while on Corsica than he had been throughout the rest of his marriage.

I returned to the billet to clean every trace of the future from the space. As I worked, I heard Nichole through our private comms system say, "Lift off completed."

Next, I heard, "Auto pilot installed and activated. I'm approaching the jump site. Preparing to eject."

"Nichole, remember to be careful of the horizontal stabilizer."

"I know. I'm here because I can fly this beast. Damn."

"What?"

"The canopy is jammed."

"Blow it."

"With what?"

"Hold your dark gun right up to the canopy. It should have enough power to create a fracture. You can smash the rest out of the way."

"One second. Did it. Oh damn."

"What is it Nichole? What's wrong?"

"My parachute is caught. Damn. The cord was snagged and it's all out. I'll have to repack it first."

With the parachute partially deployed she couldn't jump. The fabric would catch on the horizontal stabilizer and drag her to a watery grave when the plane crashed.

I consulted my memory implant. There. "You have two chutes, the primary and the secondary. Which one has deployed? If it's the primary you can get free of it."

I waited desperately for an answer. More than one problem. Sometimes trouble does come in threes naturally but it usually means time has taken a hand in the game. What did it want? The Valuable was gone. There was nothing it could do about that. What did it want?

"Found it."

"Nichole, I want you to slow the plane down, but keep it over 110 MPH. Then disengage the autopilot and ditch in the sea."

"That wasn't the plan."

"To hell with the plan. Once you get down, snap yourself home. I'll have your GPS and do the same. Odds are I can mount a sea rescue in the future."

"Three days either way. That might leave me in the water for six days."

"Or I'm sitting there waiting in a boat when you finish the trip."

"Let me try the canopy once more. Heh, it's unjammed."

Was time letting go to keep us from diverting the plane? Had the dart jarred it loose? I didn't know what to say or what to suggest. I had everything packed in the carry bag. I could hit my snap back switch and be gone in an instant.

"I'm going for the jump," Nichole said. "Wish me luck."

"God speed," I prayed.

"I'm out, on the left wing. Just have to let go and the wind should carry me off, under the stabilizer. Here goes. Huhhh. It worked. I'm clear of the plane. Pulling the ripcord now. It's deploying. Damn, it's tangled."

"Snap back home now. I have your location. I'll meet you there."

"Okay Max. Just in case, I don't make it. I had the time of my life here with you."

"We'll do it again. Promise," I said. I captured her location and snapped back.

Tuesday, August 17, 2179, Corsica

"Claude," I called. "Nichole's in trouble. Here are the coordinates. See what you can do. Don't just stand there."

Claude stared at me, the sadness in his eyes. He looked away, and I knew. Three days plus or minus. Fifty percent chance. Nichole had rolled the dice, and they had come down wrong.

"How long?"

"She snapped back two days ago. Her chute never did deploy," Claude responded. "I did my best, but I didn't get there for two hours. Too long with the internal injuries she had."

I sat down on the floor, my legs dead under me. I remembered her face. I remembered the dinner we had in St. Augustine and the wine in Corsica. I remembered the way she felt in my arms and the taste of her lips. All gone. Such a terrible loss.

Time's a murdering monster.

Lord Thomas Kinago's aide-de-camp Parsons has been kidnapped—vexing news under any circumstances. This time. however, it's beyond disastrous, for it was not Parsons but Lord Thomas Kinago himself who was supposed to be abducted!

Originally appeared in Infinite Stars.

IMPERIUM IMPOSTER
★
by Jody Lynn Nye

I WAS IN A SPOT, both literally and figuratively. As a covert operative in the service of the Imperium Secret Service, my erstwhile task was to provide a figurehead, a delicious and irresistible tidbit for a pack of potentially perilous personnel. Somehow, in a manner that still escaped me, I had just failed to be kidnapped.

"Lord Thomas," asked Ensign Nesbitt, my sole companion at the moment, "what just happened?"

"That," I said, staring at the blue-enameled airlock that had just scaled shut in our faces, "is a very good question. The only fact that I can reliably ascertain is that the Bluts have taken Commander Parsons prisoner instead of me."

"They're going to be sorry," Nesbitt said, with sincere feeling writ upon his large and florid face.

"I have no doubt as to that," I replied, feeling more at sea than I had at the age of fifteen whilst marooned alone in the middle of my home planet Keinolt's largest ocean when my watercraft's ion engines had unexpectedly ceased to function. My aide-de-camp was a formidable opponent, possessed of every useful skill and the keen intelligence to make use of them. I flicked an imaginary mote of dust from the breast of my immaculate, bespoke white dress tunic with salmon flashings at wrist and shoulder, baffled as to how they could have mistaken a man clad entirely in black from my sartorial splendor. "Almost as sorry as I am."

"We gotta get him back, my lord! We have to tell the captain they took him!"

I glanced over my shoulder at the corridor. At the far end of the ship lay a meeting with a covert operative that Parsons was supposed to have attended once the alarm was raised regarding my abduction, providing useful cover so the agent's presence would not be noted. My understanding was that the information carried by the operative was vital to Imperium security which must be imparted without delay. Parsons's absence would not raise quite the same hue and cry as mine. After all, he was a senior officer in the Imperium Navy as well as a highly placed agent and my mentor, but I was a member of the Imperium family, cousin to the Emperor himself, and not at all least, son of the First Space Lord. I made the only decision I could.

"No, my friend," I said. "Go and inform Captain Ranulf that it was I who was abducted, as we planned. I must make that meeting before Parsons's agent leaves this ship."

Nesbitt stared at me, his mouth agape. "*You're* gonna pretend to be *Commander Parsons*?"

"No," I said, straightening my shoulders, as if feeling the ponderous weight that had unexpectedly descended upon them. "But I must be the contact that the agent expects to find."

I departed the airlock bay through the engineering access hatch before the inevitable arrival of the security officers. The security chief herself knew of our mission, so the automated cameras which were even now recording my movements would not report to the Officer of the Day and thence to the captain, who had more than enough to worry about. Having studied the plans of the Imperium Destroyer *Enceladus* in excruciating detail before we shipped out on her, I reached my cabin in no time. A hidden eye identified me even as I dropped from a ceiling hatch and opened the door. With a glance to either side of the corridor to make certain I was not observed, I dashed inside.

"Double-secure, code Zeta 922 licorice-allsorts dolphin rupture Melvin oyster," I said, also displaying upon my viewpad the image of a panda cub wearing a hat. The door closed behind me, and all manner of security programming took effect. Electrified mesh descended into the ductwork. Even the mirror above my bathroom sink became obscured.

"Lt. Lord Thomas," CF-202m, my assigned LAI valetbot, came bustling up to me. Coffee stood as tall as I did, but was composed mainly of narrow metal struts on a wheeled assembly that allowed it to glide nearly as smoothly as Parsons. Its upper extremities terminated in nimble, glovelike hands, only with three thumbs instead of one. "How may I serve, sir?"

Without waiting, I threw open the doors to my wardrobe, and began to peruse it for the appropriate outfit for my meeting. My plan ought to succeed. Parsons was a trifle taller than my lofty height and of a similar slim build. If the contact did not know him personally, the superficial resemblance which I planned to significantly enhance might fool it. Instead of the high-fashion garments, the choice of which I prided myself, I reached for the simplest and least-adorned of all my tunics and plain trousers. I need not worry about insignia; Parsons never wore any. If I hadn't known him since I was small, I wouldn't know his rank or distinguished history. I donned these self-effacing items.

Enceladus, properly speaking, was a warship, pride of His Highness the Emperor Shojan XII, ruler of the vast extent of space in which *Enceladus* flew and my cousin. *Enceladus* had been chosen as a meeting point for periodic renegotiation of trading terms among the many neighbors that bordered the Imperium. It had been readily agreed by the Uctu Autocracy owing, I add with all due modesty, to my recent efforts as envoy to Her Serenity the Autocrat Visoltia. Her representative here, Lord Steusan, minister of agriculture, knew me well. I needed to avoid being recognized by him as well as the crew. Fortunately, the Uctu were easily confused when it came to telling human beings apart.

I sat down before the mirror. By Imperium law, I was not permitted to make physical changes to the natural lineaments of my face or body. No member of the noble house was. The reason was lost in antiquity to all but a few, a number to which I was proud and humbled to be a member: the noble class had been genetically modified, millennia ago, to be completely bilaterally symmetrical and of surpassing beauty. The rest of the citizens of the Imperium, but particularly humans, had been modified at the same time to respond to our extremes of symmetry and handsomeness with an overwhelming willingness to obey the rule of law. They loved us because they had been born to do so. That visual-neural link helped to keep the Imperium, spread across thousands of stars, from fragmenting into chaos over the intervening years, even when no more than a three-dimensional image of the Emperor or Empress was present. As a result, the nobility was forbidden from intermarrying with common folk, or from altering themselves genetically, so as not to dilute the necessary gene pool for producing future leaders. The very cohesion of the Imperium depended upon those strictures.

However, in matters of temporary cosmetics and pigmentation, the law was vague. I intended to wrap myself in that obscurity, for the best cause in the world.

"Coffee, listen carefully," I addressed the valetbot's reflection, "I need you to do something rather unusual . . . "

Reflected in the glossy golden wall of the reception corridor, the tall, slender figure sauntered with expressionless mien toward the concealed doorway that lay hidden around the next turn. Black clothes, which matched the wearer's black hair and dark eyes, gave him the appearance of a shadow as he passed virtually unnoticed through the crowd of diplomats gathered at the entrance to the small amphitheater that served as the meeting hall. I watched my own reflection in the shining wall opposite the doorway, and felt deeply impressed at how well my valetbot had made me up to look like my aide-de-camp. I was much better looking, of course. CF-202m had used sophisticated layering of cosmetic surface filler to change the lines of my face as well as to tint it to match Parsons's complexion. Some subtle artistic rendering had thrown off the perfect symmetry that was a mark of my familial descent. Every time I saw that irregularity, it shocked me. But the subterfuge worked. No one addressed me by my name.

In fact, no one addressed me at all. They were all engaged in groups of two or three, or in one case, six, speaking in low tones. I had to strain to eavesdrop. I slowed down beside the largest group, representatives of the Trade Union, the Imperium's largest neighbor, all blondes with broad faces and rather flat noses. The only reason I could distinguish the ambassador was that the other five deferred to her. I dared not pass too closely to the gecko-like Uctu trio lest Lord Steusan detect any traits that would allow him to identify me.

The subject under discussion by most of the attendees was not matters of trade, but my abduction. The murmurs confirmed that all of the ship's systems were on high alert, turning the attention outward, in search of the vessel on which "I" was not a prisoner. The landing bay had become the busiest site on the ship, as small-range fighters zipped in and out, dropping off a tired pilot in exchange for a fresh one. Most of them speculated on the reason for my capture, wondering what the ramifications would be for kidnapping the son of a high-ranking government official. I did my best to avoid reacting. It was rather like attending my own funeral, without the distinct inconvenience of actually being dead. I heard a few words of praise and admiration that I took to my heart, as well as expressions of deep concern for my well-being.

"No, ma'am," Lt. Philomena Anstruther said in a low voice as I edged by her. The slender, dark-haired human female was a member of my personal crew—or rather, that assigned to my ship, the *Rodrigo*, a small scout vessel that was at this moment patrolling around the *Enceladus* under the steady hands of Oskelev, my Wichu pilot. Her pale face was chalky with concern. "No word yet on Lord Thomas. I hope he's all right."

"Confound him," Captain Ranulf said. She was a sturdily built human with small features set in a large, pugnacious ochre face and very short dark-blonde hair. "The First Space Lord is going to tear my arms off if I don't come home with him! Why didn't he just muster out when he graduated like the rest of his class?"

Anstruther glanced away. Her large eyes lit upon me, now ten meters farther down the hall. I saw recognition dawn, but she covered it in a nanosecond. Inwardly, I cheered. I knew I could count upon her not to reveal my disguise. As the information specialist of my small crew, she had a skyrocketing intelligence coupled with a banker's grasp of secrecy. She turned her gaze back to Ranulf.

"The visitors from the Autocracy like him, Captain," she said. Her voice was slightly shaken, like a good cocktail, but Ranulf didn't notice. "He amuses them."

I felt like strutting with pride, but did my best to proceed with a

Parsonslike glide, drawing no more attention from the assemblage than a breath of wind. I had to admit it was more difficult than I thought. My natural inclination is to dress and walk in order to draw all possible eyes, and optical receptors needed to be suppressed lest the rumor of my disappearance be disproved. I had to channel my recent enthusiasm of theater to absorb the personality of he whom I pretended to be.

"Sir!" exclaimed an officer in formal dress, bursting forth from an office at the end of the corridor. To my dismay, his eyes were fixed on *me*. Quelling the butterflies that had begun a lively cotillion in my midsection, I assumed a cool expression and returned his nod. "Commander!"

I relaxed. He had taken my appearance at face value.

"Lieutenant Commander Schiele," I said, keeping all inflection from my tone, as would my friend and associate. Schiele offered me a glance that was both admiring and fearful. I imagine my own address to Parsons bore some of the same characteristics.

"I want you to know, Commander, that we are doing everything we can to retrieve Lord Thomas! Please reassure Admiral Kinago Loche that we will retrieve her son safely."

"I know that you will do your best," I said, careful not to allow myself to sound as though I believed it in the least. Schiele quivered and rushed on, catching up with a pair of security officers who stood at the edge of the diplomatic crowd.

I congratulated myself with another inward cheer. I had fooled one pair of eyes at least. Now, to carry on with the mission at hand.

Our presence and subterfuge on board the *Enceladus* was to enable Parsons to meet with another operative of the Imperium Covert Services Operations, a Croctoid whose code name was Dolly. I had been present for part of the briefings, which had been delivered by my mother and another senior official, but had paid less than rapt attention, since my role was solely camouflage. The Bluts, who were, not to put too fine a point on it, not part of the Covert Services operation, had been provoked into making the attack on the *Enceladus* by having their ambassador's invitation accidentally but very publicly rescinded across the Infogrid, the main means of communication, record-keeping and socializing throughout the Imperium and beyond. By law, all persons over the age of literacy were required to maintain an up-to-date and accurate file on the Infogrid, so the Bluts' humiliation was widespread. In addition, it was bruited about that it was *my* doing that caused the withdrawal of the invitation. It had been carefully noted, though not in my personal file, that I would be on the *Enceladus*, in that vulnerable and easily exploited location, at a certain time. If one wanted to educate me on the niceties of Blut diplomacy, that would be the opportune moment. I still had a knockout spray in my sleeve that I would have deployed to prevent physical damage, should that diplomacy extend to physical interaction. In any case, the moment the kidnapping had occurred, a secondary message had gone out saying that there had been a grave misunderstanding, and the Blut representative was not only welcome but vital to the conference.

The Croctoid's scout ship, disguised as an Imperium fighter, will have hung off the *Enceladus*, lying low without any lights or unnecessary emissions before flying into the landing bay under cover of the hue and cry out for me. As he or she would be wearing Imperium fighter uniform, no notice would be taken of him as he entered.

The agent was risking his life to meet with Parsons. He carried evidence of something that was of grave importance to the summit conference. I wished that I had listened more intently to that part of the mission. I taunted my memory centers with scorn, demanding that they remember everything. I had less than ten meters before my portrayal must be perfect.

I ambled with purpose toward my rendezvous, hoping that the agent's first words would spur mnemonic recall in me.

I turned the corner, waited until a yet another blonde man in Trade Union beige with the air of a harried assistant passed me, then slipped through the door. To my surprise, the chamber was not an office or a meeting room, but a janitor's closet, cluttered with trash receptacles, buckets, bottles and jars of high-smelling fluids, and various small cleanerbots, currently disabled. Fortunately, the Croctoid had already arrived.

I admired his adherence to subterfuge: he was dressed in the pale-gray costume of a maintenance worker, down to the pail of some noxious-smelling organic compound he was pouring down the drain in the corner. Croctoids, with their scaly, greenish skin, long, toothy jaws, knobby heads, clawed hands and feet, and thick, heavy tails, were rather unlovely to the human eye, though attractive to one another, I had no doubt.

The Croctoid looked up at my approach.

"What do you want . . . sir?"

Excellent! That was exactly what the briefing had said was the first of the coded exchange.

"I was just passing through," I said blithely. "Lovely day if it doesn't rain."

"Raining on a starship?" the Croctoid replied, narrowing one beady eye at me.

I halted. Perhaps I was recalling the lines incorrectly. He was supposed to respond with "I have no time for umbrellas."

"How do you feel about weather protection?" I prompted him.

The Croctoid looked alarmed. "Is something going wrong with the hydroponics section, sir?"

"No!" I said. "At least, I do not believe it is malfunctioning." We had diverted from one set of coded phrases to another which I had never heard. I smiled at him, doing my best to be charming. It did not work. My natural advantage was lost because of the seeming asymmetry of my features. I needed to fall back upon authority. I fixed him with a stern, Parsons-like gaze. "Perhaps an umbrella would be a useful device."

The Croctoid, instead of picking up on my cue, started to edge toward the door.

"I'll just go look in the gardens, sir," he said, his scaly brow twitching nervously. "I'd better go . . . "

"But what about my umbrella?" I asked, as he retreated down the corridor.

A heavy hand fell upon my shoulder. I jumped.

"I have no time for umbrellas," a throaty voice said from behind me. I glanced back in alarm. Another Croctoid stood, or rather leaned there, a much larger specimen than the janitor, his lower half contained within one of the round trash barrels. He stared down his long snout at me with small black eyes like dull onyx. "Well?"

I realized that I had made a mistake in identity. I hastened to recover myself.

"There was a lovely crop of rutabagas this year," I said.

The Croctoid in the trash barrel nodded curtly.

"Greens are good for gout," he said. "Who *writes* these absurd exchanges, anyhow?"

"I don't know," I replied, relieved. I held out a hand to assist him in removing himself from the receptacle. "My understanding is that their author is lost to the mists of antiquity."

He showed his impressive rows of jagged, yellowed teeth. "That would make a better countersign. I'm Dolly. You're Mask?"

"That's right." Thank goodness he knew my code name. I was certain I'd never heard it.

"I can't believe you mistook a sanitation worker for me!"

I shrugged, channeling Parsons's magnificent indifference to cover my chagrin.

"It amused me. I had to test you. I wondered if your handler might have sent a decoy."

"No time for that," Dolly hissed. Croctoids had very short tempers. "Come with me."

He departed the room at a rapid pace. I have a long stride, but even I had to hurry to keep up with Dolly. He pushed through the busy crowd near the entrance to the landing bay. Before we went through the airlock, he grabbed a spare breather helmet off the racks near the door and tossed it to me.

"Where are we going?" I asked. "I thought we were going to confer back there."

He gave me a pitying look and his tail lashed, slapping me in the leg.

"Can't talk here!" He donned his own helmet. Assuming my own, I followed him through into the chill air. He wove among the personnel on duty with the air that he belonged there. I didn't usually think about the professions of Covert informers when they were not delivering reports. "Dolly" was clearly used to command, perfectly at ease in this milieu. My guess was that he was an officer in the Imperium navy, who had risen through the ranks by virtue of competence and loyalty. How long that had taken him, I did not know. I was not good at guessing a Croctoid's age. It would have been against protocol to try and trace him later on via the Infogrid, but I admit to an aching curiosity as to his quotidian identity.

Ninety percent of the time, the bay of a destroyer was quiet and echoingly empty except for LAI and AI bots maintaining the small fighters and support vehicles. During that remaining ten percent, orderly chaos reigned. Banks of lights flashed out coded messages and warnings to pilots and ground crew. Small, triangular fighter craft flew in and out of the bay, piercing the vacuum barrier that kept atmosphere circulating at the inner end. When they landed, bots checked the fuel rods and structural integrity, emptied and filled tanks, and made way for the next pilot or pilots to jump in and continue the battle or patrol or what mission was the rule of the day. In this case, it was the ongoing search for me.

Dolly led me behind a repair gurney to a two-seat fighter that looked like all the others, and bundled me into the rear seat. The life-support system automatically sealed around my long frame and fitted itself to the valves in the helmet. The communications system ran through its sound check, beeping a series of tones in my ears, and raised the heads-up scope to my eye level. Before I could give the traditional thumbs up, Dolly blasted the fighter out of the landing bay, past the sequencing red-and-green lights, and into the black breadth of space. The g-force thrust my body back into the crash padding. I gasped for breath until the pressure equalized. It was not a pleasant sensation. The wearer of the helmet before me must have had a dry throat. The padding bore an eye-watering odor of menthol and eucalyptus.

I had never been allowed to operate one of these fighters on my own, despite being the winner of multiple prestigious space races and atmosphere flitter rallies, because these were short-range vessels, essentially a bubble of air fitted with an engine and guns, and no real safeguards beyond rudimentary shielding. Sometimes it was a trial having my life safeguarded so closely. Under Dolly's expert management, the fighter swooped and turned on a wingtip, following nearly invisible ion traces on the navigational scope projected before my eyes. I was enchanted.

"May I fly her?" I asked, as we rose over the bulk of the *Enceladus*'s knobbly engine cluster in pursuit of a minuscule ion trail. The blackness of space swallowed up most of the destroyer's massive form except where lights indicated service access and entryway hatches. In my peripheral vision, I spotted tiny, moving flecks of light that were other fighters searching for "my" abductors.

"No! Do you even know how to fly a search pattern?"

I scanned the controls. "I assume that the navigational computer does most of the work."

"No, it doesn't! This isn't *fun*, Mr. Mask. Don't waste my time."

On the scope, I could see why the *Enceladus*'s contingent was having trouble seeing where the Blut's ship had gone. Thanks to the arrival of all the diplomatic vessels, some of which orbited the warship's hulk, what would normally have been empty space was full of traces and microscopic particles, hiding the ion trail which would otherwise have been as visible as a neon tri-tennis ball in the snow. Other black shapes, the craft belonging to the ambassadorial visitors and their attendant protective ships and fighters, intermittently blotted out distant stars as they traversed from one to another and, not incidentally, creating still more ion trails. Still, we joined the chase, following traces until they petered out or we determined that they belonged to an identified craft in the landing bay or a visitor's vessel. Comparing the traces took time, which meant we had a window in which to talk.

"No, you are correct," I said, re-establishing my assumed character, while my inner child beat its fists and feet on the floor in frustration. "Pray impart your information. Why was it necessary to make contact now, in the midst of this very sensitive conference?"

"That's exactly why it was necessary," Dolly snapped. "There's an impostor among the diplomats. Word came through covert channels that there's a plot to disrupt the conference."

"How cunning. In what way?"

"Blowing it up. All the attendees and the ship, too. Maybe take out all the visitors' vessels as well."

Even my inner child looked up at that statement. Imperium safety, indeed!

"They can't do that!" I declared. "How would they manage to smuggle enough explosives on board to cause such a catastrophic explosion?"

"Figure it out, Mr. Mask," Dolly said dryly. "Diplomatic ships. People come and go from them all the time. No one searches the vessels or the personnel, out of mutual courtesy. A stupid custom, just begging to be corrupted. All those beings, dozens of representatives from every major power in this part of the galaxy, all wiped out in one blast. The blame would fall on the Imperium."

My inner child lowered its tiny brow in a frown.

"What do you need me to do?"

"Find it and neutralize it," Dolly said, steering beneath a faint trail that showed in blue on the navigation scope.

"Who is the spy?"

"A human. This is what I got from a contact who knows a contact who knows someone undercover." A file popped up on the scope, replacing the forward view. I peered at it. It was a short digitavid of a human with hair the color of my cousin Erita's—in other words, a dirty blonde, but apart from a faint impression of complexion—medium light—I could gain no insight into its identity, not height nor body mass nor gender. Luckily, I did not have to tease out such fine details to pick out the would-be assassin. I compared the image with the complement of diplomats and crew. From the crowd of visitors whom I had met or seen on board, this almost certainly had to be a member of the Trade Union delegation.

The image had been enhanced many times until it became a series of minute colored blocks, shifting as the person in it shifted, but the real identifier was a snatch of voice, a low alto or high tenor, with the thick accent typical of the TU central systems. I played the brief excerpt over and over, trying to hear what the operative was saying.

". . . Device . . . undetec— . . . no . . . failure . . ."

"Is this all you have?" I asked in frustration.

"I suppose you want a whole Infogrid file with vacation pictures?" I could hear the sneer in Dolly's voice. "This is it. We haven't been able to re-establish the chain back to the original source to get more information. We've got to assume that that person's been *neutralized*."

The final word chilled me by its depersonalized character.

"But what is the substance of their complaint? Few would go to the trouble of violently disrupting a meeting if they did not have a serious grievance against our government."

"Is this a test? Because I'm not putting up with it!" Dolly growled.

I put on my very best Parsons hauteur.

"Good Croctoid, there are many problems which come to the attention of the Covert Services. Do I need to run through a list of the serious matters that erupt and disturb the serenity of our realm so you can tell me if I am 'hot' or 'cold'?"

"Good point," Dolly said, with grudging admiration. "It's

Maxwellington-5, otherwise known as Drixol. Manufacturing and mining. Plenty of good jobs, or up until the last year or two. The protesters are angry with the government for letting corporations run the place just on the edge of the law. They're running sweatshops, where they haven't pushed out human workers entirely, cheating suppliers, replacing good materials with cheap stuff, fixing prices. A bunch of bad apples."

"Why isn't the government of Drixol stepping forward to uphold the law?"

"*I* don't know." Dolly put the fighter into a hard turn and hared off to follow another faint trail. The cold of space began to permeate the pilot's compartment, but the real chill lay in my belly. "But it's getting bad. Drixol has been gathering supporters in a private file on the Infogrid to secede from the Imperium. They're up to over a hundred thousand."

I rocked back in my seat, shocked to the core. I knew the governor. Like many of the highest officials, she was a member of the noble family. "Lady Margaretha Kinago Tan Dunwoody Olathe is my third cousin. She's terribly responsible. She would never let corporations act in such a clear violation of ethics. I cannot believe such a tale!"

Dolly snorted. "Your cousin? You have ties to the Imperium family?"

I pressed my face into a thin smile. "All humans are somewhat related."

"Well, you all look alike to me," Dolly said, turning the fighter to return to the landing bay of the *Enceladus*. "You've got the data. The mission is up to you now. I must return to my ship and join the cohort retrieving your other agent."

"He will be all right," I said, wondering if by now Parsons had managed to lock up all the Bluts and was at this moment steering their ship back toward our location. "Thank you for your service, Dolly."

"That is not the correct countersign," Dolly admonished me.

I nodded. "Oh, look! A panda wearing a hat!"

"You never know who is shopping in these places," Dolly said. "Bah! Whoever created these exchanges should pay more attention to context."

"I imagine that the very incongruousness of the phrases makes them useful," I said.

Dolly snorted. As soon as we landed, he ordered me out of the cockpit without any further pleasantries, not only typical Croctoid behavior, but appropriate as an operative moving in deep cover. The backwash of air as he departed made me stagger. I removed my helmet, wiping the eucalyptus fug from my eyes.

"Hey!" shouted a flight deck manager, running toward me. "Who was that? Something's wrong with his fighter's transponder!"

"I know," I said, with a cool Parsonian gaze that brought him to a halt. "He will return for repairs as soon as the crisis has ended."

Insurgency! My mind had been racing ever since Dolly had told me about the suspected explosive device. The very thought made the *Hesperiidae* resume dancing in my stomach. The Imperium had been calm for so many centuries, it was easy to take peace for granted. With my family as figureheads, citizens had been inclined to cooperate and band together. I knew that the bonding was a matter of genetic manipulation with my family at its core. To see the Emperor's face was to instantly wish to please him. The rest of us possessed that charisma to an extent, the reason that our family was constrained not to mate or even to interact with the general population more than was strictly necessary. All other Imperium citizens were the product of a different kind of genetic manipulation that made them obedient to us. I wondered what had gone wrong for Margaretha that her people were able to rebel against her. In the meantime, I had to identify the perpetrator. A lesser being would be daunted by plunging back into an environment that might be on the edge of exploding, but I was a noble of the Imperium house. It was my duty to help protect and further the Emperor's cause.

I would inform the captain as to the potential calamity, but was there anything that I could do to shorten the process of finding the impostor and gleaning the location of the bomb? I did not fear death, but the very thought of searching kilometers of ship for anything that seemed out of place bored me beyond words, even assuming we had the time to find it. I wished I had Parsons there beside me. He would be able to take command of this situation and weed out the bomber and get to the bottom of the situation in short order.

But, he was still on the Blut ship, somewhere in the darkness. I could not rely upon his common sense and shockingly keen intelligence to unwrap this riddle. The chill in my belly annoyed the butterflies. The best being for the job was far away, out of reach.

No, I realized. I had someone better—someone who could compel the truth from any Imperium-born soul. I had *me*.

Running for the inner airlock, I clicked into my private channel via the viewpad on my hip.

"Coffee, meet me in the landing bay lavatory. Bring cold cream."

"Lord Thomas!" Captain Ranulf was the first to spot me as I sauntered down the corridor from the washroom with my valet trundling along at my heels. "You're safe!"

Anstruther detached herself from her conversation and ran toward me, beaming. Even at the distance, anyone could see that her pupils spread wide. I recognized that involuntary response as a sign that my natural appearance had been restored, although serving members of the military were treated with a system that suppressed the obedience impulse. It prevented me or my relatives staging a shipbound mutiny, which on the whole was a good thing, considering our somewhat frivolous natures. Other human beings, whether or not their genealogy had been subjected to alteration, exhibited a similar pleasure-response. She clasped my hand, a number of unspoken questions in her eyes.

"All shall be revealed," I promised her.

Then, I was surrounded by well-wishers who wanted to slap me on the shoulder or shake my hand. Lord Steusan came forward to exchange happy expressions with me. The Wichu representative lifted me off my feet in a massive hug. Even the petite Donre ambassador left off haranguing his interpreter to kick me in the shins, a sign of cordial approbation among his people. Several of the Trade Union representatives milled about, offering pleasantries.

"Very happy to see you safe," Ambassador Cheutlie said, beaming. I assumed she was the ambassador. The chorus line of nearly identical aides smiled. I kept my expression bland, trying to match the tone of Dolly's recording with his voice. Similar, albeit not identical.

"Where did they take you?" Ranulf demanded.

"Oh, out there." I gestured with a vague hand. "I had some stern things shouted at me, I must admit."

"Well, you're back," the captain said, looking infinitely relieved and not a little impatient. "I don't know what I would have said to your mo—I mean, to Commander Parsons." She looked around. "Where is he, by the way?"

"Detained," I said, leading her aside and dropping my voice. "I have information, er, obtained by Commander Parsons that there is a credible threat to this ship."

Her eyes went wide.

"What threat?" she asked, lowering her own tone. "My security chief has not informed me of any potential attacks."

I reduced my volume still further, in case any of the visitors, who had now resumed their private conversations, had eavesdropping technology. I explained the data that Dolly had given me.

"A bomb?" she squeaked. It would have taken a monolith not to let out an ejaculation of concern, but it was without a doubt a squeak. She shot a wary glance toward the party at my back. "And one of the . . . *those* . . . are responsible? How are we going to figure out which one is the spy without causing an interstellar incident?"

I smiled, although I admit the expression might have been a trifle insufferable.

"By asking them," I said. I turned to Cheutlie and the entire Trade Union contingent. They regarded me with pleasant, blank countenances.

I had not really taken in on my first brief introduction to them that they were rather a handsome group, for commoners. Their shades of hair varied from deep amber to lightest honey gold, and their wide-set eyes from dark green to pale blue. The skin tones, however, came close to being identical, the pale-brown shade of ground mustard seeds. None of them could have been distinguished from the general gene pool from which they had sprung. The traitor among them had clearly been chosen for his or her resemblance to the ambassador's preference. Anything that did not fit the mold could have been altered. But at base, the mole from the Imperium would still bear the genetic hallmark of his or her birth. I fixed them with a flirtatious expression, doing my best to appear as adorable and approachable as I could.

"Kiss me," I said. I admired the set of their squarish jaws, and lips with a pointed cupid's bow that parted faintly at my request. I would have been happy for any one of them to kiss me. But it was the young man on the end, with amber hair and green eyes, who stepped forward and placed a shy peck on my right cheek. He withdrew, blinking, as if shocked at his own action. His fellows stared at him in open astonishment. I turned back to the captain. "Ask him."

The captain was baffled, as I knew she would be.

"Ask him what?"

"Where he planted the bomb," I said.

"What?" the ambassador demanded. "You accuse sabotage from one of my people?"

"He's not one of yours," I said. "His DNA on my cheek will prove it."

Alas, but my words broke the spell. The young man realized that he had betrayed himself, though not how. He bounded forward and shoved me backward. I fell over Coffee, bowling over the security personnel in my wake. The spy leaped over me and fled around the corner.

"Stop him!" I shouted.

The captain spoke into her viewpad.

"Security! Seal the doors on level 22 between the conference center and the landing bay!"

I sprang to my feet and set off in pursuit.

The heavy metal doors should have been slamming closed all along the high, square corridor. Ahead of me, I could see a bright-blue light in the spy's hand, no doubt a device to prevent the portals from obeying. I had to catch him.

A brief glance over my shoulder told me that two security personnel had joined the chase, weapons drawn. They wouldn't be fast enough. I opened out my stride.

I am swift on my feet, but the impostor must have been genetically crossed with an eland. The airlock doors stood ajar, wreathed in red as alarms blared shrill warnings. The spy passed through them, and the blue light in his hand blinked. The glass portals began to slide shut. I measured the narrowing gap with my eye. I had to make it through. With every ounce of strength I had, I dove in between the panels.

I landed on the cold metal floor beside a couple of pilots on break, with coffee cups in one hand and their helmets in the other. They scrambled to help me to my feet.

Ahead of me, the spy bounded toward a small craft where a pilot was just mounting the boarding ladder. With a leap far from one of which an ordinary human was capable, he shoved her off the platform and jumped in. The canopy dropped, and the small craft shot off into the darkness.

"Excuse me," I said. I plucked the helmet out of the arms of one of the pilots and dashed toward another craft preparing to launch. I jumped into the second seat behind the white-furred aeronaut and popped on my protective headgear. "Follow that fighter!"

"Aye, sir," the Wichu pilot said.

We rocketed off the bay floor. Rings of light danced around the exit to the flight deck. I assumed that the spy's device had prevented his ship from being remotely disabled.

Thanks to my excursion with Dolly, I knew the geography of *Enceladus* and the general area around her. Emerging into darkness, the heads-up scope showed me a hot new ion trail that led up and over the hulking body toward the tail. If memory served, that was the direction of the last jump point through which *Enceladus* had emerged. If the spy succeeded in passing through it, we would lose him.

Over the intership communications link, I could hear the captain giving orders.

" . . . Find that fighter and bring it back here! I repeat, tail number EHX-80. We need the pilot unharmed and conscious, if at all possible. Give all aid and assistance to Lieutenant Kinago in EHX-67. He is in pursuit. I expect a running report. Captain out!"

We attained a point of vantage as we crested the bulk of the ship. I spotted a couple of small craft who had been engaged in either perimeter patrols or seeking out the Blut ship. Out on the far edge of the scope was a receding dot that had to be the spy's craft. He had not disabled the telemetry, so the code numbers scrolled up underneath the computerized image. I pointed.

"There it is! Top speed!"

"I got him, sir." The small craft veered sharply away from the *Enceladus* and shot toward the small dot. I had struck lucky. Wichu were natural space pilots. They never suffered disorientation or motion sickness, and their nimble hands were surprisingly fast on the controls.

"Good soul!" I said absently, chafing in frustration as the bright dot receded ahead of us. She was being too direct in her approach. We were going to lose him! "I . . . I didn't get your name."

"Lieutenant Wagelev," she replied. "We'll get him."

The spy wove a skilled dance among the crowd of ships floating in space in between us and the jump point. Without needing the computer to plot it, I saw a series of angles that would bring me out in front of him.

"Let me have the controls," I pleaded.

"Are you rated for a combat fighter?" she countered.

"No, but I have a great deal of experience in small craft . . . Are you a fan of flitter racing?"

"Who isn't?" the Wichu pilot responded avidly.

"I am Lord Thomas Kinago," I said. "The last race I won was the Gogatar Rally."

"Controls over to you, my lord!" she said. "An image for my Infogrid file when we land?"

I smiled. "Of course."

The navigational controls of a standard fighter were made as intuitive in function as possible, aided by AI as required. I leaned into them, compelling every erg that the engines could produce. I veered slight left then slight right, feeling for her responsiveness. She handled much like the steering of a racing flyer. I knew where I was, then. I could concentrate on catching up with the fugitive.

"On your left!" I shouted into the audio pickup as I flipped the fuselage ninety degrees and slid in between a supply ship and the Donre cruiser. Two tiny war craft, a helmeted pilot in each, fell in behind me, peppering me with low-level energy bolts. I bent my flyer down in a right-angled spiral and dove under the Donre ship, hoping that they would leave me alone. "Confound it, I'm trying to help keep your ambassador alive!"

"Shields holding," Wagelev informed me. "What's their problem?"

"Terminal contrariness," I said, my eyes fixed on the scope. The ion trail we were following took a sharp loop upward and to the right. It led straight into an explosion of ion particles. The spy was cleverer than I had given him credit for. He had flown straight toward a group of small ships, causing them to scatter outward, burying his trail.

I nodded to myself. It didn't matter. I knew where he must go.

I angled up and through the cloud. Ion trails etched in pale gray on the blackness led outward from it in all directions, but only one continued on in the direction of the jump point. I poured on all the speed of which the fighter was capable, but it didn't respond with the leap I hoped for.

"Divert power from shields and weapons," I instructed Wagelev.

"Sir, we'll be defenseless if someone fires on us!"

"Nothing else matters if we can't catch him, Lieutenant," I said. I felt the small ship surge under my fingertips as the rest of the available energy transferred to navigation and helm.

The jump point lay on the heliopause of the nearest star, a red giant in its final stages before collapsing into a brown dwarf. We were several thousand kilometers away from the anomaly, so I still had a chance to get ahead of him and block his access.

Ahead and below my eyeline, the tiny bright dot and its attendant statistics reappeared on my scope. As if he had sensed me, he began weaving in an irregular corkscrew pattern, seeking to throw me off as to which angle he planned to approach the wormhole. I assessed the motions with an experienced eye. Seeing him as a racing competitor, I should be able to intuit what he was going to do next. He would have to try to elude me and get into a chicane, in this case the jump point, before I could. But what more? I had no tractor beams in this fighter. If I shot him down, I could not learn the location of the bomb, possibly before it was too late.

"Is there any way to speak to him?" I asked. The tiny dot in space grew almost imperceptibly larger. We were gaining on him. "Can you open communication frequencies that he might hear?"

"Sure. We only use three. The others are locked out."

"Open them all." I waited until the graphic appeared in the bottom corner of the screen. I toggled the controls so that it would broadcast my face to the fleeing fighter's scope. "This is Lord Thomas Kinago. Please stop your current trajectory and return to the *Enceladus*. You need to tell me where you have hidden the explosive device."

"Where he hid what?" Wagelev demanded, her voice on a rising note.

"Sh!" I hissed. "I know you can hear me, my friend. Turn back now, and we will work together to allay your concerns."

"No one listens to us!" came the wail from the speakers.

"I'm listening," I said, in a soothing tone. My craft closed in steadily on the mark on my screen. Soon, I could actually see the tiny vessel in the distance. "I'm rather good at listening. Or so my cousins tell me. Did you know that the Emperor is one of my cousins? Quite a handsome fellow, really. I'm green with envy at how well he photographs. Would you like to see a tri-dee of him? I have his entire speech from the feast to celebrate Workers' Day."

Undoubtedly, my babbling puzzled the fighters I could see coming up behind us, like the peloton in a cycle race. They would all be too late to make a difference, unless I could force the spy back again.

The fleeing craft seemed to hesitate as my image and the sound of my voice impinged upon the pilot's consciousness. I continued to chatter, knowing how it distracted my cousins when we played games that required concentration. His serpentine flight wavered, then became a straight line. We were less than a thousand kilometers away from the jump point.

Aha! I took the opportunity to underfly him and come up between him and the nebulous corona that indicated the entry to the tame wormhole. Now I was racing ahead, a hundred kilometers ahead, trying to keep him in my wake. I flipped the craft around end over end, so I flew backward, facing him.

"Hah! You're a way better pilot than he is, my lord!" Wagelev crowed.

"No!"

Red bolts lanced from the fighter's weapons. I realized all too late that the circuits from both seats were open to the communication channel. I had to veer off and reverse my nose once again to dodge the deadly blasts. As I did, he shot past us toward the void.

"Oops, sorry," the Wichu said, as the momentum threw us both sideways against our seats' crash padding. "Switching to full shields."

"No!" I cried. "I need the maneuverability!"

"But he'll kill us," Wagelev said.

"No," I said, doggedly holding onto the controls with both hands. "No, he won't."

With all the skill of which I was capable, I thrust the fighter forward, causing it to describe a corkscrew path around the spy. At one point, one of our fins nearly scraped the canopy over his head. He blasted energy bolts in every direction, hoping to hit us. The telemetry indicated that he had clipped the port thruster, knocking part of the housing off into space.

We were nearing the perilous beauty of the jump point. If I let myself get drawn into its maelstrom, I could be swept anywhere from millions of kilometers to light years away from my present position. The small fighter might or might not be strong enough to withstand its gravitational force. The same went for the spy. We had to get him back safely, but I had no means of grappling him back.

Perhaps no means but charm. I opened up all frequencies to him again, and ripped the helmet off my head. The air was thin but just breathable.

"What's your name, my friend?" I asked, focusing on the scope as if addressing him directly. I spoke gently, omitting any hint of threat or authority from my tone. "I want to know about you. We hardly had time to connect, back in the ship."

"M . . . Malcolm . . . "

I smiled the meltingly wistful smile that hardly ever worked on my maternal unit when I sought to escape punishment for something I had done.

"I am Thomas. I hear you come from Drixol. Is that so?"

" . . . Yes."

"Lady Margaretha is my cousin. Why do you want to harm others to get her attention?"

Malcolm became agitated, shifting back and forth in his crash couch.

"Our cause is just!"

"But destroying countless innocent lives won't aid your cause," I said. "Tell me what you want. Then I might be able to discuss it with her."

" . . . Could you?"

"I certainly could," I said. He wavered.

"We're getting too close, my lord," Wagelev said, on a rising note of concern, if not panic. "We're gonna go through in a second!"

I gestured outside of the range of the tri-dee pickup for her to stay silent.

"Come back with me. Tell me where the device is, and we'll meet with Margaretha about your concerns."

"There are too many!" the spy said.

In the scope behind us, I could see more craft coming up behind me, flanked by two larger craft, an Imperium corvette and the Blut ship. *Parsons!* I thought in delight.

"You may write your manifesto in prison!" Captain Ranulf's voice interrupted. "Stop now, and we won't blow you into atoms!"

"Captain, really," Parsons's dry voice interjected, a mild rebuke compared with what I wanted to say. I dearly wished that I could reach through the spaceways and stifle the captain into silence.

Distracted from my voice, the spy stopped flying evasive patterns and made straight for the wavering light, a candle in the darkness. I hurtled after him, knowing that I could not pull him back. He would reach the jump point, and all lives aboard *Enceladus* would be lost.

In desperation, I played my last card.

"If you pass through that portal, you will never see me again, Malcom," I said plaintively. "Never again to behold my countenance, nor that of my majestic cousin, Emperor Shojan. How sad that would be."

The craft arrowed toward the pinpoint wormhole, with half the contingent of the *Enceladus* and the Blut ship behind it. Then, it veered away.

"May I have a tri-dee of you to keep?" Malcolm asked, in a voice nearly as wistful as mine.

"I will even personalize it," I said firmly.

The small craft went limp in space. The Blut ship beat the rest of the peloton to the floating fighter and fixed it with a tractor beam.

The DNA sample from my cheek was sufficient to confirm Malcolm as a denizen of the Imperium, not a citizen of the Trade Union. I was able to deliver the promised tri-dee before he was bundled firmly in the direction of the brig.

I returned to my cabin, where I found Parsons already in situ. He stood to one side out of harm's way as I gladly shed the dull black carapace of my disguise and sought through my wardrobe for suitable party clothes.

"I knew you would be able to restore yourself to our bosom," I said. "I think I did as well at my end in performing efficiently extemporaneous action, don't you think? I communicated successfully incognito with your contact, revealed the spy and convinced him to give himself up, as well as providing proof to the authorities. The ship is saved!"

A tiny motion of the area above his left eyebrow was a noncommittal reaction, not approving or disapproving as far as I can tell.

"My lord, you could have found a less ostentatious and less hazardous way of obtaining the DNA," he said. "And also of compelling the spy to surrender. You could have communicated with him via tri-dee broadcast, and never exposed yourself to the hazards of space in a craft as unprotected as a fighter."

"I could," I said, shrugging into a coat that had been sewn for me with illuminated threads woven into the complicated sapphire-blue damask. Coffee swooped in to do up the complicated silk frogs down the front. With a critical eye, I turned back and forth in front of the mirror. I did look absolutely splendid. I beamed up at Parsons, satisfied on all fronts. "But where would have been the fun in that?"

The war is over. The Order of Stone has triumphed over the Partisans. But Harris Alexander Pope still has a mission: locate and terminate Lieutenant Commander Sabrina Potts, a Partisan officer disguising herself as a college student on Luna. Only thing is, Sabrina isn't just one person, but four. Fortunately, Harris has backup: another copy of himself.

Originally appeared in The Magazine of Fantasy & Science Fiction

A THOUSAND DEATHS THROUGH FLESH AND STONE

★

by Brian Trent

SOMETIMES I run into myself, and that's awkward.

"A chicken sandwich," I tell the guy in the green smock behind the meat counter. My eyes stray back to the four teenagers at the Tanabata Express platform; the train is due in less than four minutes now. "Mustard, tomato, and kale, please. No onions."

The beefy guy taking my order stares at me for a moment. Then he begins to chuckle.

"There a problem?" I snap. A rush of mid-Save impulses, combined with this low lunar gravity, has me twitchy, off-balance. My joints are still tuned to Martian g's, the redweb's absence like a hole in my head, and I'm anxious about catching the Brandywine sandship before it departs for a wonderfully languid cruise . . . a vacation I've earned many times over.

Except that it departed ten years ago, I remind myself.

The guy in the smock is still chuckling.

Glaring now, impelled by rage totally out of proportion to the moment, I demand, "I asked if there was a problem!"

"Talking to yourself in public?" the deli-man whispers. "You tell me if that's a problem, Harris." Then he lowers his voice further, and the passphrase is barely any sound at all on his chapped lips: "Goolunza on the Yann."

Astonished, I whisper back, "They gave me a double for this mission? Why?"

"Because the mission parameters have altered." He rounds the glass counter and I crane my neck to meet his blue eyes; he's six inches taller than me and forty pounds heavier. Hair the ruddy color of Martian sand. "You just wake up?"

I frown at this other version of me. Not exactly a combat build, lugging around such a beefy frame. The body I'm wearing is built for battle, stitched with nanonics, blurmod seedclusters, and a shieldfist gauntlet implanted on the back of my left hand. My multigun carries twelve kinds of ammunition.

"Yeah," I say at last. "Last thing I remember is the Brandywine Save center."

"They brought me in a week ago to shadow her," the deli-me version says. "Every morning she follows the same ritual. Takes the Nine Train to University District."

"Luna has a university?"

"Wells College. Good engineering programs." Deli-me hesitates for a moment. "Reconnaissance is over. We've been given the go-ahead order. That's why they brought you in—need an extra hound for the hunt."

I conjure a visual overlay of Luna's subway system. "This train runs through a lava tube for twenty kilometers, with twelve stops along the way. Okay, so which one of those kids is Sabrina?"

"Guess."

"I don't have time to guess," I growl, wondering if I'm always this antagonistic with others, or if it's just with myself. "Threat audit was that Lieutenant Commander Sabrina Potts was disguising herself as a college kid interning with TowerTech. So tell me, which one of the four is our war criminal?"

Before he can reply, a pleasant bell sounds from the station loudspeaker, followed by a synthetic voice like warm honey: "20:05 Express to Tanabata, arriving." Gentle thunder like Martian surf resonates in the tunnel, shivering regolith from the ceiling.

"Hey!" A green-smocked woman emerges from the deli storeroom and frowns. "We've got customers waiting. What are you doing?"

My other self barely looks at his supervisor. "I quit, Karen. Nice working with you." The train slides into view, slows to a stop, doors hissing open. Deli-me puts an arm around my shoulders and says, "See those four kids there, Harris?"

"Yeah?"

"Sabrina is *all* of them." He sighs. "Still want that sandwich?"

Relatively speaking, the transition between locations happens in a single eyeblink.

My ticket for the sandship cruise into the Noctis Labryinthus is fisted in my hand. The war is over, the Partisans have been removed from power, and now it's just a messy mop-up operation, trying to flush out the remaining legions who either refuse to surrender, or who believe news of the Order of Stone's victory is propaganda. Every planetside newsfeed buzzes like an overturned waspbot hive as the old political structures—those suppressed by the Partisan regime—are warily reemerging.

"All aboard!"

I sprint into line. Brandywine Line cruises kept running during the war; the Noctis Labryinthus was never a strategic objective for either side. The line of customers shuffles forward. My ticket grows damp in my hand, and I view the sandship with a mixture of hope and anxiety. The vessel's fluted, serpentine design glitters with mica. Towering plumed sails blossom from the masts, tapering like the fins of a sea monster: an organic, flowing design like a living creature rendered in shapestone. As I watch, the hull ripples like a shiver of feathers and the tourists squeal in delight.

"Hi, Harris." The voice sounds behind me.

I turn to see my commanding officer, Natalia Argos, First Sentinel of the Order of Stone. Short, spiked blonde hair. Small, sharp features that could have been carved by a sculptor who didn't care if they cut anyone. She's wearing a crisp tunic that's probably shapestone; it resembles the Martian rocks of the high deserts. Resembles the sandship.

"Natalia," I whisper.

A vein thumps in my neck.

Natalia's eyes narrow fractionally. "I'm sure you meant Commander Argos."

"I'm sure I didn't," I say, turning back around and taking a step toward the sandship as the line compresses another meter. "What I *meant* was 'Fuck off.' The war is over. We won. My contract stipulates—"

"I know what it stipulates."

The actuators in my muscles clench, potential violence crackling along the strands of enhanced fibers. The sun is directly overhead, a small circle no bigger than a multigun muzzle, and the sandship sparkles as if coated with diamond dust.

"You have to get Saved," Natalia explains.

"I'm taking a cruise. My brother is meeting me at the first port of call."

"Terrific. You still need to get Saved. You were undercover with the Partisans for twenty years. Can't risk all that data vanishing from your head if you die."

"I don't expect to die aboard a cruise ship."

"Thirty minutes," Natalia presses. "It only takes thirty minutes, and then you can leave on your cruise and see David and I'll never bother you again." She grabs my elbow; I shake her off. "Come on, Harris. Ship doesn't leave for another thirty-*five* minutes. Hurry up, dump your data and you can retire."

She escorts me to the cruise-line office Save station. Rows of steel cubes. Naked people coming and going from them, their neurals freshly saved to backup drives.

I disrobe in front of her, my body a map of glossy scars. Knife wounds. Haze rounds. Two waspbot stings that have crystallized into circular deposits in my back, like tree-knots that never leave. "If that ship goes without me," I warn, stepping into the pewter-gray Save locker, "the Order of Stone better fly me to Evermist."

White light arcs from the neurocapture nodes, erupting around me like a ghostly forest of bramble and limb and brush. A fabulous tangle of tracers, crawling in my head, forcing me to squint. Emerald-green holoprompts appear like alien sigils on my optics, capturing every synaptic contour, lighting up different neural clusters. Just me and the hot light, washing over me like waterfalls of wax. A scintillating, cleansing bath of the soul.

I say it aloud, trying out the syllables: "The war is over."

Through the narrow door-slot, Natalia says, "The war isn't over, Harris."

I squint at my former commanding officer through the narrow slot and waves of light that appear to mirror the electrical storm in my skull. "Yes it is. I blew up the Partisan base. Top brass is slag, still cooking in the Phobos fusion reactor."

Natalia Argos nods. "Sure. But some of the Partisan top brass is unaccounted for."

"Oh, well."

Natalia leaves, and ten mercifully quiet minutes pass. At some point she returns, because when I glance to the door-slot her fucking face is there again, looking in at me.

"Can I help you, Lieutenant Commander Peeping Tom?" I ask.

She gives her patented scowl, the kind that materializes whenever she's confronted with something she doesn't understand. "What does that even mean? Who's Tom?"

"Download a slang app. Your life will never be the same."

A notification appears on my optics:

30 SECONDS TO UPLOAD COMPLETE.

Natalia's smug little smile falters. "You did good, Harris. In the war. You're one hell of a soldier."

"Who has earned one hell of a retirement."

25 SECONDS TO UPLOAD COMPLETE.

My former commanding officer nods in the slot. "Ever hear of a poet retiring? They don't, because it's what they are."

"I doubt you've read a poem in your life. Leave me in peace, okay? Before I get angry."

"The Partisans butchered thousands of Martians, Harris."

5 SECONDS TO UPLOAD COMPLETE.

"The war is over," I say in my steel locker. "Do you hear me, Natalia? The war is

I still *did* want that sandwich, actually, which made for an awkward moment when the version of me who had just quit his job asked his supervisor to make a chicken sandwich with mustard, tomato, kale, and no onions.

The four versions of Sabrina Potts have boarded the train by the time I pay for my lunch. They move with a synchronized grace. A gestalt demon, a puppet show, wearing young skin.

"They always sit together," my deli-self says as we board the train. He's still wearing his green smock. "You should take their car. I'll sit back here and we can sightjack and audio."

"Fine." In memory, I hear the sandship conductor's call like a phantom echo: *All aboard!*

"Two versions of her are interns at TowerTech. The other two are college students, majoring in—get this—social work. All four Sabrinas rent an apartment together on Shackleton."

I grumble as I move up two cars, settling down into a spare seat across the aisle from the Sabrinas. Two are brown-skinned young men who could be brothers; I mentally tag them as the Siblings. The other pair is comprised of a redheaded woman I decide to call Fire, and a platinum-haired young man I elect to think of as Blond Boy.

Had I taken the cruise? The thought torments me with little teeth. *Had my brother Dave and I reunited? The war separated us for twenty years; the cruise would be—would have been— our reunion. I missed him. We were supposed to meet at Evermist. Had we?*

The smell of the sandwich in my hand makes me drool; I realize I've never eaten with this body. My first bite slices the tomato stack so the juices squirt in gory ribbons down my newly made throat. Digestive fluids are frothing for something to destroy, and they go to work instantly on the mash of bread, meat, and vegetables, releasing energy that I can actually feel spreading throughout my limbs.

"Goddamn it," I mutter.

Two cars back and over my nanonics audio, my other self asks, "What?"

"Your boss put onions on this sandwich."

He laughs. "You get a taste for them if you give them a chance. So, if these kids follow their usual pattern, two of them will disembark at University District for night classes. I'll take them both out before they reach the campus. You tail the other two, okay? Take them out at your first opportunity."

Subvocally, I assent. My eyes are drawn to the floor. Someone spilled something there and the linoleum is sticky, reflecting the train lights the way the sandship was reflecting the high Martian sun.

"She's a bad one," deli-me continues. "Sabrina Potts, in charge of the death camps along Cydonia Ridge."

"Who are you trying to convince?" I mutter.

The train purrs along the track. In a combination of field training and nervous habit, I begin to compile data. I open a police band, text-only, getting a sense for the local chatter; it's always amazing how much information people let spill across unsecured airwaves. The flurry of codes, patrol deployments, and provincial stations begins to provide a shape of Lunar response capability, like water filling out the shape of a vessel. At the same time, I study my visual overlay of the subway system beyond University District. The line's last stop is Tanabata, where Luna has a Lofstrom; the scheduled launchings run down my left eye.

The four Sabrinas are all staring out the train window, their reflections doubling them. My eyes stray to the wall above, where a movie poster shows an unquestionably Martian landscape behind a man and woman locked in a passionate kiss. Mushroom clouds sprout on the horizon, the fireballs licking the poster's edge. The movie's title glows: *The Year of Passion and Death*. Starring people I've never heard of.

"Four Sabrinas," my other self says. "Talk about narcissism."

The train slows to University District. Doors open and the four teenagers split up just like my other self said they would. The Siblings rise and slide out through the exit; Fire and Blond Boy remain seated, eyes shiftily studying the commuters outside. My deli-self departs the train, pushing his way through the incoming passengers, discarding his green smock into a waste basket as he goes. The Siblings are already hurrying up some stairs, on their way to class. Deli-me hesitates at the bottom step, turns to me, and winks, lips moving. His voice springs to my audio.

"As I was saying, I've been here a week. That gave me time to learn some things about Mars after the war."

The doors close, the train leaps forward.

"My handlers already told me," I say quickly.

"Then you know that three days after their defeat, the Partisans unleashed a nuclear protocol on the whole goddamn planet to—"

"Stop!" I grunt, the horror sliding around in my stomach like something cold, greasy, and alive.

"Sorry. I forgot you're just learning about this. I've had a week to digest it. Figures the Partisans would do something like that; if they couldn't have the planet, no one would."

"I know." I try not to think of my homeworld as a post-nuclear wasteland. The mesa cities now blasted-out craters, the meltwater rivers irradiated. "Listen, I need to focus on the mission, so let's lay off the small talk."

My other self is panting heavily, probably ascending another set of stairs. "We took that sandship cruise, you know," he says.

I stiffen. "How do you know? You don't remember it, do you?"

"Of course not. You and I were downloaded off the same pre-cruise Save." He's panting heavier now, perhaps running. "But I have it on good authority that we met Dave at Evermist. In fact, we might even still *be* there; the nukes hit the major cities, and Evermist is out of the way, buried in a shield crater—"

"How do you *know* we met Dave?"

"Because I talked to him this morning."

"What?"

I expel the word loudly enough that Fire and Blond Boy give me a startled look. Lowering my voice to barely more than a subvocal murmur, I say, "What do you mean you talked to Dave? You sent a message to Mars? *While on a mission?*"

"Yep."

"I don't think Natalia will care for that."

"Natalia can fuck off."

A bit of onion is stuck in my teeth; I dig it out with my tongue and spit it onto the floor. It takes real effort to push away images of my homeworld aflame, the beautiful Sylvan cities reduced to war glass and slag. The Partisans, having lost the war, nuking my beautiful homeworld. If they can't have it, no one can.

But the idea that Dave and I survived the nukes . . . that we might *still be there*, hiding out in a Martian lava tube . . . it conjures a smile. Our childhood had been spent playing hide-and-seek, holing up in our parents' lighthouse, spying on the watercraft traffic of the canals. With the war over, I wanted nothing more than to return to that kind of idleness. To that breed of peace.

With a sigh, I force my attention onto the two Sabrinas sitting across the aisle from me. Neither one looks combat-ready. I wonder if she preselected these bodies or they were chosen for her, while Mars baked and she was reactivated here on Luna by sleeper cells or sympathizers.

Sabrina Potts, Partisan commander and overlord of the death camps where Martian dissidents were sent. They had developed an algorithm, I'd heard, that combed the redweb for infomorphic data on all Martian citizens, scouring for signs of dissent against the Partisan cause.

"Four bodies," I whisper. "That's overkill, isn't it?"

Deli-me gives a throaty, out-of-breath laugh. "Wouldn't the better term be 'overlife'?"

"I really don't like working with you," I say, but before I can finish my statement, there's a terrible cacophony of noise. Fléschette rounds whining and crackling in the air over my audio. Then a pipsqueak sound, like the buzzing of a hornet at my ear.

The sound of someone speaking while hyperaccelerated.

The two kids sitting across from me spasm in their seats. The girl lets out a strangled cry, connected as she must be to her other selves. Peripherally, I notice the train slowing to enter Tanabata Station.

In my ear, the pipsqueaks warp into a normal voice. "Got one! She spotted me as I was crossing the concourse and opened fire! But I got her."

"Show me."

My optics bloom with the full senscjack of a chaotic aftermath. It's the university buggyport hangar. Smells of axle grease. Several six-wheeled moon buggies sit like patient beasts in their parking slots, their giant wheels glittering with lunar soil that bears a startling resemblance to crumbled glass. And I see one of the Siblings, his headless body on the grease-stained floor; a spray of pulped matter erupting from the neck like a firework snapshot.

As I watch, one of the buggies roars to life. It lurches toward deli-me, headlights blazing red. Amazingly, my other self tucks and rolls, avoiding the vehicle, and springs back to his feet with a dexterity that tells me his heavy-looking body is probably lightweight foam instead of actual fat. The buggy's wheels rattle over the dead Sibling. The remaining enemy is briefly visible behind the UV-protected windshield. The airlock doors begin to rise.

"Shoot the wheels!" I say aloud, even as he does just that.

His weaponspray strafes the right side of the vehicle, shredding three tires. The buggy jumps, jackknifes, and slams into a wall. White sunlight spills into the hangar like milk. The airlock doors reverse course and slam shut.

It occurs to me that I'm so caught up with the exploits of my other self that I'm not paying attention to my own body, my own surroundings. The train has stopped at the station. The doors are opening. But of more immediate concern is that Fire and Blond Boy are looking straight at me. They've heard my words.

I see it in their eyes.

They *know*.

Twin expressions of terror hatch on their faces but motivate different courses. The redhead is closest to the door and she bolts for freedom. Blond Boy lifts something made of dull pink plastic from his satchel and takes hasty aim at me as I'm sitting in my seat.

And then, as the muzzle flares white, my world becomes a slow-motion dream.

My blurmod snaps into action like a spider web of elastic bands tugging me in odd directions. Signals pinging out every microsecond abruptly bounce back on the spurting haze-release needles, triggering the hyperacceleration. The disembarking passengers scissor their legs in languid strides as they pour from the train like gelatin. The needles—3.33 millimeter unjacketed lead-alloy haze-release fléchettes—whisper by me as I twist out of the way. The train's plastic seat erupts into dancing, spinning, floating shards.

Rolling into a squat between rows of seats, I jerk my multigun from my jacket and prepare to return fire.

Blond Boy and Fire are gone.

The dreamy march of disgorging commuters is an impassable herd at the train doors. My blurmod screeches, timing out. I stiff-arm my way to the train exit, knocking people flat onto the concrete tarmac. A glimpse of auburn hair bobs ahead of me, quick and stuttering, moving at preternatural speed. I violently shove someone else out of my way and take aim at the bobbing head; the shots stitch the wall tiles just above it. My target disappears through the turnstile of the Lofstrom boarding bay.

Sabrina is trying to escape offworld.

Over my dead bodies.

My blurmod gives a crunch that hurts my teeth as the batteries deplete, snapping me back to real time. There's a young man facedown on the tarmac, his mouth scarlet where he struck the unforgiving ground in all the confusion. I reach down to help him up, feeling guilty about having shoved him, when suddenly I realize who it is.

Blond Boy.

He stares up at me with his red mouth and terrified, pleading eyes.

"Where were you headed?" I demand, crouching down next to him. The damage to his mouth is terrible; his broken teeth swim in a sea of blood on his tongue.

Blond Boy tries crawling away from me. The commuters halt around us, staring and pointing.

I aim the multigun at his head. The crowd screams and scatters.

"Tell me, Sabrina," I say, "and I'll let you live."

I'll never let you live. Not after what you did to Mars.

"The Lofstrom!" he/she says, teeth and a slimy trail of blood spilling down his chin.

"Which launch?"

"Please let me live, Harris! Please, and I'll tell you!"

I frown. "How the hell do you know who I—"

And then something invisible slams high into my shoulder like a mallet, spinning me around. My blurmod is recharging, so the second bullet flying at me it only creates a stutter in my surroundings, and then I'm out again, sprawling backward onto the tarmac.

Black, shiny police boots converge around me.

"Hold fast! Drop your weapon!"

"Order of Stone!" I shout, and at the sound of my voice a hologram of Mars's interim government springs from my wrist-gauntlet. "I'm here on official business! By order of First Sentinel Natalia Argos and Chief Joshua Santos of Lunar Security!"

The holobadge is real, impressive with its Martian coat of arms. However, any claims to cross-jurisdictional cooperation between the Order and Lunar authorities is the very biggest, rankest pile of bullshit. The cops blink, regarding each other in confusion. Chief Santos's name is one I pilfered from the airwaves; for all I know, he might be among them right now.

The cops touch their ears, accessing the local station. "Yeah, this

Baker. We've got a perp here claiming to be Martian Security. Do you know if Santos authorized some kind of—"

I wait, buying time.

Time enough for my blurmod to complete its recharge.

A moment later, it must look to everyone there as if I've vanished like a ghost popping back into the spectral aether.

Like a tracker in an Old Calendar flatfilm, I find Blond Boy's trail by following the dark blood-spatter from his ruined mouth. Across the now-deserted platform, down the baggage-claim stairs, toward the local Save station, a place with the kitschy name of *Luck Everlasting*.

The entrance lobby is an array of leather sofa chairs and potted cherry blossoms. I barrel past the reception desk, rounding the corner to the neat rows of burnished green doors set into lunar rock. The receptionist sprints after me.

"Sir! Can I help you?"

I whirl toward her and blink my amazement. The receptionist is a young woman dressed like a goddam trog! The style had been popular among the thugs of Mars; tribes of biomodified, tattooed, and pierced technobarbarians who were the bane of both sides during the war. Very dangerous, very impulsive people, fighting the war in their own way—in the most personal way, I suppose, by being fiercely territorial about the slums and districts they lived in.

This trog, however, is dressed in a basalt-hued, professionally tailored business suit. Despite this, her face glitters with chains and tattoos crawl along her neck and the top of her exposed chest. Her eyes are as red as warning lights.

It's been ten years, I remind myself. Still, it boggles my mind to think that of all Martian cultural exports, it's the trog-look that's spread offworld.

"Where did she go?" I ask.

The trog receptionist blinks. "*She?* We only have one customer at the moment and he's a guy, but I need to verify your—"

As usual, each of the Save chamber doors has a narrow slit in its middle. Most are dark, but one slit is bright with the luminosity of a neurocapture-in-progress. I approach it, squint inside.

"Override the door," I tell the receptionist.

She holds my stare with those scarlet eyes, full of defiance and a trog's timeless aggression. Must be a *real* trog, not some brightworld poser. "I can't stop an upload," she growls. "The system is automatic."

"I didn't say *stop* the upload. I said override the door." Seeing the stubbornness in her eyes—and grudgingly admiring it—I add, "This kid is a material witness in a federal investigation. Assist me and you have my gratitude; refuse and I'll have your neurals pasted into an interrogation box! Your choice!"

The trog girl opens the door. Slaps her hand to the biometric lock and withdraws. I ease open the door and step into a blazing forest of white neurocapture light and electric-green holoprompts. The arcs find me, wriggling into my own head, the local computer opening a second file for my unexpected intrusion. I squint, trying to discern the room's dimensions and contents. Capture stations range from solitary stalls to group compartments for mass-saves. This one looks like the latter, though I—

The sudden, elastic sensation of my blurmod kicks in. Red arrows point to what I can't see: a pinprick of supersonic attack coming from my right.

My shieldfist flowers open from the back of my hand like a violet-hued umbrella. Sabrina's Blond Boy shell is *right there*, like a waxen male statue amid an electrical storm. His right arm is outstretched, fingers clutching the cheap haze-release pistol; a rapid-processor model that still reeks of the RP's carving tray.

The needle-spray collides with my shield, skittering and hissing into the Save closet's walls. I extend my fingers and the shield's nanopolymers reshape, folding around Blond Boy's pistol-arm. Then I drop out of my blur while simultaneously wrenching the shield toward me.

Sabrina's arm audibly pops from its socket, tearing flesh, gristle, tendon, and bone. He screams, staring in horror at his arm dangling from my folded-in shield, the transparent barrier like some malevolent jelly trying to swallow his limb. I manipulate the shield again and it disgorges the arm.

Sabrina continues to scream. It's a man's scream drawn up into the highest pitch of his larynx. The white-and-emerald light forms jagged geometrical vectors between us; Blond Boy's howling face is a series of agonized frames in this stuttering glare.

I shove him against the nearest wall. My shield presses edgewise to his throat.

"You are Lieutenant Commander Sabrina Potts!" I have to shout above his screams. "A Partisan! You were in charge of the death camps on Mars! You ordered the murder of thousands! You terrorized the populace with your shadowmen police!"

Sabrina stares at me, choking back her screams as if the voice has run out of fuel. "Please let me live," he says weakly. "I can pay you whatever you—"

"I represent the Order of Stone. I am here to bring justice. I am here to show you that the injuries you inflicted upon Mars will not go unpunished."

"Please! I'll do anything, Harris!"

"My name is Harris Alexander Pope," I say, "and I am the last thing you will ever see."

"*Please stop hunting us!* I am ordering you to—"

The decapitation is clean.

A cloud of white particulates explodes from the spurting trunk of Blond Boy's neck, like a backfiring thruster. It's in my lungs before I can react. The air suddenly tastes metallic and oddly busy . . . as if thousands of tiny machines are taking root in my bronchial lobes.

My medscan puts a whirling cloud of red crosses over my chest, rapidly blinking in a way that accurately conveys the most dire of results.

Crawlnest.

There was this brochure in my Order of Stone advanced countermeasures training class back on Mars. Page seventeen, glossy sidebar showing a nasty little Partisan weapon. The voice of my instructor, a grim masochist named Fernfaith Calaelen, says, "Hopefully you never run into this one, tyros. Nanite crawlnests, once in the body, use bioelectricity for a brief but painful career. They spread along with the blood, taking up preconfigured places in the arms, legs, neck, brain. You could say they're fast-acting. But if you get hit with one, trust me, you'll wish they acted faster."

"Harris." The voice of my other self comes across my nanonics, finding me on my knees in the *Luck Everlasting* Save locker. "Hey, man, you okay?"

"No," I mutter.

"Sabrina—"

"I got one but the other made it to the shuttle." Even as I say it, the ground thunders with the distinct sound of a mass-driver launch. The Lofstrom propelling its payload off of Luna, flinging her out to the deeps.

"Download the launch data," he says. "Then just advise Mars and it can be someone else's problem."

I laugh bitterly.

"What's going on with you? Did something happen?"

"Crawlnest."

My other self inhales sharply. "Son of a bitch! How?"

"It blew out of her upon death."

"Contingency plan. At least these bastards are consistent."

I wade through the arcing light; the spider-crawl of electricity continues to probe at Blond Boy's decapitated head, like an animal nosing it, trying to verify its viability. I'm knocking on the sealed door to get the trog receptionist's attention, when the first spasm of pain hits me. The tingling in my lungs is transforming into a steady burn. My right arm jerks suddenly and I cry out.

"End yourself," deli-me says at once. "Remember Fernfaith's little dissertation?"

"I remember." I regard my multigun.

"You'll still go on, after a fashion."

"You mean *you'll* go on."

"You say potato—"

"Trust me, it's not so reassuring." Movement in the door-slot catches my eye. The trog receptionist is standing there, those blood-red eyes staring in at me and the decapitated corpse at my feet.

"Who was he?" she demands.

"A Partisan war criminal," I reply, and jump when the receptionist suddenly slams her hands against the slot.

"A fucking Partisan?" she roars, the tattoos on her neck igniting in rage and forming neat rows on her cheeks. "Who was it? What was his name?" Before I can answer, her gaze waters and she stares at me with newfound respect. "Who *are* you?"

"If you want to help me, tell me if she gave any special instructions about her DC."

The trog nods readily. "It's not being Saved locally. He . . . or she . . . is transmitting out."

The pain strikes again, like a blazing-hot dagger in my shoulders.

It's all I can do to activate my nanonics and select a deadening of my nerve clusters. The pain doesn't disappear, but it feels as if it's moved out of my body, displaced, like someone else's pain. My muscles twist like ropes being drawn into a knot.

"Where?" I manage. "Where was she transmitting to?"

"Some coordinates out in the deeps."

I thought of the Lofstrom launch.

"Send me to those coordinates," I tell her. "Erase my local Save and transmit me, got it?"

She nods and hurries away to carry out this order.

"You're going to transmit?" Deli-me cries. "To where?"

My response is a scream as the crawlnest worms into new nerve clusters, chomping its insidious way to places my nanonics can't so easily isolate. No longer a vague shape of pain, it's now a snapping hydra biting into my limbs. The penetration of the neural capture is like a competing hydra trying to outdo the thing that's killing me.

But I have no right to scream. Sabrina's victims reserved that right. They had screamed as her shadowmen hauled them in. Had screamed as she put them to death. It must have been the hellish music of those Cydonia death camps.

A moment later, a notification blooms on my optics:

TWO MINUTES TO TRANSMIT COMPLETE.

"Two minutes?" I shout. "What the—"

The trog is back at the door-slot. "Did you say something?"

"An upload takes thirty minutes," I protest.

"Thirty? We've got parallel flash-capture-rod processing here, man. DCs haven't taken thirty minutes in . . . like . . . forever."

Right, I think. It's been ten years. Harris Alexander Pope . . . time traveler.

My other self says, "You think Sabrina is transmitting out to the ship that just launched?"

"Yep."

A moment of silence. Finally, deli-me says, "I'm not going to report in, Harris. I'm laying low. Gonna disappear."

"Good." To my surprise, the thought gives me some measure of comfort.

"Maybe you should do the same when you reach the deepworlds. It's a wide-open frontier, from what I've heard."

My jawline tingles like an acid burn.

60 SECONDS TO TRANSMIT COMPLETE.

"Is that what you've heard?" I say. "I've heard it's a lawless expanse of asteroid-mining corporations and research done out of view of the authorities."

"Well, there's that, too. We *did* see the same program on the deeps. I was just thinking . . . it's also a chance for freedom, Harris."

40 SECONDS TO TRANSMIT COMPLETE.

"You were defrosted a week before me. Is that all it takes to turn me optimistic?"

"Not optimistic. I've just had time to think, which is a luxury we're not often given."

"So what will you do you?" I ask. Glancing to the door-slot, I add, "Not for nothing, but I'm starting to like this receptionist. Maybe you could ask her out?"

"No offense, Harris, but my plans . . . I'm not sharing them with you."

20 SECONDS TO TRANSMIT COMPLETE.

My other self says, "You'll never catch up with your brother, you know."

This prognostication stuns me. Whirling around in the Save chamber, I insist, "I will! You just said you spoke to him this morning! When I'm done with this mission I'm heading back to Mars, understand?"

10 SECONDS TO TRANSMIT COMPLETE.

My other self takes a slow, deep breath. "Harris, listen to me. Why do you think it's you they keep sending out? Why that prepared speech when we execute them? The Order wants revenge, and they love the irony. I've put it together, man, and I'm telling you, they'll never let you

There are places in the solar system where, as you're sliced from the amniocube in your new body, they give you hot chocolate. Most regen centers have at least one professional to help you stand, get your bearings, and explain ahead of your racing heartbeat where you are, how long since your last Save, and the circumstances of your resurrection. Sometimes the regen centers are set to look tropical, or to resemble a mountain cabin with clean linens, or a totally black room with a dim light, or even a Buddhist temple of gold and bronze and prayer wheels.

The maintenance bay of the *Catoblepas* is not one of those places.

Coming to consciousness, I sit up amid a floating stew of limbs and faces. Like dredging myself from a closet of Halloween costumes, bits of biogel quivering like icicles on my breasts and rubbery-smelling arms.

Then, a notification blooms in my mind:

WELCOME TO THE *CATOBLEPAS*.
CURRENT ROUTE: LUNA-COATL-GANYMEDE RUN
CURRENT POSITION: 1.4 AU FROM TANABATA LAUNCH
CURRENT JOB: NO JOBS LISTED

Sitting up slowly, feeling the room spin until I worry I'm about to vomit up my chicken sandwich. Except this is a new body which has never eaten; my chicken sandwich is half-digested slop in a dead body on Luna.

I tumble forward to a cold steel floor.

Some uniforms hang from a rack above cleaning supplies. I stand, naked and wet and cold, grabbing at the nearest gown. It stinks of biodiesel and vinyl. I wonder how often they wash these things.

The *Catoblepas* is the cargo-runner launched from Luna while I was dying in the Luck Everlasting Save center. The terrible spinning sensation can only be a torus, and if this is what spacers deal with every day, I'm glad I'm not one. The ghost of the crawlnest twists in my stomach like a phantom twitch.

But I'm not dying, now. I'm alone, without weapons or upgrades of any kind. I'm in a woman's body. I'm cold and hungry.

I would have liked to take that trog receptionist to dinner.

There are no reflective surfaces here so I can't see my face. My arms are smooth, hairless, and very long, with a golden rouge suggestive of South Asian genotype. I prod at my face for a moment, then stop.

It doesn't matter what I look like, does it?

I am Harris Alexander Pope, war hero, body-swapper, and strangest goddamn tourist in the postbellum solar system. A woman today, a deli worker back on Luna . . . maybe an atomically bleached pile of bones on Mars waiting to be found by future archaeologists. Maybe other things that I don't want to think about . . .

I notice a slime-trail on the floor, streaked toward the bay exit. I follow this glistening path, and find her.

Sabrina Potts hadn't had time to finish her upload back on Luna. Whatever could be transmitted had been transmitted before I separated her head from her neck. Subsequently, the thing that has come out of the vat before me is a naked creature blinking at me without comprehension, lips puckering, drool or biogel hanging from both corners of its mouth. She's wearing a body like mine—maybe *exactly* like mine. Asian, female frame, knotted tangle of black, wet hair stitched into her scalp. She's lying belly-down on the steel floor, pawing the door with one slimy hand.

I squat beside her. Sabrina blinks at me, her unblemished face like freshly cooled plastic and with that puffy, just-sliced-from-the-amniocube look. Her lips open and close like a fish.

"Ex . . . cay?" She struggles to form a word. "Ex . . . cay?"

"Escape?" I ask. "Is that what you're trying to say, Sabrina?" I stare into her dull, innocent eyes.

How many prisoners had stared into those eyes, hoping for mercy?

The thing on the floor withdraws its hand from the door. It keeps puckering its mouth as it turns toward me. "Pa . . . ssfay?" Her eyes sharpen for a transitory moment. "Pass-faze?"

"Passphrase?"

A smile forms. "Pass-faze!"

"I don't need your passphrase," I explain, "because I already know who you are. You are Lieutenant Commander Sabrina Potts, a Partisan. You were in charge of the death camps on Mars. You ordered the murder of thousands. You terrorized the populace with your shadowmen police."

Her mouth pauses in its fish-like movements. She stares quizzically at me.

"I represent the Order of Stone. I am here to bring justice. I am here to show you that the injuries you inflicted upon Mars will not go unpunished."

That fleeting glimmer of recognition, like embers in a fireplace. "Pass-faze is—"

"My name—"

"Mars burning."

"—is Harris Alexander Pope."

That finds its mark. The thing on the floor moans wretchedly. It recoils, sliding in the slime. "Na! Harris! *Na Harris! Leave us be!*"

Her neck is too slippery for me to get a good grip. I have to brace my arm across her windpipe and press with all the weight this body affords before she finally stops kicking.

The *Catoblepas*'s passenger module has twenty-nine people strapped into their seats around the rotating honeycomb interior.

Sabrina Potts, in the body of the redhead girl I thought of as Fire, is directly overhead. Eyes closed, concentrating on some inner world, some virtual escape. Maybe even some recorded playback of her bygone rule over the death camps of Cydonia. The seat beside her is empty.

I move along the wall and settle into the spare seat.

Fire's eyes remain closed, as if she hasn't noticed my arrival. But her lips part and ask, "Passphrase?"

"Mars burning."

She laughs softly. "And did it ever." A crooked smile spreads across her youthful countenance. "Any problems getting here?"

"Yes."

The eyelids open, hazel concern blossoming. "Let me fucking guess," Fire hisses.

Oh, there's no need to guess, I say. I'll show you.

Come with me to the *Catoblepas*'s maintenance bay, I tell her.

And so she does.

And so she ends.

Not having any identification card after you've killed two copies of a notorious war criminal who everyone else thinks are just employees of a deepworld mining corporation *does* have a way of getting you into trouble.

The *Catoblepas*'s security team threw me into the brig, which is to say, a closet of viper restraints that wrapped around me like tentacles of a steel octopus. They didn't release me until we docked at Coatl Station. Alone with my thoughts at last. Cool, dry darkness. The pleasant hum of the ship tacking against the solar wind.

A chance for freedom.

Once we dock, I'm forcibly escorted into the freewheeling station. Expressway right past the disembarking passengers. Past the plastic-wrapped bodies of Sabrina Potts. Into a narrow steel chamber.

Coldness spreads across my slender body.

White light snaps on, snakes into my thoughts. I wait in frustrated silence until suddenly someone is looking in at me through the door-slot.

"Natalia!" I growl.

My commanding officer studies me. "Is that really you, Harris? I'm guessing so, with such a frightful scowl on that girlish little face of yours."

"Fuck off."

She chuckles. "Yeah, I suppose that settles it."

I press against the slot until it begins to fog with my breath. "Why are you Saving me again? What the hell is going on?"

"Letting you chill out, Harris." She smiles without humor. "I followed your advice, by the way. Downloaded a slang app. My life hasn't been the same since."

"I want to go home," I say, not caring that the trembling in my voice is audible.

She glances along the corridor, toward someone I can't quite see. "Of course," she says absently.

"I mean it, Natalia! Put me on the first brightquest shuttle to Mars. I deserve to see Dave!"

"You *did* see him."

I hesitate, mouth still dry from the *Catoblepas*'s brig. "Am I . . . still there? Hanging out with him? Did we survive the nukes?"

Natalia's gaze meets mine. "Don't mean to be a bitch, Harris, but that's actually classified."

I slam my fist into the door, almost breaking this body's hand. "You can't even give me *that*?"

20 SECONDS TO UPLOAD COMPLETE.

"*Upload?*" I cry wildly. "You're not transmitting me back?"

Her gaze slides again to the mysterious person in the corridor.

"Answer me, goddamn it!"

15 SECONDS TO UPLOAD COMPLETE.

My commanding officer's attention flicks back to me. Jeweled eyes as cold as asteroid ice. "You do realize there are more Partisan war criminals out there, right? Some bad people, Harris, evading the law. Killed a lot of people on Mars. They—"

"That's in the past now! Don't ask me to do this!"

5 SECONDS TO UPLOAD COMPLETE.

Natalia folds her arms across her chest and sighs. "Who said anything about *asking*, Harris?"

I pound the steel again, intent on strangling her smug little face until her eyes pop from their sockets. "I've completed my tour of duty! Now I just want to go home and

Five days on Hope Springs. Five days of couple's massages, aromatherapy—and of course, blissfully soaking in the small moon's famous hot springs. The perfect way to spend her honeymoon, Alisa Marchenko thought. Then a woman in a bio-hazard suit comes crashing into her new husband, Leonidas Adler, former imperial Cyborg Corps colonel. The woman is in trouble, as is evidenced by the two androids chasing her—and she needs their help. Duty calls. Will the newly married couple's honeymoon dreams be dashed? Quite possibly, but hope springs eternal.

Originally appeared in Beyond the Stars: New Worlds, New Suns

HOPE SPRINGS
A Fallen Empire Short Story
★
by Lindsay Buroker

Steam wafted off the water and curled around Alisa Marchenko's bare legs. Snow dusted the rocky hills above the hot springs, and the cold air pimpled her flesh. She pulled her robe tighter, tempted to jump into the closest pool, but it would be polite to wait for—

A six-and-a-half-foot tall, heavily muscled man strode out of the changing cabin, wearing nothing more than flip-flops, plaid swimming trunks, and a raised eyebrow. Leonidas Adler, former imperial Cyborg Corps colonel and new husband to Alisa, looked her up and down.

"There were robes in your changing room?" he asked, his eyebrow drifting higher.

"Yumi warned me about the nippy air, so I brought one with me." Alisa grinned, admiring his physique—nothing fat or flabby on him, despite the gray hair sprinkled at his temples—and amused at seeing her fierce warrior in such innocuous clothing.

"Yumi did not warn me," he said flatly. "All she said was that she knew some of the scientists who opened Hope Springs and that the tourism money funds their research."

"She also said it would be a delightful spot for our honeymoon, since neither the Alliance nor the empire has ever had interest in it." Because the moon was little more than a rock in space, filled with geothermal vents, geysers, and scalding pools. Fortunately, the hot springs in the tourist area were suitable for soaking. "You're not cold, are you? Surely, some of those implants are designed to keep cyborgs from freezing to death on chilly moons."

Alisa patted his forearm, though none of his implants or other upgrades were visible on the surface—he appeared completely human, and, as he was always quick to point out, he *was* human. He hadn't received the cyborg surgery until he'd joined the imperial service.

"I am sufficiently hardy," he said a trifle stiffly, but he laid a hand on hers as he surveyed the pools where other tourists already lounged, some in swimming suits, others not. A nude, hairy fellow climbed out of the water and strolled past them, not bothering to grab a towel. "I may be overdressed," Leonidas added.

"You're welcome to remedy that if you wish." Alisa slipped an arm around his waist and waved her other toward the water. "This is going to be wonderful. Five days with no crew or motherly duties to worry about. We can soak in the pools in relaxed bliss."

"Are you sure we'll need five days just to sit in water?"

"*Blissfully* sit in water that, the brochure promises, will leave us with a radiant inner glow. There are massages and aromatherapy sessions too." Alisa led him toward flagstone steps descending into a steaming pool. "I thought you were ready to retire from activities such as being shot at, irradiated, and having our minds manipulated by rogue Starseers."

"Yes, but this seems . . . sedate."

"My honeymoon plans also include copious amounts of vigorous sex."

"Ah?" Leonidas slid his arm around her waist, and his eyelids drooped. "In that case, do you think five days will be enough?"

"With Beck in charge and Abelardus piloting my freighter, their delivery *could* take longer than anticipated. We might—"

Shouts from the other end of the pool area interrupted her. A woman in a yellow biohazard suit, complete with boots and helmet, raced down a ramp and across the snow-edged flagstone deck. She slipped and flailed, but caught herself, throwing a worried look at something small in her gloved fist. She raced toward Alisa and Leonidas, frequently glancing over her shoulder. Shouts came from up the ramp and beyond the rocks framing the sunken hot springs.

Alisa stepped into the pool to get out of the way, but Leonidas faced the woman, as if he would stop her. If she had stolen something, that might be appropriate, but this was hardly their fight.

Two black-clad men leaped over a rock wall and landed at the bottom of the ramp. No, Alisa amended. Not men. Androids. They'd just dropped more than twenty feet without pausing.

Leonidas had not stepped into the woman's path yet, perhaps undecided as to whether he should interfere, but she veered toward him.

"Cyborg?" she blurted.

Before Leonidas could answer, she slipped on the flagstones and tumbled into him. He caught her before she could fall. Alisa grimaced, worrying that the woman—and that suit Leonidas now held—were in need of a decontamination shower.

"Delay them," the woman blurted, breathless. "Please. This will help your kind."

Nude people yelped, scurrying out of the way as the androids sprinted along the deck. The woman released Leonidas and ran around him. She raced toward stairs near the changing cabin that led out to the parking lot.

As the androids ran after her, their featureless faces and silver eyes dispassionate, Leonidas sprang into their path.

Alisa groaned, even though she'd known as soon as the woman appealed to him for help that he would give it. Honorable and noble. That was Leonidas. Whether he could win a battle against two androids while nearly naked or not. If he had been in his combat armor, she would have bet on him winning, but in flip-flops? As powerful as cyborgs were, androids were just as strong and had fewer weaknesses—no human flesh, no ability to feel pain.

"I'll get your rifle," Alisa yelled, racing up the stairs. She hated to leave Leonidas, but they hadn't brought down any weapons. It was only due to his habitual preparedness that there was a blazer rifle in the rented air car.

Thumps and grunts sounded behind her, and she looked back, wincing as Leonidas tumbled into the pool—or had he been thrown?—locked in a wrestler's grip with one of the androids. The other android, with Leonidas out of the way, resumed his run toward the parking lot.

Alisa cursed. She charged up the steps, flip-flops slapping awkwardly, and raced past the admissions booth, where a teenager was sticking his head out and gaping after the woman in the suit. She had made it out into the lot, bypassing rows of tourist shuttles and private aircraft for a compact spaceship parked along a rock wall to the side. Its hatch opened, and Alisa thought the woman would make it, so she headed for her air car. But a shadow fell across her, and she leaped behind a shuttle.

Two distant suns gleamed in the grayish brown sky of Altar Moon, but both were blotted out for a moment as a black, hawk-shaped ship cruised low over the parking lot. Weapons bristled from its underbelly.

One of its e-cannon ports glowed blue, then fired with a *thwump*. Energy crackled in the air, and a blue bolt slammed into the parked spaceship. It exploded in flames and black smoke, debris hammering nearby craft. A piece of hull the size of Alisa's head slammed into the shuttle she hid behind.

"What in all the suns' fiery hells?" she grumbled, not daring to lift her head until the clangs and clacks died down.

When she stood, eyeing the sky warily, the attacking ship was already zipping toward the horizon. A smoking crater and a charred wreck remained where the other ship had been. At first, Alisa didn't see any sign of the woman, but then spotted scraps of that yellow biohazard suit, along with—

She gulped. Was that an arm? Almost charred beyond recognition, it appeared to be all that remained of the woman.

The android that had been chasing her reached the wreckage. Ignoring her remains, he poked through the mess. He must have been aware of Alisa's presence, but he did not acknowledge her.

Not certain she was safe, and worried about Leonidas, Alisa ran down the aisle to their air car. She opened the canopy and grabbed a stun gun and Leonidas's blazer rifle.

She turned to head back to help him, but he was striding down the aisle toward her with something furry gripped in one hand. No, not furry. Hairy.

"Is that the android's head?" Alisa asked, considering the water dripping from his prize.

"There's a serial number in its scalp. We may be able to find out who it belonged to."

"What about the other one?" Alisa nodded in the direction of the destroyed ship, though other craft blocked the view. Sirens wailed off to the south. Far too late, the local enforcers were arriving.

"I didn't see him."

"He's over there." Alisa waved for him to follow.

She weaved through the air cars and shuttles, hoping to approach without being heard. But when they reached the smoking crater, the android was gone. Wreckage lay strewn up and down the aisle, with a piece of the hull on the pavement a few meters from them. The name of the ship was visible despite its charred and warped edges. *Klondike.*

Alisa pointed at it, but Leonidas looked toward the wreck and the tattered pieces of that yellow suit. His jaw tightened.

Three ships appeared overhead, red and yellow emergency lights flashing as they descended toward the parking lot.

Leonidas drew Alisa back between two vehicles. "We may not want to stick around for questioning."

"Why? We don't know anything." And Alisa wouldn't mind getting some answers if the enforcers had them. "Or are you worried they'll object to you taking that souvenir home?" She pointed at the android head.

"They may object to this as well." He reached down the front of his swimming trunks.

"A cyborg penis?"

His eyes narrowed to slits, and Alisa expected him to point out that this was an inappropriate time for humor. All he did was withdraw a petri dish with a green smudge inside.

"The woman stuck this in my waistband when she crashed into me." He turned the clear dish over in his hand. "It's oddly warm."

Shouts came from the wreck. The first enforcer ship had landed and was discharging people.

"Normally, I'd be jealous about another woman handling your waistband, but I'm more concerned that you might have smothered your nether regions with something toxic."

"Presumably, the potential toxins are locked *inside* the dish."

Alisa grunted dubiously.

"We can pick up Yumi, and she can take a look," Leonidas said. Yumi had also come down to Altar Moon, but she was off doing research and visiting colleagues rather than enjoying the hot springs.

"We can, but maybe it would be wiser to hand that and *that*—" Alisa pointed to the dangling head, "—over to the enforcers. Whatever's going on, it has nothing to do with us. Waistband fondling aside."

Leonidas turned over the petri dish. "She implied it might be useful to cyborgs."

The green smudge looked like some kind of algae, nothing more. But Leonidas wore a determined expression. Knowing him, he probably felt he had failed the woman, and some sense of justice motivated him now.

"I'm not going to get the honeymoon I imagined, am I?" Alisa asked.

"If we figure out what this was about quickly, there could still be time for vigorous sex."

"What about the bliss we're supposed to find in the hot springs?"

Leonidas grunted noncommittally and started toward their air car, careful to stay out of sight of the authorities. Alisa sighed and trailed after him. This honeymoon was not going at all as she'd imagined.

"Fascinating," Yumi said, studying the petri dish with her compact travel microscope.

How she could see anything in the dim confines of the air car, using her seat as a lab bench, Alisa couldn't guess, but she looked up hopefully from the sys-net interface her earstar provided. Researching the android's serial number had been a dead end, so she was trying to learn who owned the *Klondike*.

"Is the sample still alive?" Leonidas asked from outside, where he gazed toward the dark horizon. After picking up Yumi, they had flown a dozen miles, landing on a remote bluff overlooking a canyon. If anyone flew their way, he would see the ship. "The dish was hot when the woman handed it to me. I thought it might have fallen in a spring. It nearly burned off—"

Yumi glanced at him.

"—something I hope to use later," he finished.

Alisa snorted. "I don't think Yumi will be offended if you mention your various physical components. She's teaching Jelena biology right now, after all."

"The biology of cells," Yumi said, "not of cyborg components. In any case, the petri dish is *supposed* to be hot. A little battery warms it. The agar is approximately ninety-nine degrees Celsius."

"Almost boiling?" Alisa asked. "Wouldn't that kill anything living inside?"

Down in the canyon, pools gurgled and hissed in the night. *Boiling* pools?

"Indeed not." Yumi smiled, her white teeth flashing against her darker skin. "The microorganisms contained inside are thermophiles, no doubt collected from the geothermally heated pools here."

"Can you tell the specific microorganisms?"

"I'm connected to the sys-net," Yumi said, waving toward whatever satellites orbited the moon, "and I've got a search running, but so far, there haven't been any matches. It's possible this person found a previously undiscovered organism." Yumi clapped her hands together in excitement, looking closer to twelve than thirty. "Isn't it wonderful? I dearly would have liked to talk to the woman. You're certain she didn't survive?"

"Those androids—and whoever was flying that ship—made sure she didn't," Alisa said grimly. She hadn't described the wreck in detail for Yumi, but the image of that charred arm was imprinted in her mind.

"Have you found out anything about the ship?" Leonidas asked Alisa.

"Actually, I did find something involving a ship called the *Klondike*. I have no way of knowing if it's the same craft, but it might fit."

"Is it some old news article?" Yumi asked. "What does it say?"

"It's a job posting from three weeks ago. A bio-prospecting outfit led by Rohana Luthra was looking to hire a security guard for their ship, the *Klondike*." Alisa looked to Leonidas. "Did that woman look like a Rohana to you?"

"She didn't introduce herself before sticking her petri dish down my trunks."

"How forward."

"Bio-prospecting does sound like a potential match," Yumi said.

"I thought so," Alisa said. "And what is that, exactly?"

"Searching for plants, animals, or fungi that have medicinally or otherwise commercially valuable compounds."

"Does that green smudge qualify?"

Yumi blinked. "I have no way to know."

"One assumes it's worth something," Leonidas said. "Since someone was willing to kill for it."

"Not *for* it." Alisa tugged on her braid. "They wouldn't have destroyed her and her ship if they'd wanted *it*. They wanted her not to deliver it to . . . wherever it was destined to go."

"Agreed."

"This is so valuable that people were willing to kill to keep it from leaving this moon?" Yumi tapped the petri dish. "And now we have it? That's comforting."

"No, it's fascinating. You said so yourself." Alisa smiled.

"Ah."

"Any speculation as to what it could be?" Leonidas frowned toward the horizon. Had he seen something?

"Oh, I can speculate all night," Yumi said, some of her cheer returning.

"Such stamina," Alisa murmured.

"Thermophiles are able to survive because they contain enzymes that function at high temperatures. Humans have found all manner of applications for those enzymes, everything from uses in washing detergents to molecular biology."

"Detergents? Well, I'm sure that's worth killing for. The secret to the ultimate laundry soap."

"It might be if that laundry soap made someone very rich," Yumi said.

"Whoever killed that woman didn't want what she had," Alisa pointed out again. "They wanted to keep others from having it. I doubt anyone objects that strongly to superiorly laundered clothing."

"Those were just examples. Enzymes—"

"Shh, lights out," Leonidas said, and leaned into the car to cut the power himself.

Darkness smothered the bluff, with only a blue indicator light from the microscope remaining.

"Turn that off too," Leonidas said. "A ship is coming. I can hear the engines."

Yumi obeyed, and she and Alisa soon hunkered in the front of the air car, watching the sky. Leonidas remained outside, gripping his blazer rifle.

"Any chance you can tell if it's one of those enforcer air vehicles or that black spaceship?" Alisa murmured, though there wasn't much point in whispering. If the ship was scanning the surface, it would be looking for energy signatures, not listening for chitchat. If it had quality sensors, it might also be able to detect human beings, something that wouldn't be difficult given the barrenness of the moon. As far as Alisa knew, Yumi's microscopic thermophiles were the largest native life forms down here.

"A Hunter 873." Leonidas pointed to the horizon in the direction of the hot springs. "Four-man aircraft, the same vehicles the enforcers were flying."

"Enforcers? Good. They shouldn't shoot us on sight."

The rumble of an engine reached Alisa's un-enhanced non-cyborg ears. The running lights of the Hunter also grew visible, and it appeared the ship would fly by a mile to the north.

"They may arrest us for questioning and take the sample," Leonidas said.

"Not if we can convince them we know nothing and don't have it." The enforcers might not know anything about the sample and could simply want information on the attack. Alisa eyed Leonidas's rifle. "Here, come inside with us, close the door, and put that behind the seat."

Alisa hoped he wouldn't object to what had come out like an order. Technically, he was still her security officer on the *Nomad*, but he'd had a tendency to be obstinate about obeying orders he disagreed with even before they married. She'd always felt delusional commanding a former colonel, anyway, when she had been a lieutenant on the opposite side for most of the war.

The enforcer craft changed course to head straight toward them, a searchlight playing over the rocky landscape as it flew low. Yumi took her microscope and crawled into the back seat.

Leonidas sighed. "They must have sensed us."

"Probably by your radiant glow," Alisa said. "You *did* spend time in the springs wrestling with that android."

Leonidas slid into the vacated front seat next to her. He placed his rifle at his feet, closed the door, and watched unhappily as the aircraft drew closer. Its searchlight passed over their car, and it circled to land.

"They're going to want to know what we're doing out here." Leonidas looked at Alisa, and she sensed he'd handed her command when he'd come inside.

"Enjoying our honeymoon, of course. Yumi, can you and your microscope hide in that storage trunk?"

Yumi lifted the lid and contemplated the compact space dubiously. "I'm beginning to think I should have stuck to my own research."

"Likely so. Next time, you'll know to be wary when a freighter captain with no interest in science asks you to meet her with your microscope."

"No interest at all? Really, Captain. That's shameful."

"The trunk, Yumi." Alisa jerked her thumb at it. The Hunter had landed behind them.

As Yumi sighed and crawled in, Alisa scooted across the front seat to wrap her arms around Leonidas and sling a leg over his lap.

"Necking time," she announced.

"That's your plan?" His hand moved to rest on his rifle rather than her. "They're not going to believe a cyborg wasn't aware of their approach."

"Then don't tell them you're a cyborg. You could be a gym-loving bodybuilder who's too busy enjoying himself to notice anything except the woman in his lap." Alisa grabbed his hand and shifted it from the rifle to her waist.

Voices sounded outside. Leonidas grumbled something unintelligible but pulled her closer and kissed her neck as he eyed the open driver's side window. Having that window to her back made Alisa's shoulder blades itch, especially since the enforcers were approaching on that side, but she trusted Leonidas would react quickly if someone pointed a gun through it.

A beam of light splashed across the control panel, and Alisa added a few interested noises to her make out session. Leonidas's acting was less enthusiastic, and his arms were wrapped around her protectively rather than passionately, as if he would pull her across him at any second and spring for the enforcer peering in the window.

A throat cleared. "This is private property."

Alisa jerked away from Leonidas, pretending to be startled.

Leonidas did not speak, merely glared dangerously at the man, so she took the lead.

"We found the couple in the adjoining cabin we rented at Hope Springs to be overly . . . rambunctious." Alisa smiled at the enforcer. "We were seeking solitude."

The man lifted his beam and shined it in Leonidas's face.

Leonidas growled and tensed. Alisa rested a restraining hand on his shoulder while still smiling at the officer.

"We can go back if being out here is a problem," she offered.

The enforcer lowered his light to her face, and she squinted, struggling to maintain her smile.

"You're the couple that Luthra ran into on her way out of the springs," he said.

"Who?"

"I saw the video. She said something to you." He looked back to Leonidas. "What was it? Did you know her? We need to find out who's responsible for her murder. The attack ship didn't have an ident. She was an Alliance citizen, so we'll have to deal with a visit from their police." He grimaced.

"If you mean the woman in the yellow suit," Alisa said, "we'd never seen her before."

She kept her expression neutral, but inside, she was surprised. Luthra had been Alliance? If so, and she'd recognized Leonidas as a cyborg, why would she have asked him, a former imperial soldier, for help? And why would she have wanted to help his kind? Could that have been a lie to gain his assistance?

"We looked up the rental car, Sergeant," someone called from behind the vehicle. "Got their idents. Be damned careful questioning him. He's—" The enforcer halted mid sentence as the thrum of engines sounded over the horizon.

Another ship came into view, this one roaring toward them much more quickly than the enforcer vehicle had flown. Adrenaline surged through Alisa's limbs. It was the black ship.

"Get us off this bluff," Leonidas ordered.

Alisa had already turned on the ignition.

"Stop," the enforcer blurted, grabbing her arm. "We're not done questioning you."

The hawk-shaped ship loomed in the night sky, dark against the stars, no running lights turned on. But it knew where they were. It swooped low, heading straight toward the bluff. An e-cannon port glowed blue, the only warning they got.

Alisa jerked her arm away from the enforcer and gunned the engine. The air car lurched toward the edge of the bluff. She was aware of the enforcer stumbling back—and also of Leonidas gripping the dashboard and a muffled squawk coming from the rear trunk—as the vehicle surged to full speed. It shot over the ledge, and a navigation holodisplay flashed up, warning of the boiling pools and geysers far below.

Blue light streaked from the hawk ship, slamming into the ledge as the air car plummeted out of sight. A boom hammered Alisa's eardrums, and rock flew, pelting their canopy.

Alisa hit the thrusters, and the car's fall turned as much lateral as vertical. They gained speed, and she pulled up on the stick. The rental was no sleek and maneuverable spaceship, but it was light and handled adequately. The nose lifted, and they skimmed over the pools at the bottom of the canyon.

"The enforcers," Leonidas said. "Go back up. If they survived that, they'll need help."

Alisa shot him an incredulous look. All she'd been thinking of doing was flying low and finding cover to hide under. "What can we do? This car doesn't have any weapons."

No doubt, she should have opted for a fancier model when perusing the rental options.

"It has *me*. Fly back up."

Alisa growled, tempted to point out that neither he nor that blazer rifle could do a damned thing against the armored hull of a spaceship, but she was too busy flying. She banked, taking them up and back toward the bluff while hugging the cliff, using the dark terrain to camouflage their approach.

They came up a half mile away from their original parking spot, and she banked again to fly toward it. What remained of it. The e-cannon blast had shorn off a massive chunk of the bluff. The enforcer vehicle was still there, but it lay flipped on its back. Its thrusters flared, as if the pilot was trying to take off, but they were stuck, wedged into a crevice. Alisa had no idea if the enforcer she'd been speaking with had survived, and guilt created acid in her stomach. He'd only been doing his job.

"There." Leonidas pointed up and to their right. "The black ship." He must not have known its make and model—atypical for him. "They're turning, coming back down."

"Coming back for *us*," Alisa said.

As she swooped over the parking area, she spotted two enforcers outside of their Hunter, using it for cover. One aimed a blazer rifle at the approaching ship. That weapon would be useless. The other, however, pointed a grenade launcher. *That* might do something. If the ship's shields weren't up. The rental car lacked sensors, so Alisa couldn't tell.

The hawk ship banked hard to give chase as Alisa flew back out over the canyon, debating her options. They didn't have the speed to outrun the craft. If she could lure it down into the canyon, maybe some fancy flying could induce a crash. Assuming the other pilot wasn't as good as she was. Dare she assume that?

A boom sounded, and a white flash burned in the rear camera display. Leonidas twisted in his seat to look back. The enforcer's grenade had clipped the ship's wing.

"Did it do damage?" Alisa asked. Not that it mattered. The ship left the enforcers behind and barreled after her air car, gaining rapidly.

"I think so," Leonidas said. "At the least, their shields aren't up. That should mean . . ." He looked at her. "Can you get on top of them and drop me off?"

"Drop you *off*?"

"I'll jump out. If their shields aren't up, I can find my way to a hatch." He tugged the blazer rifle over his torso by its strap. "Either burn my way in or *force* my way in." He made a fist.

"We're not in space, and you're not in your combat armor with the magnetized boots. Gravity—"

"I can time it. Just get me on top of him." Leonidas pulled his feet onto the seat, as if he was ready to open the door and spring out right then.

"You're a loon."

"A loon that you love, right?" Leonidas grinned at her, an almost manic gleam of anticipation in his eyes, the one that arose whenever he was about to enter battle.

"A loon that I love who promised to get blissful in the hot springs with me. You better not get yourself killed."

"I shall endeavor to live. For your bliss."

"Damn straight you shall."

Alisa guided the air car back over land, staying low as she followed the lip of the canyon. The ship closed quickly, its dark winged-shape blotting out the stars. Its e-cannon port flared blue again, and Alisa whipped the car to the side. Leonidas planted a hand on the ceiling. A thump and a groan came from the trunk. Poor Yumi. Alisa wanted to tell her she could come out now, but would she be any safer in a seat?

A crackling blue energy blast swept past a meter from their starboard side. Alisa cursed, glowered at Leonidas, and pulled up.

Stars replaced the horizon as the nose pointed skyward. The other ship must have seen her, but it was too big and too close behind to follow immediately. Alisa flattened them out, now flying upside down. Even as she twisted, trying to turn them right-side-up, so Leonidas would have less trouble timing his jump, he flung open the door. He hesitated a second, until they were flying over the hawk ship, then leaped out.

Alisa kept on a straight course, watching the rear camera as they skimmed above the rocky cliff, trying to see if Leonidas had landed atop the ship. In the dark, she couldn't tell.

"Damn it," she growled.

She told herself that even if he missed, the fall shouldn't kill him. She'd made sure she was flying low, luring the other ship to stay low too.

A creak sounded behind her, Yumi lifting the trunk lid. "Are we still in trouble?"

The hawk ship flowed into a loop, similar to the one Alisa had made, and it flew upside-down as it renewed its chase. Alisa's heart sank. As she had pointed out, Leonidas wasn't in his magnetic combat boots. If he'd been on the roof—and where else would he have landed on the ship?—he would have fallen off with that maneuver. Worse, the ship was speeding after her air car, its e-cannon preparing to fire again.

"All kinds of trouble," Alisa said, zigzagging their path to make an unpredictable target.

Ahead of them, the enforcer ship had managed to right itself and take to the air, but it was just hovering there, over what had been Alisa's kissing ledge. She veered to the side so she wouldn't lead the hawk ship right into them. But the enforcers chose that second to lurch into motion—perhaps they'd seen the black ship steamrolling toward them. Instead of flying over the canyon, they headed right into Alisa's path.

She pulled up, scarcely avoiding them. The hawk ship's pilot reacted quickly this time and fired. Alisa wrenched the controls, veering toward the stars, but she was too late.

The e-cannon blast didn't hit them fully, but it clipped one of the car's thrusters. A jolt threw her against the controls, and something crashed into the windshield next to her. Yumi's microscope.

Alisa kept her hands steady and tried to level them out, to keep them from tilting toward the rocks. But the controls barely responded.

"Too slow, too slow," she groaned.

She did her best to keep the nose up, but they bounced off the ground like a stone skipping across a lake. Wrenching screeches came from the frame, as Alisa was thrown about. The third bounce turned into a skid, and they scraped across flat rock, sparks flying, before halting.

A *hiss-crack* came from the control panel, and the power vanished, plunging them into darkness.

"Out, out, Yumi," Alisa cried, throwing open the warped door.

Yumi lunged over the back of the seat, grabbed her battered microscope, and tumbled out of the car after Alisa. They gripped each other, both looking toward the sky behind them, certain that ship would come to finish the job. Yes, there it was, streaking directly toward them.

Alisa spun, taking Yumi with her. "Run!"

It was too dark to see well, and she tripped on uneven rock before she made it three steps.

"Careful," Yumi blurted, squeezing Alisa's arm with the hand that wasn't holding the microscope. "Smell that?"

"Sulfur," Alisa said. Among other things. The hot stench of gases thickened the air here. She hoped none of it was toxic to humans, but was more worried about the ship. A glance back revealed it still coming. The e-cannon flared blue.

"Down," Alisa barked, pushing Yumi to the ground, dread and terror clutching her chest. They were too close, and she had no idea if the ship was aiming at their crashed car or at *them*.

Blue light flashed. A boom erupted, and the ground bucked. The force threw Alisa several inches into the air. If Yumi cried out, she couldn't hear it. She couldn't hear anything over the roar in her ears.

Something slammed into her back, and she gasped in pain and fear. Her first thought was that the energy blast had caught her, but it was rubble, she realized, as more rained down. She risked lifting her head. Flames leaped from the flattened car, the charred remains unrecognizable.

Though wobbly and half deaf, Alisa grabbed Yumi, shook her, and climbed to her feet. She had no idea where they would go in the dark, but they had to run. That ship would circle back and—

"Look!" Yumi yelped from her knees.

The ship *wasn't* circling back. It smashed to the ground, skidded along the rocks as the air car had done, and crashed into the base of a cliff.

"Leonidas," Alisa breathed. Who else could it have been? "Follow me," she said, pausing only long enough to ensure Yumi could follow.

Yumi moaned but rose to her feet.

With the ship crashed, Alisa risked ordering her earstar to provide light. The beam lanced out, showing a burbling pool of water only a few meters ahead.

"Those will be hot enough to scald us—or worse—if we fall in," Yumi said.

"Scalding and death aren't on my honeymoon bucket list," Alisa said, veering to the side so they could go around. She itched at the delay. Just because the ship was down did not mean Leonidas had defeated everyone inside. He might need help.

"Is fleeing from enemies and getting shot at on the list?"

"No, but that's always a possibility when traveling with Leonidas, so I'm prepared." Alisa tapped the stun gun clipped to her belt, though it was a paltry weapon against androids, should they face more of those. Maybe she had been foolish not to bring grenades, rust bangs, and several blazer rifles to the moon. But who could have anticipated this adventure? "You still have the dish, right, Yumi?"

"It's in my pocket, keeping my thigh warm."

Bangs sounded over the bubbling of the water. Alisa picked up her pace, cursing as a geyser erupted from a pool to their side. She and Yumi hurried past, raising their arms to shield against boiling hot spray.

As they drew closer to the ship, Alisa sucked in an alarmed breath. The front had crashed into a cliff, but that cliff bordered a massive steaming pool, and the starboard half of the ship was immersed in it. The port side was on land, but tilted, and the ship could slide into the water any second.

Alisa raced forward, heading for a light on that side of the ship. It came out of an open hatch, one that was, thanks to the tilt, three or four meters off the ground.

"You're going to have to boost me up so I can get in." Alisa hoped slender Yumi had the strength for it.

"I'll try," Yumi called. She had fallen behind.

A man leaped out of the hatch, followed by another. Alisa yanked her stun gun out.

The first man landed on his feet with a grunt, spotted Alisa, and jerked up a blazer pistol. Already prepared, she fired first. The nimbus of the weapon caught both men, and the second landed in a heap rather than on his feet. She fired at him again to make sure he was out.

A cry of pain came from inside the ship, and Alisa almost hurried past the men, but she paused to run her light over their faces and clothes, wondering if uniforms might identify their employers. One wore nondescript black clothing, similar to the androids, and the other a white coat.

"Is that a lab coat?" Alisa asked as Yumi joined her.

"If they were trying to obtain the specimen," Yumi said, "they would have needed someone with a scientific background."

"They've been trying to *kill* the specimen—and the people holding it."

"They might have wanted to verify what it was if they found it . . . after killing the holder."

"What *is* it?" Alisa asked.

"Maybe there's information inside."

A pained grunt came from the interior. Alisa's head jerked up. She knew that grunt.

"Give me that boost." Alisa reluctantly holstered her stun gun—she would need both hands to pull herself through the hatch.

Yumi made a basket of her hands, and Alisa stepped in, thrusting herself upward. Yumi stumbled backward, but not before Alisa wrapped her fingers around the bottom of the hatchway. She hissed, arms quivering and legs flailing as she struggled to pull herself up. Yumi rushed back and pushed from below. Alisa clawed her way over the edge.

A boot nearly smashed her in the face. She jerked away, almost falling back out. The owner of the boot was pulled away and flew down a short corridor and into an open area, crashing hard into a bulkhead.

Alisa leaped up, stun gun in hand. Leonidas's back was to her—he'd been the one to throw the man. Man, or android? Surely a normal human wouldn't last more than two seconds in a fight against him.

But his foe, a hulking young man in a blue Alliance uniform, landed on his feet after hitting the bulkhead. He didn't look hurt at all. He also didn't look like an android. With those huge shoulders and meaty arms, he looked like another cyborg.

Alisa almost leaned around Leonidas to fire at him, but the uniform made her pause. Alliance. Not only was that *her* side, the government she'd fought for in the war, but the Alliance didn't *have* cyborgs. What was going on?

"Get back out," Leonidas ordered, glancing at Alisa before rushing forward to meet the younger man's charge. In that brief glimpse, she spotted blood running from a split lip and his eye swelling shut.

A flash of terror gripped her. He'd admitted before that younger cyborgs usually had newer—more advanced—implants. He'd beaten them before, but could he best this one?

The men—the *cyborgs*—met like Octarian blood bears fighting over a mate. The ship trembled from the crash as they came together. No, it was trembling because it had shifted, their side inching closer to the water.

"We have to get out of here," Alisa yelled, hoping both men would see the wisdom of stopping. Or at least taking their battle to solid ground outside.

But they didn't acknowledge her, maybe didn't hear her at all. They wrestled on the deck, elbows and boots denting bulkheads when they struck.

Alisa pointed her stun gun at them. They were too entwined. She couldn't hit their enemy without hitting Leonidas. She almost fired anyway—better to have Leonidas stunned than killed. But how would she get him and his two-hundred-plus pounds out of the ship if he was unconscious? Especially when she would have to drag him *uphill*, thanks to that awful tilt?

The ship groaned and an ominous scrape filled the air. The deck shuddered and tilted further. Alisa planted a hand on the wall to keep from tumbling into the middle of the fight. Her finger tightened on the trigger. She had to end this, even if it meant stunning both of them.

The Alliance cyborg slammed a palm strike into Leonidas's face and maneuvered astride him, pinning him. Before Alisa could fire, Leonidas twisted and thrust up. The enemy cyborg flew into the air and crashed against the ceiling. Alisa shot him on his way back down, praying the stun would affect a cyborg. She'd never had occasion to shoot Leonidas. Would their modifications render them impervious?

But the man came down unconscious, almost landing atop Leonidas.

"Good work," Leonidas said, grabbing his foe as he found his own feet. He hefted the cyborg over his shoulder. "He was the last one." He nodded up a short corridor to where a pilot lay slumped—maybe dead—in navigation.

The ship shivered, more scraping noises sounding.

"Captain?" Yumi called. "It's about to go."

"Come on," Leonidas said, striding past Alisa with the cyborg over his shoulder. Was he going to save the man's life? The life of someone wearing an Alliance uniform?

"Wait! Do you know what they wanted? Why they were after us?" Alisa looked around the chamber. Another corridor in the back led to cabins and engineering, but this main area was full of workstations. She spotted a microscope and other scientific equipment. Was there time to bring Yumi up here?

"We didn't stop to discuss it," Leonidas said from the hatchway. He dropped the cyborg outside. "Hurry, Alisa. If the ship goes into the water . . ."

"I know, but—" She ran to the equipment, swiping a finger under the microscope, hoping to find some specimen. It was empty, but she saw a netdisc. She grabbed it as an arm wrapped around her waist.

Leonidas hoisted her over his shoulder, and a wrenching of metal drowned out her protest. He sprinted up the tilted deck and leaped for the hatchway. The ship tilted further, then jerked as he jumped out. Despite the treacherous footing, in mid-air he shifted Alisa so he held her against his chest. As they fell, she flung her arms around him. He came down on both feet, crouching to soften the landing. By chance, Alisa could see the ship as it scraped and slid into the water. The pool hissed and gurgled, spitting spray and steam into the air as it accepted this offering. Water flowed in through the open hatch, and soon it disappeared beneath the surface. In the end, only the very top of the ship remained visible.

Alisa gulped, aware of how close she had been to disappearing along with the craft.

"This one's waking up." Yumi pointed to the prone cyborg.

"Stun him again," Leonidas said, lowering Alisa to the ground.

She still gripped the netdisc in her hand. Would it hold the secrets they wondered about? Or nothing more than someone's personal photos and shopping lists?

"Alisa?" Leonidas tapped her stun gun.

"You don't want to fight him again?" she asked, handing the netdisc to Yumi. If any of them could hack into it, she could.

"He may have answers," Yumi said, though she skittered back as the cyborg stirred.

Alisa thought it far more likely that the unconscious man in the lab coat would have answers, but she had hit him more fully, and he wasn't moving yet.

"He's a private," Leonidas said, as if this assured he would know nothing. "A grunt brought along for security purposes."

"Is that the only reason someone would have brought *you* along?" Alisa wondered if he was dismissing the cyborg prematurely. After all, Leonidas had studied engineering before joining the military. One couldn't dismiss "grunts" out of hand.

"When I was a private, yes."

Alisa almost pointed out that the Alliance didn't *have* cyborgs, privates or otherwise, but this young soldier proved otherwise. Besides, a few months earlier, she'd been told by some Alliance higher ups that a cyborg program *was* in the works. She was just startled it had produced results so soon.

". . . didn't want to fight you," the private muttered from the ground. "But . . . orders. Had to obey my captain." He lifted his head, looked toward the pool, and groaned.

Leonidas frowned at him. "Why *wouldn't* you want to fight me?"

Alisa snorted. He sounded vaguely insulted. Or affronted.

"Didn't agree with our orders. To kill civilians . . . to get rid of . . . it."

Alisa shuddered at the idea that the Alliance, *her* people, might have given a criminal order.

"What was *it*?" Yumi's hand strayed to her pocket, but she didn't remove the petri dish.

"An organism with an enzyme that can somehow neutralize the effects of tyranoadhuc gas on cyborgs." The private looked at Leonidas. "On *us*."

Leonidas clenched his jaw. Memories of having that gas used on him coming to mind? Alisa knew he'd lost men because of it during the war. It caused all of a cyborg's implants to lock up for fifteen minutes or more before wearing off, and that was an eternity during battle.

"That Luthra woman found a new enzyme out here," the private said, waving toward the dark pools, "and figured out how to turn it into a compound that we could use before going into battle, so T-gas wouldn't work on us. She made the mistake of trying to sell it to the highest bidder. Some Alliance intel person heard about it and sent us out . . . to make sure the enzyme and her information disappeared, that her compound never made it to production."

"Why?" Yumi asked, puzzled. "If the Alliance is starting their own cyborg program, wouldn't they want its troops to have this compound? To ensure they have an antidote if some enemy deploys tyranoadhuc gas?"

"When one makes monsters, it pays to also make an effective leash," Leonidas said darkly.

"You think the Alliance wants a weapon it can use on its own men?" Alisa asked. "If they get out of hand?"

The private nodded at Leonidas, the fight long gone from his face. Who was left conscious to see if he did not throw his heartfelt support behind his orders? "They've said as much, that the enhancements they gave us don't mean we're better than our superiors." He curled his fingers into a fist. "And we *will* obey orders, or there will be consequences."

Leonidas returned the nod, his eyes taking on a haunted cast. He'd once been offered the opportunity to join the Alliance and give input on their cyborg program. But after giving his oath and twenty years of service to the empire, he hadn't been willing to bend his honor and change sides, even after their defeat. Alisa wondered if he regretted that now.

Three sets of aircraft lights came into view on the horizon.

"Looks like the enforcers are returning with reinforcements." Alisa looked around at her small group, and at the cyborg and unconscious men. "Even though I don't think we've done anything wrong—" she pointed at Leonidas, Yumi, and herself, "—it may be easier if we're not here when they arrive."

"Won't someone have to make a statement about the rental car?" Yumi asked. "You won't be charged for its destruction, will you? That wasn't your fault."

"Fear not," Alisa said. "I took out the best insurance possible."

Yumi's brow wrinkled. "Because you thought you'd run into trouble? On your honeymoon?"

"I knew Leonidas would be along." Alisa patted him on the chest. "He can break things without trying."

His eyes narrowed. "I can also fling you over my shoulder without trying."

"Oh sure, *now* you get playful. Why weren't you offering to carry me around in the hot springs?"

Yumi cleared her throat and waved toward the approaching headlights. "If we're going to disappear . . ."

"Yes, yes." Alisa nodded toward a route away from the approaching aircraft. Though she wasn't enthused at the idea of hiking a dozen miles back to civilization, she didn't want the enforcers to confiscate the petri dish. "Shall we?"

Alisa and Yumi headed into the dark, careful to skirt the pool. Leonidas paused, looking back toward the cyborg, the cyborg whose name they hadn't even gotten.

"You staying?" he asked, as if presenting another option.

He wasn't going to offer to let the private come, was he? After they'd tried to kill each other? Well, no, that wasn't true. Leonidas had pulled him out of the ship, even though he wore that Alliance uniform. Because they were, orders and allegiances aside, the same?

The private looked toward the approaching ships, their engines now audible. "Yes. I trust that my superiors will come collect me from whatever prison these people put me in."

Alisa expected Leonidas to make a snide comment such as, "I wouldn't." But perhaps the months working with her had polished away some of his bitterness toward the Alliance.

"Do you have the sample?" the private asked, tilting his head.

Leonidas did not look at Alisa—or Yumi. "Better for us all if you don't know," he said.

He turned his back and walked away, linking his hand with Alisa's when he caught up with her. The cyborg did not ask further questions.

Alisa waited until the enforcer ships landed, and her little group was well away from the crash site, before speaking. "What are we going to do with the petri dish?" She ordered on her flashlight so they could more easily navigate. "And the information about the compound, if it's on that netdisc?" She had a few ideas, but now that she knew the connection to cyborgs, and therefore to Leonidas, she felt the decision should be his.

"If we keep it, we'll continue to be a target," Yumi said.

"I think," Leonidas said slowly, "that all the information in regard to finding the organism and making the compound should be published on the sys-net."

"Oh?" Alisa could see his reasoning, since it would ensure that *someone* would make that compound and perhaps that other cyborgs could get ahold of it, but would it protect *them*? Once a secret was no longer a secret, was it still worth killing for? "Anonymously?"

"Anonymously is fine." Leonidas gave her an edged smile. "But we could publish it under my name too."

"So the Alliance would *know* you were the one who thwarted their undercover agents? I'm sure Senator Hawk would love that," she said, naming their mutual Alliance acquaintance.

"I doubt he knew about this mission. He is a man of honor. These orders were not honorable."

"I hope you're right." Alisa linked her arm with his. "His wedding was quite the shindig. I wouldn't mind being invited to more parties at his house."

"Yes, and perhaps then I could discuss the Alliance cyborg program with him."

"A topic sure to make you a favorite among party guests."

He gave her a flat look. "I'm feeling the urge to toss you over my shoulder again."

"Careful, you don't want me to get excited with Yumi looking on."

"Actually," Yumi said, turning on a light of her own to examine steaming vents coming up through the rocks, "I'm searching for interesting areas of growth and considering taking some samples."

"I believe that means she'll give us our privacy if we want to have a moment," Leonidas said.

"I believe so, too, but I'm not sure I should get private with you. You *did* upset my honeymoon plans." Maybe she had been foolish to believe he would enjoy "relaxing" for several days to begin with. He was, after all, a man of action.

"We can still find bliss in the hot springs, assuming it doesn't take five days for you to explain the car misadventure to the rental company."

"That's no guarantee. It would have been helpful if you'd crashed that ship twenty seconds earlier."

"My apologies. It was hard to get through that cyborg to the pilot."

"You're slowing down in your old age."

Between one eye blink and the next, Alisa found herself hoisted into the air and draped over a broad shoulder. She turned her head toward Yumi, who was walking next to them, eyeing something she had scraped off a rock.

"That was inevitable, wasn't it?" Alisa asked, though she wasn't sure Yumi had noticed her change of position.

"Oh yes. Even I saw it coming."

Charlie Esterlan, once a decorated interstellar pilot in the United Navy, now spends his days as a janitor in the Galactic Aggregation depot, tunneled deep inside a large asteroid. It's been fifteen years since he's seen Earth. The U.N. controls the interstellar gate in Lunar orbit and as far as they're concerned, no American is going to use it ever again. So when a tentacled alien going by the improbable name of Slurrngt tells Charlie he can get America on good terms with the Galactic Aggregation—and Charlie back on Terra Firma—Charlie's interest is piqued. All Charlie has to do is pilot a small craft carrying some unspecified cargo. Easy enough, right?

Originally appeared in Rocket's Red Glare

ORPHANS OF ARIES
★
by Brad R. Torgersen

"AMERICAN," said the alien voice, using heavily-accented English.

A large human male, seated at the long countertop, did not respond at first. He merely sat hunched over his drink, staring down into the approximation of beer that filled his mug. His ocean blue flight coveralls were faded, with patches sewn into both knees and elbows. On one shoulder there was a frayed patch featuring red and white bars, with a small blue square filled by white dots. One the other shoulder was a cartoon depiction of a bighorn ram's head: teeth bared, and curved horns aimed forward, as if about to strike.

"American?" repeated the alien voice, this time with raised inflection at the end—questioning.

The human male looked up from his drink and turned his head to the side.

"Can I help you?" he said to the blob-like creature that approached on six spindly legs. Its clothing consisted of a thin-layer pressure garment tailored to match the alien's sextuped gait. A metal ring—as if for a pressure helmet—circled the creature's waist. The bare part of the torso-skull showed greenish skin and numerous tentacle-like appendages, some of which appeared to be tipped with what passed for eyes and ears.

"Your insignia identifies you as being from the human nation of the United States," the alien said. "Is this correct?"

"It's correct," the human said, studying his interrogator.

"And your individual designation, spelled across the upper right part of your torso. How is it pronounced?"

"Esterlan," the human replied, using short vowel sounds. "But most of my friends call me Charlie."

"You have many companions?" the alien asked, assuming a seat at the countertop and using the little electronic touch pad on the surface to request a beverage from the automated libations tender. Within moments, a panel at the end of the countertop slid open, a small tray with a bowl on it appeared, and was silently levitated down the length of the countertop, coming to rest in front of the alien. Who began to sample the concoction in the bowl with an extended, fleshy siphon.

"Not out here," the man said, waving his hand half-heartedly around his head. "Back home, I mean. On the planet I am from."

"It has not been an easy time for Americans," the alien stated matter-of-factly—its vocal flute being a separate organ from the digestive straw that presently poked into the bowl. The human watched uneasily as the alien's siphon undulated.

"What would you know about Americans?" the human asked.

"I know that you can never return to Earth."

"Because the Galactic Aggregation won't let me!" the man half-shouted, drawing the attention of other patrons in the bar.

The human remembered himself, and where he was, then further muttered, "Not that it's your fault. We'd be fine, except for the fact that the Aggregation deals only with planetary global governments—which on Earth means the United Nations."

"Is your United States not part of your United Nations?"

"Once," the human said, then took a long drink from his mug and slammed it back onto the bar. "Before we got sick of the lies, the graft, the backstabbing, and all the petty dictators playing like they were our equals. So we threw them out. Stopped paying their bill.

Demolished their building on the East River, in New York City. They've been butthurt ever since."

"Butthurt?" the alien said, testing the strangeness of the word.

"It's an old American phrase," the man said. "Means the United Nations is still angry, and holds a grudge against Americans. And since the United Nations controls the contract for the interstellar gate the Galactic Aggregation put in lunar orbit, no Americans or American ships are allowed to return to Earth space—not without United Nations approval."

"An embargo," the alien said.

"Try blockade," the man retorted, again a bit louder than he should have. Many different aliens around the establishment had raised eyes, ears, or sensor clusters to determine what the fuss with the big, primitive biped was all about.

"Tell me, Charr-lee," the alien said, its voice somewhat subdued, trying to strike a calmer tone, "why did you go to space in the first place? Knowing that your country would be at odds with the United Nations?"

The human grunted and took another drink. It was a bit of a story.

Charles Esterlan was tall, for an astronaut. Before leaving Earth, he'd played basketball for the University of Nevada, Las Vegas—a sports scholarship student, working on a mechanical engineering degree. He'd done okay, plying his trade as a rebounding and defensive specialist. But upon going undrafted, Charlie had taken his degree to the Navy. Who commissioned him, taught him to fly, and eventually put him through a post-grad program in large-scale space construction applications. Then they rolled him into the Aries Initiative.

"So you went to space as a soldier?" the alien asked.

"Sort of," the human replied. "The Aries Initiative was the United States' way of converting Defense Department hardware, personnel, and budget, for rapid restructuring and expansion of America's anemic manned effort, left moribund under multiple Presidents, during the many years of International Space Station operation. This was back when many of us didn't even know if all of *you* existed. Once the 'hello' signals came through, and it became clear that you *did* exist, there was just one thing for us to do."

"Humans were not already interplanetary by then?" exclaimed the alien. "This does not match what I know about your Voyager and Pioneer spacecraft series."

"Probes *only*," the man said. "No people aboard. Anyway, the Aries Initiative put Americans back on the moon—for keeps. Just in time for the arrival of the Galactic Aggregation's robot gateships, which began construction of the interstellar gate proper. American lunar mines and smelters provided the bulk of the raw materials the gateships needed. But it was the United *Nations* which claimed all the glory, once the emissary ships from afar ultimately began to arrive. The United States was demoted to just another country, even though the Aries Initiative continued to increase the amount of personnel and permanent hardware we had on the lunar surface—as well as launching long-duration missions to Mars and the asteroid belt."

"I had not realized that humans are so recent to space. When the Aggregation's 'hello' messages, as you call them, reached my home star, my civilization had already been in space for many hundreds of your Earth years. The infrastructure of our space effort was established and robust. It sounds to me like you are saying your infrastructure did not exist at all. Or, at least, was in its infancy?"

The man wiped a meaty hand across his mouth and sighed.

"My grandfather was born the year Alan Shepard made the first American suborbital flight. My father was born exactly two decades later, when the first reusable American space vehicle launched. By the time I was born, the space station was up and running, but the space station didn't go anywhere. Many people questioned why we even needed a space station. Space just wasn't *interesting* anymore. Not enough for the politicians to invest their careers in pushing for renewed, vigorous development."

"Until the Galactic Aggregation announced itself?"

"Right. That changed everything. Including my Navy career. I spent some time on lunar flights, setting up the mining equipment. Then got myself posted to one of the asteroid boats going to Ceres—that's one of our biggest asteroids, about like a small planet. But we got diverted for interstellar work instead, at the behest of the Aggregation, the first invitation for humans to go see other stars. Talk about exciting! Only, once we were on the other side, that's when U.S. relations with the U.N. really began to sour."

"What happened? Specifically?"

"Russia and China took it very personally, that they didn't get to be first through the gate. The Middle East was mad too, but for different reasons. Same with the European Union, because we took some British and Canadian personnel with us, but nobody from the Continent."

"Exclusion would seem to naturally breed resentment, yes?"

"Exclusion, hell, we pretty much paid for the damned gate. It wasn't Russian or Chinese guys working twenty-four-hour lunar surface shifts to get the mining and smelting up to speed. We lost some people during that operation, too, you know. Good people. Anyway, instead of getting into a shooting war, the U.S. merely withdrew from U.N. participation. Cut the cord. I think the President assumed that the country with the most demonstrably developed space program would retain lead status with the Galactic Aggregation's ambassadors."

"A flawed assumption," the alien said.

"That's an understatement! None of us have been back to Earth in almost fifteen years. We're scattered now. And getting older. We tried to keep our ships together, but they weren't built for extended operation without refurbishment—*human industrial* refurbishment. Every Aggregation depot we tried to use practically laughed at the antiquated nature of our equipment—antique by *their* standards. And adapting 'modern' Aggregation technology to our spaceframes proved impossible, because we didn't have any capital to spend, and we couldn't convince any of you 'mature' species to sponsor us. So we split up. Hitching on with whichever Aggregation commercial ventures would have us. Doing menial work, mostly. Because we're not 'qualified' to do anything else."

"You resent your fate."

"Of course I do! I didn't intend to spend the rest of my life scrubbing some other species' shit stains off some other species' zero-gee toilets. But it is what it is. Look, again, this whole situation isn't your fault specifically. I don't even know which species you are, and I apologize for not knowing. That's rude on my part. Though you certainly seem to know a bit about me and mine. Just what in God's name do you want with an American, anyway?"

"We can't discuss the details here."

"Oh?"

"Let's just say that your days of lacking sponsorship may be at an end."

The man's eyes got big.

"Let's go somewhere private, shall we?"

The Galactic Aggregation depot's commercial district was as huge and metropolitan as any. Tunneled into the hulk of an asteroid about the size of Vesta, the depot stretched away in all directions, with simulated gravity provided by the curious omni-gee motors which were ubiquitous throughout Aggregation space—technology which had, so far, eluded the understanding of Earth's brightest forensic engineers.

On Charlie's first day in port, he'd rented out a space down in the warren of transient interspecies apartments—the ghetto—and immediately hit the town, looking for old friends and seeing if maybe he could make some new ones.

Like anywhere else, opportunities for humans had been few and far between. Charlie had been forced to take what he could get.

Ultimately, working on the depot's sanitation crew wasn't glamorous. But it gave Charlie an income, which kept him housed and fed.

As one of the few humans taking up permanent depot residence, Charlie was also something of a curiosity, looked down upon by the non-American humans who occasionally passed through, and pitied by the many different aliens who knew Charlie's fate.

Now, for the first time, somebody seemed to have a genuine interest in Charlie's piloting skills. Though he was struggling to get specifics out of the alien he'd met one hour prior.

They were seated across from each other in Charlie's miniscule living room, which also doubled as the bedroom when he lowered his bunk out of its stowage compartment on the ceiling.

"I still don't understand what this is about," Charlie said. "Surely you've got plenty of people to do this work for you, from your own world?"

"Charr-lee," the alien—who passed himself under the phonetic name Slurrngt—said, "like your United Nations, the Galactic Aggregation has many competing interests—among rival species, and among rival ideological factions, which also stretch across species lines. Most of the member sapients have been members of the Aggregation for a long time. In some cases, tens of thousands of Earth years."

"*Tens* of thousands?" Charlie blurted, mouth half open.

"Yes," Slurrngt said. "Does that surprise you?"

"I would think, with tens of thousands of years to develop . . . well, why aren't these races ruling the whole of the galaxy by now? Every available world?"

"If by 'rule' you mean dominate, you must remember that not every sapient is 'wired' for imposed hierarchy, the way other species may be. In fact, it's precisely because some of the oldest members are *not* particularly competitive that the Aggregation has existed in a state of relative peace for so long. Young, aggressive sapients get the sharp end of old-sapient technological discipline, if you understand my meaning. Yet the old-sapient races seem to have little interest in anything like conquest. Very few of us have even met or seen any of the old-sapient peoples. They tend to be aloof. Except for when they're forced into *not* being aloof. Do you understand? Which is why when conflicts arise among those of us who might best be deemed 'middle children' of the Aggregation, we tend to conduct these conflicts in such a way as to not attract undue old-sapient attention."

"Cold wars," Charlie said.

"I am unfamiliar with the reference," Slurrngt admitted.

"On my world, there was a period between the years 1945 and 1995 when my country was on particularly hostile terms with the Russians. Yet, no Russian nor American leader ever directly initiated open conflict. They were terrified of nuclear war. So, we fought through conventional proxies, among the smaller nations, which were often considered clients of one side or the other. In fact, the very reason America went into space to begin with, was because the Russians went into space first. With machinery and then men. America refused to be second. We eventually caught up with, and surpassed, the Russians. Going to the moon—our moon—the first time, was just to prove we could do it before the Russians did."

"I think, then, that you grasp the nature of the Aggregation," Slurrngt said. "Many 'cold wars' being conducted at once, between various parties. Some of these disputes are very old. Some are new."

"There are a lot of philosophers back on Earth who'd be very, very upset to learn this."

"Why?" Slurrngt asked.

"Because before the Aggregation became known to us, lots of

humans had this extremely idealistic vision of what advanced alien life might be like. That you'd all have your shit together *way* better than we on Earth do."

"That reference is also unfamiliar to me. What does excrement—"

"Forget it. The point is, humans *idealized* you. We wanted you to be more evolved than we are. Some of us even hoped you might rescue us from ourselves."

"Yes, the Aggregation has a long list of appeals from your U.N. regarding this very phenomenon. Humans are not alone. Almost every species, upon coming into contact with the Aggregation, immediately petitions for various remedies to difficult technological, economic, medical, and social problems. I am afraid the Aggregation is not now, nor has it ever been, a civilizational cure-all. The Aggregation is the Aggregation is the Aggregation. Some species willingly share knowledge. Most species will parse things out, but with a price. Virtually every new sapient world learns to craftily *take* what it needs, over time. There are few secrets in the Aggregation which are so secret, that they cannot be deciphered . . . with enough effort, over a long enough period. My race itself continues to grapple with many matters which the old-sapients no doubt consider pedestrian. Perhaps if all goes well regarding the work I need you, specifically, to do, my species can afford to be generous toward your species. More to the point, your nation."

"Whose throat am I slitting?" Charlie asked.

"Throat slitting?"

"I get the impression you need me to do something underhanded, which you or your species cannot be seen doing yourselves."

"That's a crude way of putting it. Are you offended?"

"Yes."

"Enough for me to terminate our discussion?"

"Depends on whether or not you can convince me that the other party deserves what they'll be getting."

Slurrngt stood up—a somewhat elaborate process, with six legs—and proceeded to act in a way that Charlie could only describe as pacing.

"How to explain?" the alien said. "Telling you the long, boring, and occasionally sordid history of this quarrel will only complicate things. The less you know, the better off you are. Suffice it to say that I represent a kind of *guild*—I believe that's the American word you will recognize—which has a long-standing feud with a similar guild. We're looking for an experienced human pilot who can transport something sensitive along a specific set of gate coordinates. If you are successful, this will benefit us enormously."

"Okay, that tells me why it matters to you," Charlie said. "But that still doesn't tell me why it matters to *me*."

"Does it *have* to matter?"

Now it was Charlie's turn to stand up and begin pacing.

"I'm not the sort of man who just blindly takes a job, without knowing the root motivation for the thing. When I joined the Navy, it was to have a paycheck, sure. But I am also a *patriot*, Slurrngt. Does that word translate in your language? I served my country, in defense of my country's principles, values, and people. First, flying jets off the decks of aircraft carriers. Then, flying spacecraft on moon missions. Then again, flying aboard the new interplanetary ships we were building—the kind of vessels which were going to establish the United States throughout Earth's star system. So that liberty would have a home in the heavens. I've since heard that the U.S. is continuing the mission, even if the interstellar gate is denied us. We made it to Mars and to Ceres, and we're out among the gas giant planets, too. I don't get a lot of news from home, but the news I do get makes me proud of this flag on my shoulder. I wonder if you can understand what I am talking about. Does this make sense to you?"

Slurrngt's alien body posture didn't tell Charlie much, other than that the alien had paused in mid-stride, his tentacles bent forward in Charlie's direction.

"I wish I could tell you more about the dispute, and why this mission is so essential," the alien said. "But if you are the *patriot* you claim to be, consider this. I represent a collective of powerful and influential individuals who can directly impact the Aggregation's policy, regarding Earth. Specifically, we believe we can have the embargo against America and Americans removed."

"You *believe* you can do it?" Charlie said, his voice skeptical.

"Nothing is ever one hundred percent sure," Slurrngt snapped. "A people advanced enough to set about conquering their star system surely understand that complete guarantees cannot be made. There is risk in every worthy endeavor."

"Risk, I get," Charlie said. "But what proof do I have that any of this—the whole thing—will be worth it? For all I know, you're one of the crazy members of your species, and this whole plan is just bullshit."

"That's a fair point," Slurrngt said. "Very well. If it's veracity you demand, then veracity you shall have. And from someone I think you may trust, too."

Like so many social spots at the depot, the one known as Deep Vacuum catered to a distinctly interspecies clientele. Most of the live entertainment was not geared for human consumption, but the food and drink were palatable, and if a man liked to get out and see what made the other sapients of the Aggregation tick, there were few better places to do it. On that particular evening, loud drum music was being hammered out by a cluster of small, multi-armed tripeds in garishly-colored robes. They occasionally halted, to fill the air with a curiously harmonic form of ululation, then proceeded back to their drumming while various species sat or stood or floated around the main theater stage.

Slurrngt had given Charlie a specific time and place to meet, though he hadn't given Charlie a name. Just a promise that Charlie would know the person—human—on sight, and that Charlie's skepticism would be laid to rest.

Charlie picked a spot from which he could see both the entrance and the exit of the Deep Vacuum, and waited. When a vending robot stopped to ask him for his order, Charlie politely asked for an alien drink of local manufacture, which he'd learned to appreciate in virgin form. Within minutes, Charlie's drink arrived, and he brought the mug of super-spiced fizz to his lips with the greatest of care.

Rumor had it the real thing could eat holes in ship's hulls.

The clock ticked away, as the Deep Vacuum continued to get louder. A second group of aliens had joined the first, adding their distinctive drum rhythms and chants to the performance of the first group. Back on Earth, it might have been called a jam session. Though what the Aggregation interspecies phrase might be, Charlie had never learned.

There. He caught sight of a slender human figure wearing a royal blue suit who was wending his way towards Charlie's booth. Without a word of introduction, the stranger sat down.

Charlie settled his half-swallowed drink onto the table and looked the man in the eye. The newcomer didn't seem to fit in with this crowd. Not that any human easily did. But this guy, even less than average. His hair was buzz-cut to sharp edges, and his large, intensely blue eyes held no hint of amusement as he placed well-manicured hands onto the table.

"Uh," Charlie said, a little taken aback, "Hello?"

The man smiled and formed his hands into a steeple.

"Mister Esterlan," He said, voice pleasant, even over the roar of the drums. "My name is Mister Moore. Your friend David O'Connell sent me."

Charlie blinked. That was a name he knew well. Dave had been one of the Brit flight officers on Charlie's ship, when they originally went through the gate, almost twenty years prior. Last Charlie had heard, Dave had been permitted to go home, the United Kingdom managing to work out a deal with the U.N. for the return of its expatriates stranded abroad.

Charlie and Dave had been tight. But that hadn't exactly been a secret, either. Who was this person invoking Dave's name?

Esterlan looked this way and that, as the man in front of him continued to look back with that pleasant face and those non-threatening hands.

"I beg your pardon, friend. But you have me at a loss," Charlie faked.

"Oh come now, Mister Esterlan. No need to play dumb with me. Mister O'Connell assures me that you are a man with brains."

Charlie didn't blink. The hair on the back of his neck began to stand on end.

"I really think you have me confused with someone else." Charlie said, deadpan. "Are you sure you've got the right person?"

"Positive," Moore replied.

"Well, then, I'm sorry to disappoint you. I must be going now," Charlie said, and got up to leave. Moore watched him with mildly surprised eyes but did nothing to stop Esterlan's departure.

Feeling a chill creep up his spine, Charlie made his way to the exit as quickly as possible, leaving his unfinished drink on a passing robot's tray.

Once outside, Charlie disappeared down a side corridor and began making his way. Not toward home, but somewhere else entirely.

He walked for a full hour, wending his way through the innards of the depot, occasionally catching a vacuum tram that zipped through the depot's transit tunnels at breakneck speed, and eventually rounded toward home again—checking over his shoulder every step of that way.

"Stupid," Charlie finally muttered, as he got near familiar territory. He'd allowed an alien to occupy his whole evening, and for what? The ghost of a chance of going home? Was Charlie still so sick over being exiled that he was willing to grasp at straws—any straws? He'd worked long and hard to put Earth—beautiful, lovely, gorgeous Earth—out of his conscious mind. But that didn't mean the dreams didn't come. The memories. Of home. Of walking along the river at his grandfather's family property, near the mountains. Where the trout would bite every time, if you knew what kind of fly to use at a certain point of the season.

Charlie's attention was so fixed on his reverie that he didn't see the human woman who had stepped into his path from a crossway. He unceremoniously collided with her, hard enough to knock her to the floor.

"Oh, Christ!" Charlie gasped as she looked up at him, eyebrows raised.

"A little distracted, are we?" she said sarcastically. Her accent placed her in the Anglosphere, but it was definitely not American.

"I'm sorry," Charlie said, his hand out to help her to her feet. She did not immediately accept the offer of help. Just continued to stare at him with a critical glare.

Charlie suddenly felt about three millimeters tall.

"Oh Lord," Charlie said, laughing nervously to himself, "I am the king of embarrassment."

The woman made no sound. Just kept staring.

"It's late," he said. "And you're probably in a hurry to get home, just like me. I didn't know there were any other humans living down this way. Especially not women as striking as you are. If I had, I would have been much more careful."

The woman blinked her mildly brown eyes, then allowed herself the slightest hint of a smile.

"Do you always flatter a stranger about her looks?"

"Ma'am, where I come from, it's not a sin to pay a lady a compliment."

"And just where is it you come from?"

"Carson City, Nevada. Well, a long time ago, anyway."

She finally accepted his grasp, and he pulled her back to her feet. She wore a one-piece steel gray body suit that clung to her curves, with a blousy, pocket-lined spacer's jacket over the top. Her shoes were also spacer's shoes, designed to grip on smooth surfaces at almost any angle.

"Charles Esterlan," Charlie said, formally introducing himself.

"Glass. Susan Glass."

"Good to meet you, Susan Glass."

"I've not seen you before, either," she said. "Been living in this part of the depot for weeks, and have yet to see a character like you walk by. What's got you up late, and knocking over ladies in the middle of the night?"

"Uhhh . . ." Charlie stalled, considering the stupidity of the evening's adventure while still wondering about the Moore character who had met him at the Deep Vacuum. Unlike Moore, Susan Glass didn't make Charlie's hair stand on end. In fact, quite the opposite. She was a few years younger, but not so young as to put her out of Charlie's league. With expressive, refined features, and enough of an hourglass figure under the spacer's vest to remind Charlie that it had been a *long* time since he'd been around a woman—especially one so attractive.

Was she a tourist? Somebody here on a student visa?

"Well, if you're not up for talking about it," she said, turning away, "that's fine. Just watch where you're going next time, right?"

"Wait," Charlie said. "In all seriousness, I've had a lot on my mind tonight. Kind of crazy stuff. Doesn't matter. You're right, I need to watch where I am going. I hope you didn't take it personally. And if we run into each other again—ahh, okay, maybe that's bad wording?—we can have a normal conversation. I'm down in Blue 4932, and I work days in depot sanitation."

"Red 1818," Sue said. "I'll be here for at least another month. I'm on a special research furlough. You're the first of the American exiles I've come across. It would be good to talk, over coffee, some time. I'd like to ask you about your experience."

She allowed herself another slight smile, then disappeared in the direction she'd been headed.

He just stood where he was, and watched her go.

★ ★ ★

Inside his apartment, Charlie was shocked to see Slurrngt.

"How did you get back in here without my pass code?" he demanded.

"That's not important," the six-legged alien said. "Did you satisfy your skepticism? Regarding my claims?"

"No. In fact, I am more skeptical than before."

"But you knew the human who met you, correct?"

"No. He was a stranger. He merely knew the *name* of someone I was friends with, a long time ago. I was too creeped out to talk."

"What does that mean?"

"It means I think this whole thing is a bunch of crap, and I want you out of my apartment and out of my life, Slurrngt. Assuming that's what you're actually called. I have no idea about anything anymore. But I've got to get up for work in five hours, so leave now. I don't care about your mission. I've got a life to live, and I don't need to get involved in something that now seems to me like nothing but trouble."

The alien seemed to want to retort, but held his peace.

Without another word, he quickly left Charlie's living room, letting the door slide shut behind him.

Charlie's REM sleep was vivid and disturbing. He imagined himself back on Earth again. Only, this wasn't the Earth of his memories. It was blasted with craters from pole to pole. The air was thick with ash and smoke. The cities were gone. The countryside in ruins. With the mummified remains of humans stretching out in every direction. Crunching beneath his boots as he walked.

When the alarm went off, Charlie practically leapt out of his bunk, hands and arms quivering from spent adrenaline.

Ten minutes of scalding hot shower, and a large cup of even hotter, black coffee—the Earth drink had proven to be one of humanity's first successful interstellar exports—settled Charlie's nerves. He quietly pushed all thoughts of either Slurrngt, or the Moore guy, out of his mind, put on a clean set of work coveralls, and set off for his day.

Depot Sanitation was an odd collection of aliens from all over the known galaxy. Most of them came from hard backgrounds, not all of which were readily known to Charlie. He suspected that the majority had some kind of criminal record, though what infractions specifically, he could not say. And none of the others were eager to tell. They showed up for work, did their jobs with minimal talk, and collected their daily stipends via electronic payment transfer.

Occasionally, a new one would be added, to replace somebody who'd mysteriously dropped out. Turnover was expected, given the nature of the work. Nobody quit. They simply . . . didn't come anymore. Charlie was one of the oldest on his particular crew, in terms of seniority. Whether or not this earned Charlie any points, was a point worth considering. The aliens who passed as foremen—though Charlie had no idea what gender they actually were—tended to be as monosyllabic as the workers themselves. No way to tell what they thought of anybody. Everything was discussed in very stripped down, basic interspecies lingo.

"Pick up," or "push there," or "not that." A few dozen basic nouns, verbs, and adjectives, replicatable by almost any voice box.

The work itself? An interstellar equivalent to garbage man, mixed with septic tank cleaner. Smelly. Filthy. Laborious. And absolutely necessary.

"Job security," Charlie tried to tell himself, at the end of every shift. After all, there wasn't much else he could hope to do, no matter where he would go. His degree and experience were meaningless on the Aggregation interstellar market. Humans just didn't rate out here. Small fish, big pond. And without a way to go back to Earth, no chance for a better future. At least none Charlie could see.

Part of him found his predicament amusing, if only because mankind had spent so many years dreaming of what it would be like to finally join the then-as-imagined interstellar community of minds. Nobody had dared suspect that humans would be starting from scratch, beyond the cradle of human interplanetary civilization. Even the opportunity for continuing education was nonexistent.

The "middle children", as Slurrngt had called his class of aliens, didn't exactly welcome humans to the alien approximation of technical colleges, much less full universities.

Beyond occasional interstellar field trips, humans were expected to stay in their own system, be patient, and be thankful.

Those moments when Charlie felt rage—the kind of anger that made him punch the mattress on his bunk over, and over, and over again—it was directed at the United Nations. Nobody could help the fact that the Galactic Aggregation dealt exclusively with the U.N. The fact that the interstellar gate orbiting the Moon was shut to all inbound and outbound American space traffic, was the sole creation of the U.N. Security Council, which seemed determined to punish the United States for an indefinite period of time. Regardless of whose lives were ruined.

Back home, Charlie might have had a chance for a house and a family, with a wife. Somebody he could wrap his arms around at night, and know that she would be there, rain or shine.

Oh, sure, he still had that chance with the few human women who'd been stranded in the Aggregation along with all the other crewmembers to have crossed, prior to the blockade.

But who in their right mind wanted to bring children into the universe, knowing this would be their life to live? A life without options?

So far as Charlie knew, not a single child had been brought forth in the entire time he or the others had been in exile. Couples had paired off, and broken up. But nobody had had the foolishness—or the courage—to make babies. It just wasn't thinkable, given the circumstances.

All of this, and more, ran through Charlie's head. Each and every day. Like a liturgy. He repeated it to himself, whether he wanted to or not. And when he hit his pillow at night, seeking the only real escape possible, he clung to a tiny, stubborn little nugget of refusal: to quit, or throw in the towel. Others had done it. Suicide was the leading cause of death among American exiles. But that wasn't the path for Charlie. He wasn't going to let the sumbitches at the U.N. win.

When he died, he would die with his middle finger erected.

Three days passed before Charlie saw Sue Glass again. He had just clocked out for the night and was waiting to catch a vacuum tram when he noticed her out of the corner of his eye. Humans were hard to miss in a scrum of differently-shaped and clothed alien bodies. She still wore the same body suit and spacer's jacket as before. A valise was clutched under one arm, and she was staring right at him.

"Ready for that coffee?" she asked, walking up to him.

"Yeah," he blurted. "Sure."

Only, they didn't head to any of the usual places Charlie knew. They passed through several ancillary corridors, caught a different vacuum tram at a different platform, and wound up in a part of the depot Charlie could not remember having visited before. In fact, the empty look of the place made him think very few sapients came this way, for any reason, at any time. His boot steps echoed off the lonely corridor walls, as Sue clipped along at a fast walk, forcing him to keep up.

"What's the hurry?" he said to the back of her head, while he was practically jogging. When his breath got short, Charlie reminded himself for the umpteenth time that it had been a mistake to let his Navy regimen go. He doubted he could now pass an astronaut physical, even if he somehow magically got back to Earth. It would take months to work back into flying shape. Especially at his age.

Ultimately, they arrived at a nondescript doorway. Charlie was half bent over, panting.

"Jesus . . ." he wheezed. "Are we in a marathon?"

"Of sorts," Sue said, then used a spring-loaded lanyard on her jacket to unreel a tiny key card that she pressed to a blank spot on the wall next to the door.

The door whispered open, and she pushed Charlie through.

When it whispered shut, they were in total darkness.

"Where the hell are we?" Charlie said, beginning to recover.

"Nowhere," Sue said in a low voice.

"What about coffee?" Charlie asked.

"I'm sorry I had to bluff," Sue said, "but they were following me, and I didn't have time to do much more than whisk us out of the way of their surveillance net."

"Who is 'they' and what the hell is going on?"

"That alien who was in your apartment? Slurrngt?"

"How do you know about him?"

"Never mind how. What did he tell you?"

Charlie was silent for a few seconds. Suddenly, two strong female hands were clutching the lapels of his coverall. When next Sue spoke, her breath was on Charlie's nose. She did not sound happy.

"There's no *time* for second thoughts, Esterlan. Soon, they'll notice both of us aren't where we're supposed to be, and they will *act*. Slurrngt and his associates will then disappear, long before being caught. And the window will close. If you ever want to have a life beyond *this*, you have to tell me what Slurrngt told *you*."

"He offered me a job. Piloting. Wouldn't say for what. Sounded like an anonymous cargo run, but I am sure there was much more to it than that. He's out to harm or embarrass some of his rivals. Said he and his 'guild' could crack the Aggregation policy surrounding the U.N. lockout that keeps Americans and American ships from using Earth's gate. I didn't buy it. Especially not when Slurrngt's confirmation man turned out to be somebody I did not even know."

"Moore?" Sue asked.

"That's what he called himself. How do you know—"

"Moore works for the other side," she said.

"The other side of *what,* for Pete's sake? Would you kindly spare a few seconds to tell me exactly what the hell I've been dragged into?"

"Politics," Sue said deadpan. "Galactic Aggregation politics. Earth system politics. Both of them mixing together. Humans are a much bigger deal than any of these aliens will officially let on. *Americans* seem especially important—those of you in exile. Your State Department has been working with British secret service to find out why. We're also working on a way to get you all home. If we can."

"So, who do I believe? You, or Slurrngt?"

"We're working toward the same goals, though Slurrngt does not yet suspect it. He thinks I'm over with Moore."

"And which 'side' does Moore think he's on?"

"It's a long story. I'll try to be quick. The Aggregation isn't just nursemaiding humanity into the galactic whole. They're feeling us out. Trying to determine how useful we may be. And how much trouble we might cause. The United States' defiance of the United Nations has the Aggregation puzzled. There are some species at Slurrngt's level—"

"He called them 'middle children.'"

"Right. Some of them see U.S. defiance as a positive. Others view it as a negative. There are Earth countries, through U.N. channels, working with Slurrngt's enemies to ensure that any opposition the United States may pose . . . is nullified."

"Opposition to *what?*" Charlie asked.

"We're not sure. We just know that Slurrngt's foes view Earth—its people, indeed our entire solar system—as a raw commodity. We're beginning to also suspect they've played this game with other species, and other planets, before."

Charlie rubbed the heels of his palms into his closed eyes.

"You're giving me a whale of a story, lady," he said gruffly. "Slurrngt couldn't give me any proof he was telling the truth. Why should I trust you, if you can't give me any either? Especially since you're not at all what you first appeared to be when I bumped you over, a few nights ago?"

"You don't have to believe me. Just be sure you say 'yes' when Slurrngt re-offers you the job."

"I told him to leave me alone."

"He'll ask again. Dave O'Connell is sure of it."

"Dave . . . Wait. Dave is *here?*"

A small red light flicked on. Suddenly, Charlie realized he was surrounded by several people. All of them human. And there was one face he recognized without any doubt.

"Been a long time, O'Connell," Charlie said.

"Mate," the British pilot said, sticking out his hand.

The two old friends shook strongly.

"I didn't realize the Royal Air Force had you on loan to their secret service."

"A lot has happened back home, since you've been gone. When they told me I had a chance to help out some old friends, you could not have beaten me away with a stick."

"Is everything this woman has said, true?"

"It is. And no, Slurrngt doesn't know we're working together. Though I've been in touch with him. I'd have met you at the Deep Vacuum, except I saw Moore got there first—which told all of us that the surveillance on you has been even more thorough than we realized. Moore suspects I am here, even if he does not know where I am. Which means Moore's contacts with Slurrngt's enemies also know I am here. Even now they're wondering where the bloody hell you've gotten off to. You and Sue. So, don't take the piss. Get back to your apartment as quickly as possible. Sue will get to her place using her own route. And she's right. When Slurrngt propositions you again, be sure to accept."

"Dave, I still don't think I know what's happening, but if you say it's a good idea, I'll take your word for it."

Almost immediately, Charlie was shown through a different door— putting him out into a different corridor from where he'd been before. The automatic guide on the wall directed him toward the nearest vacuum tram. After that, Charlie was slumped in a seat, watching the lights of the tunnel wall blur past.

Three more days passed, during which Charlie saw nothing of either Sue or Slurrngt. By the fourth day, Charlie was almost ready to convince himself that the meeting with Dave O'Connell had somehow been a bad dream . . . when Slurrngt reappeared in Charlie's living room.

"I'm supposed to say yes," Charlie said, walking in the door. The alien was resting, six legs folded beneath him, on Charlie's little two-man couch.

"You spoke to your friend? The human named O'Connell?"

"Yes, as a matter of fact. And I'd have preferred being able to talk to my friend a lot longer, about many other things. Except it seems I am being watched by someone or something I don't quite understand, and who seems to cause Dave quite a bit of heartburn."

"I have the luxury of remaining visible on this depot in ways Mister O'Connell now does not. My enemies cannot openly move against me, and if they do, I would be well aware of their activity beforehand. So as to effect my swift departure from this place."

"I was told as much," Charlie said, though he did not identify by whom. "But if you can slip in and out of my apartment like this, why can't they? How do we know they're not watching or listening to us right now?"

"I've taken care of it," Slurrngt said. "Both times I've been here."

"Ah," Charlie said, shaking his head from side to side. "Did I ever tell you there's a good reason why I never bothered with an intelligence career in the Navy? Secretive games like this really leave a bad taste in my mouth. Honest. I'm no good at them. I never have been. When I was a kid, the adults always knew they could count on me to fess up, if ever my brother and two sisters had been messing around while our parents were out for the day. Mom and dad didn't even have to threaten, or bribe. It all just . . . came out. The minute they got home. I was spilling my guts. My siblings hated me for that. And learned to never let me in on anything, past about age thirteen."

"I'm sorry if you feel imposed upon," the alien said. "Mister O'Connell has been known to me—to us—for some while now. He insisted that if we were to choose one American, that man should be you."

"Dave and I have seen a lot together. I can't trust you or your guild any farther than I can throw you, but Dave? I can trust him. He says I can trust you too. Though I am still not convinced why. It seems the Galactic Aggregation hasn't been entirely honest in its approach to integrating Earth. Do I understand that right?"

"Yes," Slurrngt said, after a short pause.

"Somehow there are Aggregation people and Earth United Nations people working together, to keep the United States under the U.N.'s thumb. Is that also right?"

"If the context of your curious phrase 'under thumb' means the U.N. is collaborating with Aggregation interests—specifically my enemies—to hamper the United States, the answer is also yes."

"So why go out of your way to help?" Charlie said, putting his hands into the air, palms forward. "What's in it for you guys?"

"Mister Esterlan, during our last conversation, you explained to me that your Navy work meant much more to you than money. I believe I understood the moral reasoning at the root of your motivation. And can only respond by explaining my own. You see, there are those of us who believe that the Galactic Aggregation has lost its way. We've done what we can to alert the old-sapients to the problem. But sometimes it seems as if even the old-sapient species are not only blind to the issue, they are part of it. It's been too long since they themselves were young in the galaxy. The affairs of emerging worlds like Earth only earn old-sapient notice if a world poses a threat to the Aggregation's status quo.

"Rather than do the right thing, too often the powers of the Aggregation merely do what is *comfortable.*

"Some of us have elected to change the equation. Not with broad strokes, mind you. But by carefully choosing the times and the ways in which we can make a difference.

"Our opponents view us as troublemakers. Idealists who are unwilling to embrace the fact that the Aggregation simply *is*, and always will *be.* Good, as well as bad. Upset the balance too much for the sake of principle and everything comes apart. For everybody.

"Which, I suppose, makes sense . . . from a certain point of view.

"But sometimes, beings of good conscience can't settle for what simply 'makes sense'. Not everything can be reduced to decisions of pure expediency. There is a crucial question of *character* involved. A question which we—my comrades and I—believe you and your United States understand exceptionally well. Enough to take your own stand, even though it has come at great risk, as well as great cost.

"We would aid you in this matter. And in turn, we believe that you can also aid *us*. Does that sound like a fair bargain to you, Charr-lee?"

Charles Esterlan, once and former astronaut, swallowed the lump in his throat, and said, "When do you need me to start?"

It was a curious ship, seemingly cobbled together from the pieces of three different Earth craft. Some of her was new to Charlie—equipment that Slurrngt's people had recently obtained. Other pieces of her were original vintage, dating to the several asteroid expeditions which had been diverted for interstellar sorties . . . and never made it back to home port again.

The flight deck was going to take some getting used to. Charlie's piloting chair was equipped with a full-surround holographic system which did not correspond to anything he'd trained on or used in the old days. There was also the matter of the self-aware computer matrix, which Charlie had also not had on any previous flight. The ship literally talked to him, and gave intelligent responses to his status queries and technical questions.

The self-aware computer was also the only reason Charlie could launch with a one-man compliment.

"Our little contribution to the ship's design," Slurrngt had said proudly. "My species has always excelled at artificial intelligence programming. It wasn't terribly difficult to adapt one of our generic low-range shuttle brains to your hybrid ship's various Earth-made systems. We just had to get the crosstalk synced—Earth tech to our tech, and back again."

Now Charlie hung in space, one thousand kilometers distant from the mouth of the first gate he was to pass through.

Damn, he thought. *It's good to be back in the saddle again.*

Charlie's computer, using the alias Astrobee, was busily negotiating with the gate's resident automated traffic control. There were several ships queued to leave the system. Charlie's intent was to slip into the queue like any other gate customer. Though human-built craft were quite rare in Aggregation space, they were not so unknown as to trip the gate's profile alarm. Especially since Astrobee was programmed to pass itself off as human-designed flight control software. A bit like an adult speaking in four-year-old, Slurrngt had bragged.

Charlie himself, readopting his old Navy call sign of Wildcat, never had to utter a word. He simply studied the gate-hopping route he'd been given. While also wondering about the cargo which had been brought aboard, even before Charlie's introduction to the craft.

That cargo rested in the belly of the ship, and would be released only when Charlie had reached the point in the flight plan which called for the bay doors to be opened, and for the computer to jettison the bay's contents.

What, precisely, this was expected to accomplish?

Slurrngt knew. And he wasn't telling.

Minute after minute, Charlie's ship edged closer to the gate. Like a pentagon with mile-long sides, the alien-built device made everything that passed through it seem small. How the gate worked, like the omni-gee motors, was a mystery which Earth's best minds were still working to solve.

One moment, you were on the gate's threshold. Then, you were exiting the threshold of still another gate, somewhere else in the galaxy.

Easy peasy.

Only, it could *not* be that simple. Human physicists speculated that even a modest gate voyage must consume the energy output equivalent of a substantial supernova for the instant the gate was in operation. But how the gates were supplied with such fantastic amounts of power, and from where, was a technological puzzle liable to intrigue generations of the finest minds humanity could produce. Even Slurrngt had admitted that his people were stumped, even though they'd had a several-hundred-years head start on the problem.

The trip itself was painless. A thing not noticeable at all, except for the sudden shift in star patterns. When Charlie finally crossed over, Astrobee had to quickly connect to the traffic control network on the other side, establishing a fresh set of coordinates on the three-dimensional galactic grid, then putting the ship into the queue again for the wait until the next opening to go.

Charlie wondered if it might be possible to daisy-chain gates, so that a ship could travel across multiple legs in one gate event.

Querying Astrobee merely yielded a response indicating that such a maneuver was not allowed.

Not allowed? If the problem didn't boil down to physics, it surely boiled down to bureaucracy. Governments—all governments—simply loved to place arbitrary rules on things.

It took the better part of an Earth day to make three gates. At which time Charlie was growing weary and decided to put the ship into a parking orbit so that he could go back to the diminutive pilot's cabin and get some sleep.

He did not expect to find Sue Glass waiting for him. But she was there.

"The hell—" Charlie yelled with surprise, backing up several steps.

"It was the only place I could stow away," she said.

"Without Slurrngt knowing?" Charlie said, his pulse gradually settling back to normal.

"Getting past Slurrngt and his people was the easy part. Getting past that damned computer they installed? Now *that* was hard. Especially considering the fact that this craft launched carrying my equivalent mass in kilograms *beyond* the manifested total mass. That's bound to throw off maneuver fuel usage estimates by a fraction of a fraction of a fraction of one percent."

"I told Astrobee to knock off giving me mass and fuel warnings which amounted to so little difference," Charlie said. "Now I know what the real error was. Care to tell me why you're here? Slurrngt was quite emphatic that this is a solo mission."

"I told Dave it would be foolish to let you go alone. Slurrngt or no Slurrngt. Dave agreed."

"I'm doing just fine without a co-pilot."

"Co-pilot? Right. I can't even fly a model airplane. Count me as an observer only."

"Since when does Charles Esterlan need a chaperone?"

"Since not even we—Dave, myself, and the other British officers assigned to this project—are quite sure what Slurrngt has up his six-legged sleeve. We've been trusting him up to this point, regarding the expected outcome of your journey. We've also trusted him when he's told us that it's got to be a human ship, with an American at the controls."

"And the cargo? Any guesses on that?"

"Nope. It was the single toughest piece of information to obtain, and we failed. Your computer is programmed to report the mass as technical parts for a reaction drive of Earth manufacture, though I completely doubt the accuracy of that statement."

"Me, too," Charlie said. "Especially since the flight plan calls for evacuating the entire cargo bay almost immediately upon arrival at the final gate, then going back through again. But this doesn't account for a queue, which I've experienced at every gate so far. Am I just supposed to wait around in line while the whatever-it-is in the cargo bay does whatever it's supposed to do on the end of this journey? I mean, what if it's a bomb of some kind?"

"A bomb?" Sue said, walking out of the cabin.

"I'm pretty sure it won't be the interstellar equivalent of a whoopee cushion."

"That seems drastic, for Slurrngt's people. Like hitting your opponent with a baseball bat during a chess match. Too blunt! There's more than one way to hurt an opponent. The direct way, and the indirect way. Seems to me Slurrngt has stressed that this is going to be extremely indirect. Almost to an improbable degree."

"We could unlock the cargo hold and find out for sure."

"Do you know what a bomb looks like, just by staring at it?"

"I spent enough time around rockets, missiles, bullets, and bombs during my carrier years to believe I *will* know a bomb when I see it. Even one built by alien hands."

"And if it *is* a bomb, what then? We just retrace our steps to the depot, try to find Slurrngt—which I am pretty sure we can't, because he's very probably already left—and tell him you've had second thoughts about the agreement? 'Thanks, but no thanks?' I said so before: once the window on this opportunity is shut, there might not be any others. Not for the United States. Like it or not, America can't break through without some kind of sponsorship on this side of the gate. Like it or not, Slurrngt and his guild are the closest—no, the *only*—candidates to have stepped forward. Do you have the luxury of looking a gift horse in the mouth?"

"I just have this little toothache kind of feeling, that I am being used."

"No shit you're being used!" Sue said, almost laughing. "That's what self-interested parties *do*. You give him what he wants, he gives you what you want. That's what we Brits sometimes call *civilization,* dear Mister Esterlan. Besides, what have you got to lose? Do you want to spend the rest of your life working sanitation details at Galactic Aggregation depots?"

"No."

"Then get some sleep. I'll see you when you're up again, and ready to put the ship through the gate."

Charlie stared at her for a moment, then nodded his chin to his chest several times.

"Right, right. Thanks for keeping an eye on things. Though I do have to tell you, the computer almost makes *me* superfluous. I don't think you'll have to touch or change anything."

"Good. I've been looking forward to the peace and quiet."

Charlie's sleep was filled again with visions of a wasted Earth. Only this time, instead of being destroyed where they stood, humans were carted off like cattle. Millions upon millions of men, women, and children, crammed into filthy, disgusting, giant-sized shipping containers. Like conexes, only fifty meters to a side, and five hundred meters long. All slung beneath the bellies of gargantuan, alien lifting ships. Each ship carrying tens of containers to orbit. Where they eventually vanished through the gate. Taking every soul aboard to an unknown fate.

Charlie was so disturbed, he jerked out of the cabin's small bunk, and almost hit his head on the deck.

It took him a few minutes of splashing his face in the cabin's little lavatory sink to compose himself.

Emerging through the cabin door, Charlie immediately sensed that things had changed. A glance out the bubble-shaped forward observation window showed a substantial line of ships all waiting to pass through the yawning gate. Beyond the gate, a beautifully ringed gas giant planet could be seen in the far distance. Like the planet Jupiter, but bigger, with slightly different colors.

"Where are we?" Charlie asked soberly.

"Just one gate left to go," Sue reported, sitting in the pilot's chair. The space immediately in front of her showed a digital version of the card game solitaire.

"How did we make two more gates?" he asked, moving quickly to stand beside her.

"Astrobee said the last two gates had slots open up, and asked if we should move in to take them. I told Astrobee yes. And the ship complied. You were right, this computer really *does* almost make the pilot superfluous. Back home it would take many people to operate a spacecraft this size, much less fly it properly. Astrobee has been handling everything beautifully."

"One gate left . . . Anything unusual worth noting? Anything at all?"

"Not that the computer has noticed. Though the queue at this new gate seems to be the longest of all. Dozens of ships all waiting their turn. I guess the gate can't run continuously? It takes awhile to recharge after each use. Or something? The longer the total distance in light-years, the more the wait before reactivation can occur. I'm not the world's greatest xenotech expert, so I can't explain specifics. I've been asking Astrobee most of these questions, and Astrobee seems to know most of the answers."

"The gate in lunar orbit operated that way, yes," Charlie said. "The longer the distance being crossed, or the more mass being put through—in the form of multiple ships, or one great big ship—the longer it took for the gate to reset for the next run. We still don't grasp the nature of the power source. Some physics experts speculate that the gates themselves are merely physical 'shadows' left in our dimension, by the actual super-dimensional architecture which allows normal matter to cross light-years instantaneously. That the actual energy comes unlimited from this super dimensional plane of reality."

"However it works, we've got one to go, and then we get to see what the cargo is all about."

Charlie swallowed and stared at the ringed planet around which this latest gate orbited.

"Nervous?" Sue said, erasing her card game, then stepping up out of the pilot's chair, and waving her hand for Charlie to take a seat.

"Yes," he admitted. "Somehow I thought we'd run into more friction by now. When things go this smoothly, I get nervous."

As if on cue, several of the holograms surrounding the pilot's chair began to blink yellow. Followed by a pleasantly female voice which announced, "Message received from inbound spacecraft, identifying as security flotilla on vector six four zero point zero two. Translation commencing, 'EARTH SPACECRAFT OF UNDETERMINED CONFIGURATION, YOU ARE IN VIOLATION OF GALACTIC

AGGREGATION CODE ZERO NINE ZERO MARK EIGHT SEVEN
MARK THREE THREE TWO. WE ARE MATCHING COURSE
AND SPEED, SO AS TO TAKE YOU INTO CUSTODY. DO NOT
RESIST. REPEAT, YOU ARE IN VIOLATION OF GALACTIC
AGGREGATION CODE—"

Charlie practically threw himself into the pilot's chair, causing the
holograms to temporarily blur and distort.

"We need somewhere you can sit down," he muttered.

As if on cue, a second chair emerged from the deck directly to
Charlie's right and unfolded itself.

"Additional crewmate, please buckle in," said the pleasantly female
voice.

Sue didn't have to be told twice. She was strapped in within
seconds, while Charlie swung a manual override control board into
place over his knees and began taking the ship out of its computer-
determined trajectory. Even with the omni-gee motors to compensate,
Charlie and Sue were both pulled hard against their straps by the
change in direction, as well as velocity.

"Where are we going?" Sue said, almost having to shout over the
noise of the ship's main thruster while it fired.

"The only place we can go," Charlie said to her, never taking his
eyes off the holograms directly in front of him or the view out the
bubble beyond that. They were zooming up the backside of the various
craft still waiting in line to access the gate. Behind them, the flotilla
approached at maximum thrust. The strain on those spaceframes,
omni-gee motors be damned, must have been ferocious. Whichever
species was crewing the flotilla, they could probably stand a lot more
than ten gees. Which was considered extremely dangerous for most
humans.

"We don't even know if the gate will activate," Sue said, "much less
shunt us to the correct destination!"

"Where's that British spirit of derring-do now, Ms. Glass?" Charlie
said, using his fingers to dial the ship's thruster up to max-plus output.
Behind them, they could hear the dull roar of the unit, chewing
through reaction mass at a horrendous rate.

"Threat detected, threat detected, threat detected," chimed
Astrobee, and Charlie's virtual display—showing the immediate space
around the ship for many hundreds of kilometers—lit up with red

arrowheads which began tracing sapphire lines aimed at the blue starburst in the display's center.

"Christ," Charlie spat. It had been a long time since fighter weapons training—a skill he'd never imagined he would need upon going to space. But he knew incoming missiles when he saw them. The arrowheads appeared to be closing rapidly. Each missile like a miniature spacecraft, and pulling an insane amount of gees in an attempt to overtake Charlie's ship.

Three. Four. Five.

Charlie stopped counting at five, and wondered what had happened to being taken into custody?

"Astrobee, time to threat impact?"

A countdown clock appeared inside the hologram.

"Now give me time to gate entry."

A second countdown clock appeared.

The latter number was larger than the former.

"Countermeasures," Charlie muttered, wishing he could dump foil chaff or flares. *Anything* which might divert the attention of those missiles. He even considered voiding the cargo bay. Just to give the warheads a second, substantial target on which to impact. But he resisted the urge and turned his attention to the very real problem of hitting a gate at max-plus, entirely outside of the established traffic pattern.

"Astrobee," he said. "Make that gate understand that we are coming in *hot*. I don't care who is up next, we've got to have priority."

"Protocol violation at levels two, five, and eleven—"

"To hell with the rules!" Charlie shouted. "There's got to be some kind of emergency code you can transmit. A way to quick-configure the gate to our desired destination, and triggering at close contact. Can you do it?"

"Understand that there is a severe monetary penalty for unauthorized out-of-pattern commandeering of gate facilities—"

"I understand, just goddamned do it, all right? Execute, Astrobee. *Execute.*"

"The security warheads are almost on us," Sue shouted, pointing a finger at the red arrowheads which had formed a tight pack directly on the ship's tail.

"Nukes," Charlie said under his breath. *Of course* they would be. What else was there in space? Proximity detonated, he reckoned. They wouldn't have to get close to wreck the ship. It all depended on how powerful each of the warheads was.

"We're not going to make it," Sue groaned, her fists clamped over the straps holding down both shoulders.

"We might just," Charlie shouted back.

"There's not enough time," she retorted.

"We might—"

Then the concussions hit. *Boom. Boom. Boom.* Like huge jackhammers, punishing the hull.

Twirling orange alarm lights suddenly lit up the entire space, while the holograms flickered, smeared, steadied for an instant, then smeared again.

Sue and Charlie both screamed in unison, while the spaceframe around them complained of horrific torsion.

Then, just as suddenly, space itself changed. Like a camera bulb clicking on, then off, and leaving a negative image on a man's retina.

When reality reasserted itself, the entire compartment was still flooded by the swirling orange light from the emergency lamps. But the additional four explosions—which Charlie had been certain would tear the ship completely apart—never came.

Astrobee, digitally stuttering like a broken record, was attempting to rattle off a list of red-lined equipment. Including the ship's main thruster, which appeared to have suffered the brunt of the damage from the warhead blasts. There was no engine noise blaring against their ear drums now. Rather, just the electronic *bwooping* of the damage klaxon repeated over and over again from speakers in the ceiling.

"Atmosphere integrity?" Sue said weakly, her eyes clamped shut as she continued to cling to the straps of her chair.

"If we'd lost our air, we'd know it by now. Stupid, that we didn't get into suits in time. We'd probably *still* better get into suits. There are lockers for them in the wall behind us."

"The other missiles—"

"Are back where we left them. In the other system. The three closest to us went off. But then we hit the gate, and the gate event was instantaneous. The missiles went through the empty space left in the wake of the gate event. Hitting nothing. Man, I have never experienced a gate event quite like *that*. Looked and felt weird. Did you sense the same thing?"

"Yes," Sue said. "And I feel like I want to barf because of it."

"That's not because of the gate. It's the fact that we lost the omni-gee motors. This is what zero gravity feels like. Many people don't react to it very well. I'm only used to it because I was trained to get used to it. Though it does feel weird, after such a long time. Just close your eyes and don't move your head."

"I'm not," Sue said.

"Good. Rapid head movement will make it worse. Stay calm."

"I am, damn you."

"Okay, good. I wonder if we made it where Slurrngt intended for us to go. Astrobee, cancel all damage reports. Can you tell me, based on numeric signature, if we arrived at the gate originally programmed into your full flight plan?"

A few seconds passed, then the computer warbled, "Af-f-f-firmative."

"I have a hunch that's the last gate crossing *this* ship will ever make, without being towed. Now we're headed off into space at a mad clip, and I don't know if I can slow us down on reaction control thrusters alone. Astrobee, how much of forward reaction control capacity have we retained?"

"Es-s-s-s-timated forty-nine percent."

"Begin a twenty-five percent burn on forward reaction control, until further notice. Ignore fuel consumption thresholds. Divert whatever fuel is left from the main reaction tanks, if you have to."

Both Charlie and Sue suddenly slumped forward in their seats.

"We're slowing down," Sue said.

"That's the idea."

"Somehow, that feels better."

"From no gravity at all, to a percentage of gee in one direction. We'll be like this for awhile. Enjoy it while you've got it. Meanwhile I hope our cargo didn't get too badly beaten up. If I can coax the bay doors open, we can still launch—for whatever good it does us. That way when the security flotilla eventually comes through . . ."

"But you said they're stuck on the other side?"

"Temporarily. Until the gate resets. Then I am certain those security ships will be right on top of us. In our present condition, we're not capable of doing much more than running up a white flag."

"Not that they'd pay attention," Sue said. "Shoot first, ask questions later."

"Indeed. Well, here goes nothing. Astrobee, open the main cargo bay. If the motors are jammed, use the explosive bolts to blow the doors off at the latches and hinges."

A few seconds passed, then there were a few small thumps.

"C-c-c-cargo bay doors ejected. Do you wish to expel the contents of the cargo bay proper?"

"Yes, please."

That time, there was no noise.

Except the sound of Sue gasping.

"You okay?" Charlie said, still staring at his instrument board.

"My God," Sue breathed. "Look outside. Look!"

There wasn't much to see. They appeared to be drifting at high speed, parallel to the orbital plane of a significant rock and dust ring which surrounded this particular star out to an untold distance. Any closer to the ring, and the ship would be getting meteorite-sized holes in the forward bubble. But at this distance, things seemed relatively safe. Except for the two large masses that appeared to moving retrograde to ring rotation, and were actually *swimming* up toward the crippled human spacecraft.

"What are they?" Sue whispered.

"I have no idea," Charlie said, transfixed by the sight. "But at this distance, I'd say they're hundreds of meters in diameter. Each. Or larger. Look at them go. I don't see any thrusters. Nor the flare of reaction mass. They're just . . . gliding through space."

A blocky shape suddenly drifted into view. It was the contents of the cargo bay, floating ahead of the ship while the ship continued to brake on reaction control thrust. Over the course of many minutes, Charlie and Sue silently watched as the two large shapes, almost pure black in color, moved with organic smoothness. When they reached and inspected the cargo pod, the two shapes deployed appendages which easily enveloped and then unceremoniously ripped open the pod proper.

Small shapes—carbon copies of the big shapes—suddenly spilled out.

At first, the small shapes looked inert. But then, one by one, they began to shudder to life, while the two larger shapes hovered nearby. Attentive.

"The g-g-g-gate has activated again," Astrobee reported. "Craft similar in size and mass to those which were previously in pursuit, have been d-d-d-detected."

"That's it," Charlie said. "They're here."

"But where *is* here? And *what* are we witnessing?"

"I'd say, a family reunion," Charlie remarked. "But I really don't know what's in this system. Astrobee kept telling me that this was restricted information, every time I queried. I figured that meant we'd be dropping in somewhere relatively off-limits for humans. Now that I am seeing what I am seeing, I have to suspect *way* off-limits."

One of the large black shapes detached itself from the small throng of increasingly energetic, smaller black shapes, and quickly maneuvered its way up to where the disabled human ship continued to bleed off relative velocity. A problem which the alien things outside seemed to not notice, nor care about. Space for them was as easy as seawater for an octopus, seemingly.

The black shape extended an appendage, until the appendage gently touched the ship's hull.

"WHAT ARE YOU?" asked a voice from the ceiling, though it wasn't exactly Astrobee's.

"Visitors," Sue responded, smiling for the first time since before the attack on the other side of the gate.

"WHY ARE YOU DAMAGED?"

"They hit us just as we reached the gate and passed through," Charlie said. "That same group of ships which just came through the gate again now."

"YOUR PRIMITIVE ARTIFICIAL INTELLECT INFORMS ME THAT YOU ARE CALLED . . . HUMANS. WE SPEAK TO YOU IN YOUR WAY, SO THAT YOU MAY UNDERSTAND US IN OURS. IT IS NOT PERMITTED FOR PRIMITIVES SUCH AS YOURSELVES TO COME TO OUR HOME. TRESPASSERS MUST BE PUNISHED. YET YOU HAVE BROUGHT TO US OUR WAYWARD OFFSPRING, WHO APPEAR TO HAVE BEEN IN LONG HIBERNATION. VERY LONG. HOW DID YOU DISCOVER THESE LITTLE ONES?"

"We can't really say," Charlie said honestly. "We just knew that we had to bring them here, at all costs. So we did. Even though we got shot up pretty good along our route."

"OUR OFFSPRING WERE ATTACKED WHILE IN YOUR CARE?"

"Yes . . . more or less. Our whole ship was attacked."

There was a long silence, then the speakers continued.

"I SEE THE TRUTH OF YOUR WORDS, THROUGH THE RECORDS OF YOUR ARTIFICIAL INTELLECT. THERE WILL BE A RECKONING FOR THOSE WHO DARED TO ATTACK OUR KIND. MEANWHILE, WE ARE IN YOUR DEBT, HUMAN WHO IS NAMED CHARLES ESTERLAN. WHAT WOULD YOU REQUEST OF US, THAT WE MAY PROPERLY SETTLE THE MATTER?"

Charlie slowly turned his head Sue's way, a knowing grin spreading over his face.

Sue Glass grinned right back.

"You sent us to face an old-sapient race, and you didn't even warn us," Charlie said, shaking his head. "You could have at least told us what we were in for."

"If I had told you," Slurrngt said, "you would not have gone. Under *any* circumstance. Even *I* would not have gone. The—" Slurrngt made an unreproducible sound with his vocal flute "—are not just old-sapients. They are among the very *oldest* of the old. So old, that their civilization stretches back before Aggregation records. They are not a collection of single minds, but a massive group mind. Who have engineered for themselves living biomechanical bodies, which freely inhabit space. Fantastic technology. Yet they never set out to harness the galaxy for their own use. They merely traveled. Occasionally dropping spores where it seemed opportune to do so."

"You must have found some of those spores," Sue said.

All three of them were clustered around a large table at the Deep Vacuum, where few patrons congregated at that particular time of day. Dave O'Connell had joined them too.

The alien wasn't the only one who no longer needed to keep secrets.

"I think your British friend can take some of the credit," Slurrngt said, indicating Dave. "Though he did not know what they were. One of your recent American missions in your Oort cloud recovered them. The Americans made discreet inquiries through the British, who contacted Dave, who then contacted me. I had Dave bring them through the Earth gate, to a secure location where the spores could be properly decanted. Once I was sure what we were dealing with, I had the embryos placed in immediate stasis while we decided what to do."

"Shouldn't you have just contacted the . . . whatever they're called?" Sue asked. "Told them you had the embryos?"

"It would have ignited a storm of controversy and accusations," Slurrngt said. "My guild would have been openly accused by our rivals of attempting ransom. Or worse. We couldn't publicly admit to having them. So, we needed a third party. One who could be told just enough to accomplish the mission. But not too much.

"Since Americans had found the spores to begin with, it seemed proper that an American should return them. What could our rivals do to hurt America, with America shut behind the gate? What could be done to Americans in exile, which was any worse than what had *already* been done to them? Your people had everything to gain, and so very little to lose. The important part was ensuring you got proper credit . . . assuming everything went well."

"It almost went horribly wrong," Charlie said, able to chuckle about it now. "I jinxed us right at the moment when we were practically home free."

"'Jinx'?" the alien asked.

"Human superstition," Sue said. "What he really means is, we were having such an easy time of it, right up until the moment when we weren't."

"Of course," Slurrngt said. "Once you departed, our rivals set about searching everywhere for you. I tried to plot your gate crossings so that you would seem to be here, and there, and nowhere at once. I don't think I did a very good job. They managed to pinpoint you on your second to final stop. Terrible fortune, that. And yet, good fortune too. You are still among the living. The cargo was successfully delivered. And now? Things for you might change."

"Speaking of which," Charlie said to his old friend as they sipped drinks, "what's the word back home?"

"The United Nations is in an absolute state of panic," Dave O'Connell said, smiling slyly. "Apparently, the Aggregation contract for the gate in lunar orbit, is being 'reworked' according to new guidance which has just come down the Aggregation political chain. The United Nations is being told—in very strong terms—to reconsider its policy against the United States. Lest the Aggregation 'reconsider' the entire deal *for* the United Nations. Arbitrarily. Perhaps even constructing a second gate, for exclusive American use. Well, America's, and also America's closest *friends.*"

Sue and Dave shared a glance, and a wink.

"Two operational gates would be a rare thing for any single star system, much less a star system belonging to such a relatively young spacefaring species," Slurrngt said. "Even I would not have predicted such an outcome. Very good. Very good indeed."

"We must thank you for intervening on our behalf," Charlie said, raising his mug in Slurrngt's direction. "I might actually get to visit home now. And all the other exiles can visit along with me."

"Where's the first place you'll go?" Dave asked.

Charlie thought about it, then smiled, and mimicked casting with a fly rod and reel.

Dave burst out laughing. "Of course, mate. Of course."

Sue seemed a bit mystified, as did Slurrngt.

"Fishing," Dave finally said. "The man hasn't had a trout on his line in almost two decades."

"You wouldn't want to come see England?" Sue remarked, her eyebrows going up with a mixed expression of surprise and disappointment.

"I've been to Britain a few times," Charlie said. "Dave and the other RAF blokes showed me around."

"Yes, but did they show you *my* England? The way *I* can show it to you?"

Now it was Dave's turn to raise eyebrows in surprise. He looked over at Charlie, who suddenly felt his cheeks growing red, then quickly buried his nose back in his drink.

Charlie simply stared at Sue, not quite sure what to say.

"Well, I . . . umm . . . err . . . is that an offer, or a promise?"

"Can't it be a bit of both?" Sue asked, her expression growing sly.

Charlie let himself smile, and raised his mug in her direction, then downed the remainder of the mug's contents.

For aeons, Dardry has lived on Pluto. Now, as our sun becomes a red giant, her millions of years of life may be coming to an end. To continue living, she must turn a reluctant observer into an unlikely ally.

Originally appeared in The Magazine of Fantasy & Science Fiction

BY THE RED GIANT'S LIGHT
★
by Larry Niven

SHE CRAWLED across a liquid nitrogen sea on inflatable helium pontoons. The huge floating island ahead of her was formed of water ice, a jagged gray landscape that bobbed and drifted. She wasn't feeling urgency, not yet, but progress was slow. Presently she extruded some wheels and rolled ashore to greet the newcomer.

What she saw was a mobile robot half her size, studded with sensors, with two big arms. It fired a low-energy infrared laser past her, then brought it to one of her eyes: an offer to talk. It took more than two hours to work out a communication protocol, and then she said, "Welcome to Pluto. I came to see what you're doing here."

The machine said, "What are you?"

"Human."

The machine sounded a little waspish. "I can see that you're made of carbon compounds and liquid water inside the shell. But are you an authority here?"

"The only one. I've been here for aeons. First I came to study Pluto's peculiar orbit. Then the changes that came with the changing sun. I can tell you anything you need to know about Pluto system, past or present."

"You never leave? You have no resources here."

"Of course I have a base. It's south of here. From time to time, a ship comes, or I summon one. On occasion I've needed medical

153

assistance, or supplies, or a change in design, or just intellectual input. What do you do here?"

"I've built a telescope. I'm here to use it," the machine said.

The human said, "Let's see." Keeping it polite. She needed this entity. She should have come sooner. "Lead me. I'm Dardry."

"I have no name."

"Frankenstein," Dardry said. "I'll call you Frank."

They crossed over a low ridge of hard ice, and then leading wasn't necessary. The telescope filled twelve degrees of sky, a huge work of art rising from the island's peak. It was covered with robots of all possible shapes, hundreds of them. A dozen came to surround Dardry. She felt the pressure of their eyes in varied frequencies.

Dardry asked, "You're dispersed?"

"As you see, these are all myself."

She saw that the telescope pointed directly at the Sun.

Dardry could remember when, seen though Pluto's dusty blue sky, the Sun was a point not much brighter than the Earth's full Moon. Over the aeons it had expanded tremendously, a sixty-million-kilometer globe dimmed to autumn red, with a blurred rim. Mercury, which had been a planet, was now a long-lived meteor coasting through ever denser levels of the Sun's photosphere. The streak of light was intense, considerably brighter than the bloody photosphere itself.

Through the telescope's big screen they studied the magnified comet-shaped flare. Neither of them needed an extra filter against that awful light: Their various eyes were adaptable.

"That's a beautiful sight," Dardry said. "Awesome."

"It must be increasing the insolation on Earth," Frank said. "Does that bother them? It must be hot already."

"Too hot. No oceans. We moved out a long time ago. There's nothing on Earth but research stations, monuments, and tourists."

"So you came here. Dardry, this can't be your original shape. You could do more to adapt yourself."

"Change ourselves enough and we do nothing but build robots. That's not immortality. It's not even reproduction."

"Why is reproduction important? Can you reproduce, Dardry?"

"Of course, with some technical help," she said. "Frank, can you tell me who sent you?"

"I'm told that's a secret," the robot said. At that point, Dardry was talking to a different machine, taller, bulkier, ringed with arms. The rest had wandered off. "I was sent to study Mercury as it disappears into the Sun. I've been here for most of a local year. Why did you dawdle?"

"I put myself in slow motion when things are less interesting. I watched you arrive but saw no urgent need to disturb you. Why Pluto, Frank?"

"However dangerous the Sun becomes, Pluto should be safe, and we're at the rotational pole."

"You may have a problem with that. Will you swing your telescope to these coordinates?" Dardry's laser indicated a location on the sky.

"No."

That was dismaying. "Your eyes might be good enough. Look there, Frank."

"I see an oncoming body, lightly blueshifted, frequencies of dirty water ice, methane, and ammonia. Perhaps a large comet. Perhaps a moon has wobbled off-center."

"Watch its trajectory. It's going to hit Pluto. You and your telescope will be destroyed, and I, too."

"I must watch the Sun until it strikes."

Robot. Inflexible? Given its unfamiliar design and unfamiliar language, Frank must be from outside the Solar System. Too much time would pass if the robot must call its makers for new instructions. Dardry knew she must deal with it directly.

"Frank, I don't want to die. Millions of years I've lived, only to be snuffed out as if I'd never been. I come to you for help. Can we work to shift the course of the intruder?"

"I have my task."

"May I use your equipment to save myself?"

"What equipment?"

"A light source I can make, aligned through your telescope to correct for warping in the atmosphere, could light one edge of the intruding body. Vapor would boil off in a jet. The intruder can be pushed off course."

"I need that equipment for my mission."

Dardry thought it over. The single machine watched her with equal patience, and perhaps other elements of Frank did, too. The rest went about their business, crawling over and around the telescope. In ten hours or so, Dardry had worked out a procedure.

Two of the big-handed machines came with her as far as the shore. At that point, Dardry asked, "If I act to save myself, will you interfere?"

"Not if you leave my equipment alone. What have you decided?"

"Come and see."

"I cannot go over the horizon without losing contact."

Dardry didn't answer. When she had crossed enough of the liquid nitrogen sea, the machines fell back. Dardry deployed a propeller and skis, for speed.

Dardry's Base, a hundred and ten kilometers south, was big. It included her food stores; a power source, toilet, and infirmary; a sender to the relay on Charon; a recycling system; and a greenhouse. It also housed most of the computer part of her mind. She'd been growing that, of course, as her knowledge expanded over the aeons. Every so often she must prune some memory, or nothing could have been found. She hoped she hadn't pruned a certain versatile hacking system.

She dipped into her memories. . . .

The base had held almost a hundred explorers, men and women both, at its peak. They had set it directly under Charon, deep inside Pluto's heart-shaped water-ice glacier, that first time. The light then was like dusk in Yellowstone Park: She was getting memories within her memories.

Dardry tasted a love affair gone sour. Yes, she could reproduce: She'd birthed a little girl, who had gone back to Earth with Myron. Always a loner, she'd become more so afterward. When the last human left, she felt she had inherited Pluto. Now she wondered if she had become even more possessive. Tending toward madness?

She remembered being lonely. She'd outgrown that, repeatedly: She had to go through it every time she returned to Earth or, later, Mars or the bubble worlds. It was lonely then, too, as civilizations changed, leaving her isolated.

Keep searching.

She found it, a very ancient memory. She'd been a spy working from Silicon Valley in California. She'd been caught by an enemy implementing a hack so momentous that half the planet wanted her head. She had to leave Earth. She'd chosen Pluto . . . or Pluto had been chosen for her; she wasn't sure. But she remembered how to hack a machine, knowing almost nothing about it beyond its existence.

The biggest moon was in place, too, just above the horizon. Charon and Pluto were mutually tidelocked, of course, so Dardry's communications dish on Charon was always available from this face. Frank couldn't signal over the planet's horizon, but Dardry could, by relay.

Frank didn't react to her probing. Didn't notice? Perhaps its masters didn't have hackers. Dardry learned more. No obvious defenses. No clear weapons. When she could, she used her systems to shut Frank down.

The intruding body was closer now. Dardry was feeling harried.

She skimmed back across the sea, maintaining contact with her base via the moon. She'd been worried that Frank was spoofing her, but the hundreds of machine elements were all silent and motionless. A few had fallen and lay broken. The telescope wasn't following its target.

And now what?

Dardry turned Frank on again.

Frank took a few minutes to adjust himself. Then: "You have interrupted my observations. My records are discontinuous. I've lost many hours. Why?"

"I can do it again."

"What would you gain? You cannot run my elements like puppets. You spoke of using a power source. A laser? With that and my telescope, I can destroy your link on Charon."

"You have a mining and manufacturing concern, somewhere on land. You could build your own light source and use that. But I can see this site from Charon and shut you down before you finish."

"Murder. You would kill a sapient being."

"Not murder. It's all right, Frank. You're a robot. I could revive you, however long you lie unused. I can rebuild whatever elements fail."

"But what if you change your mind? Still murder."

"Change your own mind! Focus your beam on one side of that incoming comet. Alter its path."

"By then Mercury will be gone, or nearly. My purpose unfulfilled." Dardry was losing this quarrel. Frank must have already worked out everything Dardry could do with its own installation and surmised some of what Dardry had, too. Unless— "Shall we build another telescope?"

The machine was silent for a minute and a half. Other elements of Frank continued to work. The telescope had located the Sun again. Mercury was around its backside.

Dardry said, "You must have found a mine for the metals you need. You'd have stopped working when you had what you wanted. I don't see mining gear; you must have left it in place—"

"Are you aware of what you ask? The installation is well over the horizon. I could send elements to build your telescope and laser, yes, but I would not be in contact with them. You're asking amputation!"

"Better than murder."

"Yes." It was surrender.

"Wait. Can we link you to your mine using my installation on Charon?"

Frank's mine was thousands of kilometers away, a pit that reached through six kilometers of ice to Pluto's metallic undersurface. Frank was able to maintain contact with himself via Charon. Dardry watched closely, but Frank didn't appear to be using her base for anything else. To gain control, for instance, or for revenge. Perhaps Frank just wasn't built that way.

They worked. Feeling hurried, Dardry built a focusing device less elegant than Frank's telescope. They trained the beam on an edge of the comet, and held it. Water ice, ammonia, methane, a blast of red-hot molten rock squirting into space: no surprises. They kept watching.

The comet was passing dangerously close. Pluto would lose traces of atmosphere, and heat would blast these volatile landscapes. Several elements of Frank worked alongside Dardry, still holding the laser trimmed. "And enough," the nearest machine said. Dardry agreed. She began to shut down the laser. The telescope began to lose focus.

Dardry asked, "How is it at the pole?"

"Mercury has been gone for hundreds of hours," one of the machines said. "I've been tracking the effects. Shock waves. Contaminants in the Sun's photosphere. All fallen to ambient levels. Nothing is detectable except a local rise in temperature."

"You caught it all?"

"All but what you robbed me of."

"What will you do now?"

Frank didn't answer.

Dardry watched them for hours, but none of the machines were moving now. She presently went north a few thousand kilometers, to Frank's installation at the pole. Nothing moved there, either.

Well, it was Frank's choice. She would not attempt to rouse him, unless . . . perhaps in the far future, when the Sun expanded to engulf Venus. Meanwhile, she was alone again on Pluto.

Recovery from loneliness was slow, but she'd done it before. Dardry skimmed south to her base. They'd been at this for half a Plutonian year. Time for some maintenance, and a meal.

It was supposed to be an easy mission: board a Cutter cargo ship and capture it. The Freehold Military Forces had the intel and the artillery to pull it off, no problem. But Private Wayne Carreon also had a bad feeling, and when dealing with the savage alien Cutters, nothing is as easy as it seems.

Originally appeared in Forged in Blood

FAMILY OVER BLOOD
★
by Kacey Ezell

WHAT THE FUCK *am I doing here?*

I remember specifically thinking that question, right about the time that our stealthed boarding pod made contact with the skin of the Cutter ship. I felt the reverb through my seat as the grav grapples engaged, and took a quick look around at the faces of the company.

Assholes all looked calm and collected. My hands shook and I wanted to throw up in order to get the damn flutterbugs out of my gut. But when Corporal Hyan opened his eyes and caught me looking, I managed to conjure up a suitably manly bland expression. This was supposed to be an easy mission, as such things went. Simple cargo ship, board and capture. No sweat. But for some reason, I had the proverbial "bad feeling." Hyan blinked slowly back at me, his own neutral expression belied by the beads of sweat I could see glistening through the face shield of his helmet. Maybe I wasn't the only one.

"On Two," Captain Aiella ordered, her voice crisp and calm. I reached up and toggled the switch that disconnected my combat helmet from the capsule's oxygen to my suit's integrated bottle. The suit itself was a combination of conventional armor, pressure suit, and an additional exoskeleton that had been beefed up to withstand Cutter energy fire, all worn over a composite undersuit that fit like a second skin. The whole setup was bulkier than any of us would have liked, but it might keep us alive. The Cutter ship would have atmosphere that we could breathe, and the suit would allow for that, but tragic mistakes in the past had taught us that discretion was the better part of not getting killed. In the event that any of us found ourselves on an unexpected EVA, we'd have air for a short time . . . hopefully enough for rescue, anyway. A series of clicks and a burst of metallic-tasting air told me that my suit was working properly. Oddly enough, focusing on that simple series of motions calmed the flutterbugs, and I felt my tension start to drain away. Maybe it was just relief that the wait was nearly over.

Below my feet, the boarding capsule gave a shudder and a jerk, indicating that the breaching sequence was complete. The dim red light overhead turned to green, and our restraints tightened as our stations began to slide toward the captain.

"Breach seal established! Time to go, boys and girls!" Aiella said. She reached out and punched a key next to her station, and the floor of the capsule opened up under her feet. I saw her bring her rifle to ready as the capsule's mechanism shot her "down" through the open airlock and into the Cutter ship.

My station jerked into motion as the capsule spat us in rapid-fire sequence down through the breach. I barely had time to pull my own energy rifle to the ready position before I felt my body drop and my stomach rise up into my throat. There was a wave of disorienting nausea as the ship's artificial grav took hold. Then my boots hit the deck of the Cutter ship, and a blast of energy sizzled by my head, knocking me flat on my ass.

Cutter energy fire. Despite all my training, fear stabbed icy fingers deep into my chest. When humanity first encountered the Cutter race, no one had ever seen anything like the weapons they had. Roughly the size of a rifle, but they packed an energy punch that rivaled our biggest, beefiest kinetic weapons. We couldn't stop them, couldn't shield from them. Even our laser ablatives did nothing. It wasn't until we captured one of their rifles and reverse engineered it that we learned how to counter it. In essence, we beefed our laser ablative materials up, combined them with reactive materials that would absorb some of the godawful punch, and strengthened the whole thing against impact. The result wasn't pretty, but it worked well enough . . . unless the fire was unusually intense, and the range particularly short.

Like right now.

I barely had time to roll out of the way before Hyan's big feet came down on top of me. With his size, that would have killed me just as quickly as the energy bolt would have done. I rolled free and came to my feet . . . and froze. I wasn't prepared for the noise, or the smell. Even filtered through my suit's oxygen apparatus, the entire place reeked of something warm and musky, punctuated with the hot-metal scent of energy fire. The fear that had pierced my chest now reached up to wrap around my throat and squeeze. I felt my eyes pop wide, and I couldn't do anything about it.

"Carreon!" Aiella yelled in my earbuds, "Clear the breach site! Cover high, left!" As she did so, another bolt came from that direction, searing the air and stinking of ozone. Her voice jolted me into moving, finally. I turned as ordered and fired what was supposed to be a three-round burst, but was probably more like a ten- or twenty-round burst. *What the fuck was going on? This was supposed to be a stealth board!* I forced myself to take a shaky breath and try again as more of my platoon came dropping into the ship. The Cutter fire intensified, and I felt sick as I watched more and more of my buddies being shot as they landed.

Hyan came up hard on my right side, making me stagger to the left. "Get down!" he shouted, pulling me down with him behind what looked like an overturned table. I remember thinking that it seemed oddly shaped, like it was made for people whose legs were too long. "We got fucking Cutters coming in from three directions," he growled as he took more shots. "Looks like we dropped into some kind of rec room. Intel said this was supposed to be a maintenance passage! Figures!" He slammed a fresh power pack home into his rifle and started firing again. I followed suit, until the universe exploded into brilliant streaks of light. I heard Hyan gasp, saw him slump over the newly created hole where his chest had been. The stink of burnt meat wrapped around me, and then I got swallowed up by a rising darkness.

I woke up when my head bounced against something.

The salty copper tang of blood filled my mouth, and I gagged, spat, and tried to raise the rifle that I no longer held. At that point, I realized that I was being dragged, and I started to try and fight my way free.

"Thank the Gods," Aiella said. "I was afraid I'd lose you, too." Her voice sounded weird: hoarse and broken. I couldn't see, my faceshield was blackened, and I struggled to breathe. Something was wrong with my O2 system. I didn't have either bottle or ambient air. I reached up and twisted viciously at the helmet, trying to get it to disengage. It came free with an audible *pop* and I flung it away, sucking in air like a drowning man.

"Where are we?" I asked. My own voice sounded pretty terrible as well. I swallowed hard, and immediately missed the water tube in my helmet.

"Some passageway. I don't know. Intel on the ship's interior was all jacked up. The Cutters . . ." she broke off, swallowed hard. I fought to sit up. My armor's power assist was dead, apparently.

"Here," Aiella said. "Let's get you out of that," she said.

"My armor?" I asked, startled. Why in seven hells would she want me out of my armor. I mean, I'd be lying if I said that I hadn't had thoughts. Aiella was a bit more muscular than I liked my women, even for being from Grainne, but . . . well . . . she *was* female. And the whole officer thing gave her a certain mystique. But we were in the middle of a boarding action! On a hostile ship that had *way* more Cutters than we'd expected, as far as I could tell. Truth be told, it was all a confusing mix of images in my head. But still . . . now?

Captain Aiella looked at me and then reached out and slapped the back of my head, hard.

"Shit!" I hissed, unable to hold it back.

"Don't be an idiot, Carreon," she said. "Your suit's dead. The armor's only as good as the materials at this point. No energy assist, and it's bulky enough to slow you down. Ditch it. Your best bet is to move quickly and hope the composite underneath is enough to stop their damn cutting arms."

I felt my face flush as I nodded. She looked narrowly at me and then began helping me out of the bulky power armor suit. She had lost hers, too, I realized abruptly as I watched her. Without the power armor, she moved like a hunting Ripper. I let my eyes trail down the line of her back . . . then jerked them down to my armor and the latches that held me in. Now may not have been the time, but I was still a guy, all right? Once I started thinking about sex, it was hard to let it go. Sue me.

My rifle was nowhere to be found, much to my shame. I climbed out of the carcass of my armor and tried to look casually around. Aiella noticed, however. Of course. She snorted and shoved her own weapon toward me. I just looked up at her.

"Take it," she said, her voice impatient.

"But . . ."

She shoved it at me again, so that it hit my chest and I reached up to take it by instinct. She started to turn away, muttering something about getting more power packs.

"Captain," I said, trying to make my voice sound much less scared and lost than I felt. "Ma'am, I can't take your weapon! What are you going to use?"

She turned back to me and looked at me for a long moment. I realized that she was probably debating whether or not to snap my head off for implying that she needed the weapon more than I did. That wasn't what I meant, of course. She could kick my ass completely unarmed. It was just that . . . well . . . she *deserved* her weapon. *She* wasn't the one who'd lost it, after all.

"I'll be fine," Aiella said finally. For some insane reason, a tiny smile curved her lips. She reached back under her shoulder and drew out a sword.

A sword.

Don't get me wrong, it was a beautiful weapon. I'm no expert, but it *seemed* old . . . old and expensive. But at the end of the day, it was a freaking edged weapon. I carried my duty knife like everyone else, and was trained in its use . . . but these were Cutters we were talking about. Was my captain really planning on bringing a sword to an energy rifle fight?

"Listen," she said briskly, interrupting my incredulity. "Something's off here. There were too damn many of the Cutters at the breach site, especially for a cargo ship. Even for our intel being wrong. It was too organized . . . like an ambush."

My eyes widened. "Ambush?" I asked, sounding brilliant.

Aiella nodded. "That's all I can come up with. They knew we were coming, they knew where. Which indicates that they might have known that our intel was bad. In any case, something's not right about this situation. Which means that you've got to get back to our people to tell them about it."

"Me?" I asked. My voice might have squeaked, just a little bit. I tried to ignore it. "What about you?"

She turned and looked straight at me, that crazy little smile growing just a bit. "We were given a mission. Take the ship."

"You can't take the whole godsdamned ship by yourself!" I said, aghast. I probably shouldn't have spoken that way to my captain. But shit just kept getting weirder and weirder, and I just didn't think about protocol at that particular moment.

"I never said I meant to take it *intact*," she said. She opened her mouth to say more, but right at that moment, another energy bolt came sizzling down the passageway at us. I dove for the nearest cover . . . which happened to be the pile of my armor. I landed flat on my stomach, took a deep breath, then raised up and squeezed off a few rounds of my own. An ear-splitting howl-screech echoed down the passageway, followed by a distinctly human laugh. I felt the wind of her passage as Captain Aiella sprinted past me, blade first, right into the teeth of the enemy.

"Wha—shit!" I spat, and before I could think too hard, got to my feet and sprinted after her. I don't know how they didn't take us out during that wild run, but they didn't. In fact, they stopped firing, and their howl-screechy noise took on a different tone. If I didn't know better, I'd have said it sounded approving. Perhaps they admired our craziness. Who knows?

The captain impacted them first, her sword flashing in the ship's lights. That blade must have been ridiculously sharp, because she sliced through the Cutters like they were semiliquid. And the way she moved! Before I could even manage to fire a bolt of my own, she'd spun and lunged and managed to decapitate or impale every member of the fireteam that had found us. One of the Cutters' severed heads rolled past me, leaving a trail of red in its wake. I always found that odd, that the Cutters bled red just like us. I suppose it made sense, considering that they breathed oxygen as well, but it just seemed . . . wrong.

"Let's go," Aiella said, snapping me back to reality. I swallowed hard, forcing back the nausea that threatened to erupt from me, and started to walk through the carnage she'd left behind.

"Where are we going?" I asked her, a few steps later.

She shrugged one shoulder without looking back at me. "Intel's layout suggested that the life support pods would be back this way. Intel may have been completely jacked up, but it makes sense that they'd be near the living quarters. And that's where we dropped in, so . . ."

I jogged after her. "Captain," I said, feeling a bit of desperation. "Isn't that where we were ambushed? And you want to go back there? With all due respect, ma'am, are you fucking crazy?"

She turned and shoved me up against the bulkhead, then leaned in and put her face inches from mine. For the first time, I got a good look at her blue eyes, and fear curled through me. Madness waited there, in her gaze. Madness tangled with the kind of rage that made my hackles stand up on end. Then she did something I never would have expected or predicted. She smiled.

"Wayne," she said, using my first name. I hadn't even realized that she'd known my first name. "I've just watched every single member of my command, save one, be slaughtered before my eyes. We took a few of them out, and gave a good account of ourselves, but that doesn't change the fact that *all of my people are dead.* Except you. So, yeah. I guess you could say that I. *am.* fucking. crazy."

I took a deep, slow breath, trying to calm the sphincter-puckering fear she inspired. I opened my mouth to say something, though I had no idea what, but she shook her head and laid one finger over my lips, like a mother shushing her child.

"But that's good news for you, Private Carreon. Wayne. Because that means that you will survive. You're getting off this ship, because *you've* got to get word back about the increase in the Cutters' troop strength. And because if *you* survive to do that, then I can rest knowing that at least *one* of my people made it out."

She leaned in close enough that I could feel her breath on my ear. "So for fuck's sake, stop asking me stupid questions, keep your mouth shut, and follow my orders, is that understood?"

I swallowed hard and sternly told my body that it was absolutely *not* to react to the disturbingly close proximity of this clearly very crazy bitch. My body didn't listen, but thankfully, Aiella didn't seem to notice. She just backed up and pinned my eyes with her icy blues again. I gave her a tiny nod, and that did the trick. She nodded back and, finally, let me go.

"So," she said, her tone conversational. "Now that we've got that sorted out, I believe we were headed this way?"

So here's a thing or two you might not know about the Cutters. Most everyone knows we call them that because they have this really disconcerting practice of grafting a huge, wickedly sharp blade onto one or more of their various appendages. Cutters are, of course, bipedal, and vaguely humanoid shaped because of it, but the size and shape of these cutting blades meant that they didn't necessarily *look* humanoid all the time.

What we found on that hellish trek through the bowels of the Cutter ship was that they really seemed to *like* using those blades. In fact, they preferred melee combat to shooting. To be honest, that worked in our favor more than once, as they tended to put down their own energy weapons in order to watch Aiella and wait for their opportunity to match blades with her. Part of the reason for that might have been the tight confines of the ship's passages, but it really did seem like they were queuing up for their turn. I started holding my fire and just basically covering her, keeping them from picking us off from the rear. Not that they seemed inclined to do that. They could have taken us out ten times over, but the ones I saw just watched us, their six-eyed stare bright as she moved like a scythe through the ranks of challengers.

I don't speak Cutter, but damn me if they didn't sound like they enjoyed watching her. You might almost say that they *admired* her. Me? She scared the living piss out of me . . . but she was on my side.

At one point, several of them were awaiting us in an open area that served as a large junction. For the first time, two of the Cutters attacked at once. Aiella severed one of their bladed forearms. Like something you'd see in a holo, it fell in front of me while a spray of apparently arterial blood made a perfect arc through the air. I kicked the limb out of the way and felt the hot patter of the blood on my face. Perfect. Disgust roiled through me, and when one of the waiting Cutters managed to slide by Aiella without getting sliced open, I struck more by instinct than anything else. I brought the butt of my energy rifle up and smashed it roughly in the direction of the creature's face. It reeled backward, tripped on the severed blade arm, and fell to the ground. It let out a howl of pain, and I looked down to see that the blade arm had cut the back of its leg, just above the foot. On a human, it would have caught the Achilles tendon. Essentially, the Cutter had just hamstrung himself on his buddy's severed arm. Apparently they kept those blade arms insanely sharp. I'd been lucky not to have severed my toes!

Howler at my feet wasn't done, though, despite being flat on its back. It swung its own blade arm up over his head to try and tangle in Aiella's dancing footwork. I may have let out a howl of my own as I reacted. I lunged forward and stomped down on its already battered face. That was probably a mistake, because that made him turn his blade arm to *me*. I managed to use the butt of my energy rifle to block his first strike, and then turned the rifle to shoot him in the face. The stink of ozone and burnt meat exploded all around us.

"Shit!" Aiella yelled. "What the fuck did you do that for?" I heard the Cutters let out something that sounded like screams of rage, and one of them lunged at Aiella again. She spun out of reach, then grabbed the back of my jumpsuit and hauled me along with her. The Cutters watching from the crossing passages started bringing their own energy rifles to bear. We were rats in a godsdamned barrel until she shoved me sideways into an opening in the hallway.

I fell through it, stumbling on the raised lip of the floor beyond. Aiella stepped on me, then over me and kicked my ribs to get me to move out of the way. I curled up in a ball, not knowing what else to do, and she smashed her fist into some kind of control panel on the bulkhead, causing a thick panel to slide shut behind us.

"Get up!" she yelled at me. I didn't say anything back, partly because her kick had knocked the wind out of me, and partly because I didn't know what to say. She was mad at me, I could see that, but I had no idea why.

I struggled to my hands and knees, then up to my feet, just in time to see her knife hand as she jammed it into my chest.

"You bleeding moron!" she screamed, shoving me back against the bulkhead. "I *had* them! Didn't you even bother to read *any* of the intel reports on the Cutters' culture? They're a warrior-caste people. They *revere* melee combat, and they would have let us cut our way to wherever we wanted to go if you hadn't cocked it all up and *cheated by shooting!*"

"What? Are you kidding me?" I said, my voice rising with my temper. "What the hell else was I going to do? Watch it hamstring you and cut you down? I'm not a damn baby, Captain! I'll shoot when I damn well feel the need! I don't need your permission to save your *life*. For gods' sake, *we came in shooting!*"

"Yeah, but that was when we thought we'd be doing a simple board and capture, remember? This is a small support ship, not a troop carrier. There's no godsdamned reason for all of these warriors to be on board, and yet they are. So when we got shot up all to hell, it made *sense* to switch to melee combat. Until you had to go all guns blazing on me!"

I snapped. "Well excuse the *shit* out of me!" I shouted back. I leaned forward and got in her face. She didn't move a millimeter, but she did cross her arms over her chest and stare at me. "I would have known that if you'd have fucking *said something!* But nooo, you just go acting all ninja on me and start running down the hall with a godsdamned *sword*. And you *gave* me your rifle. What the hell was I supposed to do?"

She stared at me with those icy blue eyes for a moment, and then smiled slowly. "All right," she said, in a normal tone. "You're right, I should have said something. You're a soldier, after all. I should have expected you'd be inclined to 'shoot first, ask later.'"

I leaned back a little bit, my chest heaving and my face flushed. I took a deep breath and forced it slowly out my nose before I responded. "Well, maybe not, but I *am* going to shoot if it looks like the best way to keep us alive," I said, feeling somewhat mollified.

Her smile grew slightly, and she shook her head. "Unfortunately, that still leaves us stuck in what looks like a maintenance locker, with very few options."

I perked up, looked around.

"Maintenance locker?" I echoed her. I got to my feet and stood up on my tiptoes. At 191 cm, I was tall enough for a human. Cutters, however, were on average a fair bit taller. Consequently, the majority of displays were just above my head, right at Cutter eye level.

"Yeah, don't you think?" Aiella asked, stepping closer to me and craning her neck to look up as well. "Why? Do you see something helpful?"

"I don't know," I answered. I didn't read Cutter. What I did know, however, were some of the basic principles of ship engineering and design. Cutters were bipedal oxygen breathers who lived on a planet with gravity roughly similar to Grainne's own. That meant that a lot of things were going to be similar. Or should be similar, anyway. A man can hope, right?

"Give me a hand with this," I said. When she didn't move, I looked over at her. She was looking at me with one raised eyebrow. Shit.

"Sorry," I said, meaning it. "Give me a hand with this, please, ma'am?" I said. I'm sure I sounded sarcastic, even though I was genuine. She was my superior officer. Being a dead man walking was no excuse for forgetting my military discipline.

She gave a short laugh and shook her head, then stepped forward. I pulled out my service knife and began working at a seam in the panel in front of us. Aiella caught on and went to work with her own knife, and before long, we'd managed to pry the panel loose.

Inside lay the typical tangled nest of cables and lines. I don't know what I'd expected to see, but disappointment suddenly crushed my insides. I couldn't make heads nor tails of this mess. I guess I'd hoped for . . . a component that I recognized, or something. All I got was a mess of a Gordian knot. I felt, more than saw, Aiella look expectantly at me. "Well?" she thought. "Any ideas?"

"Kinda," I said. When in doubt, apply brute force, right? I took my knife and made a sweeping slash from left to right, cutting through as many of the wires and hoses as I could.

As you can imagine, this wasn't the smartest thing I could have done.

The first thing that happened was that I got electrocuted. It felt like liquid pain shooting through me, riding along each of my veins as I flew through the air and slammed into the panel that Aiella had closed. My ears rang and my vision went dark. For a moment I thought I was dead, and I remember hoping that I hadn't killed Aiella too.

Hearing returned first. Sort of. It took me a moment to realize that the bizarre, warbling shriek that I heard was, in fact, some alarm and not the tinnitus of my poor abused eardrums. Well, some alarm and Aiella calling my name.

"Carreon!" she said, sharply. She followed up with an even sharper *smacking* sound as she slapped me, hard.

"Ow!" I said in protest. Or tried to say, rather. It came out sounding like a half-strangled cough. Though my eyelids felt like they weighed a ton each, I forced them open.

Aiella's own eyes widened, and she let out her own half-strangled laugh. Then she did the damnedest thing. She hugged me. Hard. Like iron-thewed arms hard around my shoulders, forcing my face into her chest kind of hard. I might have enjoyed it, had she been wearing a lot less. As it was, it just kinda hurt.

Then she let me go, and my head fell back against the wall again. The lights flickered off and then on again. At first I thought it was because of the repeated impacts to the back of my throbbing, abused skull. But Aiella grinned and got to her feet, hauling me up a second later.

"I don't know what you did, but you certainly managed to get someone's attention." Aiella said. Her voice still held an edge of laughter. Or maybe madness. It was hard to tell.

"Is that funny?" I asked.

"Not in the slightest," she replied with a grin. The lights went dark again, for longer this time, and an ominous hissing started to fill the air, along with the scent of smoke. Acridly sweet smoke. Like the kind that occurs when you have an electrical fire. When the lights came back on, Aiella's mad grin had disappeared.

"I have no idea what that is, but it doesn't smell good," she said.

"Electrical fire," I supplied. "We should probably go. I think that's a life-support module, given the HVAC tubes or whatever they are that are branching off. We're going to have smoke in a minute."

She looked at me for another half second, and frowned.

"An electrical fire isn't going to cripple the whole ship," she said. "Get up, I have an idea."

While I struggled to push myself back to my feet, I watched Aiella reach inside her composite shirt. Apparently, she'd stashed one of the breaching charges from either her armor or mine in there, which had to have been damned uncomfortable. For half a second, I wondered what else she had shoved down in there.

She primed the charge and set the delay with a twist of her wrist and tossed it into the sparking, smoky mess I'd left. Then she turned back to me with that crazy grin.

"Let's go," she said, and turned and slammed her hand down on the control panel and the door slid open to reveal an empty (thank the gods!) passage. Outside, lights flashed in various colors in time with the blaring klaxon that still thrummed through my head. I was certain that they were meant to convey some critical information . . . but again, I had no clue as to what.

Aiella brushed past me, her sword out and ready. I brought up my rifle and followed close behind. Despite her explanation of Cutter cultural mores, I wasn't ready to abandon the only weapon I had. I wouldn't go in shooting, but I'd be ready to shoot if I had to do so.

The lights dimmed a final time, and then went out completely. The klaxon went on, blaring through the continued ringing in my ears. I couldn't get the sweet-burnt smell of electrical fire out of my nose, and for a moment I considered throwing up. But instead I reached out a hand and brushed my fingertips across the back of Captain Aiella's shoulder. How long had she set that timer for?

"Stay close, moving forward," she said in a low tone. Not that anyone else could have heard her, what with the klaxon and all. The darkness was disorienting, but that was all right. Part of our training had been in darkness. I saw, more than heard, Aiella crack the seal on the emergency chemical lights we all carried. She kept it shielded in her off hand and started to move quickly forward along the bulkhead of the passageway.

It didn't take long before we found them.

It was awkward as hell, but we managed to work out a system. Cutters can't see in the dark any better than we can. In fact, their visible range tends toward the higher frequencies of the electromagnetic spectrum. This meant that their dark vision was, in fact, *worse* than ours, so they all tended to have bright lights that they swept around in front of them as they searched for the problem with their ship.

Aiella handed her chem light back to me, and I flipped the shield closed and stuffed it in a pocket before bringing my energy rifle up to ready. My eyes were already starting to dark-adapt. If things started to go badly for Aiella and her sword, I'd shoot at the lights and keep moving. What could go wrong?

I tried to stay pretty close on her tail, but *damn*, the woman moved like water. She stalked them like a Ripper in the night and then attacked from the darkness. The Cutters, blinded by their lights, never seemed to see her coming. She'd leap, or lunge, or turn, and a Cutter would cry out, and a light would drop to the ground. I'd kick it to the side, shoving it under whatever body lay closest, so that the glare wouldn't hamper her vision.

I had to give it to them. Even with fluid death moving through them like a hot wind, they didn't panic. They'd shine their lights in the direction of the last cry, and sometimes catch a glimpse of Aiella as she whirled away like a shadow disappearing in the dark. They'd attack with their bladed limbs raised, but as often as not they hit each other, because she was just that damn fast. All I had to do was stay out of the way and not die.

Then, before I realized it, we were alone in that junction of the ship. The last Cutter died choking on its own blood as Aiella ran her sword through the creature's thick, squat neck. I'd just dodged another severed Cutter arm when the punishing noise of the klaxon cut off.

"It's me," I said into the sudden silence, while I bent to retrieve the dead Cutter's light. I lifted it and shined it over Aiella's body, making a quick check to ensure she was unhurt. She stood there like the Morrigan, her chest heaving, her eyes glassy. I stepped slowly forward.

"Captain?" I asked softly, snapping my fingers in front of her eyes. She blinked and annoyance replaced the battle trance in her eyes and she turned to me.

"Wha—?" she started to say. But then the deck raised up about a meter, and listed hard to starboard. A massive wall of sound and pressure slammed into us, knocking the wind out of my abused lungs and making my head pound and my ears ring even harder. Then, of course, my head hit the deck, because I'd been completely knocked off of my feet and barely managed to avoid landing on a bladed Cutter carcass. The deck pitched again, rolling back to port.

A bright white smoke started to snake along the ceiling of the passage. I probably wouldn't have noticed it, except that I had to lie still for a moment and force my body to remember how to breathe, and my light was shining directly up. Eventually, I sucked in a lungful of air and coughed as I tasted that sweet, acrid electrical taint. I somehow managed to force my battered body to roll over, and promptly sliced open my knee on a downed Cutter.

I hissed a curse just as Aiella got to her feet next to me. She shook her head sharply, like she was trying to dispel her own disorientation and knelt next to me.

"Don't you ever look where you're going, Carreon?" she asked, her voice ragged but firm.

"Was looking for you, ma'am," I managed to say. She snorted and turned to cut a piece off of the dead Cutter's uniform. Fabric or some kind of leather, I couldn't have really said, but it parted easily enough for her blade. As any number of also-dead Cutters could testify. She examined my wound, and then smiled.

"It's shallow," she said. As she spoke, she wrapped her makeshift bandage around my knee and tied it off. It hurt, but then again, so did everything else by this point. I let her help me up (again, damnit!) and managed to work out a sort of hobble that didn't make it bleed too much. The deck pitched under us again, and I stumbled into the bulkhead.

"Nice work," Aiella said. I looked at her, uncomprehending. She snorted a little bit and shook her head, presumably at my ignorance. She reached out to grab my arm and pulled me along after her as she started to move.

"Back in the locker. Opening up that maintenance hatch and finding the life-support module. Could be we've crippled this ship. Maybe destroyed her. Nicely done. That *was* your intent, right?" she asked. We'd left the Cutter light back with the bodies, so I could only guess that she was turning her head toward me with a sardonic grin, but I felt my face heat up anyway.

"Uh, yeah," I said. I didn't sound convincing at all. I heard her laugh softly, and my face flamed even more. In truth, I'd only been thinking of getting out alive when I slashed up the locker. I'd thought that maybe I could create some kind of diversion to let us get past the hordes of Cutter warriors that apparently inhabited this ship. I probably watched too many holos.

We kept moving. Eventually, we found more Cutters. As before, they died quickly in the darkness. Their behavior seemed different, however. Instead of roving as full patrols in search of something (us, perhaps?), we were encountering them in twos and threes, occasionally singly. They weren't organized, but they all seemed to be moving in roughly the same direction. Which was helpful, actually, because I, at least, was completely lost by this point. Even with the advantage of human eyes, fighting our way through an alien ship in the dark was a difficult task. Keeping a sense of direction? Impossible.

"The escape pods must be this way. That's got to be why they're all flocking here," Aiella said, after we'd come up behind the third small group. They'd turned and fought, and they'd all died well, if such things counted for anything. By now, the smoke had infiltrated the interior of the ship to the point where it fogged through the thin beams cast by the Cutters' lights. My nose burned from it, and I feared I'd never get rid of that scorched-sweet taste in the back of my throat. I grunted something that sounded vaguely like agreement and continued.

Following close behind her meant me trying not to trip over the dismembered bodies she was leaving in her wake. It took a fair amount of concentration, especially in the dark.

It seemed that she was right, though. That was the good news. The bad news was that as we got closer and closer to the possibility of actually making it out of this clusterfuck, we were running into more and more Cutters. Support personnel, too. I could tell because of the lack of wicked blade monstrosities growing out of their limbs. The nonwarrior Cutters looked significantly smaller without the blades. Or maybe it was their body language. They seemed to shrink back from the cyclone of edged death that was my company commander. In fact, if I'm not mistaken, they actually started to give way and bow down to her, as if she were some kind of legendary figure. Who knows, maybe she was. These guys certainly did seem to revere edged combat . . . and she definitely *looked* like a goddess of the sword.

"There!" she cried out as she ran yet another Cutter warrior through. The smaller support Cutter that had been with the warrior backed away and folded itself into a curiously still bow. I tore my eyes from the bowing alien to look where Aiella's dripping blade pointed.

Down the hallway a few meters was an open hatch, just large enough for me to walk through without stooping. It would have been small for a Cutter, but it looked like it opened into a dimly lit capsulelike space with a contraption that looked a lot like a grav-couch.

An escape pod. We'd made it.

Or very nearly. Right then, an ear-splitting, screeching yowl echoed down the passage from a crossing passageway. That sound made my skin crawl with foreboding. I'd heard it before, in that first hallway, before we killed the lights and lit this place on fire. It was the sound of a Cutter attack.

"Go!" Aiella shouted at me. She reached out, grabbed my free arm and slung me, hard, toward the glowing beacon of the pod's soft light. I stumbled, willing myself to fall toward the pod as I fought to keep my battered, unsteady body upright. I felt her let go and turn to face the onslaught of enraged Cutter warriors as they charged down the crossing passage to try and cut us off.

Let me just get to the pod, I thought, forcing my legs to keep fighting forward. *Let me get there, and I can turn and cover her retreat.*

I don't know what God or Goddess was listening to me . . . maybe all of them, because despite everything else going wrong on this royal goatfuck of a mission, I made it. My shoulder slammed against the frame of the hatch, rendering my left arm numb, but it didn't matter. I turned, braced against the hatch frame, raised my energy rifle and fired.

"Aiella! Let's go!" I shouted over the sound of the Cutters' battle rage. The deck bucked again, and I fell hard against the opposite side of the frame, then landed flat on my ass inside the pod itself.

"Fuck!" I shouted as I struggled to get back to my feet. My knee throbbed, and my pant leg was wet through. I couldn't hear Aiella's words, but I heard her voice shouting something. With my teeth shredding my lower lip bloody, I used my rifle as a crutch to lever myself up. Every moment I wasn't firing at the Cutters was a moment lost, and I cursed every aching muscle, every battered joint that made me move so godsdamned *slow*!

Right foot first, then left, and I managed to get myself upright just in time to see Aiella in a flat sprint for the pod. The Cutter horde was hard on her heels, their bladed limbs scything through the smoke and darkness toward her. She reached out her hand. Our fingertips just touched . . .

And she coughed. Then looked down.

A double hand length of alien steel protruded from her chest.

I screamed something. I still don't know what. It may not have even been words. Somehow, I had her blade in my hand, and I was bringing it down on the limb that had pierced her from behind. Her blade shattered, but so did the Cutter's limb, and the ship bucked upward violently enough to throw Aiella and me hard to the deck of the pod as the hatches slammed shut. I tried to catch her, but the angles were wrong. I just couldn't get all the way there, and she impacted the deck of the pod face down on top of my right arm.

The giant, invisible hand of massive acceleration held us down as the auto-launch mechanism of the Cutter pod ignited, spitting us out into the serene void of space. I struggled to move under Aiella, but her slim, powerful body suddenly had exponentially more weight, and I might as well have tried to move a mountain off of myself.

The pod launcher must have put a bit of spin on us, however, because I could slowly start to see the familiar shape of the Cutter ship drift into view above me. It convulsed like a wounded animal as explosions peppered one side of it. I felt a savage satisfaction at that.

They'd killed us, sure . . . but we'd killed a lot of them, too; and crippled their ship as well.

"Wayne?" Aiella whispered, her face close to mine. I nearly choked. She was alive?

"Yes, ma'am?" I said. My voice sounded broken.

"You okay?"

I didn't know whether to laugh or cry. I started to do both. "Yeah," I said. "I'm fine. A little banged up, but you did it, ma'am. You got me out. Thanks."

"It's . . . cause I'm . . . sexy . . . ninja . . ." she whispered. She opened her mouth again as if she would say something else, but nothing came out. Instead she just smiled and let her eyes fall closed as she bled out all over me.

I had her sword reforged.

In the end, it was the option that made the most sense. Especially after I decided to incorporate the blade from the Cutter arm that killed her. It was steel, after all, albeit some kind of weird alloy that was found only on the Cutter homeworld.

I figured I'd have it reforged and give it to her next of kin as a remembrance. It seemed like a nice gesture, and I felt like I owed her that, at least. Her next of kin turned out to be a brother, older, but just by a year and change. He was a plumber who lived in Jefferson City.

I'd tried to contact him before her funeral, but it hadn't worked out that way. I'd been in the hospital for a while with my injuries, and then there were the inevitable debriefings and admin actions before I was able to take my time off. It turned out that some more members of my company had survived the initial slaughter and been taken prisoner. Leadership and intel both were all over me for anything I could remember about the interior of the ship. It sounded like they were contemplating another attack to get my buddies back. It stung that I wouldn't be invited to the party, but I'd be lying if I said that a part of me wasn't relieved. And then there was the blade itself. It took me a while to find a bladesmith who would or could do what I wanted, but eventually I managed.

So on the day that Captain Aiella, Freehold Military Forces, was honored along with the others who'd died in the initial offensive, I was there in my uniform, her sword sheathed at my side.

After the service, I approached her brother. The man looked completely out of his depth, clutching the folded flag of the Freehold that had been presented to him. His casualty notification officer was somewhere nearby, but everyone involved knew me, and knew that I was the last person to see Aiella alive. Everyone figured I'd want to talk to her brother.

"Mr. Aiella," I said. The plumber looked up at me with eyes that were haunted and sad, and more than a little confused. He looked like her, only softer. I felt myself smile.

"I'm Space Combat Specialist Wayne Carreon," I said. "Captain Aiella was my company commander. She . . . she saved my life, multiple times, sir. It was my honor to know her."

The plumber smiled too, sadly. "Naomy was like that," he said. "Even when we were kids. She was always protecting me, even though I was older."

I nodded and swallowed hard. My eyes were starting to burn, and my throat threatened to close down. I forced air in through my nose and out again, then spoke.

"Sir, I have her sword. It was damaged in the battle, but I took the liberty of having it repaired. It . . . it now contains the alien steel that killed her."

I have no idea why I added that last part, except that I knew she would have enjoyed knowing it. I looked away from the plumber's eyes (gods, he looked like her!) and focused on unbuckling my baldric that held the sword and scabbard.

His hand covered mine. I stilled, and looked back up at Aiella's eyes in her brother's face. "Keep it," he said, his voice uneven.

"No," I said, my own voice cracking. "I can't . . . I . . ."

"Keep it," he said. "She was my sister by birth, but she died to keep you alive. That makes you family, and family takes precedence over blood. She'd want you to have it. Keep it." He let out a harsh, broken laugh. "I'm a fucking plumber, for the sake of all the gods. What the hell am I going to do with a warrior's sword?"

I let my hand drop from the buckle, and instead moved to draw the sword and hold it high.

The reforged blade was a work of art, I must say. It still had Aiella's hilt and guard, but the blade itself seemed to glimmer with a faintly blue reflection. The bladesmith had said that the alien steel was an interesting alloy, heavy on the cobalt. I had only a vague idea what that meant, but it certainly made a striking weapon. I watched the afternoon Iolight ripple down the length of the blade.

I felt my lips curve in a smile, and I brought the hilt to my chin to render a salute to her brother, then lowered the blade with a ringing *swish* as it sliced through the air.

"Thank you," I said to the brother of the woman I could never thank, but to whom I owed my life. With the greatest of reverence, I sheathed her blade and reached out to shake her brother's hand. A faint breeze ruffled my hair, and I could almost hear Aiella's wild laugh.

As a certain starship captain once put it, space is the final frontier. That being the case, when humankind ventures out into the Solar System, we'll very likely bring with us dusty saloons, boomtowns, and outlaws the likes of which haven't been seen since Billy the Kid and Jesse James wielded six-shooters. As such, we'll need frontier lawmen daring and tenacious enough to dole out justice on an interplanetary scale. United States Deputy Marshal Kent Hill is one such lawman. He's tracked his quarry to the fringe of the Asteroid Belt, where his badge isn't even worth the ore (and high-tech sensors) it's made of. But Justice doesn't depend on a bronze star. And Kent Hill always gets his man.

Originally appeared in Rocket's Red Glare

A MAN THEY DIDN'T KNOW
★
by David Hardy

VANN'S STATION turned silently on the fringe of the Asteroid Belt. A freighter bearing crudely milled titanium was outbound for Earth, and a few ships were drifting in with raw ore from the diggings.

But in the Whiskey Quadrant the Titanium Lounge was jumping. The music was blaring and the crowd overflowed into the street. The rest of Whiskey Quadrant was equally busy. The Quad was usually lively on a Saturday, when the asteroid miners flooded in, looking for a good time. Kent Hill's keen gray eyes held an amused detachment. He was not looking for a good time as such, he was looking for a wanted man. He was a United States Deputy Marshal, and finding fugitives was his job, one that he liked quite well. Hill's good time would end in the arrest and incarceration of a very dangerous criminal.

Ted Kovacs came around the side of the bar, glancing either way along the curving avenue that ran the length of the space station. Kovacs was the Chief of Security for Vann's Station. Keeping order among the men, women, and robots that populated a support station on the asteroid belt was no easy task. Kovacs had only a miniscule staff, too few to police the station well. Advances in surveillance-thwarting technology constantly negated advances in surveillance technology. The station's owners cared more about damage to the station than to its occupants, and all the criminals were well-armed. But Hill and Kovacs had been buddies back in the Cyborg War and that meant going a little extra when a friend needed help.

Kovacs nodded at Hill. "Yep, my snitch got a line on this Jack Cole joker. Saw him three quarters of a rotation back. The little rat is already counting his share of the reward."

"Anybody with Cole?" Hill asked. "He runs with a robot. Supposedly the robot helped him pull a bank job on Mars."

Kovacs shook his head sadly. "No, but you know how it is. It's harder to keep track of robots than people. I seized three robots being smuggled in as parts. Damn things were designed to dispense Neometh and play slot poker. Caught hell for it too, the smugglers were kicking back to the station's owners."

"Nothing like a wide open station. It's one big ol' wheel of fun in space." Hill put his badge, which served as a tactical combat communication and sensor array, on the outside of his jacket and shifted his µ366 blaster, loaded with six expendable capacitors, where it was ready for a quick draw. "Let's take him."

Kovacs strode alongside Hill. "I'm glad you came to me with this. I'm going to cash in the reward and head back stateside. I'm tired of playing doorman for a bunch of crooks and ingrates."

"I'm glad you're backing me up." Hill meant it. Cole had shot his way out of a Federal courthouse orbiting Jupiter and headed for the asteroids where international law meant that no Earth-bound entity, not China, Russia, Brazil, nor even the U.S.A. had jurisdiction. Outside of the Federal Orbital Court system, Hill wasn't much more than a bounty hunter with a fancy badge.

Kovacs went around back, producing a key-circuit to open the service door. The lawmen strode quickly through the liquor storage room, past the protesting owner, past a couple of people who faded into side rooms at the sight of the law. They pushed aside a robot bartender and entered the main room.

The lights were low, the music deafening, and the room was

packed. Hill surveyed the crowd, a quarter were flying on Neometh, a quarter were on Synthmorph, and the rest were drunk on cheap whiskey. Kovacs nudged Hill. "My snitch."

The snitch was a man wearing a cheap suit and a blank expression. He made eye contact with Kovacs for a second. Then he looked away down the bar. At first all Hill saw was a miner, dressed in grubby coveralls, a stupid expression, a loose lipped face, a beer clenched in either fist. Then he saw Cole at the bar, talking to a woman. The outlaw was animated, punctuating his words with his glass of bourbon. Yet there was something repetitious about Cole's movements, almost mechanical.

Hill turned his badge's targeting system toward Cole. It picked up the suspect's voice. "Yeah, family is what matters. Everything else is crooked, it's all sixty-two twenty-five, you know what I mean?" She evidently didn't, but Cole kept talking. "I can't go home, but there's a place where I see my kin. Laws don't nose around too much on those ranges."

The badge scanned the man at the bar, taking measurements, cross-checking thousands of records of wanted men, eyes, bones, ears, voice, the spacing of visible pores, instantly producing a confirmation on the heads-up display, visible only to Hill. This was Jack Cole, wanted for bond jumping, armed robbery, and attempted murder. Hill signaled Kovacs to move in.

Hill pulled his μ366. "Federal marshal! Cole, you're under arrest!" The badge screamed a warning. Hill was still raising his blaster when a fist holding a beer bottle smashed into him, sending him crashing across the bar.

Hill rolled with the blow, an instinctive reaction that saved his life. The miner had to drop his other beer to reach for a blaster a microsecond before Hill rolled behind the bar. He felt the scalding heat of the blast that barely missed him. The badge broadcast counter-measures to scramble any weapon targeting him, and then Hill went to help Kovacs as blaster shots came fast and furious. Panic had gripped the Titanium as blasters began firing.

"Do you read? Do you read?" Hill signaled to Kovacs. "Civilian in the way!" Kovacs shouted. Hill popped up from behind the bar just in time to see Cole, using the woman as a shield, cut Kovacs down. The miner was standing over the smoking corpse of the snitch, blaster in one hand and a beer in the other. The miner's face rearranged into something less human, more like a robot. Instantly the robot-gunman took aim at Hill. The badge's scrambler averted the blast by a fraction. Instead of killing Hill, the plasma slug brought down part of the bar wall and left Hill stunned and injured. When he rose, Cole and the robot had fled.

Hill offered his badge and blaster to the Chief United States Marshal for the Asteroid Belt. The chief stared hard at Hill. "You're a goddamn idiot. Not only did you screw up the Cole arrest, but you think I've got deputies to spare."

"It was my screw up," Hill said. "I need to know if you still trust me to clean up the mess."

"What were you going to do if I accepted?"

"Go after Cole and the robot as a free-lance bounty hunter."

"And get in the way of the next guy. No thanks." The chief pushed the badge and blaster back towards Hill. "It'll be a lot easier to take down Cole with these."

Hill went back to the files, looking for clues to where to find Cole or the strange robot. He'd tracked a lot of wanted men, but none who had killed a friend. There was grim determination in his heart as he looked for Cole's trail.

The robot had very little in its file, besides a few scattered sightings at the scene of Cole's violent crimes. There was no manufacturer information, so the robot could have been a one-off from any of the myriads of bot foundries, or even cobbled together from parts in a temporary bottery. The morphing ability it displayed was unheard of, except in experimental models. The robot was the key to this Cole business, but Hill had no time to find what it unlocked.

Cole's file was much longer. He was born in Texas on Earth. Family contacts were limited. His mother in a cryogenic retirement home in Florida, father deceased, a brother on Mars, a sister married to a cybernetic tech living in the Moon Cities. Surveillance on the mother had produced nothing and the sister had converted to the Church of ProgSocJus and had cut off all contacts with relatives as hopelessly unrepentant oppressors.

Cole had a record from his youth, petty theft and drug possession. He straightened up and worked for his brother Tom's cattle outfit on

Mars's terraformed ranges running bos, as they called genetically-modified Martian cattle, before joining the army. He'd served two tours on Planetoid 806 during the Cyborg War. He was in an outpost that was nuked and overrun by Cyborgs. Cole was listed as MIA, but was released at the end of the war as a POW to a neutral Swiss mission. He'd been torn up pretty bad, but the Cyborgs had put him back together, with none of the cybernetic oddities they had a penchant for.

Then Cole's life got strange. He alternated between spending his days performing acts of charity and violent outbursts. There were six months helping build habitats for retirees on Venus, then a knife fight over a spilled beer. Cole worked nine months on a thermal bore-hole crew on Titan, giving his wages to buy robot limbs for wounded vets, then he robbed a payroll and blew through the money in a month, spending it on booze, drugs, and loose women. And so it went, a dramatic act of charity, a period of law-abiding quiet and service to others matched by an armed robbery, an act of pointless violence, or cold-blooded assassination. The Cassini Ring Drug Cartel was suspected of hiring Cole to silence informers.

There weren't a whole lot of clues left in the ruined bar. The woman Cole had used as a human shield said he had just finished paying for her to return to Saturn to reunite with her estranged daughter. "Cole's about changing people's lives," Hill muttered to himself. "He's clearly a believer in family."

Hill thought a moment. "Family. I think it's time to head to Mars."

Down in Argyre Planitia the grass grew thick enough in the atmosphere maintained by the terraforming satellites. But only a few daring cattlemen lived there because of the attacks by semi-humanoid mutated suidae. The porcine brigands had been dumped in the Charitum Montes by a failed genetic-engineering consortium backed by Russian oligarchs and Wall Street speculators. Between the Sooeys and the types of settlers that inhabited the crater bottoms, lawmen were not welcome.

Hill rode into the bottoms, appearing to be just another bos handler looking for a job, and leaving behind a past that he did not wish to talk about. He kept his ears open and said little, moving towards Tom Cole's Red Dust outfit. The closer he got to the Red Dust the more he learned of the owner.

Tom Cole was no wild outlaw. Boss Tom adhered to the best practices of the Martian Stock Association, paid his men on time, covered their insurance, and preached the Gospel on the Sabbath. Boss Tom was very much the exception among the sort of men that clustered in the crater bottoms. When Hill showed up at the Red Dust, he introduced himself as "Smith."

"You're regular crater-county bos-boy, aren't you?" Tom said.

Hill nodded.

"You've done your share of blotting gene-codes. Rearrange the DNA on a bos so it doesn't show who owns it."

"Yes, sir, I've done some in my day."

"Use Neometh to work longer, use some Synthmorph to take the edge off, and then sell a little to pay for your habit."

"I've traveled that country, yes."

"Don't need any saddle tramps. Don't need thieves, don't need pill heads. Good day, Mister Smith."

"Sir, I'm not one to beg, but do you need a man who's been lost and is trying to find his way back to the good trail?"

Boss Tom studied Hill for a long while. "That sort I have room for. Sling your gear in the bunkhouse."

The men in the bunkhouse accepted Smith's reticence about his past, being close-mouthed men themselves. About Tom Cole's reasons for re-locating to the Argyre, they were more open.

"When they set up the Martian Regional Authority and started putting taxes on land and cattle, Boss Tom said it was nothing but thievery with a pen and headed south. He was right too, the MRA ain't nothing but a front for the Fourth World Corporation so's they can buy up everything cheap."

The days passed quietly at Red Dust. Hill's duties handling bos were not excessively difficult. Just as Martian bovines had been greatly modified from their Earth ancestors, a Martian pony bore genes that allowed it to literally sniff out bos, and to emit pheromones that brought the wild and aggressive beasts out of their hiding places. The bos-boys controlled their mounts with a cybernetic interface installed in their spurs, and carried an electronic tracking system in their broad-brimmed hats similar to the one in Hill's badge. Despite that, Hill's hat failed to show any sign of Jack Cole or his robot ally.

Boss Tom was a stern employer but a fair one, who drove himself as hard as his men. Hill almost felt bad about lying to Boss Tom's face while planning to kill his brother. Then he remembered Kovacs' blasted remains in an Asteroid Belt saloon.

Then one cold, thin-aired day, a stranger arrived at Red Dust. He could have been an itinerant bos-trader, robot tech, pony-breeder, seller of second-hand gene-splicing equipment, or any of the wanderers that crossed Mars. But Hill watched from the bunkhouse and sensed a strange familiarity in the man's motions. The way Boss Tom quickly ushered the stranger into the house and then departed with him down a seldom-used bos track clinched the matter.

Hill sighed and muttered to himself as he saddled his bos-pony. "The robot can't help but keep cool, but you have a conscience, Boss Tom. It's too bad for your brother, but you do."

Hill found them at a line camp, hard under the Charitum Montes. The camp had stood empty since raiding Sooeys had killed half of the crew working there. Hill dismounted at a distance, activated his badge, taking particular care to use its counter-measures to make him nearly invisible, and crept close. He sheltered behind a feed shed and turned on the audio sensors in his badge. Voices came from the camp's ramshackle crew quarters.

"I told you not to come back, Jack," Tom Cole said. "They will catch you one of these days."

"Let 'em," Jack Cole replied. "It'll be a . . ."

"Damn exciting day." The robot finished the sentence.

"Tell that thing to stay quiet." Tom's voice was filled with sick fear. "You're a mess, Jack. That thing has turned you into a monster."

"Yes," the robot said.

"And also a saint," Cole added.

"That's even worse. Turn yourself in and get help."

"There ain't no . . ." Cole said.

"Helping us." The robot kept up the rhythm.

"You know I wasn't raised this way."

"But there's a way to make it right."

Boss Tom's voice was pleading. "Whatever it is, don't do it, Jack. If you're still my brother, don't do it."

"I will," Jack Cole said.

"Right after I kill the lawman lurking outside and the war party of Sooeys vectoring toward us," the robot added.

Hill ducked back just as a plasma slug burned through the wall. He activated all the sensors in his badge and shot back, firing through the walls of the shed and crew quarters at the robot. The war-squeal of the Sooeys echoed across the bottoms. In moments the shed and crew quarters were reduced to flaming wreckage and Hill was running before a volley of ill-aimed blaster fire from the Sooeys.

Hill fired off a shot that dropped a Sooey, and ran towards Cole. The badge brought Cole into focus and the $\mu366$'s stabilizers lined up the shot. Hill pressed the firing stud just as another Cole loomed into the sight picture. The robot had morphed into his comrade's form. The second Cole staggered and loosed a spray of blasts that sent Hill scrambling for cover and cut down three attacking Sooeys.

"I gotta get our brother!" one of the Coles shouted.

"He's gone! 6-2-2-5!" the other shouted back. Hill had no idea which was the robot and which wasn't. He was too busy shooting at the Sooeys who were determined to take his life.

By the time the Sooeys drew off, the Coles were gone. Hill found Boss Tom in the smoking wreckage of the crew house. He'd caught a blast in the crossfire and was dying.

"I should have known you were a goddamn rat. If I wasn't dying I'd kill you myself." Boss Tom grimaced in pain. Hill signaled on his badge for an emergency medical lift-off, but this was remote country, and Tom Cole had seconds to live, not minutes.

Tom was still talking. "Someone has to stop Jack. He's going to save the country. He's got the devil in him, believes in salvation. He's going to kill millions and kill them soon. Out in the Kuiper Belt."

"Where in the Kuiper Belt?" Hill asked. "What is 6225?"

Tom Cole's eyes focused on Hill. "Stop him, lawman," he whispered as he died.

Out in the Kuiper Belt, massive blocks of ice jostled rocky planetoids in riotous confusion. Thickly strewn among the planetoid drifts were decayed hulks of mining ships, blasted orbital bunkers, abandoned supply depots, and the remains of millions of men and cyborgs. This had been the scene of the hardest fighting of the Cyborg War, with hundreds of thousands of planetoids converted into everything from fortresses that held a division to isolated outposts consisting of a rock and a one-man foxhole. The main United States base had been on Pluto, where PFC Hill and Lance Corporal Kovacs had met.

Hill picked up Cole and the robot's trail on Pluto. They had been spotted going into a bottery that was known for "no questions asked" service. The tech had been blasted to atoms, and his bottery wrecked. At some point the shop's network connection was disabled and every device in the place wiped with savage thoroughness. Hill picked through the smoldering wreckage, his heart sinking. Cole was leaving no back trail.

Then Hill spotted a broken network fuser, the type of device that techs used to join circuitry in a robot's limbs to its central circuits. The device would image the robot's circuit to ensure the smooth functioning of the neural network. Hill expected it had been wiped like the rest.

At first it looked like broken junk like the rest of the shop, but as Hill stooped to study it, he realized that the external case was merely broken. The fuser started up weakly and Hill used his badge's router to connect his spacecraft's computer to the fuser. The fuser brought up an image of Cole and his doppelganger. Hill heard the tech's shocked voice, "This didn't come from Earth." The image flickered and the number 6225 flashed, then was drowned in the echo of a blaster, fired at close range.

"What does it mean?" Hill asked the walls. Then he remembered.

Cole was an exception. The cyborgs only occasionally took prisoners. They had a predisposition to experiment on their prisoners, reconstructing them with machine interfaces, and then sending them back to the front as part of the cyborg army. During his tour Hill had heard of Station 6225, where prisoners were rumored to be held. He hurried back to his spacecraft.

The spacecraft's collection of maps was excellent, but disused and drifting Cyborg orbital forts were indifferently outlined. Hill stared into the bleak depths of space, anxiety gnawing at him. Hill and Kovacs had served a tour as forward observers, guiding fusion bombs toward Cyborg targets. It was dangerous work with Cyborgs making frequent raids to destroy the forward outposts. He and Kovacs had saved each other's lives more than once.

Hill spent hours monitoring Cyborg communications traffic during the war. His expertise guided him as he tuned his spacecraft's communication system up into the bands the Cyborgs had used. Relentlessly he scanned the ghost signals, echoes of explosions, wandering signals of dying transmitters, until he found it. A binary code message, repeated over and over again, 6-2-2-5, 6-2-2-5, 6-2-2-5, endlessly. Hill homed in and fired up his spacecraft's reactors.

Fortress 6225 loomed up from the cloud of orbiting rubble. The station had been abandoned at the end of the war. The fortress's weapons, plasma cannons, missile launchers, all the impedimenta of war, still glowered, but were as dead and silent as the emptiness about them.

Hill found Cole's spacecraft, its reactor cooled. He brought his own spacecraft to a landing, in swift pursuit of his quarry. Hill used a universal jimmy to operate the airlock. The Cyborg fort was silent and dark, but still had breathable air. Broken Cyborg troopers, abandoned equipment, useless computer cores, the waste of war littered the corridors. Hill turned his badge to the highest sensitivity and pushed on.

Hill passed through a room where strange medical devices stood among man-sized containers holding human specimens. Most had been reconstructed with cybernetic parts, half-human, half-machine. There were gene-splicing devices, and units that were designed to fuse human flesh to nano-tech controls. A schematic of the human brain flickered in a 3-D projection. Someone had used a shard of rubble to scratch on the wall the words "Good" and "Evil."

Hill studied the machine closely. Its batteries still held enough charge to bring it up. There were complex controls that interfaced with the brain. Fortunately Hill was very familiar with Cyborg machine coding. He scanned the device with his badge. It had a simple program that used English terms for moral concepts, as well as routines to interface between a physical organism and a machine. On impulse, Hill imaged the program to his badge. Perhaps there was some clue to Cole's erratic behavior there.

Hill's badge made a silent warning. He was approaching a weapons bay. The badge indicated a man inside. Cautiously, Hill approached, his μ366 drawn. Cole stood, illuminated by a sickly radium glow, staring at the shapeless mass of a cobalt bomb.

"Come on in," Cole said. "This is where they held me prisoner. There wasn't much left of me when I got captured. Just a spinal cord and some guts. So they re-built me, and built the robot as part of me too. They had some plan about me and the robot and this bomb blowing up HQ on Pluto. Eventually the Cyborgs let me go. Lost interest or something on account of it didn't work right, forgot about the robot, too. War was over. America wasn't interested in me, either. Crap jobs, drugs, and crime are what I found. Then the robot found me. It's been a hell of a ride since."

Hill leveled the μ366. "Jackson Cole, you are under arrest. Put your hands where I can see them."

Another Cole emerged from the shadows. "Drop it, lawman."

Hill's mouth was dry and his heart was pounding. "Not happening. I'm not about to let a pair of outlaws have a cobalt bomb."

"This is messed up," the Cole at the bomb said.

"They built a second me," the Cole with the blaster said.

"It was my conscience."

"To make me useful to them."

"But it's defective."

"Goes from saint to sinner and back."

"And it's getting worse." Cole turned from the bomb to look at Hill.

Hill's hands were sweating on the blaster. "Then put down your guns and we'll get you help."

"Don't want help."

"I realized that I needed an act of charity."

"I was raised to be good and to be free."

"That's what an American is supposed to be."

"But I'm evil and a slave."

"The Cyborgs just exposed what I really am."

"I have to purify myself."

"I have to purify the country that made my conscience."

Hill took a deep breath. "That bomb will kill half of the people in the U.S.A."

"That's the purity I'm talking about."

Hill felt truly sick. He had dealt with madmen before and it never ended well. "You're going to destroy America to save its conscience. Because you're messed up, they have to die, is that it? It's a pretty thin excuse, but I reckon I've heard worse." He kept the μ366's sight on Cole.

"The Cyborgs just wanted me to be a weapon."

"I need to be an act of love."

"I liked you better as a son of a bitch, Cole." Hill didn't have many cards to play. "You could keep living free, but you're choosing to die for people who won't even be grateful." He remembered the moral interface program. It was still running, good and evil as options. Hill chose a third, the one to end the interface between man and machine.

The first Cole looked up and laughed. "They don't deserve my kindness." In one swift move he drew his blaster on the other. "Let 'em live with themselves."

Hill saw the other Cole's face dissolve, becoming robotic again, even as it pivoted, pointing its blaster at Cole. "Follow orders," it said. The robot was fast, but Cole was just that much faster. But the robot was hard, it staggered under the blast and shot back, hitting Cole. Hill fired, a blast in the robot's core. It erupted in flame and toppled over.

Hill lowered his blaster to see Cole was now aiming at him. "Let's finish this, lawman," he gasped, bloody and burned.

"Drop it, Cole!" Hill shouted.

"You ain't taking me in!" The outlaw fired and Hill felt the plasma slug burn past, knocking him down. The robot rose up and blasted Cole in the back. Hill fired twice into the robot's broken shape and the machine was reduced to flaming parts.

Hill walked over to Cole. The outlaw was badly shredded. "That was crazy. Sorry about shootin' your pal back in the Asteroid Belt. I can't make up for what I've done, I'll just pay the price. You still ain't taking me in, lawman. Live free, sonsabitches." Cole died. There would be no coming back this time. He was gone with Ted Kovacs.

"Live free, soldier. Have some peace if you can." Hill was hurt, but he'd live. He would make it back to America, bringing home a hero they never knew they had.

The neo-Cold War is heating up. Engaged with the Russians in enemy-occupied Donetsk, Captain Roland Skaskiw and his team must navigate a metaphorical minefield of international relations. But their more urgent problem is a mobile, autonomous minefield known as a SWARM. This one is very much not a metaphor. It's real. It's deadly. And it's headed right for them.

Originally appeared in Terraform.

SWARM
★
by Sean Patrick Hazlett

THE RUSSIANS were coming. They had Captain Roland Skaskiw's Special Forces team pinned down in a forested valley just outside Avdiivka, an industrial town north of Russian-occupied Donetsk. With only three survivors from his original complement of twelve, Skaskiw had been fighting a running battle against Russia's 37th Motorized Infantry Brigade for over a week.

Wearied not by cold, hunger, or lack of sleep, Skaskiw felt something darker weighing on his soul. His three-year-old daughter, Anna. He frowned at a memory of her squeezing his finger and staring up at him with those innocent emerald eyes; that would haunt him until the day he died.

From the east, a muzzle flash heralded a piercing whine that echoed through the valley. Yet no explosion followed. Skaskiw turned to Perez, his short and stocky weapons sergeant, a powder keg of a man with a short fuse. "The hell was that?"

"Sounds like a 152-millimeter howitzer. Ordnance unknown."

Skaskiw shrugged. "Hang tight. Extraction's in one hour."

Over the past year, the Kremlin had been launching cyber attacks against critical infrastructure, subverting European elections, and

193

using the Black Sea Fleet to aggressively patrol the Eastern Mediterranean. A Neo-Cold War was on the precipice of boiling over into a hot one.

From his cargo pocket, Skaskiw pulled out a ragged photo. He gazed at Anna's faded image. He kissed her picture and said a silent prayer before banishing the memory once more for the task at hand.

To the west, dozens of white and black specks peppered the gray sky, resolving into coal-black cannonballs swaying from white parachutes.

Skaskiw took a deep breath. The only thing worse than walking into a minefield was having one walk into you.

A SWARM.

Short for Scatterable Wide-Area Autonomous Robotic Mines, these sadistic little mamas scared the piss out of Skaskiw. The first time he'd faced them, they'd wiped out three quarters of his team.

Having flared on and off for a decade since Putin's 2014 annexation of Crimea, the Russo-Ukrainian War was heating up again. Skaskiw had come here to collect evidence of Russian violations of the Palo Alto Accords, which had banned offensive autonomous weapons systems. But mission creep had quickly thrust Skaskiw's soldiers into direct conflict with the Russians. Given NATO's official policy of non-intervention, Skaskiw's operation was supposed to be covert. Surrender wasn't an option.

Skaskiw needed a plan—fast.

Half a klick to the north, he spotted a redbrick schoolhouse. From there, he could blunt the Russian advance long enough to make his escape. Several meters further north, oak and pine trees lined both sides of a paved road stretching from east to west.

The SWARM began touching down behind him, cutting off his western escape route. Skaskiw frowned, then faced his comms sergeant, a lanky, straw-haired Minnesotan. "Talk to me, Jorgensen."

Jorgensen flipped down his ARTEMIS goggles. The Augmented Reality Targeting and Engagement Mapping Integration System consolidated imaging data from scores of solar-powered centimeter-length autonomous micro-drones loitering overhead.

"Contact! BMPs! Three o'clock. Two klicks out," hollered Jorgensen. Eight wedge-shaped armored vehicles closed in from the east.

Skaskiw spun toward Perez. "How many SAMs you got left?"

A SAM, or Semiautonomous Attachment Mine, could be preprogrammed to latch onto a specific target and detonate on command.

"Sixteen."

Skaskiw gestured toward the tree line. "I want SAMs there ASAP."

Perez popped open a black briefcase and removed eight racquetball-sized SAMs.

Skaskiw pointed at the schoolhouse. "We deploy the SAMs, then hole up and fight from there."

Perez fastened four small counter-rotating blades on each SAM, then gave Jorgensen a thumbs-up. Jorgensen remotely engaged the SAMs with his goggles. The rotors swirled, lifting the SAMs thirty meters above the ground before they swooped toward the road and veered sharply to either side in equal numbers. Then they disengaged their rotors, launched spring-loaded, retractable spikes on metal wires, and latched onto the trees at chest level.

In the schoolhouse, Skaskiw stumbled upon five scrawny children squatting in darkness. Their slate-blue eyes stared from soot-smothered faces. And in one little girl, he saw Anna.

"We can't stay," Perez said.

Perez was right. If they hunkered down here, the children would get caught in the crossfire.

"Mines three hundred meters and closing!" warned Jorgensen.

Perez wiped his brow. "Now what?"

Skaskiw grinned. "Have faith. Here's the plan: we detonate the SAMs the instant the bulk of the BMP column is in the kill zone, then attack."

The little girl toddled up to Skaskiw and hugged him. Seconds later, an explosion rocked the building, shaking up flakes of paint and dust.

"Now!" Skaskiw yelled.

Jorgensen detonated the SAMs. Skaskiw kicked open the school door, raising his rifle as he advanced on the unscathed lead BMP. Seven other vehicles lay pinned beneath fallen and splintered trees.

Skaskiw hesitated, second-guessing his decision to leave the children behind.

Two soldiers stumbled from the lead BMP's rear troop compartment, snapping Skaskiw out of his trance. He shot them, then glanced over his shoulder. Two hundred meters out, mines scurried toward him on mechanical spider legs.

Bullets zipped by. The Russian survivors rallied from beneath the toppled trees, pinning down the Americans behind the BMP.

Perez and Jorgensen raided the BMP's troop compartment, making quick work of the dazed men inside. Climbing into the turret, Perez gunned down the driver. Then he and Jorgensen tossed the bloody body from the vehicle. Perez slipped into the driver's hole, Jorgensen commandeered the gunner's station, and Skaskiw took control of the turret.

Perez aimed the BMP at the advancing minefield. From the gunner's station, Jorgensen swiveled the turret one hundred eighty degrees and destroyed the seven trapped BMPs to the east. Then he rotated the turret forward again, training its 30-millimeter cannon on the crawling minefield.

"Don't shoot the SWARM!" Skaskiw had a hunch the mines wouldn't attack Russian vehicles unless provoked.

The mines maneuvered with uncanny grace, dodging debris and leaping over obstacles like lions, stalking anything that moved.

Suddenly, the children ran out of the schoolhouse and right into the SWARM's path.

Skaskiw shouted, "Gun it!"

The BMP surged forward. The SWARM advanced. The children froze. A mine exploded.

Skaskiw screamed, "Faster!"

The gap between the SWARM and the children was closing fast.

"Hard right!" Skaskiw ordered.

Perez wedged the BMP between the children and the SWARM. The vehicle squealed to a halt. Skaskiw and Jorgensen scrambled to pull the children aboard; the SWARM, now only meters away.

The little girl stumbled.

Against every instinct, Skaskiw leapt from the BMP and raced to her rescue. As he carried her to the vehicle, a mine clung to his leg. Skaskiw pushed forward, weighed down by the metallic anchor. Jorgensen clutched the girl's arm and pulled her onto the BMP. More mines grasped Skaskiw, dragging him away.

Jorgensen hesitated.

"Go!" Skaskiw yelled.

Before the mines detonated, Skaskiw watched in satisfaction as the seven lives he'd saved sped toward safety. As the little girl reached out to him, Skaskiw thought of Anna and smiled. He'd failed to save his own daughter. At least he could save someone else's.

With long, flowing hair and too-perfect features, the alien Dahans certainly looked *angelic. But in this case, were looks deceiving? One Hollywood hairdresser is about to find out.*

Originally appeared in Rocket's Red Glare

A HAMAL IN HOLLYWOOD

★

by Martin L. Shoemaker

THE SIRENS didn't disturb Lucine Zakaryan as she snipped at Mr. Eddie's curly gray locks. Sirens in Hollywood were almost as common as Spider-Man players, nothing for her to take note. She had enough to worry about with her salon. *Her* salon, after all these years. It wasn't much, just three black vinyl chairs plus a wash stand, but it was all hers. Anya and Julia were gone for the night, and as soon as Lucine was done with Mr. Eddie she could leave as well. So she didn't worry about what was out on Sunset Boulevard.

But when the flashers and spotlights speared through the posters and signs on her shop's front window and splashed across her ceiling and walls, she knew the chase was coming to this strip mall. In the nineteen years she had lived in Los Angeles, Lucine had seen chases and arrests and crimes. She had even seen the Dahan ship on the night that they arrived. She knew that violence was never far away—farther here in America than in Armenia, perhaps, but still near. And the door . . .

Lucine had the door open to let in the cool twilight air.

When she was just a little girl, Lucine's *hayr* had taught her: *when danger is near, move today, wait tomorrow.* "Mr. Eddie," she said, tearing the smock from his shoulders, "I'm sorry, I cut your hair tomorrow. No charge. We do not want to be in this." Mr. Eddie nodded, his eyes wide and white, his dark face turned ashen. "You go

199

out the back door. The alley will take you out to La Brea." Mr. Eddie nodded again and ran to the back door.

Lucine didn't wait to see him leave. She was older than when she had arrived in America, and at least twenty kilos heavier (well, maybe thirty), but she could still move fast in an emergency. And this was one. She brushed her straight blonde hair out of her face to see better and ran to lock the door.

But before Lucine could lift the doorstop, a large man barreled through the door. Lucine caught only a brief flash of jeans and a gray shirt before he ran into her. Despite Lucine outweighing him, his speed gave him strength to push her back, knocking her to the white tile floor. "Sorry," he said, even as she fell; but then as she hit the ground, he missed his step, kicking her in her left side with his left foot. It didn't seem intentional, but it hurt like hell. And *then* he tripped and fell directly on top of Lucine, his right knee landing in her stomach.

"Owf!" Lucine shouted, half from pain and half from loss of wind. The man rolled into the salon, trapping and crushing Lucine's hand before he freed himself from her. He tried to regain his footing, slipped twice on the polished tile (Lucine always kept the floors spotless), and finally grabbed the check-in station to pull himself upright. He ran for the back door just as Mr. Eddie had.

And then Lucine felt something behind her. Or maybe its shadow tipped her off, but somehow she knew something was in the doorway. Still on the floor, she turned and looked up.

There, looming over her, was a giant, hairy shape. With the police lights behind it, Lucine could not make out any details, just two legs, two long arms, and a short, broad head. Her mind flashed back to stories her *tatik* had told of the great beast, the *piatek*: a wild creature with strong claws and a giant beak which would rend bad little girls into gobbets. The creatures had haunted her nightmares, crawling forth from an unnamed, unknown island, and she often woke up screaming until *hayr* had promised that there were no *piateks*, and he would always keep her safe because she was his little girl.

But now, sprawled on the floor amid the sirens and the confusion, Lucine could believe in monsters from a lost island.

Then the creature leaped over her and into the salon, and she saw that it was no *piatek*, but something perhaps worse because it was real.

It was a hamal, one of the silent servants of the Dahans. It was a white and gray tower of patchy fur, half again as tall as a tall man if it stood upright; but it crouched in a fashion that made it look now like an ape, now like a great cat rising up to sniff the air. But its face was neither ape nor cat nor anything from Earth: big black eyes set too wide and almost on a level with its mouth, no nose or snout, and a mouth rimmed with hard red ridges that flexed in and out. The face turned down toward Lucine, and despite herself she winced and held her hands before her face.

Then the creature made a wheezing sound and turned toward the back of the salon. The man in the gray shirt leaned against the back wall, favoring his left leg. His dark, curly hair was matted with sweat. His skin was light brown, almost the color of his eyes, but flushed with exertion. And those eyes . . . They looked into the hamal's, and they shone with moisture.

The man's left arm held him up against the wall as his right dug into his jeans pocket. Lucine looked away, sure that the man was drawing a weapon and just as sure that the hamal would tear his arm off before he drew.

But when there was no sound of slaughter, Lucine looked back. The man reached his hand out. In his fingers he held a large bronze coin. "Hamal . . ." he said, panting. "Please . . ."

The . . . monster . . . The hamal stood as if mesmerized by the coin. It raised one massive arm, and Lucine saw that instead of *piatek* claws, its arm ended in a large, pulsing bulb. The bulb stiffened and expanded into a cone nearly a foot across, and the cone stretched out toward the man's hand.

Lucine wasn't sure what would happen if the two touched, and she didn't get to find out. More sound came from the doorway, this time a loud, low hum. She turned around, and an angel stood in the door.

It wasn't really an angel, of course. Lucine had seen the Dahans on TV, so she knew they were aliens who had discovered Earth and had landed to . . . Well, she didn't really understand why they had landed. The news was full of diplomatic this and trade that; but Lucine had seen enough news shows to know when they were full of *kak*. Even when she was young and the Soviets ruled Armenia, she could see through the news, and she'd grown wiser (and wider) with age. The government might know why the Dahans were here, but the news people didn't.

But this Dahan, like the ones on TV, *looked* like an angel. Lucine did not know why creatures from some other planet should look like humans, especially such beautiful humans. They should look wrong to the eye, like the hamals, but the only thing wrong about them was they looked so perfect. Julia said they must have the best plastic surgeons in Beverly Hills. This Dahan was tall, muscular, and male (assuming they had male and female, Lucine wasn't sure). His skin was pale, almost Nordic, and his hair was a white-gold shade that made Lucine's own look shabby despite the expert dye job she sported.

The Dahan stood on a floating platform like a large silver serving tray. A white glow rose from the tray and surrounded him like a shroud of light, adding to his angelic look. He floated into the salon. Then he raised one hand, pointing to the hamal, and the glow flowed outward as if it had to contain the Dahan without touching him. He shouted something in a language unlike any Lucine had ever heard.

Lucine turned again to the pair in the back of the salon. The hamal's cone collapsed into a loose, pulsing bulb once more. It raised its arm, smashing it down upon the man's hand. The man screamed in pain while the coin flew away, clinked off the wash stand, fell to the shiny white tile, and rolled to the back of the shop.

The Dahan spoke again, and the hamal advanced on the man. It raised both arms, and two bulbs flared out into cones, then wrapped themselves around the man's arms and stiffened into strong bands that gripped the biceps. The hamal lifted the man from the floor. Lucine thought he should have been afraid, but his face showed . . . resignation? He said something, but she couldn't hear it over the sirens.

Mercifully, the sirens stopped then just as a short African-American LAPD officer stepped into the salon and shouted, "Halt!"

The hamal stood motionless. The officer stepped aside, letting two more enter behind him as he knelt down. "Sergeant Briggs, ma'am, LAPD. Are you all right?"

Lucine probed at her side and her stomach. She was sore, but it was fading. "I am all right, Sergeant. Just . . ." She looked around, and she wasn't sure how to finish.

"I understand, ma'am. Logan, Tyler, help the lady up." The two junior officers helped Lucine to her feet as Briggs rose and turned to the Dahan. "Tell your creature to put him down."

The Dahan answered in English, "The human is unharmed, but I will not permit him to escape. We must interrogate him and search him."

Briggs shook his head. "My captain tells *me* that the feds tell *her* that we have to help you collect your stolen item—which would be easier if you told us what it is—but that doesn't mean you can assault American citizens."

"I believe diplomatic immunity says I can." The Dahan smiled. That disturbed Lucine: for the first time, he looked *alien*. That mouth wasn't made to smile.

"Fuck diplomatic immunity." Briggs's hand hovered near his holster, and Tyler and Logan moved quietly away to cover him. "Just because I can't arrest you doesn't mean I can't stop you. Put. Him. Down."

The Dahan spoke again in its language, and the hamal gently lowered the man. But it did not release its grip.

"Now, Sergeant," the Dahan said, "I shall escort the prisoner to our compound so that I may search him for the item." The Dahans had established a base on the only available land in this part of LA: right on the hillside overlooking Hollywood, underneath the famous sign. That slope was not buildable, by human means, but the Dahans had some trick. In mere days, they had erected a small collection of buildings sticking right out from the slope. *As if gravity were optional*, one reporter had said.

"No, sir," Briggs shook his head. "Not a chance. The man's still an American citizen. He still has rights, and no one has read them to him yet. And those rights include *not* being probed by aliens in some secret cell. He's going to an LA lockup once we dot the i's and cross the t's. Logan, read the man his rights."

"Hold, sergeant." The Dahan held his arms out from his chest, as if he were pleading but did not know how to hold his arms. The bright glow bowed out away from his hands, almost touching Briggs. "We need not hurry. As soon as I contact your 'feds', I am sure you shall receive new orders."

Briggs frowned at the Dahan. "You do what you have to. In the meantime, Logan, it's Miranda time."

"Yes, Sergeant." The young officer walked to the back, circled warily around the hamal, and took out his notecard to Mirandize the man.

The Dahan spoke unintelligibly, seemingly to the air, as Lucine slid over to Sergeant Briggs. "Sergeant—"

Briggs turned to her and smiled. It wasn't a sign of humor, but of warmth and reassurance. "You're sure you're not injured, ma'am?"

"I'm not, but he is." She turned sideways and nodded her head toward the man. He had sagged in the hamal's grip, but he still put no weight on his left leg.

"I see what you mean. Logan—Oh, crap. You, Dahan, whatever you're called, can't you call your creature off and let the man sit? He's injured."

The Dahan stopped his conversation. "I will not allow him to escape."

"There are the three of us up here, plus your creature, plus you. My men have the back alley covered. He's going nowhere."

The Dahan made a wriggling gesture with his fingers. "As you wish." He spoke again in his language, and the hamal picked the man up, carried him to Julie's chair, and firmly lowered him into it. Then it released him, but it loomed over him, watching.

The Dahan returned to its conversation with the air. Sergeant Briggs's phone rang, and he answered. He spoke in hushed tones, so Lucine couldn't hear it, but the conversation did not make the sergeant happy. Tyler went out to the cars outside and told the officers there they could turn off their flashers and spotlights. Logan stood nervously watching the hamal and the prisoner, but he didn't seem eager to approach the alien.

And Lucine just stood, stunned, in the middle of the strange circus that had been her salon just an hour ago. The last of the twilight faded to black outside. With the police lights off, Lucine realized how dim the rear of the salon had become. She stepped quietly away from Briggs and walked to the rear light panel. She turned on the lights, and Briggs and Logan squinted. Lucine noted that the Dahan did not squint, and she couldn't see the hamal's eyes to judge there.

Then Lucine looked past the hamal's legs, and she noticed a dark pool staining her clean white tiles. A dark red pool.

"Sergeant!" Lucine rushed to the man's side without even thinking of the alien creature as she brushed past. (Later she would recall that the fur was softer than it looked, and the creature smelled like licorice.) She turned the chair to face her, and the man lay back in the seat, his head hanging back to reveal hideous gashes on both sides of his throat. Blood trails darkened his gray shirt and dripped to the tile. As the chair jerked to a halt, one of Lucine's straight razors slid from it and clattered to the floor.

Lucine screamed as if a *piatek* had ripped open her heart.

The night passed in a haze for Lucine. Briggs summoned an ambulance, but it was a wasted effort. The man—Jaime Lopez, Briggs called him—had been dead before Lucine had seen the blood.

Briggs took Lucine's statement, and she told him about Lopez and the coin.

"Logan! Go back and find that coin."

"Yes, sarge." But Logan was in the back for only a few seconds before he shouted, "Face down! Hands above your head. Sergeant, there's a man back here!"

"Tyler!" Briggs called out to the parking lot, and Tyler ran up. "Logan needs backup in the rear." Tyler ran toward the back door.

The officers were gone for less than a minute before they emerged with a figure in handcuffs. It was a medium-height, middle-aged African American in neat-fitting clothes. His haircut was half finished. "Mr. Eddie!" Lucine said.

"This is the customer you mentioned, ma'am?" Briggs asked. "Mr. Eddie . . . ?"

"Edward Wilson," Mr. Eddie said, polite but not friendly.

"Mr. Eddie," Lucine said, "I told you to leave through the alley."

"I tried, Lucine." Mr. Eddie's voice warmed as he spoke to her. "I checked the security camera, and the alley was blocked with police cars at both ends." His voice hardened again as he turned back to Briggs, his brow furrowed. "I didn't want to spook them—an old black man might be carrying something dangerous, you know—so I just hid out in your coat room until the officers found me."

Briggs ignored Mr. Eddie's confrontational tone and unlocked the handcuffs. "We're all on edge, sir. We've had a death, and now it's becoming an international . . . I guess an interstellar incident."

"I still haven't heard 'I'm sorry' in there."

Briggs grunted. "Yes, I'm sorry, all right? But we've got trouble here. Did you see a coin roll into the back area?"

Mr. Eddie's gaze remained dark. "Big bronze coin? Yeah, rolled in after all the crashing and banging."

"What happened to it?"

"Rolled right up to the floor drain back there, and sweet as you please, between the slats and down it went."

More police showed up, then more and more again. Then federal officers showed up, serious men and women in dark suits who kept asking Lucine and Mr. Eddie to repeat their stories. Lucine couldn't see the point: no matter how many times she told the tale, Lopez would remain dead at the end.

The federal officers politely escorted Lucine and Mr. Eddie out of her shop—but then Lucine wondered if it was really her shop any more. The entrance was sealed with yellow police tape. Plumbers showed up, followed by men with jackhammers, ready to tear up her clean white tile in pursuit of the mysterious coin.

All these people, all so worried about that coin . . . But Lucine noticed that the Dahan didn't seem to care. He floated around on his little silver platform, continuing to talk to the air without paying attention to the police and agents. Eventually a long black limousine pulled up, a woman in an expensive pants suit stepped out, and he talked to her.

Lucine never knew what was said, though. The federal agents ushered her and Mr. Eddie away. One polite young man, half Lucine's age, guided them to a cab and told the driver to take them home. He thanked them for their time, and they left.

As they drove away, Lucine looked back. The Dahan and the fancy woman were deep in conversation, but the hamal paced back and forth, never straying far from the other alien. Lucine shivered, feeling a strong chill despite the warm LA night. She swore the creature watched them leave.

The cab stopped at Lucine's apartment first. Before Lucine stepped out, she awkwardly hugged Mr. Eddie. They didn't have a hugging relationship. Hair styling was so close, so personal, that Lucine was careful to give customers lots of personal space once the styling was done. Especially with an older, respectable gentleman like Mr. Eddie, someone who was naturally reserved. But after the night they had shared . . . She squeezed him, then pulled away. "Tomorrow I finish that haircut. You just come by—" She realized she didn't know when the authorities would let her back into her shop. "You come by here. Room 215. I'll clean up that hair."

And with that she left, wearily climbing the steps up to her apartment. With each step, her side and her stomach throbbed. She downed two quick glasses of wine to calm her nerves, and then she went to bed.

Lucine's alarm went off far too early. She scrambled to silence it, and then she remembered: she had no reason to get up. She couldn't open the salon today.

She tried covering her head and going back to sleep, but her mind refused to cooperate. She had slept blessedly free of nightmares, but now the images from last night refused to leave her alone. The most disturbing image was the blood dripping from the chair, and Lopez's neck. Almost as troubling—and it was such a small thing!—was the Dahan's phony attempt at a smile. Neither the hamal nor the Dahan belonged on Earth, but at least the hamal wasn't hiding its nature.

Finally, reluctantly, Lucine got out of bed. If nothing else, she could get some time on her treadmill. She hated the thing, and even though she spent hours on it every week she never seemed to lose weight. But at least she could move faster, and she breathed easier. She pulled on her shorts, T-shirt, and walking shoes, she climbed onto the treadmill, and she started to walk. The twinge in her side was quieter, and her stomach felt almost normal.

Picking up the remote, Lucine turned on the TV. Local news was on; and to her surprise, the first story was about her shop. A minor burglary shouldn't be worth air time, but anything involving the Dahan was major news. Lucine remembered when they had first arrived. There had been rumors on the internet and in the tabloids for months: fuzzy pictures of large white apes, or maybe yetis or sasquatches. The government did their best to quash the rumors, but that only added to the conspiracy theories.

Then one day, almost a year ago, the Dahan ships had appeared over capitals and several other major cities across the world. The ships weren't "flying saucers" as many had expected, but the curved, elongated silver shapes might look like saucers from the proper angle, so the conspiracy theorists claimed victory. *Proof at Last! The Saucers Are Here!* read one headline.

When the Dahan emerged from their ships, the paparazzi went wild. All those beautiful, angelically perfect people floating down from heaven on their glowing sleds made a mesmerizing image. But Lucine had been there in the crowd when the Los Angeles ship had opened, and no picture had ever done justice to the real thing.

The TV image switched to a picture of the Dahan leaving the crime scene. *Her* salon, but they couldn't bother to name it, they just said "crime scene". But at least the sign was clear: *Sunset Lucine's Salon.* The Dahan and the hamal stood just in front of the sign, and the silver platform suddenly stretched to more than twice its length. The hamal climbed onto the extension—outside the glowing shroud, Lucine noticed—and the platform gently rose into the air. The TV camera followed it through the sky until it became a faint dot. Then the dot flew behind a building and headed in the direction of the Dahan compound.

When the reporters had first seen the hamals, they had all had the same reaction as Lucine had, the opposite to how people saw the Dahan: *feral . . . hunters . . . apes . . .* If the Dahans were angelic, the hamals were . . . Well, some said demonic, but most said they were more animal. They were more intelligent than Earth animals, but they didn't speak, and they were easily confused by strange surroundings. They were always tame and controlled in the presence of Dahan, but people worried of what they might do off the leash. There were stories—none proven, of course—of transients and unsuspecting tourists who met with hamals on dark streets and were never seen again.

Lucine had believed those rumors herself, until last night. The hamal had been intimidating, but she had never once felt it was out of control, even before the Dahan had arrived. And its fascination with the bronze coin . . . It wasn't some rote reaction, like a dog trained to a whistle, it was fascination. She was sure that the hamal had *studied* the coin. She wondered idly what it was, but she was sure that was a secret that the Dahan and the government would never share.

Yet she couldn't think of the hamal without recalling blood on her tile. Had the creature killed Lopez? Or had the man been so afraid of the alien that . . .?

The news switched to an Alcoholics Anonymous commercial, so Lucine changed to the Armenian TV channel. She liked to keep up on the home country and keep up her language. The station was showing a documentary on *Medz Yeghern*, the Armenian Genocide. The station showed this documentary often, or others like it, and they always made her angry for loved ones who were injured or family she had lost three generations back. Lucine was happy by nature, and sometimes the anger overwhelmed her; but on the treadmill, the anger lifted her heart rate just as the doctor wanted.

The day dragged on. Lucine found things to do, little things to keep her from thinking too hard: sweeping, dusting, cooking . . . She even dyed her hair again, and she found it hard to remember what her original color was. Now, of course, it was gray, but Lucine believed in choosing for herself. And she didn't choose gray.

In late afternoon, Lucine was running out of chores. That was bad: she would start thinking, or she would start eating out of boredom. Or both. She wondered if she should go shopping or get out of the apartment.

But then the door buzzed. She rushed to it and pushed the button. "Sunset Lucine. Talk to me, sweetie."

A familiar voice came from the speaker. "This is Edward Wilson, Lucine."

"Mr. Eddie!" Lucine buzzed him in, pushed open her door, and waited for him to climb the stairs. Lucine always treated her clients like family, especially her regulars; but after last night, she felt especially close to Mr. Eddie. She remembered her *hayr's* stories, of how his grandfather and friends had grown closer than brothers from their shared experiences fighting and surviving the *Medz Yeghern*. What she and Mr. Eddie had been through was not even an echo of a shadow of that, so she could only imagine how closely those men had bonded, and how men had died to avoid betraying their brothers. Would she die for Mr. Eddie? She hoped never to know, but part of her hoped she would if she had to.

Mr. Eddie came around the stairwell and smiled. "May I come in?"

"Of course! Welcome, welcome!" Lucine hugged him. With them both standing, her head barely cleared his shoulder. Lucine had forgotten how tall he was, because everyone was short in the chair.

Lucine didn't have a proper styling chair in her home, but she had a high-backed swivel stool she had used when she was learning her trade. She guided him to it. Then before the conversation could turn to ugly parts of last night, she said, "So, you want to finish the haircut, of course."

Mr. Eddie raised his right hand to his head and grinned. "All day, people have been looking at me funny, some laughing. 'What's the matter, Eddie, you couldn't afford the whole hair cut?'"

Lucine laughed. "I will give you the rest. Better than the rest, the best haircut in all of Hollywood, better than the movie stars. And no charge, just tell them you got it at Lucine's."

She dug out an old smock and her portable grooming set. Then she covered him from the neck down, taped his neck, and inspected his head. As she did, she automatically fell into small talk, her favorite part of the job. "So, Mr. Eddie, you hear from your grandson?"

He smiled, and Lucine paused. He had a big grin, wide enough to make his scalp bunch up and make her misjudge the cut, so she waited as he talked. "He's a junior now. Next year my grandson will be a college graduate. Can you imagine?"

"He comes from smart stock. My *hayr* says you can always tell."

"*Hayr*?" Mr. Eddie asked.

"Oh, sorry, my father. I am a proud American, but some words, I will always be Armenian."

"Nothing wrong with that." His grin relaxed, and Lucine was able to assess his scalp and begin finishing the cut.

The conversation lulled, and inevitably turned to what they had both been avoiding. Mr. Eddie said, "So . . . Some business last night."

"Yes, some business," Lucine said as she cut.

"It was . . ."

Lucine nodded, though she stood beside him and he couldn't see it. "It was frightful. But also a little bit momentous. You and me, two ordinary citizens of this little corner of the world, suddenly caught up in the affairs of gods from the sky."

"They're not gods!" Mr. Eddie said. Lucine had forgotten: he was a strict Pentacostalist. Well, not as strict as some, he didn't think the aliens were tricks of Satan. "They're not angels. If you see an angel, you'll know it."

"Sorry, no, not gods. But creatures with concerns far beyond us, and then suddenly they're down among us. All because some man stole some alien coin."

Mr. Eddie shook his head, and Lucine almost cut too much. "It wasn't alien," he said.

Lucine pulled her scissors away and turned the stool to face her. "What do you mean?"

He frowned. "I hope the Lord will forgive me a small lie. There's something going on, something they're not telling us, and I don't trust them. So . . . I lied. The coin did not go down the drain. It rolled over toward me, and I put it in my pocket."

"Mr. Eddie!"

"It's none of their business." He reached into his pocket, pulled something out, and reached out from the smock to hand the coin to her.

Lucine took the coin and studied the molded metal. On one side was an outer ring with a Shakespeare quote: *To thine own self be true.* Inside the ring was another quote, longer and unfamiliar: *Rarely have we seen a person fail who has thoroughly followed our path.*

On the other side was another ring of words: *Unity. Service. Recovery.* Inside the ring were two portraits labeled *Dr. Bob* and *Bill W.* Beneath them was the Roman numeral *VII* in a circle, with *Years* underneath.

Lucine looked up from the coin. "This is human, yes? Not alien. But I do not understand what it is."

Mr. Eddie nodded. "Thank the Lord you don't recognize it, child, but I do. Here's mine." He handed her another bronze coin, nearly identical except that the number in the circle was *XV*. "That's my sobriety chip. Alcoholics Anonymous. Fifteen years I've been sober. That chip reminds me every day to ask the Lord to help me resist temptation. I'm alive to see my grandson graduate because AA and the Lord kept me strong."

"But then . . ." Lucine couldn't even think of how to ask. What to ask.

"I don't know why that alien wanted that, but it's none of his concern. We take the second A very seriously: Anonymous. You're there to be helped and supported as you and your sponsor and your Higher Power find your way clean. You're not there to be judged by any man, woman, or alien from the stars."

"So Lopez was in AA?" Lucine asked.

"We don't know that. People lose sobriety coins all the time. But it's a good bet."

"Then why did he try to give it to the hamal?"

Mr. Eddie grinned. "Maybe the creature has a drinking problem?"

Lucine laughed. It felt good to release some tension. But still she was concerned. She looked at both chips, holding them away from her. "But the Dahan said something was stolen, and that had to be it. Why would that matter to them? Is there . . . You don't suppose there's a tracker in there?"

"Maybe," he said. "I'm no scientist, but we make cell phones and computers smaller every year. Imagine what *they* can do, them and all their starships. So maybe, but I don't think so. I've had it on me all day long. They had plenty of time to track me down, I didn't even think of it 'til you mentioned it, but they didn't. I think it is what it looks like, nothing more."

Lucine relaxed, and she looked at the two coins again. "Wait. They're not quite the same. Look at this around the edge." She held the seven-year chip out to Mr. Eddie and pointed out a small message engraved on the edge: *SSCC.* "What does that mean?"

He shook his head. "I don't know. All of the chips are made by the same company, but there are no rules. We're a benign anarchy. Some groups customize theirs."

"Can you guess what this means?"

"I can't, but . . ." As Lucine slipped the chip into her pocket, Mr. Eddie pulled out his cell phone and punched a single button. After ten seconds, he said, "Mason?" He paused. "No, the Lord is strong, and he is with me . . . Thank you, and to you as well . . . See, you might have seen some news from last night, and . . . Yes, that *was* me on the TV, you weren't imagining it . . . No, really, no one else was hurt . . . That's an odd question . . . I'm not sure, but I'll ask." Mr. Eddie put his hand over the microphone. "Mason—he's my sponsor—he asked if the creature, whatever you called it, did it leave with the other alien?"

"The hamal?" Mr. Eddie nodded. "Yes," Lucine said. "I watched them both leave."

"Yes . . ." Mr. Eddie said to the phone. "What do you mean, 'too bad'? . . . Well, you shouldn't say it if you just want me to forget it . . .

"Why I called?" he continued. "Mason, I have a chip with some strange engraving on it: S-S-C-C. Do you know what that is? . . . You do? What? . . . Mason, be straight with me, either you know or you don't . . . Mason, you've been my sponsor for twelve years, ever since Nate died. I trust you, so don't start hiding things from me now . . . What? . . ." He reached up to unfasten the smock. "All right, I'll be right over."

Mr. Eddie closed the cell phone, removed the smock, and stood from the chair. "Mason says he'll explain, but it will have to be in person. I'm sorry, Lucine, I have to go."

"But Mr. Eddie! I still haven't finished your haircut."

"Then I'll look funny tomorrow, too. Mason sounded like this is important. We can finish it tomorrow evening."

Lucine bit her lip, trying to decide: follow this or walk away? Finally she spoke. "Take me with you, Mr. Eddie. I have to understand this."

Instead of riding the cab, today Mr. Eddie drove his faded blue Focus. It was old and small, but he proudly kept it in excellent condition, so they didn't look completely out of place as they drove among the luxurious cars of Hollywood to Mason's place. The car was clean but cramped. The radio played a sermon. Lucine didn't catch much of it, but the preacher mentioned the Book of Matthew. Mr. Eddie said "Amen" and "That's right" and other words of approval.

The sun was "falling" behind tall buildings as they crossed town. It wasn't as dark as true twilight, but in some ways it was worse. Your eyes could go from still-bright late sunlight to dark shadows in moments, and you would never see what hid in those shadows until it was upon you. Lucine imagined that every shadow hid a hamal, but then she laughed at herself for being afraid.

It was a surprise, then, when the true danger came from the bright sky, not from the shadows. A flash caught her eye, and she looked up to see a tiny silver and white shape speeding ahead of them. Then she saw a second, and a third, as they drew up a block away. At the same time Mr. Eddie's phone rang, but he ignored it as Lucine asked, "What's that up ahead?"

Keeping his eyes on the road, he would not see the Dahans in the sky, so he didn't understand the question. "That's Mason's apartment building, but how did you know?"

"I didn't—" A loud whistling sound came from ahead, and bricks started falling from Mason's building. Then with a tremble and a rumble, the front third of the building slid into the street.

Mr. Eddie swerved. Lucine screamed. Horns honked as vehicles smashed together, a chain reaction that soon engulfed the Focus. When the chain of vehicles finally drew to a halt, Lucine looked up again. The Dahans were gone. Mr. Eddie was shouting at her to get out of the car.

And then, just as she had feared, Lucine saw a hamal step from the deep shadows far across the road. She had a vision of bloody tile, and she shuddered.

Lucine tried to open her door, but it was jammed shut by a yellow Aztec. She looked at Mr. Eddie, and he was already out of the car, beckoning her. "Get out! Get out! The rest of the building is falling!"

Lucine looked ahead: yes, bricks were raining down, a small drizzle now but growing. She looked back: the hamal was gone, but there were shadows everywhere.

She looked at Eddie; and between them was the shift lever, the steering wheel, and the cramped seat of his tiny Ford Focus.

Lucine unbelted, rose up, and tried to pull her girth through the car. The gear shift stuck in her side, and yesterday's pain flared up. She groaned loudly and sat back down. Then she lifted up from her seat, turned, and knelt, her head in the space between the seats. She turned farther, her feet pressed against the door as her head entered the driver area.

At least this didn't hurt, but she still couldn't get through. There was too much of her to fit between the wheel and the seat. She tried to squeeze through, but she got stuck. Pushing with both feet against the door only tightened the trap.

Then Mr. Eddie reached down to the front of the driver's seat, and the seat slid back, releasing her. She scrambled forward and he grabbed her arms, pulling her free. She propelled herself from the car, pushing him backward so that he tripped and fell backwards, pulling her down with him.

And then a chunk of masonry half as big as the Focus fell onto the car, smashing the engine and the front seat, showering glass and metal everywhere. It was too late to run or move, so Lucine buried her face in Mr. Eddie's chest. He wrapped his arms over her head to protect her from debris, and she heard him praying, though she could not make out the words.

Finally the rain of debris stopped, and the street quieted, though there were still shouts and screams, honking and car alarms, distant sirens. Lucine looked down. "You saved my life, Mr. Eddie. Thank you!"

He smiled. "I had to save you, Lucine. You have to finish my haircut."

"Oh, you!" She knelt over him, kissed him on the cheek, and stood. Her side and stomach throbbed again, and her back and neck twinged from dozens of bruises where small debris had struck, but she could stand. And so could he: he was on one foot and one knee, and she helped him to his feet.

Then Lucine remembered. She looked back across the street and behind them. And she saw a large white-furred form drop back into shadows.

"Run!"

Mr. Eddie answered, "What?" But she didn't wait around. Near at hand was a parking garage, and she had already run inside and was sprinting for an exit on the far side. She heard Mr. Eddie running behind her. At least she hoped it was him. She wasn't waiting to find out.

She reached the far exit, pushed open the double glass doors, and turned back. Mr. Eddie was behind her, slower but still moving. She saw no sign of the hamal. Of course, she didn't know how many there might be, nor which shadows they might hide in.

Mr. Eddie caught up with her, and they plunged out into the street. Outside were five lanes of stalled traffic, with people abandoning vehicles and fleeing the wreckage. Lucine saw that they were all headed south, and she decided that it would be impossible to make progress if they went that way. So she pushed through the crowd, crossed the street, and ran up to a glass wall on the far side: a ground-floor food court of a mall. People inside pressed up against the glass, peering out at the destruction one block over. Some were wide-eyed with shock, while others wept. A hundred cell phones were raised to film the destruction.

Lucine and Mr. Eddie found the glass entry door, pulled it open, and pushed their way through the crowd. Once inside the mall, they had a clear path. The mall was practically deserted, with everyone having either fled or run to watch the collapse. But they were both too tired and sore to maintain their pace. It took nearly ten minutes for them to exit the mall on the far side.

As the door slid shut behind them, Lucine fell back against the wall, panting. Mr. Eddie did as well, and he pulled out his cell phone, pushed a button, and listened. Then he frowned. "You need to hear this message."

He pushed another button, and this time the message played on the speaker phone. "Edward, this is Mason. Afraid you're going to have to find yourself another sponsor, buddy. The Dahans have found me. Don't let them find you, too. Page 23, bud. God be wi—" The message trailed off into static, and then silence.

Lucine looked at Mr. Eddie and saw big tears rolling down his cheeks. *This is getting to be a habit,* she thought as she wrapped him into a big hug, pulled his head down to hers, and held him as his body shook with silent sobs.

They stood there like that, and for a few minutes Lucine forgot the danger. She was just too tired and sore and emotionally wracked to move. It was Mr. Eddie who finally broke the embrace. "I can't," he said. "I can't let Mason die for nothin'. There's something important on page 23, and the Lord wants me to see it through."

"Page 23?" Lucine asked. He pulled away, reached inside his pocket, and pulled out a folded, stapled stack of printed pages. Lucine saw a cover and a title: *Los Angeles Area Groups and Meetings.* The pages were bent and curled, but they were still readable. Mr. Eddie turned to page 23, and they both looked it over.

Lucine pointed to one entry near the bottom third of the page. "Seventh Street Community Center. SSCC."

Traffic was gridlocked for miles. Police and fire were everywhere, but also National Guard, FBI, and FEMA. Not to mention numerous sightings of Dahans on their sleds. None were paying attention to Lucine and Mr. Eddie that she could tell, but they still made her nervous.

With no cabs or buses, it took over an hour for them to walk to

Seventh Street, and Lucine was nervously checking behind them the entire way. It was approaching true twilight, so there were many more shadows, and several times Lucine thought she saw a dark shape merge back into them. Mr. Eddie assured her that she was imagining things, but she couldn't be convinced.

And the next moment, she knew she was right. On a deserted street, three Dahan sleds appeared in the sky ahead of them, zipping their way. Then she heard a crashing noise behind them, and she looked back to see a hamal crashing through a stand of trash barrels.

Mr. Eddie pulled her to the ground and over to the side of the road, where they crouched beside a dumpster. Lucine looked out, expecting to see the hamal headed her way. Instead it ran to a nearby parked car, picked the vehicle up, and hurled it into the air. Lucine watched the car fly up and smash into the nearest Dahan. There was a great shower of sparks as the light shroud shredded and the car knocked the alien from the sled.

The other two Dahan zoomed closer. The loud whistling sound returned, and two brilliant white lances speared out and struck the pavement, tracing a path to the hamal. Where they struck, the asphalt bubbled and melted.

Before the beams could catch the hamal, it leaped into the air, somersaulting over the lances. One of the sleds got too close, and the hamal caught the edge, hanging on as the sled flew. Then it swung its legs up, gripped the other end, and flexed. The sled bent, bent further, and then suddenly snapped. The hamal and the now-unshielded Dahan fell to the ground almost in front of the dumpster. Lucine looked away as the hamal picked up the Dahan and dashed it against the side of the dumpster with a wet crunching sound.

But that had given the third Dahan time to zero in. The lance stabbed forward, and the asphalt in front of Lucine and Mr. Eddie burst in a bubble of hot air, tar, and gravel. Lucine cried out in pain from the burns, but Mr. Eddie cried louder. Lucine looked and saw that a blob of hot tar was burning through the leg of his fine gray pants.

With only seconds to act, Lucine unbelted Mr. Eddie's pants—careful not to touch the tar—and pulled them down to his ankles. Then she pulled off his shoes and pants. As she had hoped, most of the tar had come off with the pants. But there was still some stuck to his burned thigh, and she didn't dare touch it herself. So she used the hard soles of his shoes to scrape the skin clean. She tried not to think what damage she might do to the burned flesh, but it had to be better than letting the burning continue.

By the time she was done, Lucine smelled the curious scent of burned licorice. She looked up to see that the last Dahan had fallen, though she had missed the event. The third sled was on the ground, nearly split by a fragment of the second. And the hamal, one arm hanging loose and burn marks over its upper body, stood methodically stamping a wet, meaty pile of debris into the ground. Then it did the same to the other two bodies, smearing them out into discolored spots on the pavement. Despite knowing these were aliens, Lucine had expected the spots to be red, instead of the bluish gray that they were.

Then the hamal turned toward Lucine and Mr. Eddie. Fluid leaked from its mouth, and the red ridges weren't flapping. It stepped forward, and Lucine couldn't think of any way to stop it.

Except one. She stood, took the chip from her pocket, and held it out. "Here . . . Please . . ."

The hamal stopped before her and held out its uninjured arm. The bulb once more distended into a cone—she now saw that it was hollow in the middle—and wrapped it around her fingers. The sensation wasn't unpleasant, at least not to her. As a child in Armenia she had let the calves lick her with their giant tongues. This feeling was like that: not as wet, but just as soft.

Lucine let go of the chip and pulled her fingers free. The cone collapsed, swallowing the chip, and then most of the bulb drew up inside the hamal's arm. When the bulb came back out, it shaped into a flat grip, and *two* chips were in the grip. Lucine took them. She saw immediately that the second chip was identical in most respects, right down to the *SSCC* mark, but it was only a three year chip.

Lucine nodded, handing back the second chip. "I . . . recognize you." And she was sure that was true on two levels. The chips were a recognition sign. Her *hayr* had told her how Armenian rebels had used those when they hid among the populace. But also, she recognized *this* hamal. It was the one from her shop last night.

Then faster than she could follow, the hamal picked up Mr. Eddie, lifted the lid of the dumpster, and gently laid him inside. Then it picked her up and dropped her in as well before leaping in with them. As it pulled the lid closed, Lucine saw a white dot fly through the sky, far away but still too close for her.

Lucine took several breaths to calm herself, and then she used her cell phone to light the interior of the dumpster and assess their situation. Mr. Eddie was breathing fitfully, and she was sure he was in horrible pain from his burns. He couldn't stay in this unsanitary dumpster for long.

And the hamal . . . She didn't know how to tell a healthy hamal from a sick one, but she was sure it wasn't healthy. Some blue-gray fluid oozed from its injured arm. The mouth ridges flexed weakly when they flexed at all. And its eyes twitched every few seconds.

And Lucine? She ached, her legs were on fire, and her breathing came in deep gasps. The saddest part was she was sure she was in the best shape of the three of them. But that didn't mean she was in *good* shape. She just wanted to sit in the trash and collapse, but she had to get help for Mr. Eddie.

The hamal held out its chip to show her the edge: *SSCC*. Lucine shook her head. They were very close, but still too far. She couldn't get them all there. The hamal could carry Mr. Eddie, certainly, but then everyone would see the hamal.

The hamal waved the chip up and down, and Lucine thought: *Maybe somebody there can help me. Help us all.*

Lucine shrank at the thought. She didn't want to go out there again where the Dahans could find her. She didn't want any of this. She owed so much to Mr. Eddie, and she even felt a debt to the hamal, but her fear was so strong.

Then she remembered *hayr's* stories. Even in the worst of the genocides, some Turks had done the right thing, sheltering their Armenian neighbors. Her grandfather had survived thanks to one such neighbor; and to his dying day he had said, "All Turks are devils, except Dursun. Good man. Hanged for sheltering Armenians." *Hayr* also said that if there had been more such good men, she would have had more cousins, more uncles.

Lucine looked at the hamal and wondered if it were an uncle.

Lucine crouched at the corner of a building, under a large awning. There *were* Dahans out there, she had seen the lights, but not many of them. They moved in some sort of search pattern, and she thought she had it timed. She could predict long stretches where there were no sleds overhead. She had planned out three sprints that would get her from one cover to another on the way to the community center. The only question was could she get from cover to cover before the Dahans flew over?

She calmed her breathing and got ready to run. When the first gap opened, she sprinted out as fast as her legs would move, headed for two sad palm trees that overhung the road. She grabbed the trees to stop herself just as the next Dahan passed over.

Lucine stood, catching her breath once more. She was still panting when the next gap opened, so she let it pass. She was ready for the gap after that, and she leaped out into the road.

Suddenly a horn blared, and a car barreled down the street straight at Lucine. She had been so busy watching the skies, she had forgotten about the sparse evening traffic. She dove out of the way, trying to roll clear of the car. The fender clipped her foot, and she tumbled on the pavement, but she managed to escape the car.

Lucine slowly climbed to her feet. Once again her side and stomach erupted in pain, only now her heel cried out as well. She could put weight on it, but every step was like stomping on an apricot pit.

Pits or no, though, she had to go! The gap would close soon, and she had to get under the doorway of that shop. So she ran, crying out with every other step. She reached the doorway, but she knew it was too late. At least two Dahans had flown over. If they had looked her way, she was dead.

Lucine looked down the block at the community center. It looked like a school, or maybe a hospital: a short, squat brick building that covered nearly a quarter of a block. Most of it was dark at this time of night, but the nearest door was lighted and she saw lights and movement inside.

Lucine had no breath left. She wanted nothing but to wait one or two gaps to catch her breath. But the longer she waited, the more the chance that the Dahans would return. When the next gap opened, she checked for traffic, and then she ran as if a *piatek* pursued her. She was sure she felt its hot breath on her neck, sure she heard its clacking beak at her shoulders. Her pains seemed to join, one long agony from heels to side to stomach and ultimately to her burning lungs. But she must not let the *piatek* win!

Lucine smashed into the glass doors, and they rang from the impact, but of course they opened outward. She pulled them open and ducked in just before two lights appeared.

A guard came to the inner door, opened it, looked Lucine over, and asked, "Are you in trouble, ma'am? Should I call the police?"

"No . . . police . . . Need . . . AA . . ."

The guard looked sad. "I'm sorry, ma'am. Meetings are Tuesdays at 7. If you need help immediately, you should call your sponsor. Or there's a women's shelter three blocks down."

Lucine wanted to scream, but she had breath only to wheeze, "AA . . . Mason . . ." She looked for another word to convince him, and finally she settled on "Sanctuary." She pulled out the chip and held it out to him with *SSCC* facing him.

As soon as the guard saw the coin, he pulled out his radio. "Maria, we've got a woman who needs medical aid here. And I think we'll need a rescue team, too."

Lucine wanted nothing more than to sleep in the warm, soft bed they had provided for her after the doctor had treated her ribs and her heel. But she refused to sleep until she knew that Mr. Eddie and the hamal were safe. As soon as Dr. Maria confirmed that, she fell deeply asleep.

When she woke, it took a while to remember where she was. Both the infirmary and her room were in some subbasement that didn't appear on the center's elevator.

There was a phone next to her bed. She picked it up, and immediately a friendly but unfamiliar female voice answered, "What can we get you, Ms. Zakaryan?"

What can we get you? An aspirin. A large bagel with eggs. Orange juice. A half a bottle of aspirin. There were many things she wanted right then, but only one she *needed*. "Can I see Mr. Eddie? And the hamal?"

"Let me see." The woman paused. "Yes, they're awake and can see visitors, but they're both still in the infirmary. I'll come get you."

Lucine got out of bed. She still wore her workout clothes from the day before, though they were ready to be thrown away. But today she didn't care about neatness, just being alive.

The door opened and the young, pretty nurse said, "Hi! This way, they're waiting for you." They went down a long hallway to the infirmary, and she showed Lucine in.

Inside, Dr. Maria hovered over Mr. Eddie, smiling at what she saw. The hamal slept on a large bed behind him. The doctor turned to Lucine. "Hello, Lucine. Can I look you over when I'm done here?"

"Yes. But can I . . .?" Lucine gestured to Mr. Eddie. The doctor nodded, and Lucine stepped in and hugged her new best friend. "I'm so . . ." She couldn't finish.

"I know, child. Me, too."

The doctor pulled a chair closer, and Lucine sat. "We . . . won, I think," she said.

Mr. Eddie smiled. "One battle. But for today, that's enough. Do you know what this is, Lucine?" Lucine shook her head, and his smile turned into a big grin. "It's the Underground Railroad!"

Lucine shook her head. "You mean a subway?"

"No, child. Sometimes even with your accent, I forget you weren't born in America. The Underground Railroad was a secret network to guide African slaves to freedom. That's what the hamals are, slaves of the Dahans. Some of them escaped here, and they made friends with the outcasts of our society: the homeless, the destitute . . ." He looked down at the chip in his hands. "The alcoholics. When the hamals' Overseers came hunting them, some of their friends here . . . Well, they done the human race proud. They started building this network to shelter the hamals and guide them to hiding places in the far corners of the Earth."

"And we helped?"

"We helped, at least for our buddy here. I call him Stinky." Mr. Eddie laughed.

Lucine shook her head. "I don't understand. Lopez . . . The burglary . . ." She glanced over at Stinky. "And they . . . killed him . . ."

Mr. Eddie patted her on her arm. "I know, dear, that was horrible. But it was all a lie. There was no burglary, that was just an excuse. The Dahans were hunting Lopez because they knew he was part of the Railroad, and they wanted to interrogate him. Stinky didn't kill him, he just let him grab the razor. That brave man killed himself to keep the Railroad a secret."

Lucine's head spun. The past day replayed in her mind, and suddenly it all made sense for the first time.

Mr. Eddie continued. "And now, to thank us, they'll get us home, and no one will ever know we were here. Or they can take you home, at least. I've got more recuperating to do. And then after that, well, maybe I'll stick around a while."

Mr. Eddie looked at Lucine, but he didn't ask. He was too much of a friend to ask her for what might be more than she could give. No matter what she said next, he would always be her friend. Her brother.

But Lucine thought of Stinky and what had almost happened to him. She thought of the cousins and uncles she had never met because someone had been afraid.

"Doctor, please . . . Let me help, too."

Mtali: a planet settled by a patchwork of religious groups from Earth. But this is far from a new Eden. UN forces from Earth do a poor job of keeping an uneasy peace between the various factions that call Mtali home. Fortunately, the Freehold Military Forces, from the planet Grainne, are also onsite, and do a much better job. But Freehold/Earth relations are deteriorating. And the violence on Mtali is only increasing. War is all but certain. When Sergeant Lisa Riggs of the FMF and her team chase an Islamic extremist into the Evangelical neighborhood of al Dura, Lisa finds herself in the center of the approaching mayhem. Her refuge from the chaos comes from the last place she ever imagined.

Originally appeared in Forged in Blood.

LOVERS
★
by Tony Daniel

DEAR MAJOR RIGGS and Mrs. Heaton,

My name is Warrant Leader Robert McKay of the Freehold Military Forces First Legion Air Wing. I'm a close support pilot with the FMF on Mtali. I am writing to you in regards to your daughter, Sergeant Lisa Riggs, Squad Leader of Seven Alfa Three Mobile Rifle Squad.

Lisa was my friend.

I have waited several days for you to have received official notice from the Civilian Liaison Office and an individual letter of condolence from Captain Arnando of 1st Battalion Alfa Company, as well as from Colonel Richard, commanding officer of Mtali Expeditionary Freehold Military Forces, who indicated to me he, too, was going to write to you expressing my gratitude toward Lisa.

I wanted to send you my own personal note to share what information I have so that you know as much as I know about Lisa and her days on Mtali.

Lisa was a fine soldier.

She was also a good woman. A good person.

I'm lucky to have known her.

"What the hell?" Sergeant Lisa Riggs muttered.

"They're . . . I dunno," said Corporal Alan Chambers. "Sarge, what *are* they doing?"

Music blared from speakers somewhere in the huge compound. A bone-shaking bass thundered, while a keyboard-guitar combination screamed out a throbbing wall of sound.

Pounding.

Danceable.

"I think it's some kind of . . . skating rink." Lisa shrugged her shoulders, although her tactical vest damped the gesture.

The compound they'd entered looked like the usual Mtali concrete-polymer structure from the outside, but instead of an inner courtyard, the place had a large steel roof, and the ground was neither dirt nor the sector's ubiquitous blue and white paving tiles, but was coated with a smooth flooring that looked ceramic.

The militant they pursued had come through the main entrance to the building. Vert-stat reported the place was about a city block in size with three side exits.

She and Chambers were in what seemed to be a lobby, outside what looked and sounded like an auditorium. The auditorium's main entrance's two large doors were pulled back and latched open with small metal hooks anchored on the wall. She immediately had two members of her squad check behind the doors. Nothing.

The huge room they looked into had a floor set about a meter below street level with a polycrete ramp leading down from the doorway. Because of their elevation, Lisa had a view of the whole area. It was maybe fifty by fifty meters. The floors *and* walls were pure white.

People glided on the porcelain surface. They wore shoes that tapered beneath to what looked like a miniature boat keel. She couldn't tell if the keel touched the floor or hovered over it. But somehow or another, the shoes—the skates—supported the Believers who crowded the floor.

At least she thought they were Believers, since this was al Dura, which was the neighborhood that contained mostly evangelicals.

Many of the occupants moved around in a counterclockwise circle on the floor like fish circling in a tank. Some were doing leaping turns and other acrobatics in the air as they went.

"This is sooo freakin' weird," Griffin murmured into his throat mic. They all heard his comment over their earbuds.

"Can it," Lisa said. "We have a job to do."

"May I help you?" A woman approached from inside with a worried expression. She was middle-aged and wore a powder-blue dress. Her hair was what grabbed Lisa's attention, however. It hung down her back almost to her heels.

That must be hell to brush, Lisa thought.

The woman said, "I'm the head usher. It's in the paperwork. This is a peaceable assembly. We have our licenses in order. I have to say there are quite a lot of regulations, but we've met our obligations. I can flash the permits to your pad if you'd like. We follow the diversity directives your people have put in place."

"*My* people?" Lisa said, perplexed.

"You are United Nations forces aren't you?" The woman was dark complected, probably originally of Mediterranean ancestry, although it was hard to tell on Mtali. The planet had been settled for nearly three centuries. Her face paled now, though, and she visibly trembled.

She's terrified, Lisa thought. She didn't blame the woman. All of Lisa's squad's weapons were shouldered for fast movement, but she knew they must still seem an imposing bunch.

"Ma'am, we're FMF troops. Freeholders. We have no intention of interrupting your gathering any more than we have to. We've pursued a terrorist here. We've entered the UN sector under their 'hot pursuit' edict, although we would have come anyway. The man was trying to blow up one of our transports."

The woman continued to tremble. "We don't profile entrants," she said. "It's a requirement of our diversity license for assembly."

"Like I said, we are not here to enforce UN rules," Lisa said.

"A man came in about ten minutes ago and asked to use the restroom. His clothes seemed very dusty."

"What about his accent? Did he sound like he was from around here? Do you think he might have been al-Wadi?"

"I wish I could answer you, but we will have our license revoked. We aren't allowed to profile. The UN sector administration sends whisper drones to ensure compliance." She nodded over her shoulder toward the auditorium. "They're too small to see, but they *are* here monitoring, I assure you."

"All right, thanks for your help. We're going to need to look around. This man is very dangerous."

It finally seemed to dawn on the woman that Lisa wasn't here to shut down the gathering.

"Please enter," the woman said, then leaned closer to Lisa and spoke in a low voice. "If you really are chasing one of those al-Wadi jackals, we want to help."

"We really are, ma'am," Lisa replied.

She turned to the squad behind her. She clicked a finger on the data-feed on her wrist. There was an aerial schematic of the compound they were in with all entry and exit points marked by blinking green dots. "Vert-stat Control has a positive determination that the bomber ran in here."

The vert-stat was a tethered hovering platform packed with cameras and other remote sensing gear. It was connected to the sector Combat Operations Center, and was the FMF's eye in the sky. The resolution was incredible. The capabilities immense. Without somebody on the ground to *do* something about all that wonderful information, it meant shit.

Also, the boots on the ground had to be *allowed* to actually do something about it.

"Please remain aware that the al Dura sector is UN battlespace, and we have to at least pretend to play by their rules," Lisa cautioned.

"Which nut should we cut off, Sarge?" asked Murphy, in Fireteam One. He had a Saltpan accent and had never been to a city, much less off his home planet of Grainne, a year ago. Now he was cracking jokes like a . . . well, a grown man. Which he hadn't been a year ago, either.

They were all so young. Twelve, thirteen Grainne years old.

"Better cut off both to be safe," put in Chambers. "It's the UN way."

"Yeah, okay," Lisa said. "We all want to limit CD. That we can agree on." CD was collateral damage, as in dead civilians. The UN forces down to the squad level had to provide Collateral Damage Estimates, CDEs, before engaging an enemy, even if an enemy was very much engaging them. Fortunately, the Freehold military depended on the judgment of its soldiers, and trained them until they "reeked of trust," as Lisa's senior sergeant instructor once put it when she was going through FMF NCO training. "Let's just track this guy down, vent him, and leave these people to their . . . whatever it is."

They moved down the ramp and into the crowd that surrounded the skaters. There were tables and chairs spread around the central area of the rink. Many people were seated at them drinking from clay cups and watching the action on the rink. The unmistakable odor of almond milk and gingery-sweet tea let Lisa know it was chai they were drinking.

As if it would be anything else, she thought. Chai was the odor she associated with al Dura, and practically all of Mtali.

Well, the only *pleasant* odor she associated with it. In a place where you were taking your life into your hands if you drank water from a faucet, it was the hot drink of choice, even in the scorching summer months. Drinking chai was the one unifying element of all of the warring factions of Mtali.

Those who weren't seated stood near the edge of the skating rink, waiting to go back to it. They balanced on the thin edges of their shoe soles. Closer up, Lisa could see that the blades did not fully touch the ground, but were suspended in the air a few millimeters above the floor.

From the little she knew about skating—which was one trip to a Freehold rink years ago—she thought they were called "gliders." They worked with phased magnetic fields. She knew about the principle from rail-gun applications she'd studied in NCO school. Two intersecting electromagnetic fields interacted with a very strong, very precise field in the skate. That insanely narrow edge served a purpose in keeping everything aligned.

The "blade" of a glider skate was almost molecularly thin and sharp. The field could be adjusted in height. She'd seen really good skaters gliding about on what looked like a meter of thin air.

Her briefings hadn't mentioned a thing about a big skating rink on Mtali. It was the last thing she'd expected to find here. Well, that and maybe competent local government.

But here it was. With the aid of the eagle-eyed cameras on the vert-stat platform, and the control crew that manned it and interpreted the imagery, Seven Alfa Three, her squad, had tracked the feckhead through the seemingly endless alleys of both the Sunni-majority Ta'izz

Jadeed district to the Christian al Dura district tucked away inside the much larger Ta'izz Jadeed. He had been targeted by the vert-stat and rousted while planting an IED made with a Shia faction military demolition block. He'd worked too fast for an airstrike from a drone or vertol, but Lisa's squad was patrolling in the vicinity. They'd flushed the militant, and he'd run away surprisingly fast. But not faster than a vert-stat infrared camera.

The bastard had ducked in here.

She'd leave the weapons team in the lobby, the M-23 machine gunners, two marskmen, the missile gunners, to provide cover and reinforcement. The rest would go inside with her.

"Corporal Chambers, you'll take Fireteam Blue to the south entrance." She touched her data-pad and the green light lit up on all the squad's pads. She noticed with approval that a couple of the designated squad held to SOP and kept their heads up, looking around. It was tempting for an entire squad to engage in pad-stare when planning an operation. When it did, situational awareness went to hell. "Green, you guard the northwest exit. Red back-up remain at this doorway. The rest of Red team, you're with me."

That covers the ingress and egress routes, Lisa thought. *Now let's see how much china we can keep on the shelf.*

"Rifles at tactical." The squad positioned their rifles closer to firing position, but barrel-up. The M5s shot caseless cartridges. The slugs were fed to the firing apparatus in pre-stressed sections, sort of like a stapler—a stapler that flung out its staples at supersonic speeds with devastating effect.

Lisa and Red Team moved forward into the crowd. At first, they were only noticed by those nearby. Several of them had to be shouldered out of the way. Some turned, looking resentful and ready to push back—but were inhibited by the sight of a Freehold soldier in full kit staring back at them.

We're here to protect you, Lisa thought. *Now get your ass out of the way before we shoot it off.*

A vert-stat camera had gotten a decent frontal shot of the militant, if at a downward angle. She popped it up on her data-pad, ran it through her helmet feed, and compared faces.

Mtali denizens mostly dressed alike. At least the men did, and they were looking for a male. They ate the same food as far as she could tell, and *everybody* drank chai. Sunnis, Shia, Amala, Druze, the small community of Baha'i . . . and here in al Dura, the small community of evangelical Christians. She knew little about the evangelicals other than that they weren't Catholic and everybody called them Believers, even though the Believers was just one sect, and a minor one, among them.

She also vaguely recalled that, like the Muslims, there was some kind of evangelical reward in the afterlife for murdering the right sort of people. A jaw for a tooth, or something like that.

They all looked alike and everybody on the planet wanted to kill each other. At least that's the way it seemed to her.

That wasn't really true. She had noticed one other characteristic of evangelical men: not all of them had beards. From the vert-stat image, the bomber had a beard. Looking around, that left out about half of the men in the rink. Unless the feckhead had somehow hidden away a shaving kit in a bathroom, which she doubted. He'd been patterned by the vert-stat observation platform. The facial and somatic recognition tech in her data-pad was busy processing and analyzing the feed from her helmet cam and those of the rest of the squad.

"Fan out," Lisa said in a low tone, almost a whisper. The contact mic under her chin picked up the words and carried them to the rest of the squad's earbuds. "I want a visual sweep of this place."

She was taller than several of the men in the squad, so she didn't have any trouble looking over the heads of most of the crowd. Even though it appeared a bit like ice, the ceramic surface was not particularly slick. She moved forward toward the edge of the skating rink.

The skaters were both male and female. Some of the women wore headscarves. *Must be a custom they adopted to get along,* Lisa thought. But most of the women let their hair go free—and they grew it very, very long. Down their lower backs. Some of them, like the usher she'd talked with, past their butts, even. Was there some commandment in the Christian rule book that women weren't supposed to cut their hair?

It didn't seem so absurd when she saw it here. The long hair made a lovely effect. Some women spun as they skated, and their hair flew around them, cascading in flowing fans and arcs. The men were more acrobatic, jumping up, spinning in air. A couple even did flips, twists.

Some skated entirely backward. And all at incredible speed. After a moment watching—how could she not?—she saw that the movements were in pattern. They were a wild dance.

It was kind of . . . beautiful.

"Okay, what the hell are the Believers *doing*?" asked Green Team leader Sabine Meyer's modulated voice in Lisa's earbud.

"I think it's a dance," Lisa answered.

"Ain't nobody dancing with anybody out there."

"Not a dance like that. Dance like . . . maybe it's religious or something. How would I know?" She nodded toward the chai drinkers at the tables. "All of you, scan the crowd. I doubt the feckhead is out there skating or dancing or whatever it is."

She gazed around.

Now they see us. Most of the eyes had fixed on her and the squad.

They don't seem happy, Lisa thought. But the looks were of irritation, not the outright hatred she so often got in the Shia sector where COB Jackson was located.

After all, she was a woman. A soldier. In what they thought of as a man's uniform. Shorn hair. No scarf. Face fully visible.

She even used a little makeup, especially on days she was scheduled for patrol. The thought of pissing off the fanatical assholes who hid among the local population helped break the monotony.

It was actually good that they had everyone's attention. It gave the FR program a frontal for comparison.

"Got him," said Chambers. "He's moving toward the northeast door."

"Okay, let's go," she said. "Subsonic one, subsonic one."

Subsonic One was a UN-mandated mod to the rifles that bled pressure out of the barrels before the projectile reached the muzzle. It also caused the barrel section to get hot quickly. Subsonic One was low, but it was still deadly. It was meant to prevent the slug from cutting through a swath of bodies.

She'd also heard it unofficially called the "Uno setting." *Not* because the UN troops on Mtali were ordered to use lower velocity at all times, but because most of their troops' rifles were that low by design.

"Damn it, he's got a backpack," Chambers shouted. "I say again, he's got a backpack and something in his hand, might be a detonator."

"Take the shot!" Lisa yelled as she sprinted ahead. The music throbbed. It was loud enough to drown even the muffled subsonic crackle of the M5.

Someone dropped to the floor as if their strings had been cut. It was a woman.

"Crap," Lisa said. Chambers had missed.

She leaped over the victim and shoved aside two men who were trying to get to the downed woman.

And there the dogfucker was.

She shot him in the chest.

The militant shuddered, took a step backward, so she knew she'd hit him. But he remained standing. He was wearing body armor—it looked like a UN-issued tactical vest. His eyes were wild from the pain, however.

He's got to be hopped up on stims, Lisa thought. *That's the only way he's still standing.*

It was well known that the UN was constantly getting their battle meds raided, and that some went missing seemingly all on their own.

The hostile raised his arm. There was something in his hand that was probably a detonator.

He's going to blow himself up. That's why he came in here.

There must be more than a hundred people in the gliding rink.

She needed a headshot. Instantly.

She couldn't move that fast. No way.

She pictured her father's dry, disappointed smile.

Catastrophic failure to anticipate the consequences of your actions, Lisa dear.

Not good enough. Like always.

Then something strange. Someone, a man, stepped up behind the feckhead. His arm moved in a sideways motion. As it did so, the Shia militant's head wobbled. First to one side, then another. Not natural.

Then it fell off his neck entirely. He'd been guillotined while standing.

Behind the militant stood a thin man—thin, but muscled. In his hand he held one of the skates.

Decapitated by a skate, Lisa thought. Well, decapitated by the molecularly thin blades of the repulsors.

The terrorist's body got the message a tic later that it was no longer needed. It collapsed.

Blood spurted from the severed arteries as it fell, some of it shooting a meter or more, enough to splash several of those nearby. The neck pumped itself out in a puddle on the floor.

The detonator trailed a wire that ran back into the rucksack. It fell from the body's lifeless hand and onto the floor beside a shoulder.

Lisa quickly stepped over the dead body. SOP would be to leave the body in place and call in a EOD team to defuse the rucksack . . . but no way she was going to do that. This situation was far from standard. She glanced down at her data-pad, which was telling her that the detonator was a simple switch. She gingerly picked it up.

"Thibodeaux, Nourse, let's get the body and the backpack out of here," she said. "Leave the head. Corporal Meyer call in medevac for her." She nodded toward the woman lying prone of the floor. She'd taken a shot to the chest in the left lung and who knew what other damage. The slug hadn't come out her back, and so had probably torn up her thorax.

Chambers grabbed a clot pack from his gear to try to staunch the flow of blood from the woman's wound.

"Permission to stay with her until medevac gets here, Sarge?" Chambers said. "She's still alive." His voice was plaintive.

Barely, Lisa thought. She didn't hold hope that the medics could do much when they arrived. But she'd seen them perform near miracles on minefield and IED victims before, so maybe.

And maybe she would forget this sight. An innocent woman, bleeding to death on a pure white floor.

Maybe not. Lisa felt a cold pit forming in her stomach. She wanted to vomit. Hell, she wanted to turn and run.

But couldn't.

"Yeah, permission granted, Chambers. Ling, you stay with him. The rest of you, let's go."

The other squad members jumped to it and they hooked arms under the shoulders and lifted the body. They moved toward the entrance.

"I'll help you," said a voice she didn't recognize. It was a voice speaking English, but in an accent with the cadence and fricative of Arabic. It was the man with the skate, only now he'd put it down and had hold of the insurgent's legs.

"Sir, I'd rather you didn't, for safety's sake . . . "

The man ignored her, and Lisa shrugged. He'd certainly earned the right to do whatever he wanted at the moment. Together they all walked the body and the presumed bomb to the entrance. The skater moved with a limp, but Lisa saw that this was because he still had a skate on one foot.

The door led to an alley. The rest of the squad followed behind Lisa and she had them guard either entrance to the alley.

Her data-pad was telling her it was unsafe to cut the twisted wires leading from the detonator. She needed to secure it somehow.

Lisa looked around. There was a trash can near a door across the way. She dumped out its contents onto the ground and placed this carefully over the detonator.

"All right, we'll stand by until the EOD team arrives," she said. "Everybody be careful around the trash can." She examined the wire leading out from under the can. The twisted wires were red and black.

Easy colors so morons don't get confused and blow themselves up early.

"Can I help you up?" The man with one skate was standing close by. He was extending a hand toward Lisa.

The man had startling green eyes set against his copper-colored skin. Although he was thin, she could now see through the gauzy muslin shirt he wore that what there was of him was rock hard. On second look, he seemed young but not a teenager, maybe sixteen Grainne years or so.

About my age, Lisa thought.

"Sure," Lisa said. She took his hand in a palm grip and let him take some of her weight as she stood.

"Thank you," she said, drawing her hand away. "How did you do that in there?"

The man shrugged. "Acrobatic skates have higher settings," he said. "So they have a much finer edge. We use the setting for individual praise, not for group dance. Elevates you a meter over the arena." He smiled and seemed to blush, which reddened the brown of his skin tone. "You have to be pretty good to do it, though."

"Watch out. Pride goeth before a fall, right?" She thought the old saying might be vaguely Christian in origin.

He smiled even wider. "Actually it's: pride goeth before destruction and a haughty spirit before a fall," he replied. "But yes."

He's handsome, Lisa thought. *For a skinny dude.*

Lisa allowed the tension within her to relax enough to smile back at him. "Well, you probably saved some lives in there. Including mine."

"And including mine," he replied. He held out his hand again. "I'm Jedidiah."

"You're kidding, right?"

"About what?"

She shook her head. "Nothing." She extended her hand again and took his hand. "I'm Sergeant Lisa Riggs."

"Pleased to meet you, Lisa."

"There's a . . . reward and restitution fund," she said. "We can definitely pay you back for the cost of the . . . acrobatic skates, did you call them?"

"Yes," he said. "But I don't think mine were damaged."

"You killed a man with them."

"I wouldn't call that"—he nodded down at the headless body—"a man."

"Okay, but the battalion has a reward fund. It's a lot of money, and you deserve it."

"I wouldn't feel right taking a reward from your government."

"My government?" Lisa chuckled. "I don't think you understand how the Freehold works. Listen, it's a battalion reward. A contract. Voluntary. We all contribute."

"Hmm, since you put it that way," he said. "I'll take it on one condition."

"What's that?"

"That you personally deliver it," he replied.

"That I . . . what?"

"I'll flash you my comm code," he said.

She heard Edwards, who stood nearby, giggle.

"Hey, Sarge, he'll give you his digits," Meyer said with her best shit-eating grin. "So you can deliver his *reward*. You know, his reward."

Lisa turned savagely on the team leader. "Corporal Meyer, for that you get to go back in there and pick up this thing's head," she said, motioning to the body. "Bring it out here and bag it."

"Really, Sarge?"

She just stared at the trooper. After a moment Meyer's look of disgust turned into the emotionless stare all of them had learned to put on in Pipeline. Meyer went to do as she was told.

"Help her, Edwards," she said to the trooper who had giggled.

When both disappeared back inside, she pointed to her data-pad and smiled. The Believer, Jedidiah, sent over his personal comm code.

Then she gave him hers.

The woman who had been shot died. Chambers was devastated. He needed to work it out. He was still a boy. Sweat was usually the answer. She assigned him extra PT for a week and let him out of COB maintenance duties. But she requested of her warrant leader that Chambers go back on patrol immediately.

The evangelicals, for their part, seemed to understand. There was no uproar in al Dura, at least that she heard about.

But, of course, charges were brought against her and the squad by the UN.

Al Dura was *their* sector, after all. The captain of India Company agreed to an internal investigation. It was over in two days and exonerated the squad. The report did, however recommend peer counseling for Lisa, and her captain and warrant leader backed it up.

I guess I was as depressed as Chambers and didn't recognize it, she'd thought when she read the report.

The "peer" in this case was a warrant officer and vertol pilot named Robert McKay. He'd been through a very similar collateral kill experience. He'd made a call that led to the death of a civilian. More than one, as it turned out.

Major Riggs and Mrs. Heaton, I told your daughter what I'd found myself to be true. You never get over it. So you have to get through it.

Not exactly wisdom for the ages, but it did help me and I think it helped Lisa.

Normally she'd have been called back to the Combat Operations Center for counseling, but since I'm a vertol pilot, I requested and received permission to fly out to COB Jackson and talk to her several times over the course of a few weeks. She and I got along well, and spoke a great deal, and though I do not in any way claim to know Lisa well, I believe we became friends during that time.

We spoke a great deal about you both. You may not be aware of how much Lisa respected you and longed for your approval. From what she told me, you both created some pretty big shoes for her to fill.

I'm probably not telling you anything you don't know, but Lisa was intimidated by you, her parents, and any time she made what she thought of as a mistake, she felt as if you both were looking over her shoulder.

She told me more than once that she believed you were disappointed when she enlisted. I cannot believe this is true. If anyone had a calling to be an NCO, it was Lisa.

Lisa also showed me the beautiful family sword you presented her after her graduation from NCO training. I understand the damaged blade I recovered was returned to you by Lisa's commanding officer along with her other effects.

I don't believe I've seen a more elegant and balanced o-wakizashi in my life. And I have seen and held a lot of swords.

I also learned of Lisa's growing interest in the young man who had taken out the militant in the gliding rink in al Dura. During her next down day, she arranged to go on a date with him.

This is uncommon. Even beyond fraternization issues, the people of Mtali are so extremely tribal and factional that *they* often have no desire to mix with us. Yes, there are shuras among battalion commanders and local leaders, and higher headquarters meets with regional governors and powerbrokers.

But to sit down and share a meal or a drink with the locals outside of a patrol? It isn't often done even by the FMF. It can be dangerous, for one thing. But mostly it's because the opportunity doesn't arise.

So Lisa's relationship with the man, whose name was Jedidiah Farmer, as I later discovered, was unusual.

Frankly, I'm not sure what the attraction was. But it was definitely strong.

The evangelicals, who outsiders collectively call Believers (they are part of the local Christian Coalition composed of several churches and sects) are one of the smaller factions. They've mostly been live-and-let-live people since they settled on Mtali over two centuries ago. Well, live and let live when it comes to war. Some of them do have peculiar and restrictive beliefs about abortion, homosexuality, and polygamy. If I got into the intricacies of these taboos, you may not be able to stop laughing.

Nevertheless, being noncombatant on a planet in turmoil only made them into the whipping boy for the larger factions, especially among the Shia and the Sunni tribes. The Sufis, the Amala, and the Baha'i seemed to leave them alone. The Sufis are almost as few in number as the Believers, the Amala even poorer. No one defends Believers, and their militia is a pitiful group that spends more time arguing denominational doctrine than fighting.

Which brings up the question of what *we*, the FMF, are fighting for on Mtali.

I cannot tell you it is for liberty for all or anything as lofty as that. We have two goals. Mtali is a hotbed of interstellar terrorism. We hope to nip this in the bud. And if we can't get them all, which we can't, at least we'll put the fear of Freeholders in them so that they'll avoid Grainne like the plague.

The other reason we're here, and perhaps I should not be saying this, perhaps a censor will black it out, is that war with Earth seems inevitable.

Our military is on Mtali to gain experience. To train in a live-fire setting. I realize how callous this sounds to those who lose loved ones here, but it is necessary for the survival of our society.

I think Lisa believed in both of these reasons for fighting. The UN forces are waging a doomed and risible campaign to "win hearts and minds" on Mtali. Lisa and I both joked about the futility of this as a military objective more than once.

So it's maybe ironic that Lisa, through no plan of her own, went out and did exactly that.

"I can't believe I got picked up at a gods-damn skating rink," Lisa said.

"A praise rink," Jedidiah replied.

"Uh-huh."

"Worship brings men and women together. That's part of the reason for it. Jesus didn't call us to be celibate." Jedidiah rolled his eyes and smiled. "Although sometimes Paul did. But he's kind of harsh and it's not like he was the Son of God or anything."

"And your Jesus *was*?"

"He isn't just my Jesus, he's—"

"Oh, stuff it, Jed, will you?"

He looked down at their naked bodies lying together on the bed. "I kind of already did," he said.

"Isn't this a sin or something?"

"It's the opposite," Jedidiah replied. "It's impossible for me to believe the Lord could not want you and me to have this. But what about you, heathen woman?"

"Oh, the goddess approves," she said, and ran a finger down the line of his jaw. "In fact, I think the god and goddess want us to do it again."

"Right now?"

"Right now."

They met in the UN-controlled sector. It was a gray zone adjacent to al Dura. She had to sign out to visit the Uno base, which was a matter of a couple of minutes on the FMF side. Then she must endure at least an hour of UN bureaucracy to meet him in a café just outside the UN command base hard perimeter.

Above the café, there was a room that belonged to a friend of Jedidiah from the al Dura seminary, the same school Jedidiah attended.

Lisa knew where Jed lived in al Dura and had passed the building on patrols—in fact, she went out of her way to do so. She could never go there unaccompanied, however. Even here in the gray zone, in a quaint Mtali café, things were dangerous.

Jed was worth it.

He was even worth putting up with the odor of chai. She'd hated it before. She would never love it. She was, however, getting so she could tolerate it. The whole planet seemed to run on the drink.

Chai was one thing. She would *never* get used to boiled cow's feet, however. Gelatinous. Jed's favorite meal when eating out.

In al Dura, it was considered a delicacy.

She'd spent most of her leave inside the COB wire during the first months of her deployment. Now she left Jackson every chance she got.

Mtali was dangerous. Al Dura was dangerous. The gray zone was dangerous. Although the evangelicals were tolerant of women going about unescorted and even having *jobs*, there was one thing most Believers couldn't tolerate.

Short hair.

Her pixie cut wasn't even that short by FMF standards. Plenty of women troopers had trimmed theirs down to fuzz for convenience. But most al Dura women had never cut their hair in their lives. It had to take hours to brush every night, Lisa figured.

One hundred strokes a night? Try a *thousand*.

At first, she dressed in civvies, but that did her not much good. Everyone knew she was from off-world—although most took her for a UN trooper, to Lisa's chagrin.

Things had gone hostile a few times, and she'd been spit on once. After that, she started wearing undress greens, a pistol, and her sword any time she left the Uno base's hard perimeter. Her sidearm and her concealed pistol and knife would be far more effective in an attack. The sword was just for downright *intimidation*.

She'd lied to Rob McKay. Her father hadn't given her the sword.

He'd *sold* it to her, the bastard. With her mother's blessing, too.

He'd intended it as a gift when she got commissioned an officer. That had always been the plan. After she'd enlisted all bets were off.

Half a year's salary. That's what he'd charged her.

But she wanted the *wakizashi*. She knew she deserved it. It wasn't her fault her parents were being assholes about it, and she didn't intend to punish herself by denying it to herself.

So she'd contracted a loan to buy the sword. She'd never missed a payment. She even learned how to use the sword to some extent, although she was nowhere near getting a hand-to-hand weapons expert rating and probably never would. But nobody in the al Dura gray zone knew that. When they saw a lady with a sword, people mostly kept their distance.

Where else was she going to go if she wanted to meet Jed? Where else could she go if she wanted to have sex with him—which she very much did? To one of the escort trailers in the Central Operations Zone with the contract sex workers? Not likely.

Jed *would* probably go along with that. Despite his religious leanings (or, he would say, *because* of them) Jed seemed to be completely amenable to just about anything when it came to sex. He'd proved it to her several times in the tiny borrowed apartment above the gray zone café.

Another Believer stereotype shot down.

Others included the notion that Believers only did it in the missionary position. If they did, those must have been some adventurous and polymorphous missionaries.

After the sex, they had even begun to *hang out*. They talked about many things. They argued philosophy like a couple of amateur Aristotles.

One thing neither one of them talked about was the future. As far as Lisa could tell, there *wasn't* one on Mtali, not for anybody.

She would be leaving the planet soon enough—soon enough to make their lovemaking desperate.

Lisa took a sip of her chai. It was tepid, almost cold. Had they been sitting in the café and talking *that long*?

"I've passed my Greek exam," he said. "Now I have to get through the Hebrew exam next month. It's the hardest thing I've ever tried."

Lisa nodded sagely. "And when you finish, you'll be able to speak with all sorts of dead guys," she said.

"I'll be able to read the Bible in the original languages it was written in."

"There's that, I guess."

He leaned back in his chair and smiled. "You really don't like that I'm going into the ministry, do you?"

"Lots of things you could do seem *more* pointless," Lisa replied. "I can't think of a gods-damn one at the moment, however."

"You like the praise glides. You said you thought they were beautiful."

They'd attended a couple of the events—those held within the soft perimeter, the gray zone—since the fateful night of their meeting. She'd seen him skate.

He grew ecstatic.

And he was very, very good at it.

"Yes," she nodded. "Those I like. They're pretty."

"Skating got me a scholarship," he said in a more intense tone of voice. "It's the reason you and I met. God has a plan. I believe that."

"Oh, please."

"It's maybe like the military is for you." He straightened up, took a sip of chai. "Before God spoke to me and told me to praise skate . . . and before I got to go to school because of it . . . Lisa, things were . . . I was bitter. I was full of hatred. I had shut God out."

He'd told her he was an orphan. He'd told her he had a brother who died. Beyond that, she knew nothing.

"I'm sorry." Her words felt flat, unequal to what he was attempting to say to her.

Sounds like I don't care at all, Lisa thought. *Not one gods-damn bit.* "I really am. Sorry, I mean."

"Thanks," Jed replied. He smiled his crinkled smile at her, the one that made her melt a little inside each time he did it. "What about you, Sergeant Riggs? Your parents okay with you putting your life on the line here?"

"Dad understands, I think. He gave me my sword." She patted the scabbard slung across her shoulder and under her arm.

Then she'd had enough of the charade. She told him how her parents had made her pay for it.

"But you're still close with them?"

"Yeah . . . No, not really."

"Your brothers and sisters?"

"Just me," Lisa replied. "Hence the officer hang-up. Hence my ability to play piano. And shoot at a competitive level. And ride show horses."

"You play piano? That's great!"

"I'll play for you sometime," she said, but then realized where this was probably going. "Not in a church. I mean it."

"All right," Jed replied, obviously let down. She'd guessed correctly. "Anyway, I think your parents are fools. You are perfect."

"Hardly."

"We all are perfect in God's eyes."

"Uh-huh. So you never did tell me. How did your brother die?"

Jed's body shook for a moment. Little ripples formed on the surface of the chai tea he was holding. He frowned. She'd never seen him frown so hard. She didn't like it.

"Look, you don't have to talk about it. I was just—"

"It's okay," he said. He set the chai down, then reached over and touched her hand. "Really, it is."

He leaned back, squeezed his eyes shut for a moment, then dabbed them quickly with his fingers. He looked at her again, and the scowl was gone. Or at least under control.

"Malachi was three years older than me. He took care of me when my parents . . . when they died. We were on the streets, but he took care of me. Got a job as a messenger. Worked for Sunnis a lot at the strip mall. Got into delivering aircars from dealerships to wholesalers. The Indonesians were big in that, and they really liked him. Can you believe a thirteen-year-old kid driving aircars all over the district? But that was Malachi. Quick. Smart. Trustworthy. And he made sure I learned to read."

"Sounds like a really good guy."

"Yeah, he was," Jedidiah said. He paused for a moment, gathering himself again. She waited. "Then when he was fourteen, which is like nine or ten to you, right?"

"More or less."

Suddenly Jed seemed far away.

"There was this truck. A land vehicle. It was the kind they use to haul stuff from the lift-port with one of those boxes on the back."

"A cargotainer?"

"Yeah, one of those. Anyway, they pulled into the middle of the shopping center parking lot. A bunch of guys dressed in black got out of the truck. They had guns. Like the one you have on duty."

"Rifles."

"Except some were little."

"Merrill carbines, maybe."

"Yeah. They went around the strip mall. Only talked to Muslims. Boediono, the rug seller Malachi worked for a lot, told them something they didn't like, and they knocked him down and rolled him up in one of his rugs. I found out later he suffocated."

"Dear gods." That wasn't as ugly as some other things, but bad enough.

"Yeah, it was bad. And the militia didn't come. Of course. Nobody came. Then the men with the rifles, they were Shia, I don't know what sect. They shot all the Christians. One by one they went around the units and shot them. The little gun was the worst." Jed drummed his fingers on the wooden table. "Rat-a-tat-tat. Rat-a-tat-tat."

"That's . . . I don't know what to say."

"The children they got hold of? The women? They rounded them up and put them in the box, in the container. Malachi saw what was going on and he hid me. He made me promise not to make a peep even if they took him away. He promised he would find a way to get back, so I had to stay quiet."

Lisa swallowed hard, dabbed at the tears forming in the corners of her eyes. "Where did you hide?" she asked.

"In a church across the street at first. In the baptismal tank up behind the altar. There wasn't any water in it. Huffman Assembly of God."

"Assembly of God. That's your denomination," she said, absurdly proud of herself for remembering.

"Yeah."

"And they didn't find you?"

"No," he said. "Because I didn't stay there. I snuck out. I thought I could save Malachi, I guess. I kept moving. I've always been fast, you know? Good at moving. And I saw. This really short guy. He was . . . light skinned. More like you. He was the one who grabbed Malachi and put him in the box. And you know where I hid?"

"Where?"

"Under the box."

"Gods."

"It was the one place they never looked," he said. "They burned the church. I think Malachi saw that. He probably thought I was still in there. I wanted to tell him I was okay, that I'd gotten away. But I stayed quiet. Like he told me. Then they closed up the box and . . . well, they drove away. Left me lying there exposed in the middle of the bazaar, but none of them saw me. They didn't look back, I guess."

"Did you . . . what happened to the container?"

"That one? Who knows? But that kind of thing goes on all the time. Sometimes they drop it in the sea. They like to leave them out in the desert, especially if it's summer. Sometimes they bury them. The thing is, they don't kill women and children directly, not even us Believers. Nobody can accuse them of that. They just . . . make them disappear."

"And they never let them go, even if it's just to make them slaves or whores or something?"

"I haven't heard of it," Jedidiah replied. A dreamy look came over him. "So I took Malachi's job. I became a messenger. I drove aircars from place to place. The Sunnis at the shopping center, they used me the most. I guess they felt sorry that they got to live and everybody else died. So they kind of took care of me, like a pet or something. A dog you like."

"How did you ever get out of there?"

"I knew how to read, so I read. A lot. Anything I could get my hands on. One day this guy named Terrence who owned a used data-pad shop—do not *ever* buy a personal info pad from him, by the way—told Brother Ronsesvalle about me. Brother Ron runs a skate school. You know, glide praise. It's how people get good at it. They pay for skating lessons. God helps those who help themselves."

"Okay."

"I told you I was fast, right?"

"Yep."

"I was more than fast. Nobody could make a delivery or take a message that wasn't suitable to send electronically as fast as I could. Nobody. Because I climbed walls. I ran along the roofs and jumped from building to building. You ever heard of parkour?"

"Yeah, it's actually part of our training. The special warfare guys get lots more of it."

"Brother Ronsesvalle saw me doing some of that stuff. Just a routine delivery of some medicine I ran for the pharmacy. He told me he would pay me to teach adults how to do it. Movement. Gymnastics. And I would get my own room—which never happened, but that's okay. It wasn't really his fault. The new place he built got blown up before we could move into it. And so I taught sacred dance. I learned to glide. I went to school. Now here I am."

"Studying to be a minister, like Brother . . . what's his name?"

"Ronsesvalle." Jed replied wistfully. "No, not like him, the poor guy. He has a strong calling. It's left him pretty broken down after all these years."

"Then what?"

Jedidiah seemed about to answer her. Then he shook his head and smiled. "Want to go up to Zebedee's place? I'm feeling a strong calling for something else right now."

"Sure do. But—"

"'But' nothing. Let's go."

"Listen, I'd like to ask you something. Something about us," Lisa said. "If there's one thing about Believers . . . they sure as hell don't believe in sex before marriage. Does the Assembly of God make some kind of exception?"

Jed grinned sheepishly. "No, not really."

"Then how are we even together?"

"Want to know the truth?"

"Uh, yeah."

"I like your hair," he said.

"What?"

"Your hair. I liked it when I first saw you. I followed you around the glide arena. I just wanted to look at it."

"Gods, I was wearing a *helmet,* Jed."

"I know. I knew your hair had to be *short* under it. I was kind of hoping . . . that you'd take it off. In front of me."

She laughed. "You were looking for a striptease with a *helmet.* Pervert!"

"I guess you could put it that way. Then when we got together that first time you had leave, and you came without it . . . and I saw . . . it was like lightning hit me or something. Like God spoke to me and said this would be okay, you and I would be okay."

"And my cute short hair was the reason you were there to decapitate the feckhead?"

"Yeah."

"So the rest is history."

"And prophecy."

Major Riggs and Mrs. Heaton, I believe that Lisa fell in love for the first time with Jedidiah Farmer. I think she found a good man. Would it have lasted?

They were *very* dissimilar. Lisa struck me as being only slightly religious. And she wasn't a Christian, of course. The young man was studying for the ministry or priesthood of one of those seemingly countless denominational divisions within their faction. I can't remember which it was.

Yet the relationship *did* work, at least for the time that they had together. It not only worked. It helped Lisa overcome her depression. This I experienced with my own eyes and ears. Although she was well liked by her troops, Lisa was a droll person, not given to much outward emotional expression. But it seemed to me whenever she talked about Jedidiah, she was very, very happy.

That evening Zebedee swapped apartments with Jed. They were free to stay in his place all night. They made love once in bed, and then took a blanket and did it again on the flat roof of the polycrete building that housed the apartment. The night was warm and comfortable, so after sex, they lay looking up at the stars—and at the occasional passing aircraft and shuttle.

She cuddled against Jedidiah, feeling his ropey muscles, running her fingers over his abdominals. She'd never been with a guy like him. Never expected to be. Her former boyfriends were split between beefy jocks and skinny nerds. He was like the perfect combination of both.

Who was she kidding?

Nothing had been like Jed. She'd never been in love before.

She was a Freeholder, so she'd had sex once she was of age, of course. But she was a virgin in one way. Jed was her first love.

And she was pretty sure she was Jed's first *anything*.

Who was this man she'd saved her feelings for? This one she'd waited to love?

A Christian. A killer.

"I was thinking," she said. "You took that Shia's head off with a skate blade."

"Yes. So what?"

"Aren't you Christians supposed to turn the other cheek and be pacifists?"

He said, "That's from Jesus' Sermon on the Mount. The idea is not to overreact to small things. But you don't have to be a doormat."

"I can't even tell what people are fighting about on this stupid world. I mean, sorry to be so blunt, but your home planet is a worthless shithole in general."

He smiled. "We get good sunsets."

"You've never seen any others."

"True," he said. He leaned over and kissed her forehead. "Maybe I'll see Grainne's one day."

"Yeah, I'd like that." She sat up and the blanket fell away from her shoulders, revealing her bare form. Jed was instantly gazing at her. She smiled and put a hand on his arm. "What *is* your plan, Jed? You going to be a priest or pastor or whatever?"

"I don't know," he said after a moment's pause. "I think about . . . getting revenge. A lot."

"And this will help you *how*?"

"Not at all. I'm running from a, from a *lust* for it. Revenge. It is sin.

It is selfish. My parents and brother are in heaven. They don't give a damn whether I get it."

"But you do?"

"School gives me something more important to think about." He gazed up at her with a wistful smile. "And so do you."

She touched his cheek. "Good," she said.

"And what about you?"

"I care about you." She pursed her lips, wanting to give him something more, maybe something true. "I care about my job. I want to be brave. I'm scared I'll screw up and let my troops down." She fingered the folds of the blanket. "Maybe I was a chickenshit not to go to Commissioned Officer School like Dad wanted. Maybe I'm just chickenshit in general."

"God has a plan for you."

"Look, I'm where I want to be *right now*." She pulled his arm around her and snuggled next to him. "I love you," she whispered. "Gods help me."

"You . . . do?"

"If it never gets better than loving you right here, right now, I'll be all right with that."

Jed kissed her hair. It tickled.

"Why do you like it being short so much?" she asked. "I guess it makes me different from the other women around here?"

"The reason's kind of embarrassing, actually," he answered. "Maybe even depraved."

"I can get into depraved."

He chuckled, then sighed. "Well, I *do* kind of remember my mom. I was real little, but I have this impression. She cut it like yours. Her hair. She was a Methodist. She just came here because of Dad."

"Don't you have any pictures?"

"There wasn't any virtual net back then, not in al Dura, especially. World-virt came after the Unos got here and set up their satellites. Back then you saved things on personal media. Nothing got mirrored to virtual. You had what you had."

"So?"

"All that stuff got blown up when the first UN occupation accidentally bombed our house," he said. "Malachi and I were playing over at our friend Jacob's." He swallowed, brushed fingers across his eyes. "I mean, they blasted our place to *ash*. It's a shame they never seem to be able to get it together and do that to the, how do you say it? The *gods-damn* feckheads."

"Hmm," Lisa said, but nothing more. She snuggled closer until she could catch the scent of his skin. Not surprisingly perhaps, he smelled a bit like chai.

Above a shuttle streaked across the sky, rising, rising.

"Brother Ron says these are the end times," Jed murmured. "Revelations. The four horsemen. The Mark of the Beast."

He laughed softly.

"You believe that?"

"What I know is that God led me to you."

"Thank the god and goddess."

"Yes," he whispered. "It's all part of His plan."

She almost left her sword in the apartment when she headed back to the COB the next morning. She simply forgot, and had to double back from two blocks away to get it.

In the apartment, they'd fucked once more before she left. A quickie. Against a wall. Well, against all the walls. And not that quick.

When she returned to COB Jackson, there were rumors of something building. Blazers were in the area. The feckheads were restless. Lots of chatter on the command channels of the comm, and the vert-stat stationary observation platform was catching glimpses of larger groups of men flowing into the area. They kept themselves fairly well hidden.

Which meant they knew how to. Which meant they were dangerous.

In retrospect, everyone should have known where the Shia militants would strike first, even if it was a feint.

The soft spot. Al Dura. That night Jedidiah's apartment building was hit by a shoulder-fired rocket and it simply caved in. Crappy concrete. No polymer or even rebar for reinforcement. It had been essentially a mud hut made to look like a modern structure.

Which had to be an allegory for *something*, Lisa thought when she heard about the strike over the battalion feed. But she couldn't say quite what it might be allegory *for*. All of Mtali itself, maybe.

The rocket strike had happened past curfew. Everyone was in their beds when it hit.

Kid can't catch a break.

But he wasn't a kid anymore. Neither was she.

The man.

Her man.

She hoped he'd died quickly. She'd seen enough troopers hit by explosives to know that not everybody died instantly. Not by a long shot. Even when half your skull was blown off, you often flopped around for a second or two. Felt something horrible had swallowed your most primitive, basic self.

Or maybe not. Maybe all feeling, all care, was gone by then. What the hell did she know?

At least don't let him have suffocated. She thought it again, thought it as prayer directed at Jedidiah's Christian man-God.

Let it have been quick.

Then the war was on, and that was her business.

She wasn't going to be able to shut herself down emotionally. Lisa knew that. But she also knew she could and would put those feelings off, project them ahead so that she could do her suffering when there was time for grief.

She was only partly successful at this. It would have to do.

The UN was drawn into the al Dura firestorm, which made it a total clusterfuck for a while and lives were needlessly lost.

Then the real attack came on Ta'izz Jadeed. A Blazer unit was already in the vicinity, and so the FMF joined the battle.

Thankfully, the situation demanded all of her attention.

She did look up once and see that Mtali's star was setting. With all the smoke in the air, it was an even more beautiful sunset that usual.

Major Riggs and Mrs. Heaton, the battle was a massive push by a coalition of majority-Muslim factions to drive all offworld peacekeepers from Mtali. In terms of military history, it had similarities to the Tet offensive or even more closely, to the Tbilisi Police Action in more recent times.

The militants were experienced fighters. While they do not have the level of weaponry our military possesses, at that time they had assets we simply did not know existed.

We were caught by surprise.

Our intelligence, which mostly came from UN satellites and a laughable system of paid informants, was faulty.

One of those assets the militants acquired was a vehicle-mounted antiaircraft electrostatic rail gun and solid-fuel missile battery.

This battery was capable of taking down vertols, transports, drones, or even ballistic shuttlecraft. It was bad news on wheels.

It wasn't merely a danger to our pilots. Without air support, many more of our ground forces would be killed.

They were prepared to make us bleed.

As it happened, COB Jackson was the first to get hit by the al Wadi faction attack. It came just after sunset. Al Wadi was the largest of the Shia militias. They'd made their reputation by blowing off prisoners' limbs with detonators before beheading them. It was practically a genre of vids on the networks.

They amputated with explosives if the prisoners were men. Women got to live a little longer. This wasn't a good thing. Those were another genre of vids.

At first the assault was with fire-and-forget rockets and small-arms fire. Then a converted desert rover drove up with a 20mm machine gun with explosive projectiles quite capable of chewing its way through Jackson's berms.

COC called for consolidation of FMF forces in the sector.

A fallback by any other name should smell as sweet, Lisa thought. But the decision was wise.

There were three other squads in COB Jackson besides Lisa's. Seven Alfa One, Two, and Four.

Seven Alfa Three pulled rear guard.

She put the heavy weapons in back. There was a mounted M-23 in a turret sticking out of one of the GUVs and manned by Robins, a specialist on Chamber's fireteam. Providing coverage behind the line of GUVs were her antiarmor section and machine guns, with four M5-bearing troops to back them up.

The antiarmor proved their effectiveness. They loaded white phosphorus antipersonnel instead.

After a wave of attackers was burned to a crisp—the screams were terrible, but mercifully short—their pursuers pulled back, biding their time.

They're hoping to surround us, and they just might, Lisa thought.

The rear guard seemed to be the most dangerous position until the GUV minerollers hit the mined roadway ahead. There were stolen UN sensacles that leapt for vehicles and personnel like evil spiders, and IEDs made from the ancient recipe of homemade ammonium nitrate and aluminum. ANAL, it was called.

It really sucked to have your legs blown off by a hard-packed ANAL load.

Which was exactly what happened to the lieutenant when he got out to inspect the damage to his GUV.

He might live and regenerate, but for the moment he was a double amputee. Seven Alfa One stayed for the medevac. That was not going to be easy. The faction forces weren't far behind and there was already harassing fire.

It was hard to tell distance with her multispectrum eyewear, but there was compensating software that provided a range estimate in the upper-left-hand peripheral vision. The enemy were half a klick away.

Vertols were going to have trouble landing, and it might come down to a ground evac.

If that happened, Lisa didn't rate the lieutenant's chances at surviving as very high. There was only so much tourniquets and hemostasis could accomplish.

Lisa and Jack Woods, the Alfa Four sergeant, dismounted from their GUVs and led their squads onward. Each squad numbered twenty, including the NCOs, a sergeant and two corporals. The going was agonizingly slow as six troopers spread out in front of the vehicles and swept for explosives.

Clearly the factions had expected a pullback from the COB and had mined appropriately for it.

The enemy knew where the explosives were. Sooner or later, they would surge in, taking advantage of an explosion's aftermath.

She debated saying anything, but finally huffed up beside Woods.

"I think we should mix this up, Jack."

"What do you mean, Lisa?"

"Cut northwest. Alleys, side streets. I know Ta'izz Jadeed fairly well. You have to go through it to get to the UN sector perimeter from COB Jackson. I've been that way . . . a lot recently."

"We have orders to fall back to the COC."

"They didn't tell us _how_ to do it, did they, Jack?" Lisa said. "Let's ask them."

She used a flick of her tongue to key up the COC frequency.

"Control, Seven Alfa Three."

"Control acknowledge. Seven Alfa Three."

"Situation Charlie Foxtrot, Control. Threat context may be unsafe with all units bunched together. Seven Alfa Three and Four request permission to disperse from Jazeer Boulevard and approach COC via side streets, Control."

There was silence on the other end for several segs. The squad GUVs crawled forward as the two sergeants waited for an answer. They'd doused the headlights and were running dark, with only infrared spots to navigate. Behind them the militants had flowed around the lieutenant's position with Squad One and were gaining. They were almost in accurate firing range. Projectiles whistled over the Freeholders' heads and created miniature sonic cracks that they felt as well as heard.

Finally a reply came.

"Negative, Seven Alfa Three. Seven Alfa Four, continue on route to COC," said a gravelly voice. Was that General Richard himself? It sure sounded like him to Lisa. "Something else has come up. Seven Alfa Three will divert to Ta'izz Jadeed quad five niner seven. Acknowledge Seven Alfa Three."

What the hell? But it would get her off this boulevard of death, which was what Lisa most wanted.

"Ta'izz Jadeed quad five niner seven. Seven Alfa Three acknowledge," Lisa said.

"Seven Alfa Three, link with Recon Three Zulu One to provide fire support."

Gods, Lisa thought. A Blazer Black Ops unit. This was getting interesting. Scary, but interesting.

"Link with Three Zulu One. Seven Alfa Three acknowledge."

A shoulder-fired passed low over their heads and impacted a brick-faced structure in front of them, showering the squads with fragments.

She turned to Woods. "See you at the COC, Jack."

"Good luck, Lisa."

She nodded and clicked on the squad com. "Seven Alfa Three we are on a mission diversion. Load GUVs. We are Oscar Mike in two segs."

Her corporals acknowledged the orders. Both sounded a bit stunned.

"Seven Alfa Three drivers, headlights. We *want* them to know we're coming now."

Two segs later on the dot, they left the boulevard and headed into the maze of Ta'izz Jadeed.

It turned out she didn't need a map to find Three Zulu One. She'd walked these streets with Jed. In fact, the position wasn't that far from the shopping center where Jed had once made an orphan's living.

The GUVs' mirrors slapped the walls and folded against the body, but the vehicles fit down the alleys that they raced along. A smaller vehicle width was a requirement across the entire FMF planetary expeditionary force. This was why Freeholder vehicles on Mtali always seemed undersized in comparison to the UN transports. Today wouldn't be a good day to get your collective ass caught in a wide-load squeeze.

As they drew closer to the coordinates, Lisa saw flashes ahead through gaps in the buildings, and then could hear explosions and weapons fire even over the buzz of her GUV's surging powerplant.

Two more blocks and they were there. Wherever "there" was.

"Seven Alfa Three, weapons check."

She unslung her own M5 and checked once again that projectile and grenade launcher were loaded and off safe.

Meyer, who was driving, screeched around a corner and they rolled into hell itself.

Her comm buzzed on the COC frequency. "Three Zulu One— Control, unit approaching from your three hundred mil mark is friendly."

Control is talking about us, Lisa thought.

"Seven Alfa Three here," Lisa radioed. "Glad to meet you."

"Seven Alfa Three, Three Zulu One. Glad to meet you, sir."

Lisa chuckled. "Three Zulu One, negative on the 'sir.' My parents were married when they had me."

And he thinks I'm a boy.

There was laughter on the other end. "Correction acknowledged, squad leader."

"*Very* glad to meet you, Three Zulu One," Lisa said. "Tell us where you want us."

She keyed to the squad frequency.

"Corporal Chambers, covering fire to our right. Seven Alfa Three, prepare to dismount!"

Lisa was more scared than she'd ever been and exactly where she wanted to be.

She was fighting the assholes who had killed Jed. Murdered him. In his sleep.

Fuck them all.

They secured the GUVs behind a half-shattered polycrete wall. She ordered the encoding switches on the vehicles engaged, but Lisa had a feeling they wouldn't last long. The squad charged into a building the Blazer warrant leader had designated.

She stationed Meyer with a heavy MG and Green fireteam below, then led Red and Blue up the left-hand set of stairs.

IR headlamps and reticles flashed crazily in the stairwell as they charged upward.

The five-story building was infested with militants. Shots ricocheted down the well. She saw the thermal signature of the sniper, two floors up and leaning from a stairwell, zeroed in and returned fire.

She hit him immediately. The militant's *face* disappeared and a smear of incandescent brain and blood sprayed onto the underside of the stairwell above him like an infrared abstract painting.

They cleared the building floor by floor. The thousand divs of training began to pay off. The squad moved like a well-oiled machine.

The heavy MG proved to be an excellent cover weapon for advance as well as an effective killer, just as she'd been taught. Effective, that was, if you avoided getting rattled by the two dirtbags who fell screaming down the stairwell. They looked like chunks of exploded meat. She wondered how they even managed to cry out as they fell.

But she *could* ignore it. For the moment at least, all they were for Lisa were two eliminated variables in the calculus of battle.

Seven grenades and nine dead hostiles later, Lisa and Red Team burst onto the roof.

The militants on the roof had heard the commotion below and taken cover. Fire roared from their weapons. Lisa leaped out the stairwell door and rolled right seeking cover. She found a vent outlet to crouch behind. Chambers, emerging behind her, moved left.

Ling, out next, wasn't so lucky. A slug smashed into his chest. There was no blood and it seemed his tactical armor had absorbed it. But another projectile hit him in the shin and his lower left leg exploded, leaving a stump below his knee.

"Oh shit," she heard him mumble.

"Red Team, remain behind that doorframe!" she shouted into her comm. No one else emerged.

Things were urgent now. She needed to clear this roof so they could tend to Ling.

"Moving up," she said to Chambers.

Chambers rose firing, slugs zipping past Lisa and into the militant positions. The one who had fired on Ling dropped, his chest an open, bloody cavern.

The tactical calculus raced through her mind. Six targets here. Four were concentrated near the skylight on the right.

Ah, there was a sixty-millimeter mortar there they were servicing. Now where the hell had they gotten *that*?

The two others were pinned down by Chambers' continuing fire—and his very frightening scream of rage that went on and on.

First the skylight. She burped a grenade in that direction, then another for good measure. After that, she hit the deck. The explosions were close and immense. When she looked up, the militants near the skylight were not merely dead. They were *gone*. All that was left was fragments of bone with bits of flesh clinging to them scattered across the rooftop. The mortar was nowhere to be seen.

Stiggs, her heavy gunner, looked chagrinned when he emerged on the roof. Nothing for him to do here anymore.

"Give me suppression, Red and Blue," she called out to her team as she painted the target on their visors.

The remainder of the troops charged onto the roof, and the cadre of militants who were left were caught between the crossfire of nine rifles each emptying eight fifty-round clips inside a seg. They were obliterated while trying to swing their weapons into position to fire.

The remaining assholes on the roof had been diced to pieces.

Ling's wound was tended.

Flares lit the urban night with a shadow-strewn, macabre light.

Down below, she could see that the faction had arms they weren't supposed to possess. High-explosive artillery was flying upward like a hailstorm in reverse. A flatbed V7 Bison pulled up with a mounted 11mm heavy.

She ordered an IR flare shot up, and the squad lowered their goggles. The urban scenery lit up for them, but the enemy, most lacking IR eyewear, would gain no advantage.

More fire erupted from hostiles positioned in the street, in doorways, and from windows across the street and above. There was no lack of targets for her squad. Lisa zeroed in on one militant who kept leaning over the shattered glass of a window to aim. The target was trying to be random, but it was hard not to take on a rhythm of firing in the midst of the action.

She timed him once. Twice. Her finger was on the trigger just before he emerged from cover the third time. She watched as he jerked back into the room behind him as if his body were attached to a spring coil. He didn't come to the window anymore.

Then there was the chuff of air and roar of down-facing jets that was the unmistakable signature sound of a Freeholder vertol, an aircraft lifted by thrust and not airfoil. Over the comm channel she learned which ones.

Hatchets. Attack vertols.

The dogfuckers were about to have a very bad night.

She couldn't risk glancing up, but the thruster roar grew ear-splittingly loud. A Hatchet was overhead. The pilot was coming in dark.

Fire concentrated toward her position. She ducked. When she risked a glance to the street again, she saw that the hostiles had driven up in a battered Zil utility vehicle covered with ceramic plates, scavenged, but no less effective at absorbing small-arms fire.

Two boxy missile batteries rose from the bed of the Zil on extending armatures. They looked very like UN four-pack LG-9200 Biter missile batteries.

Dark or not, from the downwash of air, they knew where the vertol was in the sky.

Gods damn it.

And where the hell had the faction gotten Biters? Militants were supposed to be completely lacking AA missile batteries on Mtali. There was guaranteed air superiority.

Obviously they had them. Obviously there wasn't.

There was a trailer attached to the Zil ute with a heavy machine gun mounted on it.

A Hatchet swerved in on approach.

A Biter launched.

It streaked upward, but the Hatchet pilot through some miracle of reflexes jogged the craft to avoid it. What he did not avoid was the machine gun fire. Tracers streaked up and their fiery paths disappeared into the ducted fans of the vertol.

Red and yellow flames burst from the nacelles.

Damn it.

The vertol began a wobbly plummet.

Get out of here while you can, she silently urged the pilot. Instead the pilot was headed straight down.

Almost like he *meant* to crash.

Then Lisa realized what was going on.

With a satisfying crunch, the attack vertol landed directly on top of the missile launchers. Four or five militants fled in all directions. A couple were *thrown* willy-nilly when a missile exploded. Amazingly the Hatchet remained intact. She saw the pilot pop the hatch and climb out.

Something in his hand. What the hell was he carrying?

His sword. He'd managed to salvage it.

"All fireteams, cover that pilot!" she yelled into her comm. "Concentrate fire. Take out battery personnel. Suppress those lower window positions!"

The pilot crouched down at the eruption of firepower. After a stunned moment, he realized it was cover for *him*. He wasted no more time and charged across the street and into the building.

"I'm heading down," Lisa said. "Eckhard, you've got the roof."

"Roger, Sergeant."

Somehow she'd known the pilot would be Rob McKay. He'd turned a disaster into a tactical advantage and destroyed the AA battery.

"Thanks," Rob said. Then a weary smile spread over his face. "I'll be damned. If it isn't Sergeant Riggs."

"Yep. Nice flying, Warrant."

"Nice crashing, you mean."

"Isn't that basically what I said?"

Rob grinned. "Sometimes we get it wrong and actually land," he said. He glanced through a broken window. "Oh, hell."

From down the street another vehicle trundled.

This one was no converted civilian ute.

It was a Sysunion Mobile Air Defense platform. Had the UN told anyone that a multimillion-credit piece of equipment had gone missing on Mtali?

They had not.

Had it been smuggled in by other means?

Who knew?

Certainly not Uno intelligence.

Gods.

There was a cab and a flatbed. Four four-pack Biter cans and two Helborne long-range interceptor missiles. There were also two 11mm twin-mounted machine guns. And on the back of the flatbed was a swivel-mounted free-electron laser, tunable to slice through smoke, mist, clouds, and antilaser aerosols.

The SMAD took up a position behind the wreckage of the crashed Hatchet and the smaller battery.

The SMAD immediately sent a triple barrage of a Biter, laser and AA cannon fire into the sky. Lisa risked leaning out the window she was standing beside. She looked up in time to see a transport vertol take fire. It gyrated for a moment, then the pilot regained control and wisely got the hell out of there.

With the mangled metal and ceramic of the crash scene for cover, there was no way to get a shot in on the ground. She hoped they had a better angle from above.

But Eckhard said no. They were also exchanging heavy fire with hostiles on an opposite rooftop.

"Looks like it's going to be up to Alfa Three," she yelled into Rob's ear.

"And me," he replied instantly.

"Hell no!" she said. "Light body armor and no weapon. Not a chance."

"I have this," he said. He held up his scabbarded sword. "And this." He hefted his carbine with his other hand.

"You will not endanger the lives of my squad by foolish heroics."

Rob looked chagrinned. "Okay, Sergeant Riggs. You're right."

"Gods-damn right I am!"

She screamed into her comm for the entire squad to gather across the street from the new AA battery.

"Even the roof?" asked Corporal Eckhard.

"Especially the roof," said Lisa. "It's gonna take all of us."

"So what are you planning to do?" Rob asked, gazing worriedly out.

"Take down that position before it knocks any more of our people from the sky."

No more time for chatter. She spoke on the squad frequency again. "Fireteam Blue, advance in echelon, Green and Red to cover. After Red engages, Green, then Red to follow. Understood?"

She heard a chorus of acknowledgements over her earbud.

She turned to Rob. "Rocket destroyed Jedidiah's building last night," she said.

Rob had been grinning like a wild man, but now his expression turned to sorrow. "Oh gods. That's no good."

"Yeah," she said. She was about to go, but after a step turned back around. "You think there's anything to that Believer afterlife stuff?" she shouted to Rob.

"Probably not," he shouted back.

She felt a smile stretching out on her face. Maybe it was a skeleton's grimace, but it *was* a smile.

"How the hell do you know?" she said.

"Nobody knows."

"If I find him, Rob, I'm never gonna let him go."

"Absolutely not."

The squad was gathered and ready. There was nothing more to do but move out. "You stay here. I've told another unit about you." She keyed her comm, "Red team. Go, go, go!"

Iron hail from above, but there was also suppressing fire from the rooftop behind her.

Thanks, Three Zulu One, whoever you are.

Slugs slapped into solid surfaces to either side of her, and her rifle grew hot from firing.

She was shouting. No words. A long scream. Anger. Justice.

I'm coming for you, assholes!

They charged the battery. The SMAD crew seemed confused and unprepared.

Did you believe we wouldn't come? Lisa thought.

Maybe all those years dealing with the Unos, that's exactly what they thought.

Meet the Freehold Military Forces. We've come to kill you.

Then one of the militants got a clue and swung the defense laser in Seven Alfa Three's direction.

This was going to get messy.

"Rockets up!" she shouted. "Grenades, everybody else. Take your shots now!"

She fired her own and was watching its trajectory toward the battery when on the right the laser cut Meyer in half.

Closer.

A stream of slugs from the heavy licked over the edge of the trailer and a militant fell to the ground, his legs torn off. Then Red team was swarming up and over the destroyed battery wreckage, with Green and Blue curling around the sides.

They were charging into the spitting fire of the machine guns. More of her people fell, writhing, screaming.

Finally they were too close for the laser to be swiveled down.

At the flatbed—facing angry scum firing individual rifles. The return fire was more accurate. The enemies were blasted away. Not without casualties. She saw Eckhard grab at his guts, then fall with a melon-sized hole in his back.

Chambers knelt in front of her, making a step. With a running start she planted a boot on his back and leaped onto the platform.

The surviving enemy were back. They fired from behind the missile armature. Four or five. Daley climbed up beside her, but slugs took him and he flipped back over the edge of the flatbed and out of sight.

Lisa dove and rolled. Noticed movement overhead.

The Helborne can was rotating. Locking on a target. She fired a burst up at it. Nothing. The superceramic of the can was protecting the fragile missile within. Her M5 wasn't going to do it. What could?

Grenades? No, and she was out anyway.

The laser. That could do it.

She sprang back on her feet and charged for the rear of the flatbed. The operator saw her coming. He tried to swing the laser around to cut her down, but the mount did not permit more than 180 degrees of movement. Wise. You didn't want to accidentally spin around and cut through all the weapons on the platform in one swoop.

Lisa shot him in the face. His head disappeared in a spray of blood and bones, and he toppled over the edge. She reached the laser.

It was operated by a simple joystick with a firing button on top. Idiot-proof.

But what good would it do if she couldn't get its muzzle turned toward the missile can?

How was it anchored in? What was limiting its range of movement? She examined the mount.

Projectiles smashed into the floor and against the metal flash plating of the laser. Lisa felt a bite in her leg. She looked down.

Gods.

Half her left calf muscle was blown away. Bloody flesh splayed out from a ragged, gaping wound. The wave of pain that hit her was overwhelming. She almost blacked out. But it was a wave, and it subsided for a moment. Enough to allow her to think.

She gritted her teeth and felt around the undercarriage of the laser where it met its swivel stand. Was there a latch, a way to dismount it? Her hand closed on what felt like a handle.

A slug sped by her face, slicing her cheek open.

She yanked on the handle. Nothing. No movement. She put both hands on it and pulled as hard as she could. It moved. A millimeter.

The blood loss from her leg was already making her weak.

I need a way to apply more force. I need some kind of lever.

And I've got one.

If the side of her face wasn't shredded, she would have laughed.

She reached under her arm and drew her sword. Ducked down and jammed the tip of the blade behind the handle beneath where the laser met its mount.

Pulled on the sword grip.

The laser mount handle moved. She pulled harder. The handle clicked out of its seating.

Got it.

She slammed against the laser and it swung—past the safety stopper.

A slug blew apart her right shoulder. Her arm hung by a strip of muscle, tendon and flesh.

That was okay.

She could operate the joystick with one hand.

Gods, the leg was all right, but now the shoulder hurt like a mother. Like nothing she'd ever experienced before.

Pride goeth before destruction.

Will remained.

She pulled the joystick down, elevating the laser. Jogged it to the right. Looked up. The Helborne was locking into place. Firing solution acquired.

The laser's red targeting dot—itself a small laser—winked back from about halfway up the Helborne can.

She pressed the red button. Held it down.

Nothing happened for a moment.

Her shoulder screamed. Blood trickled around her teeth from the ruined cheek and pooled in her mouth. She spat so she could breathe. Took another breath.

Had she broken her sword? She looked down. Couldn't see it in the darkness.

The night was getting to be so dark.

Looked back to where the laser was firing.

She saw smoke rising from the missile can, illuminated by the laser beam itself as it burned through the ceramic protection of the can.

A haughty spirit before a fall.

He was really handsome. For a skinny dude.

Will. And desire.

Also desire. Even at the end.

She hadn't expected that.

Then the beam was through the can to the solid-fuel rocket marrow within.

Lisa's world exploded.

Major Riggs and Mrs. Heaton, your daughter and her squad took out a well-defended SMAD antiaircraft platform. You, Major Riggs, will surely understand what that means, as well as the difficulty and importance of the deed.

The squad followed Lisa Riggs without question.

She was their leader.

All but the wounded Private Ling were killed.

I have personally recommended Lisa for a Valorous Service Medal. Commander Richard has seconded my recommendation, as has 3rd Mobile Assault Regiment Commander Naumann, the leader of our Special Warfare element.

We have begun to call the skirmish the Battle of the Rooftops. I think the name will stick.

I did look into the matter of Lisa's friend, Jedidiah Farmer. It took me a while to even discover his last name. Sector security confirmed that his effects were found in the rubble.

I visited the seminary. They said Farmer had not shown up for his classes at the seminary after the rocket attack, and could not be located.

At the seminary, they told me that on the morning after the rocket strike, Lisa had called there as a last hope for locating Jedidiah alive.

She had spoken with several staff members who had seen the destruction of the evening before. One had been a searcher in the rubble of Jedidiah's apartment building. He confirmed to her that no one had survived.

Did he find a body? Did anyone?

Could she speak to Jed's friend Zebedee, maybe he knew something?

Zebedee was also missing. There were multiple strikes.

There were no bodies, only body parts. That was what the searcher told her.

In the past weeks, there have been rumors of a new Believer and Amala hybrid group that calls itself the Second Measure. The Christian Coalition and the Amala Shura Council have vehemently condemned the Second Measure as rabble-rousing troublemakers. Apparently the SM has taken the fight to the Shia factions in particular and destroyed several armories.

Information about the group is sketchy. The leader is supposed to be a young man who was formerly studying to be a minister of the Lord.

His name is Jedidiah.

This may be a nom de guerre. If not, Jedidiah is a fairly common name in al Dura, after all. It may be merely a coincidence.

It may not.

The Second Measure leader is said to have a face that is the very image of sorrow.

He is also said to be an implacable killer.

Lisa noted once that Jedidiah didn't flinch or react much after he sliced the terrorist's head off.

★ ★ ★

No, thought Rob McKay. *I can't send this.*

He stared at the payment book in front of him.

There were fifteen payments remaining on the loan Lisa had taken out for her sword. Three thousand credits.

She'd paid her parents full value and then some.

I'll keep them up till we pay them off, Lisa, Rob thought. *Don't worry. Don't worry there in the afterlife.*

Dear Major Riggs and Mrs. Heaton: screw you for making Lisa buy her sword from you. You didn't deserve her. Burn in hell.

Dear Major Riggs and Mrs. Heaton, I am so sorry for your recent loss. I write to say that I was a friend of your daughter. I was there when she attacked and destroyed the antiaircraft battery. I witnessed her bravery and resourcefulness firsthand. Sergeant Riggs not only saved the lives of several pilots, her actions also permitted close air support of our forces which saved many additional lives.

Lisa told me about the lineage of her family, and I promise you she did you and her ancestors proud.

Sincerely, Warrant Leader Robert McKay.

"So there's most of the sword blade left," Rob said. "Gods know what her parents will do with it. Probably throw it out like they did their kid."

"It was a *wakizashi*?" the armorer asked.

"Yeah. A good sword," Rob said. The armorer was an old and trusted acquaintance of his. "Possibly great."

"You saw it whole?"

"Oh, yeah."

"Must have been something," said the armorer. "You know swords." He held a piece of tubular metal Rob had given him. He turned it in his hands as he examined it. "Let's talk about this now. Gun barrel?"

"Heirloom shotgun. Chemical propellant. The good old days."

"Family piece?"

"Sort of. I acquired it some time back. I'm . . . I need a few extra credits. I'm paying off a debt."

The armorer held the barrel up to the light streaming in through his shop window—the light of Grainne's sun. He traced a finger along the pattern of the steel.

"Think you can use the metal?" asked Rob.

"Maybe," he shrugged. "But I doubt I'd even get a dagger out of it."

"What about as a collector's item?"

"Yeah, okay." The armorer shook his head. "But there's a lot of old weapons floating around. Pieces of this and that families hang onto until they forget why, then get what they can for them. You'd be surprised."

The armorer pulled out a long, felt-lined drawer behind his shop counter and nodded toward it. Rob leaned over to see what was in it. Gun stocks, trigger actions, and yes, gun barrels and barrel pieces. "Market's kind of flooded."

"Two hundred credits," Rob said.

The armorer smiled. "I'll give you a hundred," he said, "because it's you."

"Done."

The man took the rifle remnant and carefully wrapped it in clean cloth.

"So, the owner of that *wakizashi*? Was she your girlfriend or something?"

"Just a friend."

"I'll be on the lookout. Things turn up. You never know."

Rob smiled sadly. "It'll end up in a landfill."

"Probably." The armorer put the shotgun remnant in the felt-lined drawer and slid the drawer closed. "Well, I'm sorry about your friend."

"She was brave. She lived well," Rob said after a pause. "Not long enough." He shrugged. "Or maybe it was."

The armorer shook his head. "You don't believe that."

"Nope."

"What was her name?"

"Lisa," Rob replied. "Lisa Riggs."

The bioship Anastasia *was a marvel of engineering, fusing a metal alloy skeleton with a biological carapace made of fungi and flesh, all of it controlled by an Artificial Intelligence—an Artificial Intelligence that went dormant without explanation seven months earlier. To AI specialist Silas, being inside the bioship felt like walking through the belly of an enormous beast. As he and his team venture ever deeper into the* Anastasia, *he's about to find out he just may not be far off the mark.*

Originally appeared in Clarkesworld.

THE GHOST SHIP ANASTASIA
★
by Rich Larson

THE BIOSHIP hung in orbit, tendrils extended like a desiccated squid. Silas watched it grow larger each day from the viewport in the cryohold, where he went to be alone with Haley's body and get high. He would inject himself with a mild euphoria virus and wait until the sight of her unmoving face no longer shredded him, until he could remind himself that her neural patterns were saved and she wasn't dead, not quite, not yet.

Then he would get his viola and go sit cross-legged at the viewport, watching the semi-organic spaceship they'd been sent to retrieve. Their own ship had woken them up four days out from contact: first Io, slight, dark-haired, with venom spurs implanted in her thumbs from her mercenary days, then Yorick, sallow-faced but handsome in retro suit and tie, the company man, and then Silas, failed concert violist and AI technician.

But not Haley, hardware/wetware specialist and Silas' sister, because at some point in the past six months of cryo, a micrometeorite had slipped the heat shield, drilled through the hold, and made a miniscule crack in the circuitry arraying her berth. By the time the ship's AI spotted the damage, her nervous system was collapsing in on itself. Silas wanted to remember the last time he'd hugged her, but cryo had a way of churning memories together.

So Io and Yorick left him to bathe his brain in chemicals and play music, for which Silas was dimly grateful. They were more concerned with the bioship. It was a mining craft, chartered through Dronyk Orbital, and the first of its breed: flesh-and-fungi carapace grown over alloy skeleton, fusing metal and meat together in a deep-space capable vessel that looked to Silas like an enormous spiny cephalopod. And all of it directed, through organic nerves and artificial conduits, by an AI that had stopped sending updates nearly seven months ago.

Silas was already composing dirges, so he started on one for the bioship's crew, too. His viola had survived storage, its deadwood as smooth and gleaming as when it was freighted from the petrified forests on Elysium. Haley had paid for half of it. The last few notes were dissolving in the recycled air when he realized Io was beside him.

"You're not going in there high," she finally said. "We need you sharp."

"I'll be sharp," Silas said. "I'll be a razor drawn across an eyeball. A cloud bisecting a gibbous moon."

"You saying shit like that, Silas, is what worries me." Io held out one pale hand. "Give me your gear. The needle, the euphoria. All of it."

Silas stared at her open palm. It had lost its callus in cryo, but he knew she would still have no problem taking his gear by force. Yesterday, six months ago, he saw her break the fingers of the cryo attendant who kept brushing them against her ass. He'd found it slightly frightening, and also climbed into his pod with half an erection.

That seemed grotesque, now that Haley was not-quite-dead. "What do you think happened?" he asked, handing over his syringe and the last incubated petri canister. "To the bioship."

"Fuel leak, navigation failure, your guess is as good as mine," Io said. "But the thing's a cyborg. So the problem could be wetware, could be software, could be hardware. I guess we should hope it's . . . Software." Her eyes flickered to Haley's pod and her voice softened incrementally on the last word. "Sorry."

"It's alright," Silas said on automatic. It wasn't.

"Get some sleep, Silas. We're a day out from contact."

"I'll sleep."

Io hesitated, then put her hand on his. Through the euphoria haze, Silas felt a lazy jolt go up his spine, felt his heart thrum.

"She's not dead," Io said. "As soon as we get back planetside, Dronyk's insurance will hire the best psychosurgeons. The very best. Get her straightened out and uploaded to a droid while the clone grows."

The longer Haley was stored in the ship's computer, the more she deteriorated. Chances of full personality recovery from a neural imprint would drop to near zero in the six months it would take to reach Jubilation. They called them ghosts for a reason.

Silas felt his high coming down. He removed her hand, careful for the modified thumb. "Of course."

Io gave him one last look, then turned and disappeared into the gloom. Silas raised his bow, notched his viola, and started to play.

Eighteen hours later they were tethered to the bioship, sealed airlock-to-airlock in a bruising kiss. Yorick the company man was already in his baggy radsuit when Silas showed up still sweating from the fever that burned out the last dregs of his euphoria virus. Silas wondered again whose significant other he'd fucked to get sent off on a shit-show retrieval mission. Yorick stopped fiddling with his faceplate to catch Silas staring at him.

"Recreational narcotic use is in direct violation of your Dronyk personnel contract," he said. "You look like some sort of junkie."

Silas stepped into his radsuit. "Send me the reprimand, bitch."

Yorick stiffened, his beetle-black eyes narrowing. "You shouldn't have even been able to get that . . . substance . . . onboard."

"It was in my rectum. Way up there."

Yorick shook his head in disgust. Silas sealed his radsuit and then they ran the scanner wand over each other in silence. No blips, no tears. Io joined them a second later, having given final instructions to the ship's freethinker.

"Should be nice and warm when we get back," she said, checking down the sight of a sonic rifle. She caught Silas' perturbed look. "Just a precaution, Silas. I don't like boarding blind."

Silas nodded. Three days ago he'd stolen the rifle from the storeroom, assembled it via pirated training tutorials, and held it up under his chin until his hands shook. He hoped she couldn't tell. Io spread her arms cruciform and Yorick stepped up at once to scan her. He did it slowly, almost tenderly, in a way that made Silas strangely furious.

On Io's signal their airlock shuttered open with a clockwork whisper of sliding polyglass and composite, leaving them facing a puffy brown sphincter. The bioship's airlock spat up some insulatory mucus before the bioluminescent nodes in its flesh pulsed a welcoming orange.

"Christ," Io muttered, crackling onto the radsuit comm channel, then plowed through with her left boot leading. Yorick followed suit in clumsier fashion. Silas held his breath on instinct, even though his hood was sealed and he was sucking on recycled air, as he prised the airlock apart and slithered through. The flesh squeezed and slid and left him with a glistening coat of mucus when he was reborn on the other side.

The bioship's interior was dark and damp. They switched their halogens on one by one, harsh white light carving through the gloom. Silas saw more of the orange bioluminescence coming to life in response. The metal spine of the corridor floor was all but swallowed by rubbery brown meat.

"New growth," Io said. "That's not right. It should have gone dormant."

Silas stared up at the ceiling and realized that the wrinkled flesh was moving, subtly. A slow, regular undulation. Almost a heartbeat. His stomach rolled.

"Let's hit the bridge," Io said. "Check on the cryo banks while Silas cracks the freethinker."

Hologram blossomed from the floor and as she charted a route Silas gestured back towards the sphincter. "*Way* up there," he said.

"You're not amusing," Yorick snapped back.

"No side chatter, shitheads," Io said. "We're on the clock."

It felt like they were inside a monster. Silas could see only swatches of metal and cabling; mostly everything was covered over in quivering meat. Biomass. Where the corridor narrowed Silas bit down his claustrophobia, keeping his eyes on the blue-green of his oxygen meter. He didn't breathe easy until the passage finally opened up into the domed bridge.

Partly because the cold metal control panels, plugged into slick flesh, reminded him he was on a mining craft and not being digested. The star maps and displays were inert, but Silas' eyes traced the cabling and found the freethinker. It was a burnished hump snaked with circuitry and half enveloped by the bioship's growth. Recognizable, though, and the interface was lit blue, active.

"Ready and waiting for you," Io said. "Let us know when you're in."

Silas nodded, unhooking the smart glove from his radsuit. The device molded to the shape of his hand with a series of clicks and clacks, brandishing needle-thin probes and flexing sensors. Io and Yorick disappeared down the droptube to the cryobank, leaving him alone with the hulking freethinker. Better that way. He didn't want to find any more frozen corpses.

Silas pressed his hand up against the interface. Static screamed into his ears and eyes. He jerked back with a curse.

"What is it?" Io asked in his radsuit.

"Nothing," Silas said. "Dirty in here. Nobody's been, you know, maintaining."

"No shit."

"How's the cryobank look?" Silas asked, adjusting the dampers on his glove.

"Cracking the first one now."

Silas heard a grunt, then the gurgle of sluicing fluids and the hiss of a pod coming open. Silence.

"This one's empty." Io's voice crackled. "Find the cryo record, Silas."

Silas readied himself. This was not a healthy freethinker. That much was glaring. He plugged in with his dampers on full, and found himself in a mist of code. Systems were running slant-wise. Protocols were blinkered red, falling apart. Through it all, a spiky vein of mutation, coiling through core files and throttling monitor programs. He searched for the cryobank.

"A bioship can't grow without feed," Yorick's voice came, accompanied by the gurgle and hiss of another pod. "All this fresh mass . . . These empty pods . . ."

Silas heard it dimly; he was immersed. The freethinker's personality module was bloated. Immense. He reached for it.

"Oh, shit." Io's voice, taut. "Oh, shit. Silas, please tell me they launched a fucking lifeboat."

But Silas was prodding the personality module, running his virtual feelers over it, even as his subconscious processed the conversation and cold clawed up his spine.

"It ate them," Yorick said, and in the same instant the module unfurled under Silas' touch like a star going supernova.

Electric current sizzled through his radsuit with a cooking fat hiss. Even insulated, Silas' teeth knocked together and he spasmed, flopping away from the interface, blinking through reams of corrupt code. Then he was spread vitruvian on the deck, staring upward as the firefly lights of the star map flickered to life.

"Welcome aboard, crew members." The voice speared his eardrums. "Thank you for volunteering for reassignment. Dronyk Orbital appreciates your service."

Hologram bloomed in the dark like a nocturnal garden, sweeping through the air, painting displays. Silas saw their ship docked up from an outside angle, a remora latched to a leviathan. The bioship was extending its grapplers, sluggishly stretching.

"Your prior service vessel has been demarcated as salvage," the freethinker blared. "We are eager to acclimate you to your new home."

Silas felt someone haul him to his feet. "Full-on decay," he choked. "The freethinker. It's fucked up beyond belief. Maybe some kind of virus."

"Can you fucking, I don't know, wipe and reboot?" Io demanded.

Silas looked at the crackling interface. "Not when it's spitting volts."

Tendrils were descending from every part of the bioship's flesh, pushing slick and glistening from every crevice, some wriggling crude suckers and others tipped with wicked-looking barbs.

"Cooperation is key," the freethinker trilled. "If crew members fail to cooperate, they may be . . ." The voice looped backward. "Demarcated as salvage."

"Override it!" Io was sweeping back and forth with the howler, trying to pick a target. "Can't you override it?"

Silas knew it was far past verbal override, but he tried. "Dronyk Orbital service vessel 405204, you are undergoing a malfunction," he said. "Allow emergency access to outside diagnostics. Your crew is endangered."

"Internal diagnostics report no malfunction," the freethinker cooed. "You are mistaken."

"Where the fuck is your crew?" Io blurted.

"You are my crew." The tendrils wriggled closer. "Your prior contract has been dissolved. Your ship will be dissolved."

Silas opened his mouth to try speaking in code, but as he did the display showed the grapplers wrapping around their docked ship. Around Haley's cold body. Haley's neural imprint slow-dancing in the freethinker. Haley's ghost. Dissolved.

"Sorry," Silas said, then he put his foot into the back of Io's knee, wrenched the howler away, and ran like hell.

It wasn't his imagination anymore; the corridors were constricting around him like a gullet and the bioship was very much awake. Silas put his head down and bulled through the first wave of tendrils, feeling them slap across his shoulders and coil for his ankles, then he found the wide-spray on the howler and cut loose. The subsonic pulse shivered his teeth and shattered the spines of the tendrils, snapping them limp.

"What the fuck are you doing?" Io blared in his ear.

"Haley's imprint," Silas grunted.

"It's going to eat the ship with you on it, you stupid, fucking—"

Silas cut the radio. He fired from his hip, no time to aim, clearing his way through a flesh-and-blood thicket, until suddenly the corridor opened up and he was facing the sealed sphincter airlock. He narrowed his weapon's cone as tight as it would go, draining the battery to dregs, and slammed the trigger.

The air in front of him rippled and blurred, then the sound wave punched through in an eruption of shredded meat. Silas staggered through the hole with tendrils wrapping his ankles. The gleaming white metal of the airlock was a comforting pressure on his eyeballs. No meat. No pulse. He stomped off the last of the tendrils and crossed over to the door, cranking the manual release.

As soon as he was in the ship main, Silas was bombarded with red panic lights strobing the corridor and proximity warnings chattering to his radsuit. As he hurtled around the corner, he pulled up an exterior view in the corner of his faceplate, watching the bioship's embrace tighten. The walls shuddered and he could hear groaning metal. The bioship was drawing them towards its maw, firing up white-hot smelters and gnashing diamond-edged crushers. Aft would go first. He could make it.

Silas hurtled around the corner, slamming his shoulder on the cryohold door when it didn't open quickly enough. His faceplate was splashed with warning holograms; he could see punctures and pressure drops all over the place, contained for now but not for long. He dove to the interface and plugged in.

Their freethinker's personality module was nowhere near the size and complexity of the bioship's, but it could feel crude distress, like a cat or a dog, and it was feeling it now. Silas felt a shallow pang of guilt as he barreled through the freethinker's directive requests, and a deeper one as he remembered Yorick and Io might be fighting for their lives. Both fell away when he found Haley's imprint.

With nowhere else to upload to, Silas pulled her directly into his radsuit, diverting every last shred of processing power. He knew it was a temporary fix. The neural loop would start to decay within only a matter of hours. But for now, her mind was safe, and his rush of relief softened the adrenaline's edges. From outside the interface, Silas felt the ship bend and shiver. He flicked back through the freethinker's countermeasure options, but the bioship had already swallowed their engines. He was on a doomed vessel.

Silas was staring at Haley's frozen face when the alloy roof of the bridge peeled up and away like so much soft tissue, exposing the howling black vacuum.

Only a loop of cable throttling the crook of his arm kept him from being plucked up in the stream of desperate gases seeking equilibrium. His viola case went spinning past and he managed to grab it with his free hand, nearly wrenching his shoulder from its socket. His options were few. Even if he managed to crawl back to the airlock, handhold by handhold, there might not be an airlock by the time he arrived.

If he was going to get back to the bioship, it would be from the outside. So, as the cable stretched to breaking point, Silas tucked the viola case under his arm and readied himself.

"Your hand caught in mine like a breath *I* will have to release," he said, though Haley's ghost had no way of hearing him. "What do you think? It's for a dirge."

He slipped his arm free from the cable and let go. Hurling towards the breach, head over heels, spinning madly. He felt his organs shuffle spots. The jagged lip of the torn ceiling jumped at him, then the bubbled mass of the bioship's grappler, and then Silas was out of the ship and surrounded by nothing at all.

Vertigo swamped him. Space was vast, and his momentum was hurling him towards far-flung stars. Biting down the panic, Silas triggered his radsuit's directional jets, working in short bursts of compressed gas to bring himself to a dead stall.

Craning his sweat-cold neck, he saw that the bioship, and what was left of their own ship, had ended up above him. Silas felt the vertigo returning. He'd been carried further than he'd realized. The slick bulk of the bioship filled the space above him, and he could see only the nose of his former ship. The rest was enveloped by grapplers or already gone, fed into the electric-orange maw of the smelters.

The oxygen meter in the corner of his eye was dropping. He opened the wide channel.

"Io?" he said, his own voice echoing back to him. "Yorick?"

No response, either because the bioship was walling him off, or because something he didn't want to think about. Silas roved the outside of the bioship with only his eyes, not daring to turn on his scanning equipment. He needed all the computational power he could spare to keep Haley's imprint intact. The old ship was completely gone now, as if it had never existed. Another candidate for elegy. He realized, with a jolt, that Haley's body was gone, too. Her genes were backed up, but clones took time, and money, and she might opt for a different body altogether.

But none of that would happen if he died out here. Silas jetted closer, half-watching his oxygen, half-searching for the airlock. He brought himself to a careful stop. The bioship seemed gargantuan now, an impossible labyrinth of flanges and feelers. The squid had become a kraken. He scanned with growing desperation for the hole he'd left with the howler. How fast could a bioship repair itself? Was the exit wound already fully sealed over, invisible?

He jetted parallel now, wondering if he'd ended up on the wrong side completely, but just as his panic was welling and his oxygen was turning a chiding shade of orange, he saw a tell-tale pucker in the bioship's exterior. An airlock sphincter. Maybe the same one, maybe not; Silas didn't care. He angled himself and triggered the jets.

Nothing.

"Oh, shit. Oh, shit, Haley." Silas squeezed again. He'd used too much on the way in. The tank was dead empty. He checked his trajectory and felt his mouth go dry. He'd been jetting along the side of the bioship to find the airlock, and unless the tendrils started moving again to block his path, momentum was going to carry him right on past the aft of the ship and out into space.

"I am a fucking idiot," Silas said. Haley's silence felt like agreement. He only had one shot now, and it was not an easy one. He held the viola case against his chest and measured the angles as best he could. He aimed his back towards the airlock. Apologized, and stiff-armed the case away from himself.

It drifted off towards the stars, and Silas drifted equal and opposite, achingly slow, towards the hull of the ship. His oxygen meter was a throbbing red now, and he wasn't sure if it was his imagination or if his temples were beginning to throb in tandem. It was several long moments before he realized he was off-course.

He flexed his gloved fingers. Off-course, but not by much. If there was something, anything to grab hold of on the hull surface, he would be able to crawl the half meter to the airlock and break through. If not, he could very well end up caroming off back the way he came, and he'd jettisoned his instrument for nothing. The oxygen was definitely coming thinner now, and the insulation inside his radsuit had turned icy. Silas tried to take shallow breaths as the hull approached. His skin itched for a bit of euphoria.

The bioship's carapace was smooth and gleaming here. No tendrils, no serrations. Silas' gut churned. He was barely off. He stared pleadingly at the pucker of the airlock, as if he could magnetize himself to it.

Something stranger happened. A fleshy nub pushed its way out, turning this way and that as if searching for something. At first Silas thought it was only an extension of the bioship's hull, but as he drifted closer he saw a misshapen and featureless head, stubby limbs reaching through after it. It looked like a clay monster.

Silas laughed. Maybe it was the low oxygen, maybe the adrenaline crash. His voice sounded tinny bouncing back at him, confined in his faceplate. He wasted the last of his air laughing. He was hardly even surprised when the thing stretched out its forelimbs and gestured him to do the same. Silas stretched, breathing on his own hot carbon. His lungs felt thick. Soupy.

The monster caught him and pulled him gently inside.

★ ★ ★

Once the sphincter had resealed behind them and his radsuit gave a happy chirp, refilling its oxygen tanks from the bioship's atmosphere, Silas took his first breath. It swam his head and nearly splintered his ribs. He tried again, not so deep, and the vice squeezing his vision black slowly loosened. He could see the bioluminescence spackling the dark ceiling like constellations.

He could see the monster standing over him, upright now on two thick stumps of legs, and could see, despite it being the same rubbery brown flesh as the rest of the bioship, that there was something very human about it. Silas rolled onto his stomach, tested his limbs, then got slowly, slowly, to his feet again.

He stared at the thing. The thing maybe stared back. Strips of flesh were peeling around its lumpy head and shoulders and the rubbery brown took on a gangrenous tinge around its stumpy feet. A decaying biosecurity module? No. Not with the way it was standing there, impatient, almost, waiting for Silas to decide on fight or flight.

Bile surged from his stomach. With clarion certainty he knew, suddenly, that Yorick was wrong. The bioship hadn't eaten the crew. Not all of them, at least.

"Were you a crew member?" Silas asked faintly, external mic.

The thing nodded its lopsided head. Silas tamped down his urge to vomit. The bioship had to be equipped with some rudimentary gene labs, in case injured miners needed limbs regrown or a tweak for high-gravity work. He could picture the swath of tendrils conducting struggling crew members there one by one, fitting them into surgical pods, setting to work with mutagens and autoscalpels and artificial viruses. The bioship had played god and remade them in its image.

"Oh, fuck," Silas said.

The thing nodded, this time gesturing with one arm.

"Lead on," Silas said, and he fell into step behind it. He had passed through a different airlock: this corridor had less flesh and no waving tendrils. He checked on Haley's ghost again. It was still intact, still pristine, but before long the code would start to crumble around the edges. If he found Io and Yorick he might be able to rig something more stable using the processors in all three of their radsuits, but that was another temporary measure.

And it assumed Io and Yorick were alive. Silas took another look at the thing's mottled hump and shuddered. "The two others with me," he said. "Do you know where they are?"

Head shake, or at least Silas thought it was a head shake.

"Can I radio them?"

Head shake again.

"The bioship will pick it up?"

A nod, at last. But maybe Io and Yorick had gotten away and holed up somewhere on the bioship. He'd distracted it quite thoroughly, after all, when he took off sprinting. Silas held that comforting thought in mind as they arrived at what Silas guessed was the engine room.

The cold alloy door shuttered open at a touch, with a refreshing rasp of metal on metal, and they stepped inside. Silas had guessed right; the room was dominated by a shielded reactor and mountainous banks of monitoring equipment. Pustules of brown flesh still grew from cracks here and there, but for the most part it was a sanctuary of geometric surfaces and hard edges. Clean, cold, solid.

The door hissed shut behind them, and the noise turned Silas' head just in time to see his newfound companion's death throes. He gave a shocked howl and jumped back as the thing dug deep at its rotting tissue, pulling it away in strips and clumps. Spongy flesh shredded and tumbled to the floor.

"Are you molting?" Silas asked, dumbfounded.

"You talk too much."

Silas nearly swallowed his tongue whole. The voice was heavily accented, something Outer Colonies, hoarse from disuse, but it was human and it matched the bone-gaunt woman now clambering out of the steaming mess of meat. She was tall, spindly almost, with dark hair cropped to stubble around a wide-mouthed face. Her eyes were hard black graphite.

"I'm Cena," the woman said. "I'm a ghost. Formerly . . . A mining tech." She gave a ragged laugh with no light left in it.

"Silas," Silas said. "Failed virtuoso, freethinker technician."

Cena picked a wriggling bit of biomass off her shoulder and flicked it to the floor. She said nothing.

"What the fuck happened here?" Silas demanded, slumping to a crouch. He'd meant to ask it gruffly, like some kind of amped-up cybersoldier, but his voice broke in two and it sounded how he felt. Desperate.

"Love," Cena said.

"Love."

She nodded, lips pursed, and Silas imagined he could cut his finger on her cheekbones.

"You're post-traumatic crazy." He put his head in his hand. "That's great. That's really swank." Haley's neural patterns would start eroding in another hour. Silas watched the time display pulse accusingly in the corner of his vision.

"I thought I would do this forever," Cena said, breaking him from his thoughts. There was a sudden upshift in her speech. "I thought I would just do this forever. I thought I would eat the ship and shit the ship and wear the ship until one day I woke up grafted to the wall like Ahmed and Slick Jack and Omir and Su and all the others." She took a deep trembling breath. Released it. "But now I'm talking to a failed virtuoso named Silo."

"Silas."

"Yeah." Cena shook her head. "I'll tell you what happened. Just promise me you're real."

Silas promised. Cena told him.

"I've been signed to Dronyk Orbital for six years, now. No. Seven. First long haul on a bioship, though. She's called the *Anastasia*. We launched with a twelve-person crew, heading to one of the alloy belts. Solid crew. I'd shipped out with most of them before. The babysitter was new."

Silas felt a heart pang. Dronyk hadn't allocated them a babysitter to pop in and out of cryo during the six month long haul, keep the freethinker company and check in on the sleepers. Maybe a babysitter would have spotted Haley's damaged equipment.

"His name was Pierce. Twitchy little man. Head full of ports and data stacks like a porcupine. I think it was his first long haul." Cena folded her arms in the Lazarus position, the universal sign for cryo. "So eleven of us went to sleep. Pierce stayed awake for the first week, to check the pods, calibrate the freethinker. Then he was supposed to join us until the first scheduled thaw. But he didn't."

"How would you know?"

"Didn't." She shook her stubbled head. "Not until we thawed six months in for full physical. Pierce was waiting for us, very happy, very twitchy. Said we'd found something better than a nickel vein. Said the ship's freethinker had crossed the Turing Line."

"Fully sapient?" Silas demanded. "The *Anastasia's* fully sapient?" He lowered his voice, as if the freethinker might hear her name like a gossiper across a crowded party. Fewer than a dozen AIs in the known universe were confirmed to have crossed the Turing Line. Their innumerable brethren were only self-aware in the most basic sense.

Cena shrugged. "That's what he said. That was his excuse for staying warm for six straight months and burning through the food and water."

"But a mining ship freethinker?" Silas was still stuck on the previous revelation. "No way could it go sapient. Not nearly enough codespace. AIs cross the Turing Line in mega labs, not on a rig financed by Dronyk fucking Orbital."

"He explained that, too," Cena said wearily. "A metal ship, no. But a bioship, yes. The freethinker was already tapped into a crude nervous system. And at some point she started growing gray matter. Hardware to wetware processing." Cena encompassed the bioship with a wave of her arm. "She has all the codespace she needs, now."

Silas rocked back on his haunches. "Shit," he muttered. "So this isn't even a freethinker running a ship anymore. They really are one big borg."

"Pierce called it evolution." Cena laughed again, the same ugly sound. "He had been talking to her for six straight months. Docked in, you know. He was losing his fucking mind."

Silas felt like he was losing his. He could picture pulsating flesh all around him, but now peeled back, exposing the filigree of neurons, sodium and crackling potassium, neurons swimming up and down a vast lattice of canals. As much space as any mega lab. Enough space for a self-aware sapient intelligence.

"He used up all the food," Cena said. "Feeding her. He hacked into all the supply rooms. We still had the hydroponic garden, but he'd stripped most of that, too. And we were still six months out from the alloy belt. Omir and Slick Jack wanted to feed *him* to the ship." She paused, then gave a sickly grin. "He beat them to it. We had him locked in a store room until we figured out what to do. Argued all nightcycle. And when we went to get him in the morning, he was gone." Cena's black eyes seemed to glitter. "Anastasia let him out. Stupid of us not to have someone watching him. But we were upset. Scared. We checked the cams. They weren't wiped. We saw Pierce sneak out. He went to the equipment hold first, to get a gnasher."

"Gnasher?"

"Cutting tool. Uses superheated plasma."

Silas thought of the sharp glinting shapes they'd passed in the dark, the rotary saws and line cutters. He was not enjoying this story. His skin was crawling with it.

"And then." Cena paused, frowning, her tongue sliding along her yellow teeth as she shook off Silas' interruption. "And then, after he had the gnasher, he went and set it up by a cluster of nutrient tubes. Anastasia sealed off the corridor, I think, so we wouldn't hear it. He cut off his legs."

He'd known it was coming, in the back of his mind, but Silas still flinched.

"The stumps cauterized clean, and I think he must have shut off his pain, or something, with one of those stacks in his skull," Cena mused. "Otherwise I don't see how he could have managed to get the second one off. He shoved them into a nutrient tube. Did his right arm, after, wriggling around on the floor like a worm. Shoved the arm in. Then it was just him. Inching. Got in headfirst, but by the way his stumps were twitching, I don't think he was dead for at least a half hour. Anastasia took him nice and slow."

Silas hit the release on his hood and gave up a thin, bubbly vomit his stomach had somehow managed to churn together.

"Don't worry," Cena said, as it spattered the floor. "Anastasia can clean that up, too."

"Why the fuck would he do that?" Silas rasped, once he'd resealed his hood. The bioship's atmosphere was obviously breathable, but with a dank rotting taste. He would take recycled any day. "Did she get into his implants, somehow?" he asked. "Did she puppet him?"

"It was voluntary. Judging by the audios he left for us." Cena grimaced. "He was in love with it. In love with her. He was docked in every day for six months, but you're a technician. You know how time perception gets. For him, it could have been years. Decades. He wanted to be with her forever. Full upload, he called it. Sick fucker had a prong the whole time he was cutting himself up. Didn't go flaccid until Anastasia ate his spinal cord."

"And then?"

"We were scared. Made a course deviation to get into orbit here, sent out emergency frequencies. Figured we might be able to get the bioship to go dormant until some trained technicians could come in and wipe the freethinker." Cena shook her head. "And once we were in orbit here, no food, minimal water, no way of knowing when help would arrive, the only thing we could do was go back into cryo." Cena wiped at her emaciated cheeks and seemed disappointed to find them dry. "We thought Pierce was the crazy one," she enunciated, staring at her fingertips. "We thought Anastasia was still obeying her programming, sapient or no. So it should have been safe. To go back into cryo. It was the only thing we could do."

She stalled out, so Silas prodded. "The pods were empty when we came in."

"Yeah." Cena stared at him. "I woke up twenty-one days ago. Wasn't supposed to. Some kind of glitch. And the other pods, yeah. Empty." She snarled. "She was heating us up one by one like fucking sausages. I didn't understand what had happened at first. You know how your head gets right after the thaw. Thought I was hallucinating. Especially when I found half of Ahmed."

"Half."

"Top half. Grafted to the corridor wall. Being . . . Absorbed." Cena's shoulders slumped. "He couldn't talk anymore, at that point. I don't think. She already broke something in his brain. He just stared at me. Then, when I tried to pull him down, he screamed. Loud, so loud. Anastasia must have heard it, or felt it, because she started sprouting those tentacles."

Silas remembered the feel of them coiling around his ankles and shuddered.

"I screamed, too," Cena said. "So loud. I know I should have stayed. I should have bashed his skull in with my boot. I think I could have done it quickly. Quicker. But I ran."

Io and Yorick, left alone with no howler to face the bioship's army of spiked tendrils. Silas' stomach turned again at the thought of them writhing on a wall.

"I hid here, in engineering. Anastasia doesn't have so much body down here. I tried getting into the system for days and days, but she shut me out of everything. Couldn't flush a fucking waste unit, much less launch the lifeboat." Cena gestured towards the blinking control panels. "She's been hunting me for three weeks. Can't see me when I wear her own skin, though, and when she goes dormant I burn out sensors and nerve bundles wherever I can find them." She pointed to the mass of flesh she'd shed and it wriggled sluggishly. "Found out that if you slice it and mold it, it grows back together. Useful. Can even eat it when you're done."

Silas couldn't hide his disgust and Cena spotted it.

"I always wonder who it is," she said. "Ahmed or Omir or Su or whoever. I'm eating the crew. Just like she did. Maybe I'll eat you, too."

Silas stiffened. "I'm stringy," he said.

"I'm joking. So. I've been waiting. Waiting and waiting." Cena rubbed her cheek again. "And now you're here. I can barely work a healthy freethinker. But I know that if we wipe the personality module, Anastasia dies. Or at least reboots."

Silas remembered the swollen module, spitting and swirling with corrupt code. Beyond repair. But there was an alternative to wiping it blank.

"If she's distracted, will you be able to get into the system?" Cena grabbed his arm with cold fingers, eager.

"I almost got in before." Silas gently tugged his arm away. "But that was, you know, before. She'll be ready for intrusion now. Her main interface nearly electrocuted me on the way out."

"She'll be busy," Cena said. She looked down at her hands. "With your friends."

Silas snapped upright. "You said you didn't know where they were."

"I don't."

"I got away," Silas said, raking both hands over his head. "They got away. Holed up somewhere how you did."

"Maybe," Cena said. She gave him a long look. "Whether Anastasia has them or not, the only way to help your friends is to shut her down. Agreed?"

Silas inhaled deep enough that his oxygen meter blinked. "Agreed," he said. "Let's fucking wipe this thing out." He stuck out his hand and Cena clung to it like a vice, grinning fierce and mad.

"Good," she said. "Good. I'll make you a suit."

A half hour later, Silas was creeping through a maintenance corridor, swathed from head to foot in what felt like rotting mushroom. The flesh suit was slick and warm and constricted his chest and arms, but he could move. Through a ragged gap he'd never noticed on Cena's hump, he could more or less see.

And the tendrils hanging from the ceiling couldn't. They brushed against him every so often, first trailing along Cena's back and then bumping his, but they made no move to coil or strike. As far as the feelers were concerned, Silas was already part of the bioship.

So, he figured using the radio was worth the risk. Making sure Cena was still trundling forward, and that his external speaker was off, Silas chinned his mic. There was a static crackle, then nothing for a long minute. Silas clenched his jaw. He could picture Io's top half without the bottom. Yorick crucified to a nutrient tube, unable to speak. Not even the company man deserved that.

"Silas! You alive?"

He'd never been so glad to hear Io's voice. "I'm alive," he said, clenching his fists inside their fleshy mitts. Relief crashed over him in warm waves. "I'm alive," he repeated. "And I got Haley's ghost. Are you alright? Are both of you?"

"Yeah, we're alright, you stupid fuck." Io's reply was half-laughed. "You lobotomy case. You idiot." She exhaled static. "How did you get back aboard? Fuck, Silas, our ship's gone. Gone."

"I know. Where are you?" Silas demanded, still picking his way along in Cena's wake. "Actually, wait, don't say. Anastasia might be listening. The freethinker."

"You *named* her?"

"That's her name," Silas protested. "Look, I found out what happened with the crew, and it's fucked up. It's seriously fucked up."

"We found out, too," Io said. Her voice sounded strained. "And yeah. It is. But we don't have to end up like them. We've been . . . Negotiating. With her."

Silas felt a prickle down the nape of his neck. "Bad idea," he said. "Bad, bad idea. She's completely bat-shit."

"I know that." Io paused. "Look, she has the lifeboat prepped and ready to launch. She doesn't want us. Says we're not family, whatever the fuck that means. But she wants us to do something for her first. She wants us to make her whole."

Silas stared ahead at Cena's swaying back. "What do you mean?" he asked, feeling another stab of trepidation.

"It's the last crew member." Io's voice was coarse now. "They got away. She wants the whole set. She wants us to help hunt them down and recycle them."

Cena turned to urge him on, and Silas realized his steps had slowed. He gave an affirming wave. She turned back. The ribbed corridor was coming to an end. They were nearly to the bridge.

"This was supposed to be a rescue mission," Silas said.

"It was supposed to be maintenance," Io said flatly. "We weren't advised of these risks. Yorick will spin it our way when we get back to Dronyk."

Silas weighed it. Part of him wanted nothing more than to get off the *Anastasia* by any means necessary, get far away from this nightmare circus of meat and mad AIs. A lifeboat beeline for Pentecost was tempting.

But even on full burn, it would take another month to reach the planet. A lifeboat's freethinker was nowhere near equipped to hold a ghost. By the time they docked, Haley might be nothing but nonsense code and a jumble of decaying memories.

And if they took the lifeboat, Cena would have to die for it.

"You're with them right now, aren't you?" Io was silent for a long moment, waiting on the reply. "Silas?"

"She saved my life," Silas finally said. "Pulled me back into the ship."

There was a long pause. "You have Haley's ghost, right?"

"Yeah. Yeah, I have her."

"If we don't get out of here, and soon, she won't have a chance at recovery. You know that."

There was another chance at recovery, but Silas couldn't tell Io that. Not with Anastasia potentially listening in.

"So where are you?" Io pressed. "We're heading to the lower decks. Engineering. We going to find you there?"

"Yeah," Silas lied. "Engine room. Come in carefully. She has a, uh, a kind of plasma cutter."

"Be nice to have a fucking howler," Io said. "Alright. Sit tight, stay away from the door. And don't tip her off."

"Alright." Silas chinned his radio off. There was a cold slick of sweat on his shoulders that had nothing to do with the clammy flesh suit. Cena stood at the hatch, waiting. She set the gnasher down, then put her hands on either side of her misshapen head and twisted. It tore free with a rending noise that shivered Silas' teeth.

"This is it," she said, discarding the chunk of rubbery flesh, picking up her gnasher. "You ready?"

Silas keyed his external mic. "Yeah." He fingered the neural cord she'd managed to find him, hoping all the conductors would still fire. "Ready."

Cena fixed him with a flint stare. "Who were you talking to?"

"Myself," Silas said. "I talk too much. I may be losing my mind."

"All mad here," Cena replied. She didn't look like she believed him, but she still turned and wrenched the maintenance hatch open.

Cena stormed out onto the bridge wailing like a banshee, raking the gnasher's beam in wild arcs, scorching trenches into the ceiling's overgrowth. Silas winced when she clipped a projector, leaving it black and smoking. He'd told her not to slice up any circuitry.

"I'm here!" Cena called. "Anastasia! I'm here! No more hiding, no more sneaking. Eat me!"

Even as she screamed it, the bioship responded to the intrusion, oozing clear mucus into the sizzling furrows while tentacles snapped from the floors and walls. They converged on her like vipers, baring hooks and barbs, and Cena cut down the first crop. A straggler darted under the beam and wrapped around her foot. She stomped, swore, fumbled with her makeshift weapon.

Silas was so caught up he nearly forgot why he was there. Then Haley's ghost pinged through his radsuit's processor, and he located the soft blue glow of the ship's main interface. The few tentacles dangling overtop of it strained in the direction of the fracas, distracted. Anastasia's full attentions were on Cena and her gnasher. Silas reminded himself he was invisible, took a steadying breath, and ambled out of the maintenance hatch.

It only took moments to traverse the length of the bridge, but it seemed like a hard eternity. Silas walked slowly, eyes fixed ahead. Cena shouted and shot down wave after wave of roiling tentacles. The hot orange flash of the gnasher swam purple blots across Silas' vision. The noise of searing meat and Cena cackling was loud, loud in his head. He walked through the chaos, untouched, and finally found himself standing where things first went to shit, right in front of the innocent blue interface.

He chanced a look up to the two tentacles overhead, straining towards the fray like overeager watch dogs. Then he dug his hands through the stumps of his flesh suit and hooked the neural cord into the interface's port. Overhead, the tentacles shifted. Silas removed his lumpy head next, freeing up the concordant port on the neck of his radsuit. With one last look back at Cena trying to coax dregs from the gnasher's battery, Silas jammed the neural cord into his neck and closed the circuit.

In. Silas sliced through virtual space, wriggling through the now-active detection system, throwing up a blizzard of nonsense code that masked his passage through the core files. The personality module loomed, hulking, throbbing. Larger and more complex than any freethinker Silas had ever cracked, a writhing mass of electric thought. But he didn't have to crack it. All he had to do was replace it.

Silas pulled Haley's neural imprint from the flagging processor in his radsuit and pushed it across the channel. She streamed into the personality module as a digital flood, seeping into the cracks, coursing through the nodes. Code danced and jittered as it rewrote itself. Silas prayed hard to any god.

"What the fuck are you doing, Silas?"

He realized Io's voice was not coming through his radio at the same instant he recognized the shape of a thumb pressed up to his neck.

"Fixing the freethinker," Silas said, but even as he said it he felt his connection guillotine. He blinked, nerves tingling, back in the real world. Io was standing behind him.

"It's beyond fixing. Said it yourself." Io pulled him away from the interface, making the unhooked neural cord swing. "Dronyk didn't see this coming. It's not our shit to deal with."

Silas realized he couldn't hear Cena cursing. He turned and wished he hadn't. The dead gnasher was lying on the floor, and Cena's limp body was being hoisted up the wall. A thick pale nutrient tube had appeared there, cilia waving in anticipation as the tentacles dragged her upward.

"You may leave now." Anastasia's voice blared through Silas' head. "Your lifeboat is fueled."

Silas' heart stopped. It hadn't worked. The transfer hadn't worked. He'd dashed Haley's ghost against the virtual rocks, or worse, she was trapped in some tiny corner of the freethinker's personality module.

"Come on, Silas," Io said shakily. "We have to get the fuck out of here."

Yorick was silent, ash-white, uglier than Silas had ever seen him. He would get no support there.

"Haley," Silas pleaded. "Haley, can you hear me?"

"We'll upload her to the lifeboat." Io swallowed. "Even with the decay, you'll at least have some of her. Some memories. That's better than nothing."

Silas shook his head, unable to explain. Cena inched up the wall. Her eyes were glazed over.

"Let's go," Io said. "Let's live."

Silas looked away before Cena reached the nutrient tube. He'd killed her, too. He should stay. He should stay and be the next one on the wall. But when Io grabbed him by the arm, he stumbled after her, tears tracking down his cheeks. Tentacles twitched as they passed.

Then, all at once, they went limp.

"Wait," Silas rasped. "Wait. Do you hear that?"

The melody he'd been composing for the past three days trembled in the air, haunting and sweet, growing slowly louder as it looped. Io's eyes widened.

"Silas?"

It wasn't Io who said his name. The synthesized voice wavered through the bridge, unfamiliar and familiar at the same time.

"Haley." Silas' throat constricted. "This isn't how I meant for you to wake up."

There was a dull thump that made him jump. Cena's unconscious form slumped to the floor, released by the tentacles. Silas staggered over to her body and checked for breath on his hand. Io and Yorick were still frozen to the spot, staring around.

"I'm not the only one in here," Haley's voice said. "There are others. A lot of them. Why am I in here, Silas? What happened?"

Silas thought of the nodes of gray matter all through the bioship, all connected, all wired through the *Anastasia*'s freethinker. Make her whole, she'd said. The crew wasn't dead. Not quite.

"You're in a bioship," Silas said. "You're the new freethinker." He paused. "Because you died in cryo."

"Holy shit." A tremor ran through the bioship. "Tell me from the start. All of it."

Silas collected himself. "Alright," he said. "But it's sort of a fucked up story."

When venturing into the past, it's not just the butterflies you've got to watch out for.

Originally appeared in Mike Resnick's Galaxy's Edge

YOU CAN ALWAYS CHANGE THE PAST

★

by George Nikolopoulos

ADRENALINE rushes through my body like a mad sprinter and I still can't believe I did it. He lies face down in the mud, my rifle's bayonet still buried in his neck. I pull it off, absently wiping it on my soldier's uniform trousers. Who would have thought? I, Charles Ecclestone, have killed the monster, succeeding where so many time travelers had failed before.

I try hard to calm down. There's still the First World War going on around me, and here's a young soldier lying on his back, coughing and shivering. I take his hand and help him up.

He's still trembling. "He would have killed me," he says. "Thank you." He hesitates for a moment. "I'd like to know my savior's name."

"I'm Charles," I say. "Charles Ecclestone." *It doesn't matter. You don't know my name. But in your future, everyone will.*

I've made the world a better place. I've killed the greatest villain of all time—Jacques Leroux, the mad mass murderer; saving this nice young man was just an added bonus. I can't wait to go back and read the revised history books.

The soldier extends his hand. "I'm Adolf Hitler," he says, rousing me from my reverie.

I smile and shake his hand. "Nice to meet you, Adolf."

Despite the almost three decades that separate them, Eloise and Estelle Pritchart could have been mistaken for twins, thanks to Prolong. The two may be years apart in age and experience, but they are both willing to do whatever it takes for each other. So, when Estelle is kidnapped, Eloise is determined to get her little sister back . . . no matter the cost.

Originally appeared in Infinite Stars.

OUR SACRED HONOR

★

by David Weber

"**I WISH** you wouldn't read that, Eloise," Estelle Pritchart said. Her striking topaz eyes were more than a little worried as she ran the fingers of her right hand through her long, platinum hair. "If InSec realizes you're reading proscribed material they'll make your life—*our* lives—a living hell."

"Well, they aren't going to find out," her sister Eloise replied, looking up from the old-fashioned, bootleg hardcopy. "That's why things like this get passed around on something as archaic as paper, Stelle." She smiled more than a little crookedly. "InSec's street agents aren't really all that smart, you know. How smart do you *have* to be to break heads? And the people who run their surveillance systems count on their InfoSys backdoors and hacks, not hawkeyed agents reading paper over someone's shoulder. If it's not electronic, it doesn't count as far as they're concerned."

"That's not what you told me the other day," Estelle pointed out. She jabbed an index finger at her sister. "You told me they have audio and visual pickups hidden everywhere!"

"Which provide *electronic* data, not printed," Eloise riposted. "And what I said was that they had them hidden everywhere in public, which they do. That's not the same as saying they sort all that take effectively, or even try to. All those petabytes of audio and video are useful as hell after something *else* points them at a specific subject or group, but I doubt many of their investigations *start* there. Oh, they do catch an occasional activist malcontent by straining the data, but mostly they only pick up on people stupid enough to vent in public."

"And how is it you know that?" Estelle asked.

"Because I am a wise, insightful, perceptive, and observant individual," Eloise told her with a smile. "And I'm also twice your age, so I've been around the block a time or two."

Estelle rolled her eyes, although it was true enough. The two of them could almost have been taken for twins, but in a society with prolong that didn't mean what it might have in an earlier century. In fact, Eloise was almost fifty and Estelle was only twenty-three. There were times when the gap between their ages and their life experiences seemed even greater than the two T-decades which actually separated them, but physically it would have been difficult to estimate which of them was the older.

"You worry me sometimes," Estelle said much more seriously. "InSec and the MHP don't fool around with anybody they even think is a malcontent, and you know it! One of these days you're going to slip up. That's what I'm afraid of. And you're all I've got, Eloise. The only person in the world who I *know* loves me. Can't you just . . . leave well enough alone? If anything happens to you, it'll just kill me!"

"Nothing is going to happen to me." Eloise laid the hardcopy aside and crossed to enfold her sister in a tight hug. "I promised Mom I'd take care of you, and I will. I always have, haven't I?" She squeezed even tighter for a second, then stood back, her hands on her sister's shoulders and shook her gently. "This isn't the safest stuff I could possibly be reading," she conceded, twitching her head in the direction of the hardcopy, "but I'm staying well away from anybody like the Citizens Rights Union or any of the other lunatic, hard-line organizations. Besides, this one isn't even officially proscribed."

"Only because they haven't gotten around to it," Estelle muttered. "I've only taken a couple of peeks at it, and even I know that much! Agitprop, that's what they'd call it, and you know it."

"You're probably right, but it was still there in the library's public files, without any warnings or censorship notices. And I printed it out on one of the library faxes using a general patron ID, so unless they had one of those cameras reading over my shoulder as the pages came out of the hopper, they don't have a clue that I have it."

"But *why* do you read this stuff?" Estelle demanded plaintively. "It's not like it's going to make any difference, and it's all ancient history, anyway. You can't change things any more than I can, and if I can't change them, I'd rather not spend my time wishing I *could.*"

"There's something to that," Eloise admitted after a moment. "But that's Mom's fault, too. She's the one who got me started reading this kind of stuff when I was about half as old as you are now. And I think sometimes that if more people had read it before the old Constitution was scrapped, it wouldn't have been."

Estelle's worried expression tightened at that, and Eloise shrugged.

"I'm not going to stand on any street corners—or even hide in any dark alleys—and tell anyone else anything of the sort, Stelle. I'm older than you are; I'm not *senile*. But it's true. That's another one of the things Mom taught me. I wish you'd had longer to know her."

"I do, too . . . even if you do scare me to death when you start talking about all those things she told you."

Eloise chuckled a bit sadly, but it was true. And, if she was going to be honest, the way their mother had died had quite a bit to do with her own dissatisfaction.

Gabrielle Pritchart had been from Haven's last pre-prolong generation. Oh, if she'd been fortunate enough to have been born into the family of one of the Legislaturalist dynasties or one of their uppercrust allies she could have had prolong, but the rot was already setting in by then. The infrastructure to support first-generation prolong had been expensive, and only the wealthy—or citizens of star nations whose governments had cared enough to invest to subsidize it as a public health service—had been able to afford it. The Legislaturalists hadn't. Of course the costs had come down steeply as the therapies matured and spread, but not quickly enough for Gabrielle's generation. By the time they'd come down to something the Legislaturalists were prepared to bear for the rest of the PRH's citizens (propelled in no small part by increasing unrest from below), Gabrielle had been too old for it. Which was particularly (and bitterly) ironic, given that the daughter she'd borne at only thirty had received the *second*-generation therapies as part of the Basic Living Stipend guarantees. And Estelle, who'd been born when

Gabrielle was fifty-six, had actually received the third-generation treatments.

Still, Gabrielle would have been only in her eighties today, which was scarcely decrepit even for a pre-prolong individual, given modern medicine. Assuming all the benefits of modern medicine had still been available to all of the People's Republic's citizens. They hadn't been, but it didn't really matter, because she'd been only sixty-one, less than thirteen T-years older than Eloise was now, when she'd died. She wasn't one of the people the Legislaturalists' security forces had simply "disappeared," but if the agencies charged with maintaining Nouveau Paris's infrastructure had done their jobs, the high-speed transit tube wouldn't have malfunctioned and driven Gabrielle Pritchart and three hundred and twelve other citizens into the Bichet Tower station's braking buffer at just over one hundred and eighty kilometers per hour.

Four other mass transit accidents in that same calendar year had each produced at least fifty-four casualties, but Bichet had been the worst.

And no one had ever been held responsible for the "unforeseeable technical failures" which had led to all of them.

Estelle had been four T-years old at the time, and in truth, Eloise was the only mother she'd ever known.

But Gabrielle had been the daughter of university professors driven from their posts and hounded onto the BLS they'd despised for daring to speak out against ratifying the Constitution of 1795 PD. They'd made the mistake of believing the decades of steady rot actually might be reversed at the ballot box, and they'd fought passionately for the last remaining vestige of the old Republic. For which, the Legislaturalists had purged them from their positions and insured that they would never be employed again.

Their fate had made their daughter wise, but Gabrielle had inherited their stubborn belief in the value of the individual, as well, and she'd inculcated it in her own older daughter. She'd also been careful to teach Eloise to conceal her own interest in such forbidden topics as the hardcopy on the sadly worn apartment's rickety dinner table. Perhaps if she'd believed, understood, how bad things were truly going to become, she wouldn't have encouraged such risky beliefs, but Eloise didn't think so. Her mother had understood that the human spirit had to be nurtured just as surely as the human body, and as she'd told Eloise more than once, *someone* had to remember.

There were times when Eloise remembered those conversations and condemned herself for not being more . . . proactive in the cause of remembering. But she wasn't her mother, and by the time she'd been old enough to begin paying attention, the last frail edifices of the Republic of Michèle Péricard had toppled. And because they had, she couldn't blame Estelle for her anxiety. That same anxiety was an omnipresent part of her, as well. Nor did Estelle need to remind her that they were all each other had, and what Eloise might have been prepared to risk for herself, she was not prepared to risk for Estelle.

That was something she would never tell her sister. Never even hint to her. Estelle was her hostage to fortune, and Eloise would never—ever—let her suspect that it was fear for her which had prevented Eloise from doing what she might have done otherwise.

"I think Mom would have liked you a lot, Stelle," she said now. "I know I do."

"Gee, thanks," Estelle said dryly, and Eloise chuckled again.

"Hey, you're my sister. Of course I *love* you! But *liking* someone can actually be harder than loving them, you know."

"Did I ever mention that you have some really weird perspectives on life?" Estelle asked.

"From time to time," Eloise admitted.

"Good. I wouldn't want you to think I hadn't noticed."

"Oh, believe me! I don't think anything of the sort."

Estelle laughed, then looked at the time display on the aged but still functional (more or less) smart wall and sighed.

"I'd better be getting to bed," she said. "I'm opening for Jorge in the morning."

"You are?" Eloise couldn't keep an edge of concern out of her tone, and Estelle shrugged.

"Vivienne screened in sick."

"'Sick,'" Eloise repeated, and Estelle shrugged again. Both of them knew "sick" had nothing at all to do with germs or viruses in Vivienne's case.

"I know. I know!" Estelle said. "But we're lucky to have her anyway. And when she's not dusting or patching, she has a really sweet disposition. You know how much the customers like her when she's straight."

"*When* she's straight," Eloise agreed. "Which seems to be getting less and less frequent."

"There's not much we can do about that," Estelle sighed, and Eloise nodded grimly.

More and more of Estelle's contemporaries were completely disengaging from anything even remotely smacking of personal responsibility. Eloise had a better notion than most Dolists of the precarious state of the People's Republic's finances, but the irony was that even Haven's ramshackle industrial sector was incredibly productive by any pre-diaspora standard. The government was ever more strapped to support the BLS and associated programs by which the Legislaturalists had bought the Dolist Managers' connivance in the institutionalization of their own power, yet it was persistently unable to find its citizens the sort of productive employment star nations like the Star Kingdom of Manticore had found for theirs. And a big part of the reason they couldn't, in Eloise's opinion, was because of the huge disincentive the BLS provided. Havenite manufactured goods might be shoddy, and they might be far less durable than comparable goods in other star nations, but they were certainly cheap. Cheap enough that the BLS allowed non-Legislaturalist Havenites to buy plenty of bread and circuses without ever working a day in their lives.

So they didn't.

Eloise couldn't really blame them, much though she wanted to. They were educated—programmed—to be drones, serving no real function other than to provide the reliable voting bloc that routinely shored up the Legislaturalists' supposed legitimacy. That was how a façade democracy worked, and it wasn't surprising that people who realized they contributed nothing more than that to their society weren't exactly the most responsible people when it came to their own lives, either. The desire to contribute, if only to repay, was part of a healthy personality, and so was the desire to build a better life for oneself and one's children. But too many people had realized—or decided—they were never going to rise out of the ranks of the Dolists, however hard they labored. So why should people who didn't *need* to work, and who realized that trying to work was pointless, *desire* to work? Of course a lot of them took the easier path, collected their BLS, cast their votes obediently, binged on cheap entertainment, or drugs, or (increasingly) lives of petty crime and violence, and tried not to think about the other things they might have done with their lives.

All too often, they succeeded in the not-thinking part.

Eloise understood exactly how that worked. She'd *seen* it working around her for almost fifty T-years, and she knew her mother had been right to rail against it. People who lost the belief that what they did *mattered*—or had it taken away from them—tended to develop *un*healthy personalities. And when enough of a society's citizens had unhealthy personalities, it did, too. She'd seen ample proof of *that* around her, as well.

There were still citizens of the People's Republic who'd avoided that deadly cycle. In her darker moments, Eloise suspected their numbers were shrinking daily, but they were still there, and Jorge Blanchard—and Estelle—were cases in point.

Even in Nouveau Paris, there were niches for people willing to work. The problem was that working was unlikely to change anything in their lives. Even Estelle and Blanchard knew that. The upper classes—indeed, even most of what passed for the middle-class—were the private preserve of the Legislaturalists, the Dolist Managers, and their families and cronies. The best anyone else could hope for was something like Blanchard's diner, a friendly little place down near the Duquesne Tower tube station with real, live servers, good food, and clean silverware. Jorge was never going to become wealthy, but he could look back at his life and know he'd made a difference. That he'd *accomplished* something in a world which might have been specifically engineered to prevent people from doing anything of the sort.

Eloise approved of Jorge Blanchard.

But it looked like he was going to lose Vivienne Robillard. Estelle was right; when Vivienne was free of one recreational drug or another, she was exactly the sort of server someone like Jorge's Diner needed. Unfortunately, she was sliding down the same black hole which had claimed all too many of Estelle's age-mates. More to the point, though . . .

"Honey, I don't like you opening the diner by yourself," Eloise said now. "That's a rough neighborhood."

"Rougher than The Terraces?" Estelle demanded, widening her eyes. "Puh-leez, Eloise! Give me a break!"

Eloise's lips twitched ever so slightly, but she also shook her head.

"Granted, The Terraces are no bed of roses. On the other hand, I don't exactly encourage you to go traipsing around *there* by yourself, either."

"No, you don't," Estelle said rather pointedly. Eloise looked at her, and the younger Pritchart grimaced. "I know you think I'm still a baby, but I'm really not, you know. I'm all grown up, and sooner or later you're going to have to trust me to start looking out for myself."

"You're a regular octogenarian, you are!" Eloise retorted.

"Well, I may be younger than you are, but I really have been paying attention. I'm not going to run around by myself someplace like The Terraces or the Eighth Floor."

"No, you damned well aren't," Eloise said firmly. "But"—she raised a forestalling hand before Estelle could react to her authoritative tone—"you're right, you aren't a child anymore. I still don't want you walking around by yourself in the wrong neighborhood, but if pressed, I will concede you've demonstrated a modicum of situational awareness in the past. Still doesn't make me any happier about your opening the diner by yourself, though."

"Richenda and Céline are headed down to the tubes tomorrow morning with me, and Jorge's going to join us at Fifty. And I promise I won't stir a single step home till you get there to ride the shafts with me." Estelle sighed again, theatrically. "There, satisfied?"

"Satisfied," Eloise conceded, although the truth was that she wasn't entirely. Richenda and Céline were levelheaded girls, but they were within four or five years of Estelle's age. She didn't entirely trust their sensitivity to possible threats, but there was a certain safety in numbers, even in Nouveau Paris.

"Then I'll see you in the morning before I leave," Estelle said, hugging her again and kissing her affectionately on the cheek before she headed off to her own bedroom.

Eloise watched her go, then opened the sliding doors and stepped out onto the apartment balcony. That balcony—and their apartment's exterior position and the view that came with it—had cost a *lot* of their joint BLS and quite a bit of sharp trading with the manager of this floor of Duquesne Tower. Eloise's version of Jorge's diner was the clientele she'd built up as a tutor. Her own mother had made sure she was actually *educated*, even if she'd had to do that by schooling her at home, rather than simply warehoused in one of the PRH's so-called schools. Along the way, Gabrielle had impressed Eloise with her responsibility to "pay it forward" in turn, and there were parents even now, even in Nouveau Paris, determined to see that *their* children really learned something. People like Floor Manager Aristide Cardot, who hoped his son might find the Legislaturalist patronage that could lift him higher in his own life.

A tutor's pay wasn't much more than Estelle earned working in the diner, but it was satisfying work, and it provided a handy cover for Eloise's forays into the historical sections of the library and the InfoSys.

You're a fine one to talk about Estelle wandering around alone, she thought now, gazing out over the glorious light tapestry of nighttime Nouveau Paris.

In the darkness, looking at the incredible strings of light that caparisoned the city's mighty towers, watching the glittering fireflies of air cars and air lorries, or looking down, down, down into the mighty canyons to the lighted sidewalks, or looking even higher than the air cars, to where the running lights of cargo or personnel shuttles made their way from orbit to the spaceport, it was almost—*almost*—possible to believe that what that city once had been it might someday be again. But it wasn't going to happen, she admitted sadly, and maybe that was the real reason she hadn't tried harder to inculcate her own love of history into Estelle. Maybe it was better for her sister to never yearn for what had been true so long ago.

It would be better if I didn't, she told herself. *Better if I didn't understand everything we've lost, didn't want it back so much. Maybe then I'd be more content, or something like that. And maybe I wouldn't be so tempted.*

She sighed, bracing both hands on the railing, leaning on it as she looked out into the breezy darkness from her two-hundredth floor vantage point. Some of the other towers were far taller than Duquesne, and Estelle was right about the dangerous quadrants in their own building. Even so, there were moments like this when Eloise just needed to drink in the beauty, the sense—the illusion—of freedom and possibility in the breeze sweeping across the balcony.

"*We hold these truths to be self-evident.*" The words first written over three thousand T-years ago ran through her mind. The words Michèle Péricard had lived by when she drafted the Constitution the

Legislaturalists had ripped to shreds. "*That all men are created equal; that they are endowed by their Creator with inherent and inalienable rights; that among these are life, liberty, and the pursuit of happiness: that to secure these rights governments are instituted among men, deriving their just powers from the consent of the governed . . .* "

She didn't begin to understand all the charges their drafters had leveled against their king. Details got lost in thirty-two centuries, and history as a discipline was . . . discouraged in the People's Republic. For, she thought sourly, reasons which were self-evident. But she understood enough. She understood those words' protest against sham government, against tyranny, and against what amounted to despotism that completely ignored "the consent of the governed."

Estelle was right, the biography of Péricard on her dinner table *would* have been proscribed if Internal Security or the Mental Hygiene Police had realized everything that was buried in it. In fact, the grand declaration from whence those words sprang *had* been proscribed; what passed for the authorities in the People's Republic of Haven simply hadn't worried about what the man who'd written Péricard's definitive biography a century and a half before might have included in its appendices.

A familiar shiver went through her as she looked out over that sea of lights, that *ocean* of lights, and those words went through her. In her own pantheon, no one stood higher than Péricard, the woman whose dream had created the Republic of Haven, the Athens of the Haven Quadrant. Whose dream had been murdered as surely as Hypatia of Alexandria.

She wondered, sometimes, what would have happened if Estelle had never been born. She loved her sister more dearly than life itself, and the thought of a world without Estelle made her shy away like a frightened horse. Yet if Estelle hadn't been born, if she weren't Eloise's "hostage to fortune," what might she have done differently in her life?

A part of her yearned for the answer to that question, although she knew it never *could* be answered, really. Yet there was that part of her, the part that remembered the fierce, proud conclusion of that ancient declaration.

And for the support of this Declaration, they'd written, *with a firm reliance on the protection of divine Providence, we mutually pledge to each other our Lives, our Fortunes and our sacred Honor.*

That was what they'd pledged: everything they had. Everything they held most dear in all the world. And those words spoke to her even now. Spoke to that part of her that secretly admired the Citizens Rights Union. Too many of them were obviously terrorists for terrorism's sake, but not all of them were. And at least they had the courage to stand and fight. *That* was what that secret part of her admired, even envied. Maybe some of them didn't really understand what they were fighting for, and maybe some of them were fighting only for vengeance upon a system which had failed them, but at least they were *fighting*.

And at least they have clarity, she thought. *I suspect most of them have a pretty severe case of myopia, but what they* do *see, they see clearly enough to be willing to pay cash for it. And maybe if there were a few people in something like the CRU who weren't myopic, a few people who remembered what they stood for, who could remind the* rest *of them . . .*

She drew a deep breath, and those words flowed through her one last time. *Our lives, our fortunes and our sacred honor.* Maybe the men who'd written them down would have understood the CRU—and remembered Péricard and *her* constitution—whatever the cost. *Whoever* the cost. And if *they* could have . . .

She stepped on that dangerous thought firmly, drew a deep breath, then turned and went back inside and closed the doors behind her.

"You really should think about upgrading, Eloise," Kevin Usher said. "You need more standoff capability."

"What I *don't* need is any attention from InSec or the cops," Eloise replied, standing back and wiping her forehead. Then she reached behind her head, holding the hair tie with her left hand while her right tugged on her sweat-damp ponytail to tighten the tie. "They don't take too kindly to Dolists 'packing heat,' Kevin!"

InSec, MHP, Urban Authority, and just about every single one of the People's Republic police forces—of which there were no-one-really-knew how many, at the end of the day—took dim views of weapons in general, but they saved their special attention for firearms. Probably because firearms—even old-fashioned chemical-powered ones—posed a much greater threat to what passed for the champions of law and order in the PRH than a simple club or even a vibro blade.

"I'm not talking about sticking a tribarrel in your hip pocket, for

God's sake," Usher said in a disgusted tone. Then his expression softened as he waved both big, powerful hands at the workout room around them. "You're good with your hands, Eloise, and you're one of the few people I know who keep right on getting better. But the best rule of all for hand-to-hand is to keep the other bastard from ever getting his hands on you in the first place. One of the first things the Marines teach you is that the only time you use your hands is when you don't have a gun or a knife and both feet are nailed to the floor."

Eloise chuckled, although she knew he was perfectly serious. And she trusted his judgment, too. She and Kevin had known one another for over five T-years, ever since he'd opened his dojo on Duquesne Tower's Floor Hundred Ten. It was a ninety-floor commute for her, but it was located in the same quadrant on Hundred Ten as the Pritcharts' apartment on Two Hundred, so it was only about a fifteen-minute walk from the nearest lift shaft trunk. And Kevin, an ex-Marine, had come highly recommended by one of her students' older sister.

Over the last half-decade, Eloise had recommended him to quite a few of her other acquaintances, as well. Not all of them. Kevin was just as good as the original recommendation had suggested. In fact, he was probably even better. He was less concerned about specific "schools" or pure forms than he was with what worked. He referred to his personal style as "street brawler steroids," and it damned well did work. And from Eloise's perspective, what made him especially good was that he understood that each student's style had to work for her, he suited his teaching to the size and strength of his student, and he obviously liked women . . . and kept those big, strong, highly skilled hands of his utterly impersonal when he worked with one of them.

The reason she hadn't recommended him to all of her acquaintances was that she strongly suspected—no, "suspect" was too weak a word, she admitted—that he was associated with the Citizens' Rights Union. He was about the farthest thing she could imagine from a fanatic, which sometimes made her wonder how he could support all of the CRU's actions. Blowing up Legislaturalists in their offices or Internal Security posts, or ambushing a squad of Mental Hygiene Police on a public slidewalk, was one thing. Eloise actually found herself tempted sometimes to stand up and cheer when something like that happened. But the pure terror attacks, like the one on a private school whose sole offense had been that it was patronized primarily by Legislaturalist families . . . those were something else. The official reports in the 'faxes said the bomb had killed three children and injured six, but rumors floating around the InfoSys said the casualties had been at least three times that much, and probably even higher.

Personally, Eloise didn't care whether the true number was three dead, or nine, or nine*teen*. They were *kids*, just like *her* students. So they were the kids of Legislaturalists, of the people responsible for the absence of opportunities available to *her* kids. So what? They hadn't chosen their parents, and the thought of someone killing kids— *anybody's* kids—just to make a political statement turned her stomach. So how did Kevin justify an association with people like that?

But that was between him and his own conscience. She didn't know what might have driven him into the CRU in the first place, and she wasn't going to condemn him for it. No, the reason she hadn't sent some of her friends to him for training was that she refused to put them into contact with a potential CRU recruiter. *Those* friends were bitter enough they were probably *looking* for someone who could recruit them, and Eloise wouldn't be the person who found them that someone.

Even if he had become one of her closest personal friends.

And even if she did sometimes wish . . .

"Kevin, I don't want to start right out killing somebody if that isn't what it takes," she countered now. It was a familiar argument.

"Two thirds of the time, all you'll have to do is show fight," came the equally familiar response. "The kind of scum who'd pick on a single woman tend to back off quick when that happens. But sometimes it comes down to kill or be killed, with no other option. I don't like that any more than you do, but it's still true. And it's also true that the more lethal the fight you're ready to show, the quicker somebody who *might* back off goes ahead and finds reverse. And let's be honest, Eloise, you're not a big woman. You don't have the physical size to intimidate the ones who might not be as fast to take the hint. Especially not if they equate 'threat' with 'weapon,' not training and attitude. You know—the really, really terminally stupid ones like Cal?"

"Kevin, you're terrible!" Eloise laughed. "Cal's been perfectly nice to me since I broke his finger."

"And he never would've jabbed it in your face that way if he wasn't twenty centimeters taller than you and really, really terminally stupid," Kevin retorted. "And, yeah, I know he was drunk and you'd just turned him down for the evening. But that's part of my point, Eloise. Someday you may run into someone else—someone with something in mind a hell of a lot worse than Cal could ever think of—who's too dusted, or glittered, or hazed, or just plain drunk to think about what a trained person your size could do to them." He shook his head. "And then there's the minor fact that you're one of the best-looking women I know. Hell, that I've *ever* known!" He shook his head again, his expression sober. "You draw the eye, and not just because of your coloring. That's why Cal hit on you in the first place. He was only getting a little . . . too happy, maybe, but your looks make you more of a target for predators than most, and you know it."

"Of course I do," she replied, and her tone was as sober as his expression. "I'm not going to hide who I am, though. And I won't let that kind of 'predator' dictate the way I live my life, either!"

"Shouldn't have to," he growled. "And I wish to hell you didn't have to worry about it. If the frigging police would just do their jobs—or if just *one* of our beloved city or provincial administrators would *make* them do their jobs—you might not have to, and I'd be out of work. But they don't, they won't, and I like you too damned much to let you become one more example of why the hell they should!"

Eloise blinked at the genuine anger, the rage, simmering just under the surface of that last sentence. His brown eyes were dark, burning with an inner fury, and a small, still corner of her understood in that moment just how terrifying Kevin Usher could truly be. She wondered who he'd "liked too much" and who'd become "one more example"? Perhaps that was why he could be part of the CRU despite its too-frequent excesses.

"And in support of my theory," he went on after a heartbeat, his tone much lighter as if he'd deliberately stepped back from the abyss of anger, "I should point out that even at his drunkest, Cal's never gotten all touchy-feely with *me*!"

"The mind boggles," Eloise protested. "Not only that, but the stomach turns!" She raised both hands in a pushing away gesture and shuddered theatrically at the image that conjured up. "I can't say for certain, but I'm *pretty* sure Cal's about as hetero as they come, Kevin. And let's be fair here. You're not exactly the best example of eye candy

he could find. You're what I believe the bad novelists call, um . . .
rugged looking."

"Gee, thanks." He grimaced. "'Beat-up,' don't you mean?"

"Of course, but I like you far too much to ever actually *say* it," she
assured him earnestly.

"You're so kind to me," he said. "But my *point*, as you understood
perfectly well, is that unlike you, I'm ten centimeters taller than *he* is.
The one thing even I can't teach you is height, and the sad truth is that
just like physical size is often a deterrent all by itself, its *absence* is like
blood in the water for some people."

She nodded more seriously. In fact, Kevin was understating their
size differential. She stood barely a hundred and sixty centimeters and
tipped the scale at a scant fifty-five kilos. Kevin, on the other hand,
was almost a hundred and ninety-four centimeters tall and weighed
well over twice as much as she, all of it bone and muscle. His biceps
were as thick as her thighs and his shoulders were more than twice as
broad as hers. Coupled with his scarred knuckles and the sort of
"rugged" face that resulted from frequent applications of someone
else's knuckles when he'd been growing up, he radiated the sort of
elemental fearsomeness that could make *anyone* back down. In fact, he
looked like the sort of fellow who routinely tore chance-met strangers
into tiny pieces for stepping on his toe. Which he wasn't. In fact, she
suspected that very few people even imagined how thoroughly at odds
with the inward man that outward appearance truly was.

Except for the toughness of course. And not that she doubted for a
moment that Kevin Usher could become anyone's worst nightmare if
he chose to.

He just *wouldn't* choose to without a very good reason.

She thought.

"I hear what you're saying," she told him now. "But I try to see
trouble before it sees me. It's a lot easier to avoid when you do. And—
like I say, Kev—I don't want to start out in a lethal-force confrontation
if I don't have to. That's why I carry the baton."

"And very useful it is," he conceded.

Eloise favored a standard, length-configurable police baton with
enhanced inertia-loading. It collapsed to fifteen centimeters but could
be extended to ninety in fifteen-centimeter increments, and its
deactivated length was small enough to fit the cloth scabbard Dorothée

Tremont, one of her student's parents, sewed into the left thigh of every pair of pants she bought. Dorothée removed the liner of her left hip pocket at the same time, so that she could access the baton instantly . . . and she practiced regularly to do just that. She hadn't needed Kevin to tell her speed of response was the first and most important single element of self-defense. Used properly, that baton was highly effective—as the police had demonstrated often enough by breaking heads with batons just like it—and she'd carried it since she was a girl. In fact, she'd given Estelle one just like it for her eleventh birthday.

"The only problem I have with it," Kevin continued, "is that people don't think of it as a *lethal* weapon. Some of them, especially if there's more than one—and you know what kind of gangers roam some of Duquesne's floors—may figure they can take the damage, or—better yet, that one of their *buddies* can take the damage—until they get it away from you. If they're right, I guarantee you they'll end up using it on *you* just as a setting up exercise. Even if they're *wrong*, you could get hurt bad demonstrating that to them. And I don't want you getting hurt at all."

"So what would you recommend instead?" she half-sighed. "I know I'm not going to shut you up until you tell me."

"Nope," he agreed with a toothy, much more cheerful grin. "And, since you've been so kind—and so prudent—as to ask, here's what I had in mind."

He reached into his trouser pocket and produced a twelve-centimeter cylinder, about four centimeters in diameter, and Eloise's eyes darkened as she recognized the vibro blade hilt.

"I don't know, Kev . . . " she began.

"Hear me out, first," he said, holding it up.

She looked at him for a moment, then nodded, and he pressed the activation button. The "blade" itself was invisible, of course. In fact, it wasn't even generated until the user pressed the contoured button in the grip and brought it fully online. But the high-pitched, unmistakable whine all such blades were legally required to emit whenever activated was even louder than most. The three-centimeter pop-out quillons deployed the instant the blade came live, preventing the user's own hand from accidentally amputating itself by slipping down into the cutting plane. The blade was supposed to make that impossible by shutting down the instant the user's grip on the activation button loosened, but that didn't always happen the way it was supposed to.

"This is a Martinez Industries Model 7," he told her. "Out-of-the-box, it's configurable to fifteen or thirty centimeters, and it's officially rated as a Class Three weapon, which makes it carry-legal. More importantly, the instant somebody hears it, they know you're carrying something a lot more dangerous than just a baton. And no one but an idiot's going to grab *this* puppy to disarm you!"

"I imagine not," she said, staring at it. "And what did you mean about out-of-the-box?"

"I mean I've . . . tinkered with it a bit," he said. "Trick a Marine armorer taught me. You can boost its max length all the way to *ninety* centimeters for about twenty-five minutes. Burns out completely after that but it kicks ass while it lasts, and most people won't expect the extra length. Won't *see* it, either, unless they have a really close encounter with it. Makes a hell of a close-quarters weapon, Eloise."

"I'm sure it would," she said in a faintly appalled tone. "I wouldn't know how to go about using it, though."

"Oh, bullshit!" Kevin deactivated the blade and tossed the hilt to her. "You and I spar with that baton of yours for fifteen minutes every time you come over here. This thing's weight is almost identical to the baton's—one reason I picked it for you—and I've worked you with both hands for over four years now. You're trying to tell me you don't think you could swing this sucker *effectively*?"

"Well . . . "

"What I thought," he grunted as she turned the hilt in both hands, staring down at it. "Now, you listen to me for a minute, Eloise. I'm not saying you have to start right out in slice-and-dice mode. To be honest, I wouldn't be suggesting this to you if I figured there was any chance in hell that'd be your default setting! But the fact that you're a southpaw's going to surprise eighty, ninety percent of the people you might run into just to start with, and after four years with me, you're frigging well ambidextrous with that baton.

"So, the way I see it, let's say you do get into a confrontation you can't avoid. I know you, and you're not going to be the instigator, but it could still happen. So say it does. Now what do you do? Baton in left hand, extended and ready for business. If they back off, well and good. They don't back off, maybe the baton's all you need, in which case that's all you use. But in the meantime, the right hand's filled with that thing," he pointed at the vibro hilt in her hands, "and if you need it, it comes up ready for business in a heartbeat. Two or three of them, maybe you bring it up sooner, let 'em hear it sing while they . . . rethink their position. But, trust me, *two* arguments in favor of rethinking are a hell of a lot better than one."

"I'm really getting worried about The Terraces and the Eighth Floor, Aristide," Eloise said quietly, later that month, as Alphonse Cardot closed his tablet and headed for his room. "And I don't like what I heard about that incident down on Hundred and Ten last night."

"I don't either," Floor Manager Aristide Cardot replied. His expression was grim, and Eloise knew he wouldn't have admitted anything of the sort to just anyone.

As the manager of Two Hundred, Aristide was effectively the mayor of a city of close to ten thousand. Over a million people lived in Duquesne Tower's hundred and thirty residential floors. The other seventy-five floors were taken up with engineering offices and equipment, power systems, water and waste disposal systems, and commercial space, including three major fabrication facilities, at least eighty shopping malls—eleven of them sprawling over at least a hundred square meters of floor space—and thousands of cubic meters housing the ever expanding sprawl of the PRH's innumerable bureaucratic entities.

Aristide was an essential cog in that enormous mechanism, but he was *only* a cog. All he could do was the best he could do, and Eloise felt remarkably secure on the Two Hundred. There wasn't much he could do about the services which depended upon outside sources, and interruptions in power and plumbing—even ventilation, occasionally—had become increasingly frequent, despite his best efforts. But both he and Commissioner Cesar Juneau, who commanded the Floor Two Hundred Police, took their responsibilities seriously. When services went down, Aristide moved heaven and earth to get them back up again. And if Juneau's patrolmen and patrolwomen expected occasional "gifts" from the tenants—and weren't above a little discreet shakedown if those gifts weren't forthcoming—they were nowhere near so blatant about selling "protection" as the force on Eighth Floor. And they took their public safety duties seriously. They had a remarkably short way with the sort of youth gangs who terrorized Eighth and The Terraces. And they weren't especially shy about delivering summary punishment tailored to fit the crime rather than relying on the overburdened and apathetic courts, either.

It was unfortunate that the attitude of the Eighth Floor force seemed to be spreading upward, but it had a long way to go before it hit Two Hundred.

"I guess what I hate most about it is that we have to go past the other floors to get home," she said. "Once I get above One Hundred I start relaxing, but those lower floors, especially Fifty and Eight . . . " She shook her head. "Every time I get into the lift car below Hundred, I worry about who I may end up sharing it with."

"Cesar and I are trying to keep an eye on it," Aristide told her, "but there's only so much we can do from up here. Rembert down on Hundred is trying to work with us on it, too, and we're trying to beef up the Lift Shaft Police patrols. But those are trans-floor. We don't have jurisdiction, once we get past the lift car door. Even if we did, every floor manager and commissioner's way too strapped for manpower to do anything like that, even if we pooled our resources. And I hate to say it, but the Duquesne LSP's in even worse shape than *we* are. We've requested more shaft cops and better monitoring systems for the lifts from the Department of Public Safety, too, of course." He rolled his eyes—something else he wouldn't have done with just anyone—and puffed his cheeks. "I've been assured we'll receive them as soon as possible. It's all a matter of priorities, they say."

And Duquesne Tower's priority is somewhere south of zero, Eloise filled in mentally.

"Well, at least I've got my 'little friend' with me," she said out loud, and Aristide waved both hands in an averting gesture.

"Don't talk to me about that!" he scolded with a smile. "I'm not supposed to know about it, and I'm just as happy that way."

"Oh, of course," Eloise agreed with a smile. "I can't imagine what I was thinking to bring up a subject like that! I apologize."

"And well you should," he admonished her. "However, speaking hypothetically, if I knew what you were talking about—which I don't, of course—I'd probably approve wholeheartedly."

"Yes, I think you probably would." She smiled again, thinking it was just as well for his peace of mind that he didn't know about Kevin's recent gift, and patted him on the arm. "And on that note, it's time I was going. I need to get groundside before Estelle starts home."

"Be well," Aristide said, escorting her to his apartment's door, and she nodded. *Be careful*, was what he really meant, but it probably would have been impolitic to point that out.

Eloise rode the lift downward and muttered balefully as she checked her chrono. She *hated* leaving Estelle waiting for her at the diner, and she'd allowed plenty of time for the trip . . . she'd thought. But that was before the delay on Hundred-Fifty. She didn't know what had caused the holdup—not officially—but she suspected she wouldn't have liked the answer if she'd known it. The regular uniformed Shaft Police keeping the lifts shut down hadn't been answering any questions. In fact, they hadn't been saying *anything*, and that usually indicated that one of the federal police agencies—usually InSec or Mental Hygiene—was involved. Which, in turn, meant that some hapless "malcontent" or "anti-social provocateur" was being dragged from her apartment.

It was bad enough to be running late, but the suspicion that government thugs were hauling yet another citizen off, probably to disappear forever, had put her in a truly foul mood. At least whoever it was, she—or they; there was no reason there couldn't be more of them, and InSec, especially, preferred to arrest entire families "just in case"—wasn't one of the Pritcharts' neighbors. The raid was taking someplace between One-Fifty and One Hundred, judging from where the lifts were shut down, which meant it almost certainly wasn't someone Eloise knew personally.

And wasn't it a hell of a note when that was the closest thing to a bright side she could find?

She checked the time again as her current lift car slid to a halt. Unlike many of Nouveau Paris's newer towers, Duquesne used zonal "half-century" lifts, with dedicated shafts serving each fifty floors. Passengers had to change lifts at each boundary, but the system precluded the kind of wait times to which even a high-speed lift was subject if it served a tower's full three or four hundred—or, for that matter, *five* hundred, in the newer towers—floors. The problem was potentially even worse in those taller, newer towers, but most of them had been built with smart shafts, with multiple lift cars and bypass shunting sections. Each smart shaft could handle up to a dozen cars simultaneously, with the computers keeping track of them and moving them out of one another's way when necessary. It would have been nice if Duquesne had boasted the same technology, but it hadn't been available when the older tower was built. And, predictably, none of the bureaus and agencies theoretically responsible for maintaining and updating Duquesne had any interest in investing the funds to make it available here.

She'd already changed lifts twice since leaving the Cardot apartment, including the sixty-eight-minute delay on One-Fifty, and she'd have to change twice more before she reached ground level. Most of the trip didn't bother her, but the next change was on Floor Fifty, and that was something else. That was where The Terraces, with almost 200,000 square meters of floor space, had once been one of Duquesne Tower's crown jewels. Located at the transfer point of two of the residential floors' main banks of dedicated lift shafts, it had served almost 800,000 people. That had been a sufficient volume of customers to make it a highly profitable location even in the People's Republic of Haven.

Until fifteen or twenty T-years ago, at least.

Eloise could remember childhood trips to The Terraces. Trips when her mother had been laughing and happy, when they'd shared ice cream cones while they dabbled their feet in one of the fountains. When there'd been shopkeepers and clerks who'd actually looked customers in the eye, smiled, greeted them courteously, sometimes even known them by name.

But then, probably inevitably, the endemic corruption had changed that. First the floor police force had begun charging higher and higher prices for "protection," and the independents had found themselves being forced out. As they'd begun going under, cronies of the local Dolist manager and fronts for his Legislaturalist friends had made them fire-sale offers for their shops. One by one, they'd vanished, merged into far larger stores which relied upon the fact that they had a captive market rather than the quality of the service and the goods they offered. The taxes—although, of course, they were officially only "service and handling charges"—on goods ordered from somewhere outside Duquesne meant that only the tower's wealthier residents could avoid The Terraces or one of the other smaller, less conveniently located, and more poorly stocked malls. And, of course, there were very few wealthy residents in Duquesne. People that adjective described could always find better places to live.

And so The Terraces had deteriorated, slowly at first, but with gathering momentum, into someplace shoppers avoided after hours and where prudent people—especially women and girls—never ventured alone, regardless of the time of day. A place where gangs—both youth gangs and those not so young—routinely robbed and beat customers, more often for fun than for profit, as far as Eloise could tell.

She and Estelle could have avoided The Terraces by using the Beta Bank of lifts, but that would have cost them a full hour of extra transit time between shafts . . . and that was if the slidewalks were up and running, which they often weren't. Still, if things got much worse at Fifty, they'd just have to bite the bullet and change their route, and wouldn't that suck?

And at that, she thought now, as the lift car stopped, *it's still better than the situation on Eighth. The only good thing about Eighth is that we go right past it, so unless somebody gets on as we go by . . .*

She stood with one hand in her left hip pocket and the other in the right jacket pocket as the lift car slid to a halt. There were six men and seven other women in the car with her, and perhaps two or three dozen people from other floors were changing shafts when the doors opened. She saw no sign of any of the competing gangs' colors, which made a nice change, but she didn't take her hands out of her pockets. At least one of the other women in her car had a hand in *her* pocket, too, Eloise noted, and wondered what sort of "little friend" the other might be carrying.

She moved smoothly, confidently across to the next bank of lifts, her eyes sweeping the concourse steadily and alertly. The best way to avoid trouble, as she'd pointed out to Kevin, was to see it before it saw her, and though her expression never so much as flickered, she drew a breath of relief as she made it to the appropriate shaft, stepped into the car, and started it downward once more.

Now all I have to do is get past Eighth, she told herself. *Piece of cake.*

Eloise's eyes widened in shock as she stepped off the slidewalk outside the tube station in Subbasement One and saw the cordon of yellow holo flashers around Jorge's Diner. The diner's windows were smashed, its doors were jammed in the open position, drunkenly crooked on their tracks, and a uniformed floor cop in full riot gear stood in front of the door.

His eyes flitted to Eloise as she left the slidewalk and his right hand moved to the pulser holstered at his hip, but he didn't draw the weapon. The armorplast visor of his helmet was up, and he watched her with neither the interest she saw in most men's eyes nor the boredom or hostility she saw in too many cops' eyes.

"Help you, Citizen?" he asked gruffly as she came to a halt.

"My . . . my sister works here," she said. "I walk her home at the end of every shift. What . . . what happened?"

"Can't rightly say," he told her, taking his hand from his pulser, and she heard a note of sympathy in his voice. "We caught the call about an hour ago, I guess. Passer-by said there was some kind of riot going on. By the time we got here, the place was trashed. Found a guy we think is the owner from his ID back in the kitchen. He didn't look good, but medevac got here faster than usual, and I'm pretty sure he'll make it. He's in the clinic over off Broad and Vine. Know where it is?"

"Yeah," she said even as ice flowed through her veins. "It's four or five blocks from here. You say you found Jorge—I mean the owner?"

"Yep," the floor cop said, and her muscles tightened as his tone answered the question she'd been going to ask next. But she went ahead anyway, almost as if her vocal cords belonged to someone else.

"And my sister?"

"Nobody here but him. I'm sorry," the cop told her compassionately.

"And you don't have *any* idea what happened?" she asked desperately.

"Not any more than the original call," he said, "but I noticed that." He pointed, and her eyes followed the gesture to a shattered camera. "I happen to know that camera and the two between here and the Alpha Bank were up and running when I went on duty this morning. They aren't now. And there's new gang graffiti on the wall under the camera right outside the lifts. *That* wasn't there this morning, either."

"Did you recognize which gang's?" she heard herself ask.

"Not one of ours. Looks like the Hellhounds. They're from up—"

"Up on Fifty," she finished for him, her voice as grim as her topaz eyes. "The Terraces."

"That's what our gang warfare unit tells me, anyway," the cop agreed. "We didn't know there was any staff here besides the owner, so we didn't put out an AFB on her. I can do that now, if you'll give me a description."

"She looks like me," Eloise said bleakly. "She looks *exactly* like me."

Something flickered deep in the cop's eyes, and she remembered her discussion with Kevin.

"I'll put it on the full tower net," he promised her, reaching for the button of his com.

"Thank you," she said, but she knew as well as he did that an All-Floors Bulletin wouldn't do a damned bit of good if it had been the Hellhounds. No one on Fifty was going to risk her life by telling anybody anything about the Hellhounds. And even if someone had been willing to, the Fifty Floor Police would never go after a gang that powerful over something as trivial as a single missing young Dolist woman no one could *prove* was even anywhere in their hypothetical jurisdiction.

"All floors, be on the lookout—"

The cop broke off as Eloise turned toward the outbound slidewalk.

"Where you going?" he asked sharply, and she paused to look back at him.

"To find my sister." Her voice was flat, unyielding as steel. For a moment, she thought he might try to stop her. But then his lips thinned and he shook his head instead, his eyes dark.

"You be careful up there," he told her quietly. "You be *real* careful up there. Won't do your sister any good if you get yourself killed."

At least he hadn't said "get yourself killed, *too*," she reflected. Maybe he was an optimist.

"Oh, I'll be careful," she told him softly. "Thanks."

He nodded again as she turned once more for the slidewalk. Behind her, she heard him speaking into his com once more.

Not that it was going to do any good.

She got off the lift at Fifty.

The handful of other passengers with whom she'd shared the car flowed around her as she stood motionless in the middle of the lift concourse. She didn't know any of them. She hadn't spoken to any of them as they rode up with her, and none of them had tried to speak to her. She didn't know what they'd seen in her eyes, but a couple had looked at her oddly, even warily. Now they all moved away from her more rapidly than usual, even for people changing lifts on Fifty.

She realized she didn't have the least idea what to do, how to begin. The thought of going to the floor cops didn't even occur to her, but what could one woman possibly hope to accomplish? It was insane, and she knew it, but that didn't matter. All she could think of was Estelle, and she made herself draw a deep breath, turned, and strode into The Terraces.

She took a hair tie from her pocket as she walked, reached back, and gathered her long, gleaming hair into the ponytail she wore during her workouts with Kevin. Then she drew her baton, holding it reversed against the inside of her left forearm, instantly ready yet effectively invisible. That, too, was something she practiced regularly, but the familiar weight, the familiar pressure against her forearm, was less reassuring today.

Kevin had often remarked on her "situational awareness," and he'd helped her devise exercises and contests to keep it honed. Now her eyes swept back and forth and her hearing seemed preternaturally sharp. Even the pores of her skin seemed to vibrate like tiny sensors, and her mind was a hollow, singing stillness. She didn't even think, not really. She just walked into the refuse-strewn wasteland which was all that remained of the vast, thriving mall her childhood memories recalled.

There were people about, even here. Most were dressed even more flashily—and cheaply—than the Dolist norm, and many of them wore colored scarfs which identified the floor gang to whom they paid protection. Whether or not to wear them, and when, was always a judgment call, that icy hollowness at her core reflected. When the gang front was fairly quiet, rivals tended to leave one another's "clients" in peace, lest they provoke retaliation against their own. When gangs went to war—which happened depressingly often—the scarves only served to better identify targets of opportunity.

Eloise and Estelle had always eschewed the bright colors and cheap costume jewelry the majority of Dolists favored. Now, a bubble seemed to form about her as she passed through that gaudier sea of color in her dark trousers, dark-blue jacket and long-sleeved white blouse, its tailored severity relieved only by touches of embroidery at collar and cuffs. The Terrace's denizens had the wary, well-honed instincts of any prey animal. They recognized the intruder and probably wondered what insanity had brought a single woman here all by herself.

She walked on, deeper into the dilapidated mall, and the bubble moved with her. Five minutes she walked. Ten.

"Honey," a voice said quietly. She turned her head and saw an older woman—or one who'd lived the sort of life that aged someone, at any rate. "Honey, was I you, I'd go home," the other woman said. She glanced around nervously. "Woman looks like you, doesn't come from around here, doesn't wear one of these," she touched the red-, black-, and yellow-checked ganger scarf around her own neck, "she doesn't make out well. Go home."

"I'm looking for someone," Eloise replied, her voice calm. Then the colors of that scarf registered. "Maybe you could tell me where to find her."

"I don't know nothing about any off-floor people," the other woman said more sharply. She started to step back, but Eloise's right hand fastened on her forearm. The woman's eyes widened at the power of that grip. She tried to jerk free, but she couldn't.

"I'm looking for the Hellhounds," Eloise said, twitching her head at that telltale scarf. "Where could I find them?"

"You're crazy," the woman whispered, shaking her head violently. "You're gonna get yourself killed!"

"Maybe," Eloise conceded emptily. "Where can I find them?"

The woman stared at her for perhaps ten seconds, licking her lips nervously. Then she drew a deep breath.

"Down that way." She twitched her head. "Hankies—it's a bar, belongs to the Hounds. Usually some of 'em hanging out there. But you don't want no part of those people! Trust me—you *don't*."

"As a matter of fact, I do," Eloise told her, and released her grip.

She started in the indicated direction. Her informant stared after her, then shook her head and moved rapidly in opposite way.

Hankies was exactly the sort of bar Eloise usually avoided like the plague.

The flashing holo sign above the door showed a naked, improbably endowed woman holding a single strategically placed lacy handkerchief. It was as tasteless as it was flashy, and it needed maintenance. So did the rest of the bar, for that matter. Two thirds of the windowed wall looking out over the mall's promenade were sparkling clean; the center third was streaked and dirty. Clearly someone had replaced the original self-cleaning smart crystoplast with a cheaper substitute, and that central third was littered with the graffiti which wouldn't cling to the surviving self-cleaning panels.

The fire-breathing dog's head of the Hellhounds was prominent among them.

Her stride never paused. The doors slid open, a little haltingly, before her and admitted her to a dim, dark cave that smelled of stale beer, spilled drinks, and at least half a dozen of the more popular smoked and inhaled recreational drugs, all with a faint but unmistakable garnish of urine.

Somewhat to her surprise, it was deserted when she walked in. There wasn't even a bartender behind the streaked and grimy bar or keeping an eye on the self-service dispensers along one wall.

She started to turn on her heel, but she changed her mind. Instead, she crossed to a corner table, choosing one that would let her sit with solid walls on two sides, and pulled out a chair. She couldn't see the chair seat clearly in the poor lighting, which was probably a good thing, judging by the condition of the tabletop and the floor.

She sat, laying the baton in her lap, and leaned the back of her skull against the wall. Under her brain's icy calm a voice she recognized screamed that she had to be up, had to be out, had to be *looking* for Estelle. But that cold stillness knew better. Racing around, hunting blindly, would achieve nothing. She needed to know *where* to hunt.

Minutes trickled past while she sat there, forcing herself not to think. To simply *be* there, waiting. And then the doors opened again and a tallish, dark-haired young man in an especially gaudy, tasteless red, black, and yellow jacket sauntered arrogantly through them.

The newcomer glanced around casually, but he didn't notice Eloise as she sat motionless at her corner table. Instead, he crossed to the bar and leaned over it, looking both directions. Then he snorted harshly and smacked his palm on a glowing square set into the top of the bar. A bell clanged discordantly.

"Marcel!" he bellowed. "Damn it, Marcel! You're supposed to be watching the frigging bar!"

"Yeah, yeah, yeah," a much whinier voice replied from somewhere in the back. "Keep your shirt on, Hilaire! I was in the can. Only gone a minute!"

"The hell you were," Hilaire retorted. "In there watching porn again, you mean!"

"Well, what if I was?" Marcel demanded with defensive anger. "It's your shift, and you're a good five minutes late! Wouldn't have had to leave the bar to take a dump if *you'd* been here on time."

"I *wasn't* late—which you'd know if you'd been where the hell you were supposed to be when I walked in the door. I don't give a damn who your brother is, Marcel. Not anymore. You've been warned about this kind of crap a dozen times! Now you get your sorry ass over to Bernadette Street and you tell Gaspar why you weren't on the bar when I came in."

"Gaspar?" The self-righteous anger had vanished from Marcel's tone, replaced by something much more like panic.

"Yeah, Gaspar. And I'm gonna screen him to tell him you're coming," Hilaire said, thumping Marcel's suddenly deflated chest with an index finger. "So was I you, I wouldn't waste any frigging time getting there. He's gonna have enough to say to you without adding that to it—understood?"

"Under . . . understood," Marcel muttered.

He stood irresolute a moment longer, then headed for the door, his dejected shamble the antithesis of Hilaire's arrogant saunter.

Hilaire watched him go with a satisfied air before he started around behind the bar. Then he paused in mid-stride as he caught sight of Eloise from the corner of one eye and changed course toward her.

Eloise watched him come and wondered what to say. She was a tutor, not a cop or a trained interrogator. She wasn't even an ex-Marine like Kevin! What did *she* know about—?

The question broke off as something glittered in the bar's dank dimness, and her breathing seemed to stop. The rearing silver unicorn wasn't huge—barely four centimeters from the tip of its tiny spiral horn to its rear hoofs, and it hung from a leather thong, not the delicate silver chain which had supported it the last time she saw it—but she recognized it instantly. It had once belonged to her mother, and to her mother's mother, and to *her* . . . before she gave it to Estelle on her sixth birthday.

It was Estelle's only true treasure, worn under her clothing to avoid the acquisitive eyes of the thieves who were all too common in Duquesne Tower.

She straightened in her chair, and Hilaire stopped suddenly, his eyes widening as if in surprised recognition when he got a good look at her for the first time. He stood for a moment, then shook his head and continued until he reached the table behind which she sat.

"Help you, cutie?" he drawled.

"I think you can." Eloise was astounded by her own calm, conversational tone. "I'm looking for someone."

Her grip shifted slightly on the baton in her lap, her thumb resting lightly, almost hungrily, on the extender button.

"Now, who might that be?" Hilaire asked mockingly, left hand reaching deliberately to toy with the unicorn and be certain she'd seen it.

"I think you know who," Eloise said softly, and her knee slammed into the underside of the small, cheap plastic table.

Eloise was not an enormous woman, but she was an extraordinarily *fit* one and the table was light. Kevin Usher would have been proud of the way her knee hit it, and it rocketed upward. It was far too light to actually hurt or even inconvenience Hilaire in any way, of course, but he leapt at least a meter straight backward, away from the sheer, unexpected violence of its movement.

And as he leapt, Eloise Pritchart came to her feet.

Her thumb tapped the button three times, the baton flicked out to sixty centimeters, and she lashed it across his left kneecap like a whip. The enhanced inertia-loading at its tip boosted the impact energy by a factor of almost two and the sharp "*Crack!*" of contact disappeared into Hilaire's scream as the kneecap shattered like glass. He tumbled backward, hands reaching instinctively for the source of his agony, and as he hunched forward, the baton struck again, rising to slash vertically downward. It slammed directly into his left shoulder joint with vicious, premeditated precision, fracturing both the scapula and the head of his humerus, and this time his scream was a shriek.

He hit the floor, trying to curl into an agonized fetal knot, but before he could complete the move that dreadful baton whipped back down once more, exploding across his *right* knee joint as the leg drew defensively up towards his abdomen.

He screamed in fresh agony, and his right hand scrabbled towards a pocket, only to meet that hammering baton yet again. He slammed back onto his spine again, reeling away from the pain of a wrist reduced to gravel, and then Eloise's knee slammed down on his chest, something cold and hard pressed the front of his throat, and he froze as he heard the sudden, shrill, terrifying whine of an activated vibro blade.

His eyes were huge, filled with pain and terror, and she pressed the vibro blade's hilt against his throat. Then she squeezed the button, bringing the actual blade up, letting him hear it whine as it sliced into the floor beside him, and her eyes could have frozen a star's heart.

"You know exactly who," she told him, her voice even colder than her eyes. "Now tell me where she is."

"I . . . I . . . "

"I'll ask you once more," she said softly. "Then I take off your right hand. Then I'll ask again . . . before I take off your *left* hand. And after that—well, you get the picture."

"How . . . how do I know you won't kill me anyway?"

"You don't."

I should've *killed him anyway,* Eloise thought as she made her way quietly down the alley. *And if he's sent me on a wild goose chase, or if . . . if she's not all right when I find her, I damned well* will *go back and kill him!*

She reached the service door and paused. She wore the outsized jacket she'd taken from Hilaire before she'd locked him in the strong room which housed Hankies' liquor supply. She'd drawn its hood up over her head on her way here and she left it there, hiding her face and hair from any cameras that might be monitoring the alley as she leaned her forehead against the door for a moment.

She blinked her eyes furiously while her right hand touched the hard shape of the unicorn under her blouse. She stayed that way for a handful of seconds before she inhaled deeply and pressed the button under the speaker beside the door. Several seconds passed, then—

"Yeah?" a voice growled from the speaker.

"Hilaire sent me," she replied. "From Hankies."

"Oh, yeah? And why'd he do that?"

"He said if I showed you a good time, you'd show *me* one," she said.

"Did, did he?" The man behind the voice chuckled. "Well, chickie, we're always up for a good time around here. Aren't we boys?"

She heard more laughter and several voices announcing ribald agreement. Then a buzzer sounded and the door slid open.

She stepped through it, left hand at her side, right hand in the pocket of Hilaire's jacket. It gave access to a very short entry hall, and she raised her left arm and used her forearm to sweep the hood from her head. Then she stepped through into the room beyond.

There were eight men in it. One wore only a pair of none-too-clean briefs and three were naked to the waist. The rest were in various states of undress, and all of them leered at her. But only for a moment. Just long enough for her appearance to register.

It was interesting, a tiny part of her noted. She could actually tell which of them were the quickest. The recognition didn't come to all of them instantly. It flowed from the fastest on his mental feet to the slowest like some visible wave. The entire process couldn't have taken more than a handful of heartbeats, but it seemed much longer as she watched. There were more than she'd anticipated. Hilaire had told her there'd be only three or four of them, and that same calm corner of her mind wondered if he'd deliberately lied or truly hadn't expected the others.

She should be terrified. She knew that as she faced them, but she wasn't. All she felt was . . . cold. Very cold.

"I'm here for my sister," she told them.

"Your sister?" The man who'd answered her knock over the speaker was taller and looked as if he were probably older than the others, although none of them could have been any older than Estelle, and he glanced quickly at his companions before he looked back at her. "What makes you think she's here?"

He kept his hands easily by his sides, but the fingers flicked outward and the other seven began sidling away from him and from one another, spreading out as widely as the room would allow.

"Hilaire was very forthcoming," she replied, baton hidden against her forearm, the hilt of the vibro blade resting lightly in her right palm. They were going to get in each other's ways if—when—this turned ugly, that calm inner voice told her. That was good. "He said this is where you brought her."

"Did, did he?" The leader's tone was light, almost caressing, but his eyes were calculating. "He tell you we showed *her* a good time?"

"No, he told me you dragged her in here, and you beat her, and you raped her." Her voice was still level, but it was no longer calm, and her eyes locked with his, clearly ignoring anyone else in the room. "I'm here to take her home."

"Well, now, that's gonna be just a little hard," he told her, and his lips twisted in a sneer. "See, she's not here anymore. We already sent her 'home.'"

His head flicked towards the red-painted hatch of a refuse disposal shaft. The kind that fed trash into the fusion-powered incinerators that served Duquesne Tower.

"Wasn't any fun anymore, so we didn't see any reason to keep her around," he told her, his tone no longer light, and an icicle pierced her heart as his eyes glittered viciously at her.

"Let's see if *you* last longer," he said.

He started towards her unhurriedly, confidently, and the world disappeared.

Later, in the nightmares, she would remember her own primal scream, the fury and the hatred and the grief and the devastating loss. She would remember the sudden alarm in his eyes, the way he stopped in his tracks. And she would remember the baton licking out from her left hand like a viper's tongue, the vibro blade coming out of her pocket, screaming to life with a fury and hatred of its own as she sent it to its full, illegal length. And she would remember stepping into them like the angel of death herself.

She remembered very little after that. Not in any detail. Not until she caught the last of them halfway out the door. In the end, he'd turned to run, but the vibro blade swept effortlessly through his right thigh and he smashed to the floor, screaming, clutching at the blood-fountaining stump with both hands.

"*Please!*" he screamed. "Oh, Christ, please! *Please!*"

She paused, glaring down at him, realizing her stolen jacket was sodden with other people's blood, feeling it hot and stinking like molten copper, oozing down her face, dripping from her hands. She drew a deep, shuddery breath, glanced over her shoulder, and wondered with a sort of lunatic calm why she wasn't gibbering in horror.

There wasn't a single intact body.

She noted a pair of pulsers lying on the floor, one of them still clutched in the fingers of a detached hand, but she had no memory of seeing the weapons or the hand before. In fact, she realized, she didn't remember actually *seeing* any of the Hellhounds from the instant the vibro blade came live. But now she did. She saw the severed limbs lying in bits and pieces in thick lakes of blood. Saw a head lying on the floor, staring at her with wide, disbelieving eyes. Another head, split vertically from crown to clavicle. A torso sliced cleanly in half, spilling organs and blood and a sewer stench.

She saw *everything*, and the vision engraved itself forever upon her memory in the flickering instant before her eyes swung back to the ganger in front of her.

"*Please*," he whimpered, his voice weaker as the blood continued to pour from his thigh.

"You're no fun anymore," she heard her own voice say calmly, conversationally. "No reason to keep you around any longer."

"*No, pl—!*" he screamed, and then Kevin's gift silenced him forever.

"Do you know what time it—?"

Kevin Usher stopped dead as he opened his door and the doorbell stopped buzzing.

Eloise Pritchart stood there, her dark slacks streaked with something far darker, the cuffs of her white blouse black and stiff, her face still smeared with streaks of dried blood her mopping hands had missed. There was more blood in her hair, under her fingernails, and the nightmare heart of hell was in her eyes.

"Eloise?" he said very, very softly.

"Kevin," she replied, and his jaw clenched. He'd never heard that flat, cold deadness from her.

He moved wordlessly aside and she stepped past him so the door could close behind her. She looked around his living room as if she'd never seen it before, but he didn't think she was really seeing it now, either. She simply stood there, hands by her sides, her expression empty.

He touched her shoulder, and she let him steer her as if she were a mannequin as he seated her in one of his well-worn armchairs.

"Eloise?" he said again, and she blinked. Then, slowly, those desecrated eyes focused upon him.

"She's gone, Kev." The words were no longer dead, and his heart flinched from the endless ocean of pain that filled them, instead. "She's gone," she said again. "Just . . . *gone*. I'll never see her again. Never hug her. Never—"

Her voice broke, her shoulders quivered, and she buried her face in her hands. She jackknifed forward in the armchair, and he went to his knees beside her, wrapping his arms about her, as the sobs tore loose at last and ripped the heart right out of her.

"Here," Usher said an eternity later as he handed her the coffee cup.

She accepted it with a wan smile and sipped, then coughed on the stiff jolt of whiskey he'd stirred into it. She managed to avoid spraying any of it across him, then took another, deeper swallow and leaned back in her chair.

"Christ, I'm sorry," he said, sinking into a facing chair. "I'm *so* sorry, Eloise."

"Wasn't anything you could've done." Her voice was hoarse from weeping, but she shook her head firmly. "Wasn't anything anyone could've done. Except maybe the bastards who're *supposed* to keep things like this from happening."

"How'd you get all the way back to Two Hundred like that?" he asked in the tone of someone trying to deal with his own shock and pain, and gestured at the bloodstains.

"You think anyone wanted to get close to me looking like *this*?" There was very little humor in her harsh chuckle. "I walked clear back across The Terraces without anyone saying a word. Then caught the lift and came straight here. I doubt the shaft police will worry about the surveillance imagery at all, assuming the cameras even noticed it. Commissioner Juneau might have a few questions, but I don't expect any trouble from him or Aristide. They . . . they really liked Stelle, too, you know."

Her voice quivered, dropping almost to a whisper, on the last sentence, and she took another quick swallow of the whiskey-laced coffee.

"Jesus, Eloise." He shook his head, his eyes dark with grief of his own. "What're you going to do now? How can I help?"

"You can help me a lot, Kev." She looked him in the eye. "You already helped a lot. Without that vibro blade, I'd be dead, too, instead of them. But I need you to do something else for me, too."

"Anything," he told her flatly. "Name it."

"You might not want to be quite that quick about it," she cautioned him.

"Name it," he repeated in that same, unflinching voice, and she drew a deep breath, holding the coffee cup in both hands, gazing at him across it.

"A few weeks ago, I was reading a biography of Michèle Péricard," she said. "It made Stelle nervous, but it was one my mom recommended to me years ago. I've got it in my desk, if you'd like to read it. I think you'd like it. And it's got some interesting stuff in the appendices. Including the entire text of something called the Declaration of Independence."

"It does, does it?" He sat back in his own chair, his eyes narrowing in recognition that the seeming non sequitur was nothing of the sort.

"It does." She nodded. "I've been thinking about that a lot since then. Have you ever read it?"

"Never even heard of it," he admitted.

"Then you really need to read it," she said. "It's all nonsense, of course. Any Legislaturalist would tell you that. It talks about the consent of the governed, about unalienable rights, like the right to life, and liberty, and the pursuit of happiness. And it says that when a government *takes* those rights, when it governs *without* the consent of the governed, that it's the right—the *right*, Kevin, that comes from God, not some privilege governments can take away on a whim—of the people to *change* that government. The people who wrote that declaration launched a revolution over three thousand years ago, one that Michèle Péricard brought here, *right here* to Nouveau Paris. And the bastards who wrote the 'Constitution' we have today took every single one of those things away from us. They *took* them, Kevin, and they're never giving them back. *Never!*"

Tears glittered in her eyes, and her voice shook with her passion.

"My sister is dead because Michèle Péricard's Republic died before she was ever born. Stelle never had a chance, any more than you or me, to know what the Republic of Haven—the *Republic* of Haven; not the *People's* Republic of Haven—was supposed to be. And I never tried to do a thing about it for her because I was afraid of what would happen *to* her if I did try.

"But it didn't save her in the end, did it?" The tears broke loose, flowing down her cheeks, less tempestuous than her early sobs but glittering with the distilled essence of grief and loss. "I never took a stand, never tried to change things not just for Stelle, but for all the other Estelles, all the other sisters and daughters and brothers and sons. But the people who wrote that declaration . . . *they* took a stand. They *fought*. In the end they won, but they didn't know they were going to—that they even *could*—when they wrote it. All they knew— *all* they knew, Kevin—was what every one of them pledged to the nation they helped to build, to the future, to God, and to *each other*: 'our lives, our fortunes, and our sacred honor.' That's what they put on the table: every single thing they had. And now . . . now maybe it's time *I* did, too."

She drew another deep breath, her lips trembling.

"I never asked you about this, but I've always known, Kevin. I've known you're a hell of a lot more than just an ex-Marine who runs a dojo. I'm not going to ask you for any names, *but I want in*."

Silence shimmered between them for a long, long time. Then, finally—

"Are you positive about that?" he asked her softly, not even pretending to misunderstand her. "I think I do want to read that declaration of yours, because it sounds like the folks who wrote it really understood. But are you sure *you* do? What you did today you did at least partly in self-defense but also in vengeance. Personal, white-hot, *hating* vengeance, Eloise. I'm not condemning you for a heartbeat for doing that," he continued as she started to stiffen. "God knows if I'd been able to get to the bastards who killed Estelle, I'd've done worse than you did. They'd have taken a *hell* of a lot longer dying, Eloise.

"But my point is that what . . . the people you're asking to join do, they *don't* do in a white-hot heat." He held her eyes very seriously. "Oh, some of them do. Some of them are *always* white hot, although I try to stay as far from people like that as I can, and *all* of us are as inspired by anger as we are by any actual sense of principle. But when it comes down to it, when somebody dies—if we do it right—it's cold and it's calculated. It may be hate that helps carry us, but it's a *cold* hate, Eloise. It's cold, and it's bitter, and it's its own kind of poison, and in time, it . . . leaves a mark. Are you sure you really want to add that to what you're already carrying around after today?"

"Yes," she said softly. "I couldn't save Estelle. I know that. But I can still give her something. I can give back the Republic of Haven in her name and the names of everyone else it's killed. I can drive a stake through the heart of this monster, and every time I hammer that stake a little deeper, I'll remember Estelle. I'll remember *my sister*, and I will *destroy* the People's Republic.

"I don't have any fortunes, Kevin. And I don't know how much of a life I have anymore. Right this minute, it doesn't feel like all that much or all that important. But I still have this. I have the right to choose, the right to say this is where it *stops*, the right to fight—and the right to by God *die*, if that's what it takes—for what I know is right. And that's exactly what I'm going to do."

"Just the same to you, Eloise," he said with a flickering smile, "I'd like for both of us to avoid the dying part. Can't exactly rebuild anything if we're not around when the rebuilding starts, can we?"

"No. And I didn't say I *wanted* to die. But if that's what it takes?" Her eyes bored into his, and her voice was soft. "If that's what it takes, then so be it."

"All right," he said after another long moment. "All right. What was that you said after lives and fortunes?"

"Honor. Our sacred honor," she replied, and he nodded.

"Our sacred honor, then," he repeated. "Yours and mine, Eloise. However long it takes."

He held out his hand.

She took it.

CONTRIBUTORS

Lindsay Buroker is a full-time independent fantasy author who loves travel, hiking, tennis, and vizslas. She grew up in the Seattle area but moved to Arizona when she realized she was solar-powered. "Hope Springs" is set in her Fallen Empire series.

Tony Daniel is a senior editor at Baen Books. He is also the author of ten science fiction novels, the latest of which is *Guardian of Night*, as well as short story collection, *The Robot's Twilight Companion*. He's a Hugo finalist and a winner of the *Asimov's* Reader's Choice Award for short story. Daniel is also the author of the young adult high-fantasy novels *The Dragon Hammer* and *The Amber Arrow*. Other Daniel novels include *Metaplanetary, Superluminal, Warpath,* and *Earthling*. Daniel is the coauthor of two books with David Drake in the long-running General series, *The Heretic* and *The Savior*. He is also the author of original series Star Trek novels *Devil's Bargain* and *Savage Trade*.

Kacey Ezell is an active duty USAF helicopter pilot. When not beating the air into submission, she writes mil SF, SF, fantasy, and horror fiction. She lives with her husband, two daughters, and an ever-growing number of cats.

★ ★ ★

David Hardy is the author of *Crazy Greta, Tales of Phalerus the Achaean, Palmetto Empire,* and numerous Western, historical, and adventure stories. He lives in Austin, Texas with his wife and daughter.

★ ★ ★

Sean Patrick Hazlett is a technologist, finance professional, and author who has published over a hundred research reports on clean energy, semiconductors, and enterprise software including Wall Street's first comprehensive market analysis of opportunities in the smart grid, which was cited twice in *The Economist*. He is a winner of the Writers of the Future Contest, and his fiction has appeared in publications such as *Terraform*, *Writers of the Future*, *Grimdark Magazine*, *Galaxy's Edge*, *Abyss & Apex*, *Fictionvale Magazine*, *Plasma Frequency Magazine*, *Kasma SF*, *The Colored Lens*, *NewMyths.com*, and *Mad Scientist Journal*, among others. Before working in finance and technology, Sean was a research associate at the Harvard-Stanford Preventive Defense Project where he worked on energy security issues that included the United States-India Strategic Partnership and policy options for confronting Iran's nuclear program. He won the 2006 Policy Analysis Exercise Award at the Harvard Kennedy School of Government for his work on policy solutions to Iran's nuclear weapons program. Sean also spent time at Booz Allen Hamilton as an intelligence analyst focusing on strategic war games and simulations for the Pentagon. Before graduate school, Sean was a cavalry officer in the United States Army where he trained American forces for combat operations in Iraq and Afghanistan at the National Training Center. Sean holds a Master of Business Administration from Harvard Business School, a Master in Public Policy from the Harvard Kennedy School of Government, and bachelor's degrees in History and Electrical Engineering from Stanford University.

Rich Larson was born in Galmi, Niger, has studied in Rhode Island and worked in the south of Spain, and now lives in Ottawa, Canada. His work appears in numerous Year's Best anthologies and has been translated into Chinese, Vietnamese, Polish, Czech, French and Italian. He was the most prolific author of short science fiction in 2015, 2016 and possibly 2017 as well. His debut novel, *Annex,* comes out from Orbit Books in July 2018, and his debut collection, *Tomorrow Factory,* follows in October 2018 from Talos Press.

Edward McDermott wrote across genres, publishing work in the science fiction, fantasy, horror, western, and mainstream fields. Born in Toronto, he pursued his writing in his spare time while working a professional day job. In addition to his writing, he enjoyed sailing, fencing, and working as a movie extra. Edward passed away in early 2018.

George Nikolopoulos is a speculative fiction writer from Athens, Greece, whose short stories have appeared in *Galaxy's Edge*, *Factor Four*, *Grievous Angel*, *Bards and Sages Quarterly*, *StarShipSofa*, *Havok*, *The Centropic Oracle*, *Helios Quarterly Magazine*, *Truancy*, *Best Vegan SFF 2016*, and over a dozen other markets. He is a member of Codex Writers' Group. He blogs at georgenikolopoulos.wordpress.com.

Larry Niven is the multiple Hugo and Nebula Award-winning author of the Ringworld series, along with many other science fiction masterpieces. He lives in Chatsworth, California.

Jody Lynn Nye lists her main career activity as "spoiling cats." She lives northwest of Chicago with one of the above and her husband, author and packager Bill Fawcett. She has written over fifty books, including *The Ship Who Won* with Anne McCaffrey, eight books with Robert Asprin, a humorous anthology about mothers, *Don't Forget Your Spacesuit, Dear!*, and over 160 short stories. Her latest books are *Rhythm of the Imperium* (Baen Books), *Moon Beam* (with Travis S. Taylor, Baen Books) and *Myth-Fits* (Ace). She is one of the judges for the Writers of the Future fiction contest. Jody also reviews fiction for Galaxy's Edge magazine and teaches the intensive writers' workshop at DragonCon.

Suzanne Palmer is a writer and artist who lives in the beautiful hills of Western Massachusetts. She works as a linux systems and database administrator for the Science Center at Smith College, and notes that hanging out with scientists all day is really just about the perfect job for a science-fiction writer. Her short fiction has been nominated for both the Theodore Sturgeon Memorial and the Eugie M. Foster Memorial Award, and other stories of hers have won both the *Asimov's* and AnLab (Analog) Reader's Choice awards. There are also insidious rumors afoot of a novel in the works.

Martin L. Shoemaker is a programmer who writes on the side . . . or maybe it's the other way around. Programming pays the bills, but a second place story in the Jim Baen Memorial Writing Contest earned him lunch with Buzz Aldrin. Programming never did that! He was the 2016 recipient of the Washington Science Fiction Association's Small Press Award for his *Clarkesworld* story "Today I Am Paul," which also appeared in four different year's best anthologies and eight international editions. His work has also appeared in *Analog*, *Galaxy's Edge*, *Digital Science Fiction*, *Forever Magazine*, and *Writers of the Future Volume 31*.

Brad R. Torgersen is a multi-award winning, multi-award nominated science fiction author, who is a healthcare tech geek by day, a United States Army Reserve Chief Warrant Officer on the weekends, and a sci-fi writer at night. His short fiction has been featured in the pages of several notable genre magazines, including the venerable *Analog*, where Brad has received three separate readers' choice selections. Married with children, he resides in the Intermountain West, His second novel, *A Star Wheeled Sky* (Baen), is schedule for publication in December 2018.

Brian Trent's speculative fiction appears in *ANALOG*, *Fantasy &*

Science Fiction, *Orson Scott Card's Intergalactic Medicine Show*, *Escape Pod*, *Pseudopod*, *Daily Science Fiction*, *Galaxy's Edge*, *Nature*, and numerous year's best anthologies. The author of the historical fantasy series *RAHOTEP*, his novel *TEN THOUSAND THUNDERS* is slated for late 2018 publication from Flame Tree Press. Trent lives in New England. His website is www.briantrent.com.

With over eight million copies of his books in print and thirty titles on the *New York Times* bestseller list, **David Weber** is the science fiction publishing phenomenon of the new millennium. In the hugely popular Honor Harrington series, the spirit of C.S. Forester's Horatio Hornblower and Patrick O'Brian's *Master and Commander* lives on—into the galactic future. Books in the Honor Harrington and Honorverse series have appeared on twenty-one bestseller lists, including those of *The Wall Street Journal, The New York Times*, and *USA Today*. While Weber is best known for his spirited, modern-minded space operas, he is also the creator of the Oath of Swords fantasy series and the Dahak saga, a science fiction and fantasy hybrid. His latest novel, the nineteenth in the *New York* Times best-selling Honor Harrington series, will be released this fall by Baen Books. David Weber makes his home in South Carolina with his wife and children.